APPREHENSION

APPREHENSION

MARY ROBINETTE KOWAL

SAGA PRESS

LONDON NEW YORK TORONTO
AMSTERDAM/ANTWERP NEW DELHI SYDNEY/MELBOURNE

# SAGA PRESS

AN IMPRINT OF SIMON & SCHUSTER, LLC

1230 AVENUE OF THE AMERICAS, NEW YORK, NEW YORK 10020

This book is a work of fiction. Any references to historical events, real people, or real places are used fictitiously. Other names, characters, places, and events are products of the author's imagination, and any resemblance to actual events or places or persons, living or dead, is entirely coincidental.

First Saga Press trade paperback edition October 2025

SAGA PRESS and colophon are registered trademarks of Simon & Schuster, LLC

Simon & Schuster strongly believes in freedom of expression and stands against censorship in all its forms. For more information, visit BooksBelong.com.

For information about special discounts for bulk purchases, please contact Simon & Schuster Special Sales at 1-866-506-1949 or business@simonandschuster.com.

The Simon & Schuster Speakers Bureau can bring authors to your live event. For more information or to book an event, contact the Simon & Schuster Speakers Bureau at 1-866-248-3049 or visit our website at www.simonspeakers.com.

Interior design by Lewelin Polanco

Manufactured in the United States of America

1 3 5 7 9 10 8 6 4 2

Library of Congress Control Number: 2025939771

ISBN 978-1-6680-9915-5
ISBN 978-1-6680-9916-2 (ebook)

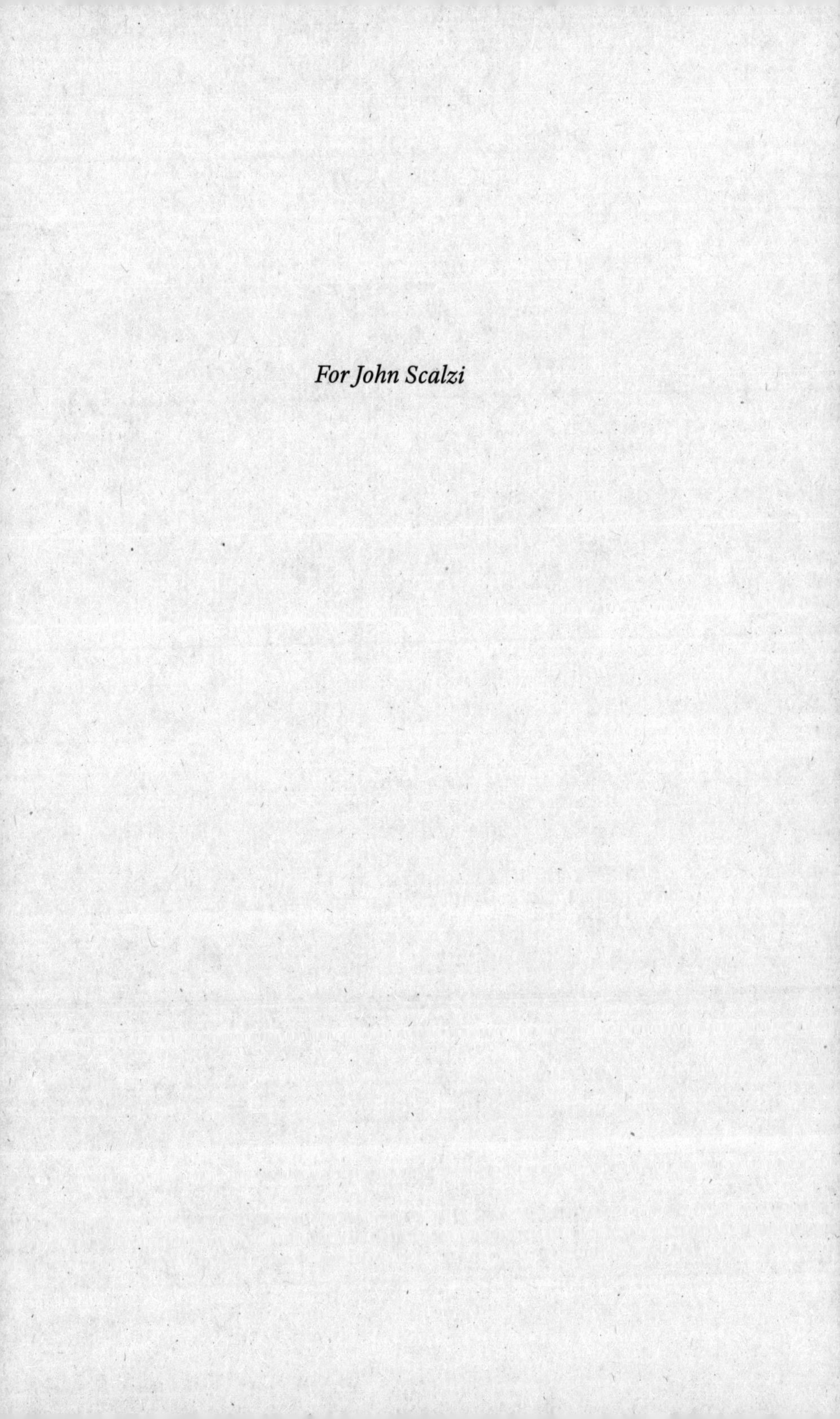

For John Scalzi

ONE

Back when I was in my thirties, I'd spent five long and weary years living on the surface of Namhatanu while the dust and rubble of war had hidden the modern cities beneath corpses both human and Herl. And here I was, forty years later, voluntarily stepping out onto the surface of the planet without a piece of protective gear in sight.

Before, I'd dropped on an Interstellar Service Corps ship with a squad in a streak of plasma. Now, I glided down in first-class seats with my son-in-law and grandson on the orbital elevator from Piper Nine Station to its terminus in Tali Province, at the equator.

And walking out of the terminus onto the street, I knew I had a problem. It was crowded with vendors and so many Herl. I thought I'd be fine. I'd thought the PTSD was long behind me. But sweat coated me, and I knew that old rabbiting in my chest. So many Herl, with their backward knees and long noses. I started looking for snipers that weren't there and drafting escape routes in my head.

Why the hell had I come back here?

Because under the lie of war had been the Herl's culture of reckless generosity? Or because the upcoming Unification vote marked the real end to the war I'd been here to fight? Or simply because Namhatanu was not Earth?

I had memories here, sure, but not of Sam.

And my son-in-law and my grandson had no memories of Namhatanu at all. Maybe we could all lie our way past grief.

I glanced over my shoulder to make sure that Jax kept one hand on Tristan as we worked our way through the crowd. It wasn't that I didn't trust my son-in-law to keep an eye on my grandson, it was just that I didn't trust a six-year-old to stay focused, period.

"Grandma! Where's the hotel? How much farther is it?"

"Not too far, sport! I got the route pulled up on my HUD!" I sounded so goddamned cheerful.

"Awesome!" Jax gave a thumbs-up with one hand, and with the other kept Tristan from darting for a display of wooden puzzles.

Indications of when the ISC had occupied the planet after the war were still everywhere, with signs written in Herl, English, and Chinese. We passed a small group of activists who carried signs in all three languages urging people to vote for Unification. ONE PLANET, ONE PEOPLE. The area closest to the elevator had cookie-cutter kiosks that catered to tourists, all with terrible pun names like "NamHATanu," which sold hats. And a tanning salon—so you didn't become orbital-pale—named "NamhaTANu." Hell. Somewhere around here, they probably had a restaurant named "NOM NOMhatanu." The overlay path glowed on my subdermal heads-up display. God. I remembered the days before subdermals—hell, I remembered the days before HUDs, and I did not miss navigating with a handheld.

Herl vendors kept calling out to us and to the other passengers disembarking, and I had to work to keep from flinching for no damn reason. I had plenty of Herl friends that I'd served with and kept up with over the years. I knew the difference between nose sacs puffing up in pleasure and feathered crests rising in threat. Damn it all, I was just out of practice at managing old scars. The rabbit in my chest was getting more frantic. I bent my head as if I were attending to our robosuitcases, but they were trundling along dutifully.

Around us, representatives of various species peeled away from the elevator hub. There were more Herl than any other species, which made sense on account of Namhatanu being their home. Some of them wore human-style suits, which accentuated their ostrichlike legs. Others wore the long traditional robes of Sati Province. Most, though, had the close ribbon bindings of Tali Province. And I saw more than a few of their feather-like crests fluff in irritation at having to dodge a tourist. After the Herl, I saw fewer humans than had been deployed here during the war, and then the occasional fuzzy orb of a Fealif or the slender shape of a Pimin.

Tristan piped up, "Daddy, are we the ones who look funny here?"

Jax made a pained face, and I did not envy him navigating that bit of childish questioning. "Good thought, buddy. But remember what we said about talking about how people look? If it's nothing they can change in less than thirty seconds, then we don't need to point it out."

"Oh, right! Like the bags under Grandma's eyes."

"Um . . . A better example would be that we *could* talk about your favorite shirt." Jax shot me a chagrined look with his face while my HUD pinged with an incoming message. *Sorry about that.*

Tristan held out the hem of his green-and-white Space Mouse shirt as if discovering for the first time that he was wearing it. "I love my shirt!"

"It's a great one."

I subvocalized a message to send back. *No worries. At seventy-eight, I know I'm old and tired. You're doing great.*

That was the thing about Jax. Even in the midst of a depressive cycle, he always put on the mask for his son. He was doing a damn fine job of solo parenting. Together, he and Sam had been amazing parents.

My heart squeezed at the thought of my child, and it crowded out some of the fear. Then another Herl came up, and I turned faster than I needed to. My arthritic hip seized up and sent an ice pick through my pelvis. I stumbled and knocked one of the robosuitcases over.

"Bonnyjean!" Jax had me by the elbow, and I nearly slammed an open palm into his nose as if he were an enemy combatant.

"Don't—" I caught my tongue, just barely, and switched tactics, burying my panic under a layer of Southern sweetness. Forty years. I was a POW forty years ago. And not even in this province. I rested my weight on the remaining robosuitcases and faked a grin. "Don't you worry none. It's my gosh-darned hip. I just need a minute."

Jax studied me and looked away with the rapid eye motion of someone using their HUD. "I'm going to call a cab."

"The hotel is within walking—"

"I'm calling a cab." His shoulders were tight and his voice had flattened the way it had done when he'd been nursing Sam and his spouse had gotten stubborn about treatment.

I swallowed my protest. "Okay."

"Thank you." He turned. And then he looked worried and kept turning, rising onto his toes. "Tristan?!"

"Tristan!" He had been right there. I pulled up his tracker on my HUD, and the damn thing said *Tristan Low is with you right now*.

"He is *not* with me, you stupid machine," Jax growled, probably in response to the same goddamn message I'd gotten.

"But he's close enough that the proximity check thinks he is." I rose to my full height, looking for his green-and-white Space Mouse shirt with that stupid purple logo.

A raised voice, chattering rapidly in one of the Herl languages, pulled my attention back to the main street. And Tristan—

My grandson stood in front of an angular Herl, and he was holding a red sash in one plump little hand. The other end trailed on the ground.

Oh hell. That was a prayer scarf, and half the war had been about doctrinal differences. Oh no . . . No, no. The Herl's crest of feather-like plumage was spread wide in clear agitation.

The drumming was back in my chest, but this time it was rage that someone was threatening my grandson.

"Oh hell, no—" I stalked toward them. I had to dodge pedestrians to get over to where Tristan was.

That Herl looked furious. Didn't matter that he had good reason to be mad; I had uncomfortable memories of what an angry Herl could do.

The Herl rattled his plumage together, towering over my grandson. The other people in this part of the main street were either vendors or people who had just gotten off the orbital elevator, and all they'd done was activate their cameras to catch the spectacle. Lovely.

Jax sprinted over to Tristan and clapped one hand on his shoulder. "You okay?"

"I wanna go home!" The little boy drew back, still clutching the length of red cloth.

I got between my family and the Herl. The alien turned his deeply lined face toward me and scowled down the length of a narrow nose. My heart kicked up like someone was step-dancing in my chest. The Herl seemed to be aiming his monologue at me now, but none of the words matched the clicking, rattling High Herl I'd learned.

I sent a ping to my HUD, asking for translation.

Translating from Mandarin—

Oh, for fuck's sake. I sent a reset command. A Herl was in front of me. *Translating from Mandarin.* Whatever he was saying was angry. I canceled the translation request and held up both hands, low and to the sides. I had learned High Herl, but not this dialect, and I couldn't dredge a single useful word out of memory. My brain kept giving me words like "forceps" and "clamp."

"Hang on—hang on. We're all friends here. . . ."

The Herl continued to talk, pointing a two-thumbed hand at Tristan.

From out of the crowd, a young human woman pushed through the spectators. She wore a neatly cut suit, bound at the cuffs and wrists in the Lunar fashion, which complemented the deep sheen of her skin.

She smiled at us. "Excuse me." With a single aggressive pivot, she faced the Herl. From her throat came that same rolling waterfall of language.

The Herl's plumage fluttered and flexed in response to her words. Once or twice she gestured back to Tristan. He made a snort, blowing the sides of that long nose out like a bullfrog's throat.

What the devil were they talking about? Again, the Herl pointed at Tristan, who continued to cower next to Jax.

The young woman glanced back and gave a decisive nod. She turned her back on the Herl and, with all the spectators furiously filming, walked over to Tristan. She gave the little boy a wink before plucking the red scarf out of his hand.

Holding it in both hands, she lifted it over her head and turned back to the Herl. In a very clear ceremonial gesture, she lowered it in a graceful arc to the alien and barked a short phrase.

The Herl snorted again but took the cloth with an odd twist of the head. The fierce plumage hissed as it settled back into a smooth drape across the Herl's shoulder.

I let out a sigh. "Good lord . . . Thank you. My system kept trying to translate from Mandarin."

"Well—" The young woman looked a little embarrassed. "He was speaking Mandarin."

For a moment, my mouth hung open.

Jax made a sort of breathless laugh. "Seriously? My family's Chinese—granted, fifth generation, but still. I don't speak it, so why would a Herl—I mean, we're not even on Earth."

It took my brain that long to catch up. "Oh . . . We're in Tali Province. Darn it, I'd clean forgotten that."

"Very good! And correct."

Jax raised an eyebrow. "Tali Province?"

"During the war, China had most of the troops in Tali." I rubbed the back of my neck, where the old wound was. "Most English speakers, like me, were in Sati Province. Well . . . In any case, I'm really grateful for your help."

The young woman smiled with a shrug. "A simple thing, friend. On our journey, we are each sometimes the helper and sometimes the helped. Today? I was the helper. Tomorrow? Perhaps our roles are reversed."

"Be that as it may, I'm grateful for you smoothing things out." I stuck out my hand. "Bonnyjean Stephens."

"Desta Kessell." The woman's grip was firm; there were calluses across her palm as if she used her hands frequently.

"My son, Jackson Low." That wasn't strictly true, but I found that when I introduced him as my son-in-law, people asked him about his spouse. They expected that I wouldn't bring a son-in-law without my actual child. It had been hard enough losing Sam without that reminder.

Desta Kessell offered her hand to Jax with a disarming smile. "A pleasure, friend."

Jax grinned in answer, and I allowed myself a momentary fantasy that he might find romance on the trip. Or at least a fling. "Call me Jax." And a slight pause there, to see if she recognized Jax Low. When she didn't, his charming smile got broader. "And thank you, Mx. Kessell."

"Jax? Then I am Desta, please."

Was it my imagination that their handshake was a little longer than it should be? But then Jax was clearing his throat. "And the troublemaker of the hour . . . my son, Tristan."

"Ah, but Tristan and I have already met, have we not?" She held out her hand to Tristan as if he were an adult.

Peering up at her like she was a curiosity seen through a window, Tristan shook her hand. "You talk like an alien."

"Mmm . . . Technically, yes. We are on their planet, so we are the aliens, and thus Mandarin is an alien language. Here, but not on Earth."

Jax looked after the Herl, who had disappeared down the street. Most of the spectators had wandered off now that there was nothing dramatic to record. "Is that why he was so angry? I mean, Tristan's obviously a kid, right? It was a mistake is all."

She crouched next to Tristan but otherwise addressed him seriously. Made me like her that much more. "Let me explain the 'mistake.' During the occupation, Earth soldiers did not permit Herl to wear their prayer scarves. Now they wear them as a matter of pride, and to remove one is . . . upsetting."

"I didn't mean to."

"I am certain you did not, but you see that you stumbled onto an unhealed wound, yes?"

The pride of my heart cocked his head in confusion, and I could see him trying to understand. "Like a laceration?"

Desta's brows rose toward her hairline. "That . . . that is an impressive vocabulary."

I raised my hand. "My fault. Doctor, right here."

"Grandma's a neurosurgeon!"

"Oh." Desta laughed and tapped Tristan on the end of his nose. "And you sound like one as well."

I gotta admit, I grinned with pride that could power this entire space station. "Ask him to spell cerebellum, and he's your man. Cat or dog, though? Stiiiiill a little trouble."

Desta's laugh spilled out, sparkling like bells. "Your practice is here, Dr. Stephens?"

"Now, now . . . If you're Desta, then I'm Bonnyjean." I winked. "But to answer your question—Earth."

"Earth is a large planet." She winked back at me.

"Fair enough." I grinned at her. "Chattanooga, Tennessee. At Erlanger."

"What brings you all the way from Chattanooga to Namhatanu?"

"A spaceship," I deadpanned, and ignored Jax's eye roll.

"Naw. I know what you mean. I've been planning a vacation for a while and . . ." And I'd kept putting it off while Sam was sick. "Anyway, decided to make it a big one. I wanted to show the boys Namhatanu."

Tristan tugged at Desta's sleeve. "Grandma saved the world!"

I winced at the gross exaggeration, even though Desta was laughing at his earnestness. "In my younger days, I was a military surgeon. Stationed here. Well, in Sati Province."

Jax cleared his throat. "How about you, Desta? You live here?"

She smiled blandly and shook her head. "I am also a visitor." Turning her attention back to me, she said, "Was it a direct trip from Earth?"

Jax tilted his head to the side with a frown, studying Desta. Why had he suddenly gone unhappy?

"We stopped at the Lunar Station for a few days. For the transfer."

"And may I guess as to your hotel here?" She pretended to study us, rubbing her chin. "Either the Sanderson or the Meacham?"

Jax's brows came together and he frowned. "Why those two?"

Thank heavens Desta didn't seem to notice his frowny face and just smiled. "Their advertising optimization is very good for English-speaking visitors."

"What an interesting thing to know. Are you sure you're just a visitor?" Why the devil was he suddenly being rude after this nice young woman had saved our hides? And here I had thought he might take an interest in—oh.

Oh. I'd bet dollars to donuts that just the idea of flirting with someone was probably making him feel unfaithful to Sam, even though it had been over a year since the funeral. Hell. The boy had to get out of his shell at some point.

I gestured to the kiosks that dotted the length of the street. "Can we buy you a drink?"

Desta pressed her hands together. "That's kind of you, doctor, but unfortunately I have some business first."

My son-in-law stuck his hands in his pockets and was about as casual as a skunk in the summer. "What business are you in, Mx. Kessell?"

But Desta held up her finger and looked into space in the universal sign that she was using her HUD. Then she lowered her finger and said, "Pardon, but perhaps we might have a drink together later?"

I grinned. "All right. We're at the Meacham. Drinks in our suite?"

Desta tipped her head. "Charmed. And then you must let me take you to dinner."

Oh, no. I'd never met a politeness battle that I was willing to back down from. "No. Now that's not a fair bargain."

Desta gestured at the area around us. "But I know the town. May I assume that you wish to escape the tourist traps?"

"Well—" I did want to give the boys a sense of the universe, and if Desta knew the town, that would be swell. As for letting her pick up the check? Ha! I knew how to pretend to go to the facilities and grab the check from the maître d'. "That's what we came here for. Okay, Jax?"

He smiled, and I willed Desta to see how charming he was. "Okay, but I make no promises to be entertaining. Shuttle lag, you know?"

Desta twisted her head and bowed like a Herl. "To be the

one who is entertaining is my fondest wish. Until later." She nodded to Jax and me and patted Tristan on the head.

"See you later. And thanks again," I called after her.

Desta gave us a cheerful wave and strolled off. She tucked her hands into her pockets and seemed utterly at home. I had a wave of envy because I hadn't felt that comfortable anywhere outside of surgery since I was . . . since maybe not before the war.

While we waited for the car to take us to our hotel, Tristan danced beside me and was clearly hitting his limits. "Can I look at the puzzles?"

"That's a question for your dad."

"Not today, buddy. The car is nearly . . ." Jax's voice trailed off, and he was staring back in the direction of the orbital elevator. I turned to see what had caught his attention so thoroughly.

Big street, thronged with people. The ubiquitous Herl murals curled around the elevator building, in reds and golds. Above it, stretching up into low Namhatanu orbit, was the trunk of the elevator. I didn't see anything to catch his attention.

Our car rolled up from the opposite direction, so it wasn't that, although the sight of it made my heart sink. He'd called one of the Herl-style transports, and the seats were all wrong for our bodies. Herl knees bent opposite the way ours did, so they straddled stools. It was going to be hell on my hip.

"Jax? Car's here." I grabbed a suitcase and headed toward the vehicle. "Need you to authenticate."

"Oh, right. Sorry." Jax turned toward the car and gave his passcode. Which I could tell, mostly because the trunk and doors opened. He picked up a suitcase, glancing back the way we'd come. "Bonnyjean . . . Desta Kessell was talking to that Herl."

There were about a half dozen just in easy sight. "Which one?"

"The one that was mad at Tristan. Looked like they were old chums."

So that was what he'd been staring at. I glanced back and didn't see either the Herl or Desta. "Okay . . . So they know each other. So what?"

"Doesn't that strike you as odd? That she wouldn't mention that?"

"Culturally, maybe she couldn't. I dunno." I hadn't been stationed in the equatorials. I didn't know what was culturally appropriate here.

Jax put Tristan in the car and paused. "How the hell do the seats work?"

"Just use them like stools." I shoved one of our cases into the boot at the front of the car. "What's got you so bothered?"

Grabbing two of the cases, Jax came to join me in loading up the vehicle. "She set off every single one of the red flags I had from when a fan was trying to get information."

"You think she's a fan?" This was one of the problems with being the lead singer in a band that almost made it big. Would have too, probably, if Sam hadn't gotten sick.

He shook his head, placing the last of our suitcases in the boot. "All her questions were about you. Seriously, she now knows that you're from Earth and live in Chattanooga, Tennessee. A doctor at Erlanger. You have a son—or, well, that we're related. Your grandson can spell 'cerebellum.' You went to Lunar

Station. You once served on Namhatanu with a military hospital. I think she's a scammer preying on tourists."

"Honey . . . These are just the things people talk about when they're getting to know each other." Which he would remember if he would get out and meet people.

Jax shook his head and took my arm. "She deflected every one of our questions. If she's a scammer, you may as well have handed her your system ID."

"There's not a darn thing there, including the cerebellum thing, that she couldn't have gotten from one of my social streams." I wouldn't deny that Desta had been curious, but none of the questions she'd asked were out of keeping for when you met new folks. I might be a neurosurgeon, but I could still recognize his survivor's guilt, and paranoia was a really common form of expression.

"And who's to say she hasn't?" He pointed back the way we had come. "Isn't it convenient that she just happened to come to our aid? To 'save' us from someone she knows?"

"All right. I'll stop being social." I nudged him, hoping to tease him back to good humor. "Bet you're just mad 'cause she didn't know who you were."

Jax glared at me for a minute and a wave of emotions went across his face, and I had this hope that he would yell at me. But he just shut down again. "Is that your formal diagnosis?"

"Jax—my formal diagnosis, and prescription, is that we ought to have drinks and not worry about it."

The car dropped us off at an elegant facade that stood out from every other building on the street and fairly screamed *COME TO ME, PEOPLE OF EARTH*. The elegant doorway was covered in faux gilding and fabricated to look like an art nouveau masterpiece.

"Here we are." I winced as I got out of the car under the curved glass canopy.

The Meacham Hotel's system made a connection with our identification modules, and the door hissed open. A real human porter stood inside, smiling a greeting.

In the height of affectation, the human porter addressed us in High Herl. Which, really—what was the point of that if they catered to English speakers?

Oh sure, my HUD would translate. But it annoyed me that he was using language like a costume.

I'd learned High Herl and remembered enough to be polite. *Please. I'm sorry. No. I'm hungry.*

I shook my head, chasing old memories back into the

corners. None of that would be helpful here. "My name is Bonny-jean Stephens, Dr. Stephens."

And the porter responded by switching to English, but with a Herl accent, like he'd grown up on Namhatanu. "I'll take care of everything, *pulukulpa*."

In isolation like that, I recognized the High Herl honorific for a woman.

Well, maybe some of the old language would come back to me. Sighing, I beckoned Jax and Tristan into the hotel. Three shallow stairs led up into the main lobby, and I had to grab tight to the brass handrail to make my stride look even. Stairs always made my right hip feel like someone was driving an ice pick into it.

"There's a ramp over—"

"Just want to get to the room." My pride forced a smile. "Make sure you got Tristan."

A couple of humans were coming toward the entrance, and I did not want my grandson to cause any trouble with them. Both of them were well-dressed and had that sort of pleasant polish of people who read only magazines and have personal stylists but no personal taste. The man was middle-aged and had a carefully trimmed beard and waxed mustache and seemed the sort who made a hobby out of being offended. The young woman with him couldn't have been more than eighteen and had the same almost white-blue eyes, so I was guessing she was his daughter. She did a double take and stared at us with our luggage and six-year-old in tow. Yep. Not the sort that tolerated noise, I'd bet.

The man beckoned to the porter, who hadn't even begun to manage our luggage yet. Then, just like they were showing off, the man opened his trap and spoke what sounded like a long string of perfect High Herl. I did my best not to gawk at him.

The porter nodded—which was not the way Herl indicated

agreement unless a lot had changed in the forty years since I'd been here. But he said, "*Kuma,*" which was High Herl for "yes."

Jax leaned over to whisper in my ear. "We're being watched."

If my eyebrows went any higher, I'd have to shave my head to find them. When I looked over my shoulder, the fancy-schmancy woman was still staring at us. And there was no question about if she was a fan.

Because her lips were rounded into a soft O and she was staring at Jax. Or more specifically, Jax Low of the Math Turtles.

Desta Kessell leaned against the balcony parapet of our suite, admiring the view beneath the amber blushes of a Namhatanu sunset. The young woman had exchanged her suit from earlier for a deep purple silk pantsuit with full belled trousers, bound at the waist, wrists, and ankles with gold satin ribbons. Given that it was another Lunar fashion, it was a fair bet that she had lived or grown up there. I wanted to nudge Jax and say that see, I did know something about Desta.

The broad glass doors had been swept wide, erasing the barrier between in and out. Jax stood by the side table sipping, appropriately, a Namhatanu. I willed Desta to look away from the garden at Jax. See how nice he looked. A starched white shirt over a flowing floor-length skirt in amber set off his skin nicely. He'd gelled his hair so that the dark strands stood up in the orbital style, and he had even pressed a bit of gold powder to his cheeks.

Tristan burst out of the suite's bathroom with his toothbrush in one hand. "Bedtime song! Bedtime song!"

Jax cleared his throat and glanced at Desta. "We have company, Tristan."

"Pleeeeeeease? I'll sleep better." And really, that face and those huge brown eyes were why I spoiled the child.

Jax didn't stand a chance. He smiled at his son. "One song."

Bouncing on his toes, Tristan said, "'Don't Borrow Trouble.' The way you sang it with Bibi." He referred to Sam with a six-year-old's blissful lack of awareness of his father's grief—or mine, for that matter. But then, a year was an eternity in his life. "I'll be Bibi."

Jax cleared his throat. "Deal."

"Showtime!" Tristan did a little flamenco on the carpet as a way of introduction, and you could see the ballroom dance classes we'd put him in. Then he stopped and struck a pose that made my heart beat sideways.

Sam used to stand like that at concerts. Hard to say if Tristan remembered, since he'd only been three when Math Turtles had stopped touring, or if he'd watched vids of his parents' band from before Sam got sick. Either way, I could see my child's joy reincarnated in Tristan's rooted feet and that cocked elbow when he held the toothbrush in front of his mouth like a microphone.

Tristan's voice wasn't huge, but given his legacy, it was good.

"When I was lost in the darkness,
my fate a set course,
my love found me,
lifted the shadow
and pulled me back,
by offering this key."

Jax stepped in with a voice like a campfire wrapped in silk.

"Don't borrow trouble.
That's a spiral down, down.

Turn around now, turn around.
Don't borrow trouble.
Don't spiral down, down."

Sam had loved his voice, and Jax had sung bedside serenades for hours in the hospital. God. Grief caught me at the worst times. I slid a thumb under my eyes to wipe away any betraying tears and glanced at our guest. Desta had turned on the balcony, mouth parted a little in wonder.

Tristan danced a circle around his dad.

"Still I grew up afraid to love
and told my sweetheart, 'Don't be misled,
I can't promise you endless summer.'
Here's what my sweetheart said."

Jax caught his son's hand, and they twirled around the living room, his skirt flaring out as he sang,

"Don't borrow trouble.
That's a spiral down, down.
Turn around now, turn around.
Don't borrow trouble.
Don't spiral down, down."

Tristan's face glowed with happiness, watching his dad sing, and he puckered up his rosebud lips to whistle an accompaniment. Harmony, even! Sam's little boy for sure.

Jax crouched down, skirts puddling around him, so his head was level with Tristan's, and they sang in harmony.

"Don't borrow trouble.
That's a spiral down, down.

Turn around now, turn around.
Don't borrow trouble.
Don't—"

A loud knock sounded on the door to the suite.

Tristan kicked the floor. "Aw . . . blew the ending."

Shaking my head, I went to the door and pulled it open. A Herl waiter was outside, crest smooth and unruffled against his scalp. "Good evening. I have your room service and will be the babysitter you requested."

I glanced at Tristan to see if he was okay with the Herl after his adventure that afternoon. And . . . he was playing air guitar with his toothbrush. Thank God for the resiliency of a six-year-old. I pointed to the smallest bedroom, which we'd allocated to Tristan. "Come on in."

The Herl bent down, knees going the wrong way, like a giant emu. "Hello, little. My name is Ravi."

"I'm not little."

"No. Indeed, but I do not want anyone to be alarmed to know that there is a giant in their midst." He winked.

"I'll get you two acquainted." Jax headed for the bedroom and hauled Tristan along after him. Hopefully, with a meal, Jax would be able to get my grandson settled for the night. Macaroni and cheese. The magic food of the ages.

I hollered after them, "Wash your hands!"

Desta picked up the Namhatanu she'd set on the parapet. "Your son has an astonishing voice."

"He ain't too shabby." Didn't have to be a blood relative to burst with pride.

"Breathtaking. I had no idea. It is a shame it was interrupted."

I thought of the tour he and Sam had been on when my baby's first fainting spell had hit. "You have no idea how true that is."

"Has he ever made an album?"

Before I could answer, Jax walked back across the main room and onto the balcony. "Flattering question." He settled on one of the faux-iron chairs, waiting until Desta leaned against the parapet. "Yes. I was in a band, Math Turtles. Had a number one Billboard single. Toured all over, even some off-planet gigs."

"Oh?"

"For a bit, I was wondering if you'd seen me in New Athens—being Lunar and all."

Desta shrugged. "Going to concerts requires leisure time, which I so rarely have."

"Ever been to New Athens, Desta?"

Over the rim of her drink, Desta studied him briefly. "It's my hometown."

Jax took a sip of his drink, brows coming together with a hint of frustration. "And what takes up so much of your time that you can't go to concerts?"

"Business."

"Oh? What do you do?"

Desta shrugged. "This and that. Finding profit where I can."

Setting his drink down on the balcony parapet, Jax looked back at me. I shrugged, spreading my hands a little. I could see his point. On the other hand, business was dull, and here she had a professional singer in the room.

Jax drew a breath, and I moved toward the balcony to cut him off before he could be outright rude and—another knock at the door. Jax grimaced and stood. "I got it."

I paused, facing Desta. How the devil do you apologize for

someone going prickly like that without betraying their pain? Behind me, the door opened, and a string of High Herl rippled into the room punctuated with a single Earth name. ". . . Reyes."

Jax stood at the suite's door, facing a slate-gray Herl who stood with shoulders stooped and crest rustling in agitation. "Um . . . Give me a second for my translator to calibrate."

Like I'd never stopped speaking High Herl, the phrase "How can I help?" offered itself up.

The Herl cleared his throat and focused on me, as if I were a lifeline in space. And he answered in High Herl. I caught maybe three words and shook my head. "Sorry. Don't actually—"

In English, the Herl said, "Seek I am the habitation Mx. Reyes for to drink tonight."

I shook my head. "Got the wrong room. Sorry."

The Herl twisted his head with an odd flourish. "Regret. Regret and sorrow for to disturb."

"Ain't no bother."

When Jax shut the door, Desta had come farther into the room and was staring at the door with her brows drawn together. Without a smile, her cheekbones seemed drawn with a knife. Then Desta smiled, but it was clearly forced.

She pressed her hands together. "Forgive me, but I must ask for a launch delay for dinner tonight. A piece of business, I'm afraid, requires my immediate attention. I hope to see you another time. . . ."

Without giving us time to respond, Desta walked to the door and was gone.

• • • • • • **FIVE** • • • • • •

The restaurant that the hotel concierge recommended catered to humans. That was not at all interesting to me. I wanted the food that I'd had when I lived here. Did I have bad memories of being a POW? Yep.

But I also had memories of training and the friends that I'd made. So, I used my HUD to track us down a place that served food from Sati Province. Sure, we could have ordered room service and stayed in after Desta's abrupt departure, but we already had the babysitter booked.

The moment we walked in, the tangy-sweet smell hit me, and I started salivating. The walls of the restaurant had actual murals—not just projections, but the sweeping abstract curves that I remembered from my time on Namhatanu.

Herl waiters moved with quiet efficiency among the low couches and sofas. The Herl version of a maître d' looked up from the host. He inclined his head with that odd twist to the side, as a sign of respect like bowing. And then I realized I was in trouble when he greeted us in Tali Herl, followed by Chinese.

"Um . . . *Suruts*." I wet my lips and figured I'd try what I could remember of High Herl. "*Ilveki om?*"

"*Suruts, pulukulpa ta rolukulpa.*" He twisted his head again and replied in High Herl, which I mostly recognized as a sort of "hello, lady and gentleman." Tapping his fingers together, he dipped his head. "Would English be easier?"

"Oh, thank God. Yes." I sagged a little. "Sorry, it's been a real long time."

"Not at all. I am pleased that you made an effort to learn any High Herl." He picked up two menu sticks and gestured deeper into the restaurant. "This way, if you please."

Beside me, Jax made a small hum of surprise. When I followed his gaze, we were passing the couple from the hotel—the expensive folks who had stared at him. The young woman looked up and did a double take, eyes going wide in that way I'd seen fans of Sam and Jax do before.

Naturally, the maître d' stopped at the table behind theirs. "Your waiter will be with you momentarily."

Jax grimaced and looked around, as if he were trying to find another table. But he sank onto the cushions of the low bench with a grace I envied. It took me a little more doing to ease down onto the cushion of the bench opposite him, and lord knew how I was going to get back up again. The thing was practically on the floor. Which I remembered from when I was here before, but I'd also been in my thirties.

Jax glanced furtively at the table behind me. He sent me a ping. *And now she's just staring.*

I glanced over my shoulder and somehow thought that I could be subtle about it, but I looked right into the lady's eyes.

Her manicured eyebrows were raised in an expression of

delighted interest. "Oh! Hello." She leaned a little so she could look past me to Jax. "I'm so sorry I've been staring. So rude, I know. Daddy is appalled. It's just . . . You're Jax Low, *the* Jax Low from the Math Turtles?"

Across the table, Jax visibly relaxed. This was a script I had seen him deploy countless times when he and Sam were touring. His voice dropped a little lower, letting the campfire smoke of it wrap around his words. "You have me."

The girl turned to the man next to her. "I told you so!" She gave a little wave. "I'm Emma she/her and this is my father, Noah he/him."

"I did tell her not to stare." The man had all the plummy vowels of the British upper crust that I had sorta expected from his stylist's wardrobe choices.

I grinned. "Nice to meet y'all. I'm Bonnyjean she/her."

"Emma was telling me that the Math Turtles played at Orbitalooza some years ago."

"Not that we got to see you." Emma rolled her eyes at her father. "I make do with your albums."

Noah twisted a waxed end of his mustache, looking a little embarrassed. "And she's got me hooked—that one song. What is it? 'Pennies from heaven, tears in rain, something, something . . .'"

Jax laughed at the awkward compliment. "'Keep coming round, but you remain.'"

"That's it! By George, that's catchy. When is your next show?"

For a moment Jax Low, singer, flickered, and Jackson Low, widower, looked out. But he shrugged. "There . . . there won't be another show."

Emma's manicured hand flew out to catch her father's sleeve, but the man just kept talking. "Come now! I promised Emma that we would go to the next show."

"Daddy—"

"I can't break my word, now can I?"

"It's just that we're on vacation." I tried to save Jax from having to talk about it. "And after Namhatanu, we thought we might go . . ." Hell. I had no idea where the sentence was going, because all I could hear were echoes of Sam telling me, *Keep him happy*.

"What Bonnyjean means is that my partner died last year. Sam Stephens." Jax looked up through his dark lashes. "Math Turtles doesn't exist without Sam."

Noah frowned at his daughter, seeming to finally realize that she'd been trying to stop him.

Emma wrung her hands. "I know. It was just the worst thing I'd ever read when I heard the news. I'm so sorry."

I saw Jax pull the performer mask back up. He waved a hand. "Thank you."

She still fluttered for a moment and then fixed her attention, rather desperately, on me. "So . . . vacation? What have you seen so far?"

I needed to extricate ourselves from this conversation quickly, partly to protect Jax and partly because my bones were protesting from the twist in my spine. "I'd be happy to tell you— only I'm getting a dreadful crick in my neck."

Jax looked across the table at them. "Why don't you join us?"

That shocked the hell out of me.

"Oh!" Emma looked like she'd gotten Hanukkah, birthday, and graduation presents all at the same time. "Oh, I don't want to intrude."

Jax's mouth curved and got that sideways grin he wore in their publicity photos. "Please. It would be nice to talk to someone who remembers Sam."

And what was I? I was Sam's mother. I remembered my baby every single day.

Grease coated my fingers as I scooped up some of the fragrant truddra, which was a tuber-like vegetable native to the southwestern continent. The best description I had come up with was that truddra was the love child of a yam and bacon grease. In Sati Province, Herl cooked it with a range of fiery spices that lit the inside of your sinuses like a beam of light from heaven. I could get it some places on Earth, but it was never quite right. This . . . this was glorious.

Noah had proven to be an affable and gregarious dinner partner, despite his ridiculous mustache. His father had settled on Namhatanu after the war, and Noah spent dinner sharing all sorts of useful information. "To mimic the Sati Herl, use only your first finger and thumb, never the smaller fingers. It does not matter which hand, simply keep the other fingers tucked out of sight."

Jax imitated the motion. "Is that a religious thing?"

I knew the answer to that. "Not really. They have opposable thumbs on both sides of their hands, so the interior thumb and finger are for fine work, while the outer ones are more for heavy grasping. That means they are more likely to be dirty." I shrugged. "You could compare it to human religions where things are 'unclean,' but it's just practical here—more like, 'don't pick your nose.'"

Jax reached for another bit of truddra patty, swiping it through the thick, dark, mole-esque sort of paste. "I'm just thinking about all the time I wasted getting Tristan to use utensils."

Noah laughed. "I had the same problem with Emma."

She blushed. "Daddy . . ."

He winked at her and ostentatiously licked his fingers, making her laugh. She snorted, which was goddamned adorable, and shot a look at Jax, blushing even harder. Poor kid had it bad.

Jax cleared his throat and made a saving throw for her. "So, Noah, you were telling us about the family estate?"

"Right. Where was I?" Noah snapped the fingers of his clean hand. "Ah, yes. Gorgeous place in the highlands of Sati, right on a line of geothermal vents, so we have a thermal waterfall. You must come up to visit."

"Sounds like heaven." Jax smiled, but at Emma again, and I went on high alert.

He wasn't foolish enough to fall for an underage fan, was he? But grief does weird things.

"As long as it lasts. I would offer to send you the reports on water rights. . . ." Noah's shoulders slumped. "But it is . . . ahem . . . dry reading. Ha ha."

As I reached for some more truddra, I noticed Jax staring at the entrance. So did Noah. Any further conversation just dropped out of my head.

Desta was standing in the entrance of the restaurant. On her arm was an exquisitely dressed older Herl woman, with a peacock-blue gown setting off her copper crest. Desta scanned the restaurant, looking for the headwaiter, and stopped on me.

I waited for Desta to smile or nod or—well, anything really, but the young woman's gaze moved on without any sign of recognition and kept moving until she spotted the headwaiter. My jaw just dropped.

Uncomfortably, I turned to Jax, who looked about ready to cut Desta.

The headwaiter approached Desta, and she exchanged a few words with him, which I couldn't hear, but I could feel the young woman not looking at us. The waiter guided them away from the entrance to a set of cushions in the farthest corner from us.

I couldn't account for it.

I knew that Desta had seen us. But she apparently had no intention of speaking to us or even acknowledging that we existed. Oh, good lord. What if Jax was right and that woman was just a scammer? I toggled my subdermal HUD to see if any of my accounts had been compromised. Everything seemed fine.

But watching her walk through the restaurant made my guts clench.

Snorting, Jax reached for his drink. "Now I'm really wondering what her 'business' is."

"Fair." I scowled across the restaurant, for all the good it did. "You were right. I was wrong."

"Thank you." Privately, he sent me a ping. *Sorry. She just set off every red flag.*

And your fans here don't?

He set his drink down. *No. Emma's a good kid. And her dad's motivation is clear enough. He just wants a good story to tell.*

Noah cleared his throat and leaned across the table. "I say, why don't you let us show you around tomorrow? Emma here knows all the best shops on Central Corridor."

Jax gave a charming smile. "That would be great. Thanks."

I would sit here and enjoy the damn company. I picked up a patty of truddra and tried to find joy in good food. There were perfectly nice people right here, and they didn't have mysterious motives. I glared in Desta's direction to send the heat of my wrath across the room.

Desta listened to something the woman said, then nodded and turned to look right at me.

The next morning, Noah and Emma led us off the beaten path to a covered outdoor market, where Tali Herl craftspeople sold their handmade wares. A weavers' collective, with lush textiles made from the hair of the small doglike vrindra of the Vahati Province, sat next to a bookbinder, who worked in the style of the Dani Province but cut his pages in the boxier shape of human books rather than the long, narrow ones Herl preferred.

Jax picked up a tiny book threaded on a cord like a pendent. It was the soft teal that Sam had loved, and I could almost see the sadness come back over him. My baby would have snatched that up in a heartbeat.

I looked around for a distraction. And his son was the best option. Tristan was standing with Emma in front of a Herl who had a small booth on which she was projecting a shadow play.

"Looks like Tristan found a puppet show."

"Hmm?" Jax had the little book in his hand and was at the register.

"Think we should save Emma from Tristan?"

He snorted as he tapped the payment portal. "Probably. She's been an absolute saint."

"Handy having fans." I was honestly ashamed of myself for thinking back at the hotel that Noah and Emma didn't like children, especially when it turned out they were just fans of Jax.

"Sometimes." He looped the cord over his neck and tucked it inside his shirt, resting a palm against it for a moment. It was like I and the rest of the market didn't exist. Jax looked over to where Emma stood with Tristan. "I mean, yes . . . I'll admit it's nice to know that someone remembers us. It's been so long since the last Math Turtles album that I—I dunno. I'm just surprised and pleased."

It would hurt to see him perform without Sam, but if it made him happy . . . I swallowed. "Maybe . . . maybe you should think about trying some solo work?"

"People always think that just because you were a performer once, it's all you want to be. What I loved was performing with Sam."

"Grandma! Daddy!" Tristan ran up to us, having escaped Emma's grasp. "There's pu-KA-ti-YON-gi . . ." He screwed his face up as he recited the unfamiliar syllables. "She's a puppet lady because 'pu' means girl, and Emma knows all sorts of stuff you don't!"

Jax laughed. "I would not doubt it." He crouched down by his son. "What's your favorite part of the show?"

"There was a MONSTER!"

I leaned over to Emma. "Let me know if you need a break."

Grinning, she shook her head. "This is the most fun I've had on Central Corridor in years!"

"The monster is back!" Tristan tugged on her sleeve with an

infectious grin, pointing at the screen. He dashed back, and she barely caught up with him.

God. He reminded me so much of how full of energy Sam had been at his age. Talk about a child powered by joy. . . . I looked sideways at Jax. "You really content not to perform anymore?"

Jax didn't ask me to explain the non sequitur; he followed well enough. "Look . . . It was fun. I loved doing it, but now? I like being a dad. I enjoy it. This life—it's not the one I would have chosen, but I like it."

"Does that include sharing a home with an elderly crone who always smells of disinfectant?"

He laughed. "As my favorite mother-in-law would say . . . 'Crone? My aunt Fanny's ass.' Besides, I don't have to look sexy in the carpool line or worry if the *Times* reviewer doesn't like my mac and cheese."

"Your mac and cheese is excellent."

That earned me a full-throated laugh. I wanted to punch the air with victory.

He put his hand on his chest where the little book was. "I just think about how Sam and I missed out on so much of Tristan's childhood when we went viral, thinking that there would be a Later. There was for me. But there wasn't for Sam."

It wouldn't do any good to dwell on that. I did a comic double take. "What the hell is a French bakery doing here?"

"Would you—" Jax clenched his fists, not turning to look at the bakery. "Listen, Bonnyjean. There's a thing I've been meaning to say. . . ."

The look in his eyes made my stomach tighten with apprehension, and I didn't even know why. I gestured at the hubbub surrounding us. Acrobats, sewing machines, and just the sheer swathe of sentience walking through the market. "Ain't no one listening but me."

"When are you going to stop erasing Sam?"

You could have picked my jaw off the floor. "Ex-excuse me?"

"Every time Sam comes up, you change the subject."

"That's ridiculous." Erase my own child. The nerve.

In the distance, someone shouted. More cries of alarm rose in the air. My heart sped up, as old memories of Herl screams echoed in my mind. It had been an evac mission—get in, grab some wounded soldiers. Get out. *Explosions and screaming and hiding in bright, multicolored rubble.*

Herl blood the same color as humans. Bright arterial red.

"Tristan!" Jax's smoky voice tore on the two syllables of his son's name.

I snapped back to myself. It had been a long time since I'd had a spell like that. A long damn time and not long enough. I shuddered, swallowing, and everything around me had changed while I'd been frozen.

A white-robed Herl ran down the length of the corridor with a passel of local police hard on his heels. Some were human, some Herl.

One of them had a rifle.

"Tristan! Tristan—get back here this instant!" Jax was caught in a knot of people.

Flanking them, Emma went around the people and cut through the open space created by the acrobats. She reached out and grabbed Tristan's shoulders, spinning him toward her.

Breathing heavily, she steered him back toward Jax. "Don't borrow trouble . . ."

Tristan was craning his neck, looking toward the chase. "I wanna see!"

Jax swept my grandson up into a fierce hug. "You can't—Tristan, buddy—you can't run off like that."

I managed to get out of the memories I was tangled in and over to my family. In the distance, shouts and commotion made it clear that the police hadn't caught the fellow yet. Good lord. "Is this sort of thing normal?"

Emma's cheeks were pale. She wet her lips, shaking her head. "I've never seen anything like it."

Old instincts that had never really gone away had me assessing the space for escape routes and cover. With my HUD, I could route a clear path out of here. I pointed to a side street that would lead us around the commotion. "We should head back to the hotel."

Thank God, no one protested—I mean, no one except Tristan, who desperately wanted to stay. Jax picked him up. I took point without thinking about it, scanning the area as if I had a weapon to fight someone off with.

In the distance, something crashed like a tower of pottery shattering. Away. We needed to get away and quickly. The sounds of the chase echoed off the overhead canopy and reminded me uncomfortably of being in surgery during the war. *Just keep on, steady as you go, and never mind the carnage outside.*

I rounded the corner and—

The Herl that the police had been chasing was directly in front of me.

I inhaled so sharply that my lungs ached. What the hell. He stared at me, crest flat against his head. Staggering, he took a step toward me, and all my doctor instincts went off at once. He was hurt. Badly.

Herl bled the same color as humans. Bright arterial red.

The devil could take the police and their rifles. The fellow was injured. My training had covered Herl emergency medicine. I could stabilize him until help arrived.

I stepped forward to meet the Herl as he collapsed. I tried to catch him, but my hands missed his shoulders, and one of them brushed past his cheek.

The hell? I reacted to the wrongness of the sensation before realizing what it was. Latex or faux skin or something, but lord— if that wasn't human flesh showing through the tear in the fellow's cheek . . .

And a knife, bloody and wicked, lay on the ground.

I dropped to my knees by the fellow. He'd been stabbed in the back. How far were we from a hospital? I needed to improvise a bandage and—

"*Kulpani chima . . . kulpani baris chima . . .*"

I had no idea what he'd said, but the voice—that was a human woman's voice. I knew that voice.

Desta. Desta Kessell was lying on the ground, covered in a Herl disguise. She gasped with the ugly bubbling sound of blood in the lungs. I glanced at the fallen knife. Oh hell, no. I grabbed Desta's shoulder, so I could turn her over and get to the wound.

She reached up and grabbed my arm with a shockingly firm grip. "Bonnyjean—listen—listen!" She pulled me down toward her. Her voice was barely a whisper—more of a strained rasp. "A lawmaker . . . is to be killed . . . assassinated . . . in Vatri." That was the capital of Sati Province. "Soon . . . very soon . . . tell them . . . in Vatri . . . to try Murray Chappell . . ."

Desta's head fell back. I reached for her carotid artery but already knew the diagnosis. Desta Kessell was dead.

· · · · · · · **EIGHT** · · · · · · ·

Around me, a crowd had closed in, yammering in what felt like a hundred different languages, all wanting to know what had happened.

I sat back on my heels. What the hell. Who was Murray Chappell? I looked up, turning to make sure that Jax and Tristan were all right. They stood in a shocked cluster with Emma and Noah. What. The. Hell? I tried to stand and gasped as my arthritic hip seized up.

Goddamn aging and goddamn arthritis. I shifted my weight over to my left leg to try again.

Jax took a step toward me, but he was still holding Tristan's hand. He hesitated.

"Do you want me to watch him?" Emma held out her well-manicured hand.

"Yeah . . . Yeah. Thanks." He made sure she had a grip on him, then hurried forward to help me.

Thank God. I needed his hand under my elbow to stagger to my feet. But what I needed more was something to write on. If

I saved it to my cloud storage, anyone could hack in. Paper was safest. I patted my pockets, breath coming fast. God. Did I even have a tissue?

"Bonnyjean." He swallowed when he saw the blood. "Who is that?"

"Desta Kessell." I turned to Jax. "Do you have any paper?"

His mouth dropped a little. "Is she . . . ?"

"Dead, yes." I was being curt, but by God, the woman had just been murdered in front of us and was apparently a . . . a what? A spy? From one pocket, I fished out a bright orange crayon. I couldn't think of when Tristan and I had last been coloring. Oh, who the hell was I kidding? I couldn't think at all. Desta Kessell— who'd had drinks in our suite just yesterday—was dead. I needed something to write on.

From around his neck, Jax pulled the thin woven cord from which hung the tiny leather-bound book. "Will this—"

I snatched it and saw his eyes widen. Let him think I was rude; I would explain everything just as soon as I finished writing down what Desta had said. In my peripheral vision, the police had finally arrived. And there was Noah, coming over to be nosy, and all these damn people just gawking when a woman was dead. I slipped the cord of the little book around my neck. I let it drop beneath the collar of my shirt and shoved the crayon back into my pocket.

The police addressed the crowd in two or three different languages. I wiped my hand over my face. My heart would not slow down. I couldn't catch my breath.

One of the Herl police officers approached us and said something, but I hadn't a clue what.

Before my HUD could calibrate and start translating, Noah stepped forward and made himself useful. He rattled off a string of rolling syllables.

In response to the police officer's nod, Noah turned to me. "He would like to know if you know who this is."

Before I could think what I should say, Jax sputtered, "We—we had drinks with her yesterday." He pointed at the body lying on the ground. "That's Desta Kessell."

Those police officers didn't need to know a lick of English to follow what he'd said. The one closest to us, a heavyset older Herl with freckled jowls, fluttered his crest. "Desta Kessell?"

He took a step away and gave some instructions to the other uniformed officers. The police officer gestured at Jax and me. "*Kulpani demedas?*"

Noah answered, "Jax Low *ta* Bonnyjean Stephens."

Well, I could recognize my name, at least. Then came a long string of syllables from the Herl officer. He gestured away, down Central Corridor.

Noah nodded with a frown, and turned back to Jax and me. "I'm afraid that he needs you to go make a statement at the police station."

I grimaced. "Really?"

"There's no getting around it." Noah beckoned Emma over, stepping so that he was between Tristan and the body. Fat lot of good that would do, but I appreciated the effort. "Darling—I'm going to go down to the police station with them. Help translate and such. Why don't you take Tristan back to the hotel? Babysit him, eh?"

"I'm not a baby!" Tristan scowled up at him.

"You're a giant." Jax crouched in front of his son. He hesitated for a second before looking at Emma. "Would you be willing to come watch him at the station?"

Emma still clutched Tristan's hand. Her eyes were wide, and a line had managed to crease the perfection of her brow. "Sure. It's no bother. I . . . um . . . giant-sit my cousins all the time."

The police officers gestured toward what I presumed was the station. Noah and the police officer led the way, chatting about the crime—at least that was my best guess. Tristan tugged Emma forward so they were behind her father, as if this were all an adventure.

Wetting his lips, Jax leaned into me and sent a ping. *I don't get it. Why was she dressed up like a Herl? I mean makeup?*

I'd rather know why she was murdered.

He winced. *Do you think she was a spy? Or something like that?*

Had he seen what I wrote? Or was that just the logical conclusion when someone wears a disguise and gets murdered? It could have been a LARP gone horribly wrong.

Bonnyjean, what did she say to you?

I looked around at the police officers in front of and behind us. Ordinarily, I'd tell them what she'd said, but there were two problems. First, they had been chasing Desta. But the bigger problem was that Desta had said that a lawmaker in Vatri would be assassinated, and if the politics from the war held, that threat would probably come from Tali Province.

Which was where we were.

I needed a moment alone to think.

Later. Please. I looked at my hands, half expecting them to be stained with Desta's blood.

Aloud, Jax said, "You okay?"

I clenched my fists and shoved them into my pockets. "Feeling guilty about the names I called Desta. That's all."

The police station was off Central Corridor, through a warren of twisty little passages perfect for ambush. We sat in the lobby on hard benches designed for different anatomy, low and backless and evil. Waiting. Well, the adults sat. Tristan was spinning in circles with his arms out. Jax kept touching his temple as if he were trying to get his subdermal to connect. I didn't know why he kept bothering, since the police department was blocking them.

Noah caught him touching his temple and leaned over. "I'm sure that the police inspector will be more reasonable. I'll do my best to help speed things along, but with the Unification vote coming up, I'm afraid Herl have been a bit touchy about protocols."

Bureaucrats. They seemed to be the same in any species.

"To give you some context . . . Since the war, the Herl youth have a saying, '*deras dhahumani dharuts.*'" He chewed his lower lip, watching the desk sergeant. "It translates, roughly, as 'lie like a human.' Add to that the fact that much of the controversy around the vote has been tied to the protected tax status that humans have had in Sati Province, and well . . . we are not well regarded."

"Well, I reckon they'll have to deal with me telling the truth. We met her yesterday and don't know her beyond that."

"Just try to see their point of view." He shrugged as if it were the most reasonable thing in the world. "She whispered something to you, and then you wrote it down. It hardly looks like you were strangers. Will you show them?"

I had no idea. The thing I kept chewing over in my mind was that Desta said I had to tell "them" in Vatri. Not this province but back in the capital of Sati.

It had occurred to me that whoever killed Desta was still out there. And that the murder had happened while she was running from the police.

Tell the police? What if the police were the problem?

A door slid open halfway down the hall, and a broad-shouldered Herl stepped out wearing the gold-banded ribbons of a police inspector's uniform. He had a curling scar alongside his nose that had punctured one of the air sacs, leaving him a lopsided look. His gaze flicked to Jax and then back to me. He beckoned to us.

"Tristan." Jax snagged his son and swung him up into a spin, which made the little boy giggle. Squeezing him, Jax rested his forehead against Tristan's. "Stay out here with Emma? You make sure she feels safe, okay?"

"Okay!" Tristan wriggled to get down.

Jax let him down, and the little boy ran dizzily to where Emma sat, then hopped up beside her. "I'll protect you."

Jax looked like his heart was going to burst from pride. I know mine was.

Noah got to the Herl while I was still getting my feet under me. "*Dekulpani dha vatri demani* Jax Low *ta* Bonnyjean Stephens. *Kulpani deherl nesha rit ta kulpani dha danuneshi yavi nesha.*"

The inspector held up both hands. "Much appreciated. As you see, I do not require a translator." His English sounded as though he'd learned it from someone in Ireland. He stepped back, gesturing to the door, with his gaze fixed on me. "Please come in." As Noah attempted to follow, the inspector held up a hand, with all four of his fingers spread wide. "Later, I should perhaps like to speak with you. For now? Please wait here."

A shivery twitch ran down my spine as Jax and I went into the office. It sure would have been a mite more comfortable if we could have had someone with us who knew his way around modern Herl customs. What I knew was forty years out of date and from wartime, besides. And mostly medical stuff.

The office had a low desk, with a Herl kneeling chair set beside it. A hand-loomed rug in blue and yellow swirls gave the room a little cheer, as did the fronds of the vaguely fernlike blue-green plant in the corner. Low leather cushions faced the desk.

The inspector waved us to the cushions. Hell. I was going to have a devil of a time getting back up again. Using my left leg, I lowered myself to the cushion, then stretched my right leg out to the side.

Straddling his kneeling stool, the inspector squatted with ease and rested with his knees splayed flat on the floor. "You traveled into the Namhatanu system on the ship ISC *Wukung*?"

"Yes"—I dredged the masculine honorific out of my brain—"*rolukulpa*."

He looked thoroughly unimpressed. "A doctor? What is your area of specialty?"

"I'm a neurosurgeon, specializing in implants." Surely he had to see that we just happened to be in the market when everything happened. "Otherwise, just a tourist, and a Terran citizen."

He grunted and turned back to his screen, studying whatever details about our lives lay there. "You spent time at New Vegas?"

"A medical conference."

"Then you travel to Piper Nine on the same shuttle as the deceased, stay at the same hotel, have drinks together—in your suite—and then dine at the same restaurant."

Jax leaned forward. "We weren't together. She snubbed us. Sat at a different table."

The inspector's eyes flicked to him briefly, as if dismissing a bug. When he stared at me again, the depths of those dark eyes seemed endless.

I held my hand up, as if swearing on the Bible. "I met her yesterday—outside the orbital elevator—for the first time in my life."

The undamaged air sac along the inspector's nose filled, and he let out a snort. "I find it curious that in a city of five hundred thousand people, in the middle of Central Corridor, this 'stranger' gives her final words to you."

I straightened my spine and stared down my own, much smaller nose, as best I could. "I'm not denying she recognized me, but I don't know a blamed thing about her."

"Really?" The inspector's crest puffed for a moment. "For instance, you didn't know that she was with Delukulpa Srikshivi?"

Now I was genuinely flummoxed. When I'd been here, that had been an all-Herl bureau doing intelligence work for Sati. "Excuse me?"

His air sac pulsed again with a snorted breath. "Shall I also believe that you have never heard of the Terran Interpol?" Heaving a sigh, which seemed universal in its exhaustion, he said, "This would go faster if you would lie less."

"How dare you—" I drew my leg in, as if standing and storming out were an actual option.

"Here is what I think." The inspector held up his inner thumb. "The dead woman was a spy who had discovered something." The inner finger. "She was killed for it." The outer finger. "She passed that intel to you." And then the outer thumb, and he waved his hand at me as if serving me on a platter. "A stranger? I think a colleague is more likely."

"Don't know why you need me here, when you got all the answers." My accent was going more country with each tick of anger. I crossed my arms over my chest and cocked my head at him. "Now let me propose a question."

"I await eagerly."

"If I were a spy, like you think, why the hell would I tell you a goddamn thing?"

The inspector gave a studied shrug, as if he were using the body language deliberately for a human. "It does seem foolish for me to ask a human to understand the law."

I jabbed a finger at him. "You wanna talk the law? I'm a tourist on vacation with my family. We saw someone get murdered."

"A tourist? But you have left out your military service." He tapped the screen. "Lieutenant Bonnyjean Stephens."

The room got cold. And then hot. The High Herl words for "please" and "I'm sorry" pressed against my lips. I shook my head and couldn't get a full breath.

"Many in Sati Province owe a debt to you. So why come to Tali Province?"

Beside me, Jax had turned in his seat, eyes wide.

"That's kind of where the orbital elevator touches down." My palms were slick with sweat. "Now look. I came down here to try to be a helpful witness, and instead, you start treating me like a suspect—"

Before I could get going, my subdermal suddenly connected.

The gentle *connecting* startled me into silence. It immediately rang. I didn't care who it was, I was going to ask them to call the embassy and get us out of here.

The inspector stared at me and I just set my jaw as I sub-vocalized, *Hello.*

The line had an ungodly amount of distortion, so it almost sounded as if it were in a high wind. Through the hiss, a voice said, "Dr. Stephens?"

I closed my eyes and tilted my head down, as if I were just taking a little nap. I was seventy-eight and would play the elderly card when needed. *That's right. Who's this?*

With a huff, like air sacs inflating, the voice said, "You say a word of what Desta Kessell told you and you place in danger your little boy."

The distortion silenced.

Connection lost.

My heart stopped and started triple time. The spaces inside my knees felt like boiled jelly. Not Tristan.

Who could cancel a police block of my subdermal? The simplest answer was that it was the same people who had been chasing Desta and had killed her. The Tali police. Ironically, the inspector across from me was probably the only one I was sure I could trust, because otherwise there was no point in telling me not to talk to him.

Keeping my eyes closed, I tried to breathe some of my panic away. What the hell. What the hell was I going to do? Tristan was in the police lobby. If they harmed one hair on Tristan's head, I was going to feed them to wolves.

Jax touched my arm. "You okay?"

"Just an old lady getting tired out." Think this through, Bonnyjean. This wasn't the inspector, but maybe it was people who worked for him. Or maybe it was the Delukulpa Srikshivi wanting to keep their agent's information secret. Regardless, that phone call meant that I had to assume whoever they were would absolutely know anything I said. "We're done here."

The inspector rose from his kneeling chair. "Only a moment, please. I do need your formal statement."

I ground my teeth together. They had threatened Tristan. I would kill people real soon now and that—that was not a skill I'd used in a long time. And killing people would not make Tristan safe. When we left here, the police would follow. What I needed right now was to be nonthreatening and get someplace where we could assess.

I grimaced, rubbing my hip and making a big show of how much it hurt. "You got two minutes."

"Naturally." He pulled a lens up from his desk.

Jax tilted his head, looking at me like he knew something was going on. Well, sure he did. We'd seen someone murdered today, hadn't we? He just didn't know that his son had been threatened. Not yet. "Bonnyjean . . ."

I gave the smallest shake of my head that I could. We would give our statement, and then we would go. And then I would have to tell Jax that someone had threatened his son.

TEN

When we walked out of the inspector's office, my entire spine was tight because every step I took was a lie. Jax didn't know that Tristan had been threatened. And I kept lying by omission because I wasn't going to tell him in public. And that threat also put Emma and Noah in danger. We needed to get all of them to safety—the embassy made sense. Letting my limp show, to make myself seem helpless, I turned toward the long bench where we'd left Noah, Emma, and Tristan waiting.

Jax cleared his throat. "I thought you were a surgeon on Namhatanu."

"Those are the stories I tell." And that was as far as I was going to go.

"Did Sam know?"

"Nope." Telling your child about how you'd almost died was not the sort of bedtime story I'd wanted to share. I rubbed the back of my neck, where the old scar was. I didn't want to dredge up my past for all sorts of reasons, but the biggest right now was that the bench where we'd left Tristan was empty.

I tried pulling up Tristan's tracker, but my subdermal still had only local access. "Damn it. You see them?"

Jax frowned, looking around the waiting area. "Emma probably took Tristan to the restroom."

"You check, and I'll ask."

"We could just wait."

"We really can't." I rested my hand on my hip and made a rueful grin. "Gotta get back to my medications."

"Now I know it's bad." Jax winked at me, but I could see the concern in the line between his brows. He waved at the bench. "You sit and I'll do both."

"That bench is made by the devil." I looked at the door to the police station, beyond which I ought to be able to access the net again. "And truth to tell, I could use some fresh air. Wait for you outside?"

Jax squeezed my elbow. "And then we're hiring a car to go back to the hotel."

"Deal." I limped out the door, and my hip really did hurt like fire. When we got back to the hotel, I was going to burn through one of the corticosteroid shots I'd brought. I needed better mobility than I had now.

Outside, I got about a meter from the door when my subdermal said, *Connecting*.

Breathing out a sigh of relief, I pulled up Tristan's tracker.

It showed that he was at the hotel.

I sagged, nearly going to my knees with relief. While I didn't love that they'd gone back without telling us, there was every chance they'd left a message and it hadn't gone through. I called Emma. My call went to her voicemail, and all the panic started climbing my throat again. It was fine. Tristan was distracting. I sent a ping instead. *Hey, we're out of the police station and heading your way.*

And then, because I'm a paranoid old fool, I called the hotel directly. "Hey there. This is Bonnyjean Stephens, we're staying in the Chara suite. I'm trying to get ahold of Emma . . ." I trailed off, realizing that I had no idea what her surname was.

The man on the other end said, "I'm sorry, *pulukulpa*, but Miss Emma is no longer our guest."

"What? Wait—she checked out?"

"Yes, *pulukulpa*."

I grabbed the rail of the stairs outside the police station. This was a mistake. This was a misunderstanding. "No . . . no. You've got her confused with someone else. Her father has a ridiculous mustache. . . ."

"Yes. I did—I did see you with the Varnhams earlier. I know who you are talking about."

Varnham. That was their name. What a fool I was, not to have even known that. The brass of the rail bit into the palm of my hand as I clung to it. "And they're really—"

"Checked out."

"They were with my grandson. Is he in our suite?"

"I—I'm sorry. I have not seen him since you left this morning."

I pulled up Tristan's tracker on my HUD and sent a ping to it. My heart tightened as I looked at the glowing dot on the map again. "His tracker says that he's at the hotel."

"Again, I'm very sorry." I could hear distant tapping as if he were using a manual keyboard. "I can see the key log, and your door has not been accessed since your departure."

"Look for him!" I clenched my fists in empty air. "Please."

"I-if he is missing, perhaps it would be best to report this to the police?"

"No." I didn't know for certain that the police were involved, but it seemed like a sure bet that whoever had called me wouldn't like that. "No . . . I'm sure he's there. We'll just . . . We'll just come back right away."

As I disconnected, Jax jogged out of the police station. He was frowning, and I knew what he was going to say as he walked up to me. "They left right after we went in to talk to the inspector." He looked up and to the side, like he was accessing something on his HUD. "Tristan's tracker says he's back at the hotel."

I scrubbed my face with both hands, because the last faint hope that maybe my app was frozen had gone away. "Okay . . . let's start back to the hotel."

I let my limp stay real visible, which was maybe good for making me look harmless, but it made Jax duck his head to look at me. "You okay?"

"Just stiff is all." Because I couldn't tell him that Tristan was missing, outside the police station, where a scene might cause someone to think it was safer just to kill all of us. I pulled myself together and let Jax take my arm.

He guided me down the sidewalk to the main pedestrian way. "When we get home, you're making an appointment to have that replaced."

I shook my head. "They have to put you under general."

"So . . . ?" He gave a little laugh. "You're telling me you're afraid to go under? You're a neurosurgeon."

"That's why I'm hesitant." My hip hurt, but I could still move on my own. "The increased risk of medically induced dementia in patients over seventy is well documented. I'm seventy-eight."

"Oh come on—"

"I said, no!" I winced at the snap in my voice. "Sorry. I didn't mean to—it's been a long day."

"Of course." Jax stood at my side, silent.

I spotted a pedicab of the sort that every city on every planet seems to have, to appeal to tourists. The geometry was different on this than one on Earth, with a bright pink canopy over a long backless bench. I waved it down and dragged myself up into it, giving the Herl driver our address.

Jax sat down beside me. "Tristan is going to be real mad that we took this without him."

I sat backward on the bench so I could watch the direction we'd come from, as if I were just touristing. Smiling and watching the streets roll back behind us, I patted Jax on the knee. "Okay, turn off your subdermal."

Jax tilted his head. "Six months ago you were begging me to turn it back on."

"Six months ago you weren't even leaving your room."

"That's got nothing to do with this."

I took another deep breath. "It's got to do with your brain, and I sorta make my living with brains."

"Neurosurgeon is not the same as psychologist."

"It's not." I nodded. "Not saying it is. But I know subdermals. Under duress, sometimes our subdermals react to impulses that later we might wish we hadn't had. All I'm asking is that you turn yours off while we talk."

He crossed his arms over his chest. "You're serious."

"Serious as death and taxes." Maybe I could have picked a better aphorism. "Look. There's some stuff about Desta and all this that I've been holding back. It'll be a shock, and so for me to share it, your subdermal being off is my asking price."

His brows rose. "You wouldn't even know. I could say I'd turned it off."

"But I trust you."

"Oh . . . that's not playing fair. Fine." Turning his gaze away to the street, Jax muttered to himself and used whatever cues he'd set for his subdermal to turn off. He nodded. "Okay, Dr. Stephens. I'm now disconnected from the larger world. For the second time today, I might add."

I rested my hand on his knee. Holding his attention, I swallowed to clear my throat before I could talk. "While we were in the station, remember when I went still and quiet? I got a call on my subdermal. It was someone—sounded like maybe a Herl—who threatened me. If I say anything about what Desta told me . . . they are going to hurt Tristan."

The muscles tensed as if he were going to jump out of the cab. I saw his eyes dart as if he were trying to pull up his HUD.

"Emma—did something happen to her? Is that why Noah left the station?"

Shaking my head, I kept my hand on his knee and wished I could hold both of his hands. "They've checked out of the hotel. Tristan's tracker shows that he's there, but the hotel hasn't seen him, and no one has been into our suite since we left."

His breath was fast, and he kept swallowing. *Keep him happy,* Sam had said. That was it. Not a big dying wish, and look how well I was doing. Jax turned his gaze away from me and stared back down the street. He swallowed again and turned back to me. Jax held out his hand. "Can I see the message?"

Grimacing, I pulled the woven cord and drew the book out from under my shirt. I slipped the cord over my head and handed it to Jax. In bright orange crayon over three of the tiny pages, I had written the words, as best I could remember them. *A lawmaker . . . is to be killed . . . assassinated . . . in Vatri . . . Soon . . . very soon . . . tell them . . . in Vatri . . . to try Murray Chappell.*

Jax sucked in his breath. "Jesus. Why the hell didn't you give this to the police?"

"Did you forget the police were chasing Desta? You sure showing them would have been the right thing?" I reached over and pulled the little book out of his hand. Slipping the cord around my neck again, I kept spinning thoughts around, trying to figure out what to do. "In hindsight, Desta must have been watching us on the shuttle over. You were right."

Jax covered his face. "I did not want to be right."

There was nothing I could do. The only promise Sam had asked of me, I had broken. *Keep him happy.* Hell. I couldn't even keep him safe.

"We'll find him. But we got to be smart about it. We got to be careful, you hear?" I kneaded the ball of my hip, thinking it through. Why had Desta approached us? "My bet is that she was looking for a human couple—from Earth."

"We're not exactly a couple."

I nodded. "But she had to check us out anyway."

"So you're saying this hypothetical other couple had to murder her before she found them?"

"No. No, she found them. Last night. At the restaurant. And that got her killed."

Jax's jaw dropped. Then he wiped a hand over his face, rubbing his eyes. "You're telling me it was Emma and Noah."

"I am."

"That sweet teenager is not a murderer."

"No . . ." I shook my head. "She was with us the whole time in the market. But where was her father?"

"Shit." I saw the guilt wash over him, because he'd trusted them.

I grabbed his hand and held on fast. "This isn't your fault. Being trusting isn't a fault."

If it was anyone's, it was mine. Jax hadn't wanted to come on the trip. I'd bullied him into it because, I'd said, *It will be good for Tristan*. But really, it was because grief had hollowed him out and just left a shell of a father.

Their fans kept posting tributes to Sam, and every single one was beautiful and like another nail through the heart. He'd shut off, so he didn't have to—

"Holy shit." I opened my eyes. "Jax. Your fans."

That beautiful voice was a lead monotone. "What?"

"The hotel said that their last name was Varnham. We can't go to the police, but if we ask the questions right . . ."

He lifted his head. "Mobilize the Math Turtles fan base. Really? After my last fan kidnapped my son?"

"That's the thing, though, right?" My voice was sour as I remembered choices I'd made in the POW camp. "The worst thing has already happened."

His mouth hung open for a moment; then he half turned on the bench to face me. "There was a girl. A data crawler. She could track them."

"Good. Yes. But Varnham may be an alias."

"Math Turtles. Math. Our fans are good with data." Jax straightened on the bench. "I am turning my subdermal on and I'm going to fucking find my son."

Outside the balcony, the golden light of sunset reflected on the plush blue-green velvets of our suite. Jax lay on his side on the sofa, with a throw pulled up around his shoulders, eyes twitching behind his lids as he accessed file after file on his subdermal. While he'd been channeling fans, I had packed our things and then, when I'd run out of stuff to do, I'd thrown money around. Room service, a bottle of Jack Daniel's Reserve imported from Earth for us, and a Space Mouse plushie dressed like a Sati Herl for when we found Tristan. . . .

We had a private suborbital waiting to take us . . . somewhere. Wherever it was that Jax's data-crawling fan told him to go.

This was probably the only still moment I would have. I picked up the corticosteroid injector and my medical kit and carried them both into my bedroom.

On the bed, our suitcases were all packed and waiting. Tristan's, too.

I rested a hand on the Space Mouse emblazoned on the front. Gritting my teeth, I walked over to the dresser and set down my medical kit. We would find him. In front of the mirror, I pulled the waistband of my trousers down past my buttocks. The skin hung loosely on my flanks, with large blue veins mottling the skin. I probed the edges of my hip and found the orbital socket and the femoral head with my fingers.

Carefully, I placed the injector so that the tip pointed into that groove. Letting out a slow breath to steady myself, I stared at my reflection. Looked like someone had bruised me, the bags under my eyes were so swollen and dark. I squeezed the trigger.

The injector popped.

Bright white pain lanced through me, chasing nerves up and down my leg and spine. I let out a grunt.

"Bonnyjean?"

"Don't come in!" Maybe it was more than a grunt. I braced my free hand on the wall. "Got my pants down."

Course you could probably say that about the whole day if you had a sense of humor, which I'd lost somewhere in the marketplace. I pulled the injector away, and a single bright red drop of blood bloomed on my hip. I fished an antiseptic wipe out of the bag and tore it open.

In the other room, cloth rustled and the sofa creaked. Jax cleared his throat. "Got some news."

My heart twisted around hope, and I stared into the mirror as if the angle were right to see into the suite. "I can hear you. Go on."

"Vicky—my data crawler—found Emma. Her social feed shows that she just had her eighteenth birthday. Backgrounds in Vatri. Multiple posts with our music in them." Glass clinked on glass with a burble of liquid. "So I think that she might be an actual fan."

"Jax, they took your son. You can't excuse that away as—"

"I'm not." His breath shuddered. "What I'm saying is that if Desta Kessell hadn't come into that restaurant, they would never have drawn a connection between us. Which also means that if we can convince them we're harmless . . ."

"Well, we're damn near helpless, if that counts." I tossed the antiseptic wipe into the wastebasket and pulled my trousers up. I turned toward the door and limped back to the sitting room as my hip protested at having a literal needle jabbed into it.

"Damn near is not the same as entirely helpless." Jax stood by the sofa, blanket trailing off one shoulder like a cape. "The Varnhams had a private suborbital. That ship could go anywhere on the planet, but . . ."

"But your data crawler found the flight path, didn't she."

He nodded. "They landed in Vatri."

"In Vatri." Tugging on the cord, I drew the little book out from under my shirt and walked over to Jax. He took a step back, which nearly broke my heart. I stopped and opened it and read aloud, "A lawmaker . . . is to be killed . . . assassinated . . . *in Vatri.* Soon . . . very soon . . . tell them . . . *in Vatri* . . . to try Murray Chappell."

"I don't care about the assassination."

"That's not what I mean." I laid the book on the coffee table and sat down on the sofa. With the remote, I activated the large wall screen and connected my HUD to it so Jax could follow along. It only took a moment to call up the Vatri directory.

Jax grabbed a bottle of water off the wet bar and wandered over to stand behind the sofa. "What are you up to?"

"Murray Chappell. I figure we try to find him." I started anonymous browsing. I entered the search terms and started reading, "Manas Chappell—Maruts Chappell—Murray Chappell!"

Jax sucked in a breath behind me. "He's based in Vatri."

For a moment I stared at the screen as if it would provide some additional information, before giving my head a shake. Time was a-wasting. Wetting my lips, I clicked the highlighted name and read through the search results. He ran a special effects shop in Vatri. "Prosthetics . . . He could have given Desta the makeup."

"So . . . does that mean he's an ally?"

"Hell. That's a good question." My heart was tied into a knot so tight it was pulling my lungs out of place. "I'd been thinking that he was in on the plot, so I was going to offer him money and our silence in exchange for Tristan. But if he's a friend of Desta's . . . god damn it."

"Let's send something vague. See how he responds?"

"Okay . . ." I wrote:

> *This is Bonnyjean Stephens. I have some business that I wanted to discuss with you. Is there a time or place where we could meet?*

I looked at Jax before I hit send. "How does this look? I'm trying to keep it vague, since we don't know which way he's leaning."

Jax chewed his lower lip for a moment. "Okay."

I let my breath out, and for a weird moment remembered learning to fire a gun back in my military days. The way you breathed out, so your pulse was steady on the trigger. Then I hit send.

I stared at the screen, and there was nothing else I could do. "Now what?"

"Let's head to Vatri." I stood up and walked to the bedroom, and my hip might have been moving a little more smoothly. "Bill is paid. The ship is waiting."

Jax followed me into the bedroom. He saw Tristan's suitcase and his armor just . . . shattered. He bent forward at the waist, both hands resting on the Space Mouse. "God, please." Curse or prayer, the sob sounded like it had ruptured his diaphragm.

Opening my arms, I pulled him in—alert to any flinch—but Jax folded against me and buried his head in my shoulder. Where was Tristan? God, I wished I knew.

During the flight to Vatri, I refreshed my inbox religiously, like any moment I might get a miraculous message that Tristan had been found and was well. I did not.

But I did get a response from Murray Chappell.

> *Thank you for your inquiry. Meetings at my shop are the recommended course. We are open from 800 to 1700. I am attaching a link to my booking calendar, and you may choose a time that works for you.*

I pulled out my handheld and showed it to Jax. "So, either he's also playing it close, he doesn't recognize my name, or this is a red herring."

He grimaced, looking at the message. "It's 1600 already. We can't wait until tomorrow."

"Time zones are in our favor." I tapped my handheld. "Vatri is north and west of Tali. It's five hours behind, so only 1100."

"Let's just pick a time." He rubbed his hands together like he was trying to warm them. "First available."

There was a slot at 1400. That would give us time to land, check in, and get to the shop. I booked the appointment and got the confirmation and then . . . we waited. The remainder of the flight to Vatri provided no new information. We simply sat while the autopilot followed the set flight plan and brought us in for a landing at the main Vatri spaceport.

I had arranged for a car to meet us and take us to the Denila Grand Hotel. At least having a private suborbital meant we could skip baggage claim and go straight to the car instead of having to deal with a line.

At least, that had been my plan.

But as we approached the exit for the secure area, Jax started to slow down. "Oh . . . Oh, shit."

Someone squealed. Multiple someones. "OH MY GOD! JAX LOW!"

Just on the other side of the secured area, a throng of kids—human and Herl—stood in Math Turtles shirts and held big signs that said things like, I <3 JAX LOW! or DON'T BORROW TROUBLE or SAM STEPHENS RIP.

I clenched my fists and stumbled to a halt. Jax grabbed my arm. "Smile." His jaw was clenched in a rictus of a grin that he spoke through like a ventriloquist. "It hurts. I hate it. But you have to smile for them."

Through my teeth, I somehow managed to smile back.

Jax turned as if he were looking back to make sure our luggage was following us. "This is wild. We never even played here."

"Maybe that's why they're so excited. Didn't think they'd get a chance to see you." My cheeks hurt from holding the smile.

"I didn't even tell Vicky where we were." He gestured at the fans and—holy hell—press badges, too. "Oh hell . . . Data crawler. She figured it out."

The group was a churning mass of noise and excitement. Even passengers who had probably never heard of Jax Low or the Math Turtles were stopping to stare at the commotion. A squat young Herl woman, with a dusty gray prayer scarf draped over her shoulder, stared at Jax as if she were trying to understand what the fuss was about. Another Herl, holding a sign in swooping letters that said something about beauty, waved it in front of her, and the young Herl frowned and stepped back, disappearing into the crowd.

Jax acted like a champ, smiling and waving to the fans. How the hell were we going to get through that gauntlet?

A slender Herl woman stopped next to us. She wore a neatly pressed burgundy Sati-style business suit with divided skirts flaring beneath a tailored over-tunic. Her crest gleamed an iridescent red-black and fell gracefully around her shoulders. For a moment, I thought she was just an airport traveler trying to figure out how to get past the blockade we'd involuntarily created. Then I spotted the airport logo on her name badge.

She tilted her head in the Herl manner to indicate respect. "We're so honored that you have come to Vatri, Mx. Low." She gestured to a side door, away from the crowd. "I suspect you do not want to face so many fans. I have another route that promises to be easier."

This was a very Herl thing. They had this aphorism: *A problem for one is a problem for all.* That was part of that reckless generosity I remembered. I dredged up my High Herl. "*Kuma, daverbha.*" And then for Jax, I said it again in English. "Yes, thank you."

The air sacs on either side of her nose thrummed with pleasure. "*Kulpa deherl nesha?*"

I snorted, which has a very similar meaning for human and Herl. "*Deherl nesha rit.* Forty years ago, I was pretty fluent, but not now."

"Well, we will stick to English then." She led us toward a side hall marked in High Herl FOR AUTHORIZED PERSONNEL ONLY, which is one of those phrases I had good cause to remember. The door unlatched as she approached it. I glanced back toward the crowd of fans. The squat young Herl woman stood near a wall, lips moving as if she were carrying on a conversation via subdermal. As she spoke, she stared directly at Jax and me. That did not feel great.

And then we were through the door and it was too late to change my mind. A human man, with matching moles in the center of each dark brown cheek, waited in a navy Sati business suit. He had dressed his hair in locs that had been cut to mimic the shape of a Herl crest.

The airport agent stopped and turned to us. "I do apologize for the subterfuge." She took a small black identification binder out of her pocket and held the artifact up for inspection. Inside was an enameled disc, embossed with swirling High Herl. "Many pardons. I am Inspector Idusvati from the Crime Unit of Delu-kulpa Srikshivi—People's Investigation Bureau."

Jax's eyes widened, and he turned to face the inspector. "Is that so?"

I scowled. "And here I thought you were being helpful."

Inspector Idusvati cocked her head toward the crowd of fans. "You can, of course, go the way you intended. But I think it would be best if you did not."

It sounded all polite, but I didn't have a doubt in my mind that it was just barely a request. I glanced at Jax, whose brows had drawn together in a frown. He swallowed, looking at me, and I figured we were thinking the same thing. This wasn't about Jax Low, musician. This was about Desta Kessell.

But I didn't see a good way out of it. Even if we pitched a fit, what good would that do Tristan? We had an appointment, and we needed to get through this as fast as possible. "Well now . . . that's right kind."

Idusvati gestured to the human man. "This is Agent Woodard—Dr. Stephens and Mx. Low."

Woodard inclined his head and spoke with a faint High Herl accent. "How do you do?"

Okay, so this fellow was raised on Namhatanu. They must have brought a human in to make Jax and me feel better. "Y'all going to tell us what you want?"

His smile looked weirdly alien, even though he was clearly human. "Please. Inspector Shivsati requests a moment of your time."

Shivsati. Sweat covered every part of me. It was not a common Herl name. But still, it might be someone else.

Jax looked at me, then back at Woodard. "Inspector of what?"

"Special Branch, Delukulpa Srikshivi." He walked a short distance down the hall to a door, which had a poster with WEL-COME TO NAMHATANU on it in a dozen languages.

With an inclination of his head, he gestured to us to enter the room. My insides ached with a desire to run away, but I went down the hall and through that doorway, leaving Idusvati outside to take up what looked a helluva lot like a guard position.

Inside, a long, low conference table was surrounded by Herl kneeling stools. Tourist posters on the walls declared the natural beauty of Namhatanu, with pictures of the Eight Gorges water falls and the Moss Gardens of Vridretika. An elderly Herl man, with the thick, leathery skin of the very old, looked up from a cup of tea—incongruously, a blue Wedgwood cup of what smelled like Earl Grey. His crest lacked the sheen of youth but had been carefully tended with pomade and kept in glossy order. Forty years changes people, be they human or Herl.

Woodard twisted his neck in the Herl fashion for greeting a superior. "May I present Inspector Shivsati—Dr. Stephens and Mx. Low."

The inspector put both hands on either side of his cup and pushed himself up. His back curled a little with age, but his eyes were bright. "Bonnyjean. Sorry about the circumstances." His English sounded as if he'd learned it from someone Southern.

Because Tadevi Shivsati had learned it from me.

"Tadevi. Hell of a long time." My voice rasped as if the air had been sucked out of the room.

"It did not need to be. I let you know when I was on Earth."

"You did." I had panicked then the way I was panicking now.

Jax's eyes were huge as he looked between us. "How . . . how do you two know each other?"

I opened my mouth, not sure how to answer in a way that wouldn't unpack a bajillion other questions.

"We were in a POW camp together." Tadevi gave an answer that only touched the surface. He looked at Woodard. "That'll be all, Woodard."

The human man stepped out to join Idusvati and shut the door behind him.

Tadevi gestured behind us. "Please, have a seat?"

Against the wall were two human chairs, side by side. Jax hesitated for a moment and then sat down. I dropped into the other one because honest to God, I wasn't sure how much longer

I'd be able to keep standing. What do you say to your lover from forty years before?

What do you say to someone that you left behind?

Tadevi put his hands on the table and lowered himself back to his kneeling stool. He picked up a small teapot and poured for both of us, and age had not robbed him of a whit of the fluid elegance of his hands. "Mx. Low, I want to say, right up front, that we're shocked that your son was taken from you and are deeply sympathetic."

Red alarm panged in my gut. "How did you know he was missing?"

"The hotel reported it." His gaze turned to me, and the wrinkles surrounded those same amethyst eyes that I remembered from forty years ago. "Your name had already been flagged because of your encounter with Desta Kessell. I then asked to be assigned to this because of our history."

"That's . . ." I swallowed guilt. "That's very kind of you."

The air sacs on his nose pulsed with a soft *hmm*. "The price for his return is, I believe, your silence?"

Jax leaned forward in his seat. "Have you found him?"

Tadevi slid a cup of tea across to Jax. "Sadly, no. The name that Noah Varnham gave the hotel was false. The form of payment was also fraudulent." He pushed the other cup toward me. "We are pursuing other methods to find them. In the meantime, I think it would be fastest if we collaborated, and I know that Bonnyjean is worthy of trust."

I closed my eyes, swallowing bile. He sounded so kind, but that was a knife thrust straight to my heart.

"Desta Kessell was sent to Tali by the Interplanetary Special Forces on our behalf, to block an assassination plot. It was dangerous, which she knew, but she was an excellent agent, and yet . . ."

And yet she got murdered anyway. What a pleasant way to remind me of exactly how over our heads in shit we were.

Picking up his tea, Tadevi inhaled, air sacs flexing with appreciation. "Desta found you to be worthy of her trust. She trusted you, specifically, to carry vital information to us."

The notebook around my neck pressed against my breastbone. Desta had asked me to *tell them, in Vatri, to try Murray Chappell.* But that was before Tristan was kidnapped. "Did she know who I was?"

"Only what is in the public record about your service." Tadevi set his cup down and turned fully to face me. He laid a hand on the table, fingers spread wide. "I know that forty years ago, you had the skills to track down the culprits and retrieve your grandson. I do not know if you have kept up those skills."

An evac mission gone so wrong. *Rubble and explosions and bending over a body as it bled and bled and bled.* I tightened my fingers in the fabric of my trousers. I stared at the tourist poster across from me, tracing the waterfalls that sprayed the Eight Gorges.

"I haven't. Helluva neurosurgeon, though."

Swallowing, Jax stared at me like he'd never seen me before. His gaze flicked to the place where the little book rested below the neckline of my shirt.

Tadevi didn't miss that movement. I bet he'd looked at security footage and seen that I'd written something down. He tilted his head, regarding me. "May I know what message Desta gave to you?"

I was holding my breath because if I let the air out of my lungs, I wasn't sure I could inhale again. My stomach was a tight knot. Regardless of the time that had passed, regardless of the way I'd gotten repatriated out of that camp and never looked back, Tadevi was someone I could trust.

"Yeah." I pulled the notebook out of the cord and put it on the table. "Here's what she said to me."

Beside me, Jax suddenly stiffened and the color drained from his face. He slapped his hand down on the book, covering it. With the other, he pointed to his temple in the universal sign for *I'm taking a call*.

"Hello? Emma?" Swallowing, he lowered his hand to fumble in his pocket. "Where's Tristan? Is he with you?"

Tadevi's gaze went wide. He pulled his hand away from his teacup and reached for a notepad.

"Just please tell me. Please?" Pulling out his handheld, Jax blinked twice to transfer the call to it and pushed the speaker function.

Emma's voice sprang into the room with tinny fidelity. ". . . probably want to talk to Tristan?"

"God, yes. Please. I've got you on speaker so Bonnyjean can hear." He chewed his lower lip. On the other end of the line, cloth rustled and someone made a small sniffle. Jax clutched the handheld. "Tristan? Buddy, you there?"

Emma answered, "Give me a moment."

Tadevi held up the notepad, on which he'd written, *KEEP THEM TALKING AS LONG AS POSSIBLE.*

"Daddy?"

My heart nearly gave out. Jax clapped a hand over his mouth, squeezing his eyes shut.

Even after taking a deep breath, his voice still sounded hollow. "Tristan. Hey, buddy. You okay?"

"I'm scared, Daddy, but only a little. I think. But—but—but I miss you, Daddy. I wanna come home. I miss you, I miss you, I miss you."

Jax slapped his hand back over his mouth, choking back sobs, and thrust the phone at me.

I could barely form words myself. "Tristan, sweetie. This is your grandma."

"Is Daddy crying?"

Hell yes, he was, and my own eyes were leaking tears like God was going to flood the earth with them. I swallowed oceans of tears and found my voice. "We miss you, sweetie."

"I'm sorry! I didn't mean to make him cry. I'm so-sorry." His little voice broke.

God damn those people to hell and back. "It's okay, honey."

"Tell me where you are. Tristan, where are you?" As those words left Jax's mouth, I pulled the phone away to try and stop him, because that was the wrong way to keep them on the line.

Tristan sniffled and then, bless him, "Dhri eight—"

The sound snipped off.

I shook the handheld as if that would do a damned thing. He was gone. I hurled the handheld across the room, and it smacked into the wall next to the door, shattering the glass on a poster. Jax stood, grabbed me and pulled me in. I wasn't sure if I was hugging him or he was hugging me, all I knew was that I was going to either vomit or collapse or kill someone.

Tadevi looked at the broken glass and his crest rustled.

Jax stepped back, wiping his eyes with his sleeve. I just let the tears stream down my face. There wasn't a sleeve big enough to catch all my terror.

Tadevi looked up and to the left, as if he were accessing his HUD. "The call came from within Vatri city limits." His air sacs flared with a quick breath. "A kiosk phone. Tower seventeen."

Jax spun in a circle, like he was trying to walk every direction at once. He stopped, facing Tadevi. "What's Dhri eight?"

"Part of a street number. I've already passed it to my agents." Tadevi tapped his temple, and I wondered how many people he'd had listening to the call. "We're sending a car, but likely they'll be gone."

Jax scraped the book off the table. "They know we're here. It's not safe to talk to you. You get Tristan back, and then we'll have something to say to you."

"She knows you are here in Vatri, yes. But does she know you are with me?" Tadevi leaned across the table, eyes intent on Jax. "Did she say that she knows you are with me?"

"Not in those words, but the timing of the call . . . I mean . . . She's got to know."

"No." My skin was cold, and old memories of pincers and tie-down straps and blood crowded the edges of my vision, making it hard to see. I swallowed, closing my eyes for a moment, but that just made the images more vivid. I looked at the scarred edge of the table. "She doesn't know we're here. If she did, she'd have to believe that we'd already talked. They would have to make different choices at that point, and Tristan would not . . . You got to talk to him. She doesn't know we're here."

"So, what? You think it was a coincidence?" Jax looked desperate. I know I was right there.

Tadevi looked out the windows toward the tarmac. "The press. She called because they know that you are in Vatri. What is your next move?"

Jax and I looked at each other and I pinged him. *If we can trust anyone, this is the guy.*

He took a deep breath, staring at the ceiling, his hands wrapped around the book so tightly that his knuckles were white. Swallowing, he lowered his head and put the book back on the table. "You know everything in there except the name."

"Murray Chappell." It was like I had set down a weight.

Tadevi's crest rustled with tension as he reached for the book. "That is not a name on my radar at all. Human."

"We looked him up before we came. He has a special effects shop here in Vatri. We figure that's where Desta got her Herl disguise."

Tadevi looked up sharply from the book, his air sacs pulsing with surprise. "No. That was something Desta got from us."

"We—" Jax wiped his hands on his thighs. "We have an appointment at his shop. This afternoon."

"Hmm . . . then that may be the other reason for the call. Perhaps contacting him alerted them that you know his name." Flipping the book's pages with his inner thumb, Tadevi stared at one of the walls, eyes twitching in that way that happens when someone is using an HUD. "Nowhere near tower seventeen . . ."

Jax asked, "What does that mean?"

I answered for Tadevi. "It means that the shop isn't near where Emma was when she called. So Tristan's probably not there."

"True." Tadevi rested the fingers of the other hand on the end of his long nose, bending down the tip in the way he used to when we were playing word games. Blowing out the air sacs in a loud, thrumming decision, he looked to the door.

Idusvati stepped in, answering a silent summons. "Sir?"

"I need reconnaissance of Murray Chappell." Tadevi could have sent all this via a ping. He was saying it aloud, in front of us—in English—for our benefit. "The child may be a hostage there, but I think it unlikely. Still, until we are certain, observation only."

"Understood."

Tadevi picked up a cane that had been leaning against the wall. He limped heavily as he rounded the table and stood in front of Jax and me. "I will supervise setting up the surveillance myself."

For a moment Idusvati's crest ruffled with surprise. "Sir . . ." She looked at us and then away, as if she were subvocalizing.

"Mm . . ." Tadevi also looked at us, but responded to her aloud, and I knew that was also for us. "I have time before Adusandika. This is important."

"Thank you." My hands were shaking so hard that I clasped them together behind my back. "What can we do?"

He inclined his head to me. "May I request that you remain here, while we investigate?"

"Shouldn't we keep the appointment?" Jax moved to the front edge of his seat. "See what we can learn?"

"What would you do with that information?"

And that was the crux of the problem. I was seventy-eight years old with an arthritic hip. Jax didn't even have training to have forgotten. When he looked at me, I could see the despair in his gaze.

"My people are very good. Now . . . I suspect that Emma will call you again. If she does, I am leaving Woodard here. Let him know at once. Keep her on the phone as long as you can." Tadevi's gaze turned to me, and even with all the wrinkles surrounding his eyes, I recognized the plea. "Please. Let us do our job."

It felt so much like being trapped again, but I nodded. So did Jax. We would wait.

For now. But if Emma called again and there was a chance in hell of getting Tristan back, I would do whatever it took.

I kept checking the time, which seemed as if it had come to a complete standstill. No more than half an hour had passed since Tadevi had left the office. That would be enough time for them to get to Murray Chappell's place and that was about it. I kept shifting and opening windows on my HUD as if I could pay attention to anything.

With a grunt, I shoved my way out of my chair. If I sat in the damn chair a minute longer, my hip was going to freeze solid. I walked back and forth, trying to keep it limber.

And then, I realized that I was counting in Herl in my head.

Did Tadevi still count in English when he exercised?

Base eight and base ten. Our fingers touching each other in the dark with a mismatch that he made up for by offering the soft palms of his hands for five and ten. I stopped, remembering the tender skin of his nose sacs pressed against the side of my neck as we lay face-to-face after lights-out. Knees bending opposite, we could face each other and form a perfect spoon. His voice was a low murmur in my ear, telling me that he would keep me safe. First in Herl and then, later, in English.

I was one of six humans in the camp. There had been nine of us when I'd arrived.

Heart tight, I stopped in front of one of the walls, staring blankly at the tourist poster in front of me.

Behind me, Jax shifted in his seat. "What did Shivsati mean by his 'history' with you?"

"POW camp."

He waited for me to say something else, and he could keep waiting. "POW camp is a place. What's the history part of it?"

I scrubbed my hands over my face. "It was a long time ago."

He sighed. And the thing about Jax was that he never shouted. As loud as he could get onstage, he was the quiet one in the marriage. That sigh was a scream of frustration in anyone else. "You asked me to trust this person you erased out of your life. Is this what it's going to be like with Sam?"

"No!"

"Okay then. Tell me about Shivsati. Give me some reason to hope."

I bit my lips and braced myself with my hands on either side of the poster frame. "Tadevi kept me alive."

"Jesus." His chair scraped against the floor as he stood. Footfalls brought him closer to me. He didn't try to touch me, thank God. Even having him that close made me want to bury myself in the corner.

I held myself still and stared at the poster, concentrating on the lines. It was a map of Old Town. I let my gaze trace streets with old, familiar names mixed with stuff I'd never heard of. I spotted Enirodi, which we'd used for training when I first arrived. Now it was the Herl equivalent of a shopping mall.

Jax still stood next to me, waiting, the way he used to wait for Sam to find energy for one more word toward the end.

I dipped my head under the weight of his attention, turning away a little and focusing hard on that goddamned map so I wouldn't have to answer his concern or pity. So I didn't have to tell him that I had, in fact, erased someone that I loved from my life.

A decade after the war, Tadevi had come to Earth, to study. He had contacted me. I hadn't replied. It wasn't that I was ashamed of having a lover who was not human. But every memory of him was wrapped in another one of pain and fear. Sam was maybe five, and I couldn't figure out how to explain to my child or my husband who Tadevi was.

So I just kept putting off answering. And the longer I waited, the more ashamed I was for not reaching out after the war ended to find out if he was safe.

Then he finished his studies and went back to Namhatanu.

What piece of that did I want to share with my child's widower?

I closed my eyes, trying to steady my breathing. And when I reopened them, my eyes focused on the map directly in front of me.

DeluMary Danuyongi Yeima.

The mix of English and High Herl caught my attention, and my brain unpacked the High Herl rather than have to think about Tadevi. Possessive Honored Mary Over Ghost Place.

Spirit place. Church.

St. Mary's Church.

No—St. Mary's Chapel.

"Shit." I took a step back from the poster, then leaned down again to stare at it. "Shit. Shit. Shit."

"Bonnyjean, are you okay?"

"No. It's not that. Wait. Wait . . ." I pulled up a map of service towers in the city and laid it over the map on the wall. Tower seventeen, where Emma's call had been routed from, was five streets from the chapel. I put my finger on the building. "It's a place. It's not Murray Chappell. It's St. Mary's Chapel."

"Oh God." His eyes widened as he stared at it. "So Shivsati has gone to the wrong place."

We both started moving for the door at the same time. Jax beat me to it by a lot and jerked it open. "Agent Woodard!"

The human man had been sitting in a chair opposite the door. He was on his feet by the time the door finished opening.

"We were wrong. My son is at St. Mary's Chapel."

The agent tilted his head the way a Herl would, from the base of the neck, and it looked so weird on him. "Did you receive another call?"

I shook my head, beckoning to him. "No. I just wrote it down wrong. There's a map in here and—doesn't matter. Look up St. Mary's Chapel or DeluMary Danuyongi Yeima and overlay the service tower map on it. It's near seventeen."

He squinted, staring into the space over our heads. "I will let the inspector know."

Jax shook his head. "We need to go there. Tristan has to be there and in danger."

"It's not that simple."

"Fuck you. It is." I stomped forward. "Let me talk to Tadevi— Let me talk to Inspector Shivsati."

"He cannot be reached." Woodard spread his hands apologetically. "We have people watching the place you identified earlier, and they have the inspector's highest trust."

"But that's not where my son is." Jax pointed back into the room, past me, at the map. "He's at St. Mary's Chapel."

"And earlier you thought he was at a special effects shop." Woodard sighed. "I'll arrange to send a car to do a drive-by, but Herl have very clear laws about religious institutions. We can't just barge in."

I rolled my eyes. "St. Mary's Chapel? It's not for Herl. It's an expat thing."

"The laws are the same, regardless of planet of origin. A drive-by is the best I can do without something more."

My jaw was set so tight that it ached. I squinted at the man. "Any rules saying I can't go there?"

"I would not recommend that."

"I'll take that under advisement." I caught Jax's eye and used my subdermal to send him a text. *Stay here.*

He shook his head, messaging back. *I want to come.*

Not a good plan. I'll be safe. Promise.

He set his jaw and shook his head again, glaring at me.

I reached over and took his hand, drew him back into the room, and shut the door in Woodard's face. "Listen . . . No one watches old ladies. You? With the press?"

"My son."

"My grandson."

"You shouldn't go alone."

"You can listen in. But you aren't coming." I gave a little shrug. "Which of us was in a military infiltration team?"

"Forty years ago."

"I know." I looked at the map again and headed toward the door. "I'll bring him home."

FOURTEEN

The Namhatanu sky had gone to a deep purple with salmon-pink clouds glowing against it. As my autocab stopped at the corner, evening shadows muted the murals lining the streets. Except for a plain white stone wall surrounding a green lawn, in the center of which stood a church that might have been at home in Maryland or maybe London, but here all that white stone looked like a Herl house with the murals painted over for mourning.

I tilted my head back to follow the belfry up to the evening sky. Tempting though it was to barge in, I took the time to walk around the building, looking for routes in and out. A side door on the north side. Windows up in the belfry. Stained glass everywhere, and no view into the interior. Clenching my fists, I took a breath, and then I walked through the gate onto the grounds and followed the stone sidewalk up to the front doors.

They were wood, with brass handles, and had more stained glass inset. For once, it helped, because it masked my approach. I stood to the side, listening to sounds from the interior. A hymn drifted out, mingling voices and organ music in the air. So, a service was happening. That would help and also reduced the chances that this was the right place.

Still. I had to know. Opening the door a crack, I peeked through into the dim vestibule. The angle let me see the far wall, which had a hanging of the Madonna rendered in the embroidery style of the Sati highlands. There was a carved screen separating the entry from the main chapel. Directly opposite the door, the screen part of an arch that opened onto the main aisle. No one in view.

I wanted a weapon in my hand in ways that felt familiar but had been made alien by time.

Unarmed, I slipped through the door and into the vestibule, crossing as quickly as possible away from that open arch to the cover of the screen. My palms were sweating and my throat was tight.

I got to the cover and my brain had the urge to say *loerku*, as if I were clearing the way for a squad mate.

Through the piercings in the pale wood, I could see pops of color from the interior. Murals lined the walls, but not with the abstract seascapes that Sati favored. These were renderings of the stations of the cross in the same vivid colors as the surrounding streets.

Beneath softly glowing chandeliers, the chapel was empty.

The sound of the organ and the voices came from speakers.

I messaged Jax. *Looks like another dead end.*

We would bring Tristan home. This might be another wild goose chase, but we would find him.

And then—Christ on a hound dog. Emma was walking down the far aisle toward the vestibule.

I looked around for an escape, because Emma hadn't seen

me yet. Back out the main door, but then what? Crossing the vestibule to the aisle she was coming down would mean crossing the arch that opened onto the main aisle.

Could I grab her and use her as a counter-hostage? I scanned the area around me, looking for anything I could use to restrain her. The wall hanging, maybe, but it wouldn't be fast. There would be plenty of time for her to scream.

And then Emma was there. She stopped on the far side of the vestibule, too far away to even try to grab. The color drained out of her face.

There wasn't much else I could do, so I stared straight at Emma. Her eyes showed white all the way around as she stared back.

At the front of the church, a door opened, and Noah walked into the room in conversation with a couple of Herl and a human woman. One of them laughed, but with the organ music, I couldn't make out even what language anyone was speaking.

"Emma?" Noah stopped, looking across the church at his daughter.

She wet her lips and then turned and walked back up the aisle. "Yes, Daddy?"

Hidden behind the carved screen, I had a fairly decent view of Noah's face as he looked at his daughter and frowned. He obviously knew something was wrong, but not what.

Emma and Noah were both here, which meant that Tristan was very likely in the building. I pulled up my directory on my HUD and opened a channel to Jax. *Tell Woodard that Noah and Emma are here.*

Noah asked Emma something. She shrugged, pointing toward the side door, away from me. As if . . . as if Emma had *not* told him that I was in the vestibule.

I held still. Please God, don't let him see me. Please let Emma be the good girl she seemed to be.

Jax replied, *He says you should exit the chapel and wait for the police.*

No. My fingernails bit into my palms, and my jaw ached from clenching. Letting out a breath, I pinged Jax again. *Tadevi said he had an event at Adusandika. It's a concert hall. Can you get to Adusandika and find him?*

Why do you think he'll do anything? I'm coming to you.

I bowed my head as if I was praying, and I guess a part of me was. *We were lovers. That's who we were to each other in the POW camp. Tell him that the Varnhams are here and he will come.*

There was a very long lag before Jax replied. *Okay, and then I'm coming to you.*

Fair.

At the front, Noah beckoned to Emma and took her by the arm, whispering to her. A moment later, with her shoulders stiff around her ears, Emma walked through a side door by the altar.

The door behind me opened. The Herl who had shown up at our hotel looking for "Reyes" stood in the entrance. He held a gun.

The skin between my shoulder blades tightened. I held my hands up and out to show that I was unarmed. Stepping all the way in, he kept the gun trained on me and with the other hand, locked the door to the church.

Raising his voice, he said in High Herl, "The old woman is here."

Noah gave a smirk. "Dr. Stephens, how serendipitous."

The Herl gestured for me to head down the aisle. I limped openly, letting my leg drag. The meds were kicking in and I could walk without that feeling of bone grinding on bone. It wouldn't last, but I didn't need good movement forever. Just until we had Tristan.

And they didn't need to know that I could move.

I stopped in front of Noah. "Where's Tristan?"

He shrugged. "Upstairs. I'm delighted you're here, actually. Emma could use a hand with his dinner. Finicky eater, that one."

For a moment, his gaze flicked to the back of the church. I glanced over my shoulder as a heavy clang sounded through the chapel. The door that Emma had gone through was shut. The squat Herl woman who had watched us at the airport slipped an analog key into a iron lock. Even from where I was, I could hear the lock click home.

The woman dropped the key into a pocket.

Oh hell, no. Turning back to Noah, I pushed off with my left leg and closed the distance between us. Before he could pull back, I grabbed his collar and spun him so he was between me and the Herl with the gun. "Look. I don't care about your politics. I just want my grandson."

He grabbed my hands, prying at my fingers. "And Jax? Where is he?"

"At the hotel. Just give me Tristan and we'll leave you alone."

Noah's mouth twisted under that ridiculous mustache. "You want to see him? That could be arranged."

Still holding Noah, I shouted, "Tristan! Tristan Low! Tristan! Honey, where are you? Tristan! Tristan!"

The sound echoed through the chapel as the Herl man with the gun tried circling around us.

A thin voice echoed from deep in the chapel. "Grandma? Grandma, I'm here! Gran—"

I was going to kill them. I shoved Noah at the Herl with the gun. As they tangled together, I headed straight for Tristan's voice. The Herl woman got between me and the side door, and I just tucked my head down and slammed my shoulder into her side. Pain flared, but that bastard stumbled back and out of my way.

Then a double-thumb grip grabbed my arm, spinning me. Something slammed into my midriff, driving the air out of my lungs. Arms wrapped around me and I went down.

Time stretched out and blended with the past.

I am lying under the weight of a body—Peters, I think, but I hadn't looked to see which of my buddies I'd dragged on top of me. My vision is filled with blue-green rubble, slicked with blood. Beyond my line of sight, the rubble shifts with the footsteps of the bastards who ambushed us. Blood trickles down the back of my neck, and I don't know if it's from me or Peters.

No. No. That was hard, clean stone under my cheek. The footsteps were those of the bastards who took my grandson. I blinked and swallowed. I was in St. Mary's Chapel.

One of them had a knee on my back, arms twisted around behind me. I used to know how to get out of this hold. Of course, I'd also been in my thirties and ripped. I'd need him to give me a bit of slack if I had any chance of breaking free.

A young Herl woman, probably the one who'd barred the doors, spoke in High Herl, and I understood both words. "They've gone."

They. That was probably Tristan and Emma. I tried to activate my subdermal, hoping they hadn't thought to turn on a blocker. I got no response at all. Nothing. Not even a local-access-only notification.

My HUD wasn't just blocked, like at the police station. Or "off" the way I'd asked Jax to do with his. Noah had used a contact remote to turn it off. We used them to completely deactivate subdermals for surgery. I was fucked. The only way to turn it back on was with another contact remote.

"Seyeli?" Noah stood just at the edge of my field of vision. Clicking footsteps preceded a pair of Herl tabbed shoes, with double-toes capped in black enamel. He said something in High Herl, and it took me a minute to parse each word. "Here are the concert tickets for Adusandika."

I caught my breath. Adusandika Hall. Where Tadevi had gone tonight. The question was: Had he gone to stop an assassination or was he the target?

The Herl did not speak, but paper rustled against cloth and the bottom edge of his tunic billowed. Maybe he put the tickets in his pocket?

The next part, I only caught some of the words. "A box" and "across from your target" and "Do you remember the . . ." but not what it was he was supposed to remember.

"You sent a recording." The ragged edge of the Herl's voice placed him. Seyeli was the Herl who had shown up at the hotel. And then a word I didn't know.

I counted people and placed them in a map in my mind with my head being at twelve o'clock. The goon on my back. The woman at four o'clock. Noah and Seyeli at ten o'clock. I breathed through my mouth, eyes mostly closed, and listened for other people.

"Good. Good." Noah clapped his hands together, mimicking a cymbal crash. My High Herl was so rusty that all I got was "In an . . ." and "No one should hear, so that should" and then a string I didn't get at all. But then words I knew. "A second shot is risky."

"I'll take no risks."

"I'm pleased. I would hate to have gone . . ." Then the English words "Piper Nine Station" popped out. He turned away from Seyeli, his feet pointing at me, and I just kept playing possum. "Your target should be at Adusandika Hall by now."

"Payment on completion?"

"It will be in your account."

Seyeli snorted through his air sacs. "All humans are liars."

Noah sighed and switched back to English. "Out the back door, if you please. And I do apologize for the rear exit, but we have our front to maintain. Ha ha. Our front . . ."

I watched as best I could without letting my head move. The assassin went out. Same door that Emma had gone through earlier. It meant that there was probably only the fellow on my back, Noah, and the Herl woman.

Someone pounded on the front door. The goon on my back jumped and damn it—I hadn't been ready for him. He got a grip again before I could move.

Noah's feet shifted. "Irmani, look outside."

The woman's feet passed me—that must be Irmani. She headed to the door the goons had come out of. A moment later, she was back. "Police. One car. Four police."

One car. With my face pressed against the floor, I cursed buckets at Woodard. One car. Four officers. Now I knew how little they cared about Tristan.

"Out the rear, then, for all of us. Bring our friend, eh?"

On my back, the goon shifted, and this time I was ready. I

pushed down with my left thigh, sliding my right leg up. My hip screamed, and I screamed right along with it. His grip slipped. Not a lot, but enough that I twisted my left arm free.

I rolled, slamming my elbow back into the goon's crotch. With a strangled cry, he fell sideways off me. I wrenched free and staggered to my feet. Noah ran toward me. I grabbed the first thing I could lay hands on and flung a chalice at him.

He flinched, just long enough for me to make a limping run for the nearest door. I closed the door as soon as I was through and fell back against it, fumbling for the lock.

The door slammed against its frame. Muffled voices and then the sound of metal on metal.

Oh hell. The woman had had a key to the other locks. My heart was a trapped animal inside my chest. The only thing in the room was the foot of a narrow, curving flight of stairs. "Double hell."

I pushed away from the door and grabbed the handrail. I got maybe five stairs up before my hip started squawking. Jaw set, I hauled myself up another turn and then, even with the corticosteroid shot, my hip seized in a wall of blinding white pain and I tripped.

I clutched the rail with both hands and just managed to keep from going down the stairs like a slide. My breath rasped in my ears.

That was it. It didn't sound like anyone was climbing after me. I sat for a minute, straining my hearing. Not a goddamned thing. Wetting my lips, I hauled myself to my feet. One limping step at a time, I went a little higher until the curve brought me to a small stained-glass window set in the stone. I had to bend a little to peer out.

Below me, Noah stood wearing a wig and a surplice, like he was the vicar. He was casually talking to the police. Laughing with the police.

"No!" My voice echoed inside the bell tower but didn't appear to go beyond the glass of the window. I yanked my shirt over my head. As I wrapped the cloth around my fist, the cool air raised gooseflesh on my arms. I punched the glass.

The jolt sent fireworks up my arm. The glass didn't even flex. Stupid reinforced safety window. It had a micro-thin layer of high-tensile strength glazing smoothed over it. I wouldn't be able to break it with anything short of a sledgehammer driven by John Henry himself.

Scrambling, I hurried down the stairs, trying to get the shirt back on and not trip at the same time. I fetched up at the bottom with an awkward shuffle.

At the door, I stood staring at it and then rested my ear against the wood. Nothing. Not a noise or a vibration. Maybe they were trying to bluff me into coming out. But the way Noah had been outside, I didn't think that was the case. I unlocked the door and yanked.

It didn't budge. I pushed, in case I was being stupid. But the door was barred from the outside.

The only potential way out was back up.

The thing about a corticosteroid shot was that it would reduce inflammation for three to four weeks of normal activity. Normal activity. Normal. I leaned against the wall of the church's bell tower and grimaced against the throbbing in my hip. It wasn't the usual ice pick, just a constant, pervasive ache. A breeze cut through the wooden slats at the top of the tower and seemed to pick up a chill from the enormous brass bell in the middle.

Whoever had originally built this church had been pining for home and digging their heels into denial about being on Namhatanu. I tried my subdermal again, just in case, but my subdermal wasn't just asleep, it was off.

Outside, the sky had turned to twilight and streetlight puddled on the sidewalks. The completely empty sidewalks. Hellfire and damnation, there wasn't anyone I could holler at for help. All right . . . what did I have to work with? Paper in my pocket. Throwing a note down would do jackshit if there wasn't someone to see it. Might as well wait for someone.

The top of the belfry was distressingly tidy. Wooden slatted windows. Big ole bell—huh. A bell. Folks used to signal things with a bell.

The pull rope disappeared through a hole in the floor, but I was not going down all those stairs again when I could just lean on it right now. The bell was about a third of my height, attached to a stout metal yoke that pivoted on a wheel. A lever came off to one side, with the rope attached to it so you could haul down to get it to ring.

Wrapping my hands around the thick brown rope, I pulled down on it. The bell weighed more than I'd thought. Its yoke rolled a little on the wheel, swinging the bell on its side, but not quite far enough to make a sound. The bell swung back to center, and momentum pulled it through to the other side. Still silent.

I hauled down again, using the bell's motion to try to get sound. This time it arced far enough that the clapper struck the side.

I flinched. The toll vibrated through my hands and punched me in the ears. Gritting my teeth, I hauled down again as the bell arced back and forth, clapper slamming into the sides. It felt as if the ice pick from my hip had found my eardrums. Probably doing some damage, but that didn't much matter. Not when Tristan was missing, and I'd just sent Jax to where the assassin was.

When I got it swinging, I let go of the rope, clapping my hands over my ears. Even then, it felt as if the ice pick was slipping through my fingers and straight down the ear canal. I ran down to the nearest clear window, ready to drop my hands and wave to get someone's attention.

The police car was gone. How the hell did Noah convince the police officers to leave?

Behind me the bell continued to toll. It slowed. More time came between strikes. And then it was silent, rocking in its yoke. I walked around the belfry, peering out through the window slats.

A few people turned and looked curiously toward the tower, but they kept moving. None of them seemed to recognize it as a distress call. None of them thought it was worth investigating.

Goddamn it. How the hell was I supposed to get out of this tower?

I put my hands on the louvers covering the nearest window and felt around for the latch. It had been painted over, but prying at it with my nails, I was able to scratch the paint away enough to unlatch the screen. I leaned out and looked down. The roof of the church was about a story down and steeply pitched.

To the right, an iron fire escape clutched the side of the main building, which would be great if I could get down to it. The side of the bell tower was rough stone that once upon a time, I might have been able to climb down. I wasn't enough of an idiot to think I could do a free climb now. Wrong shoes, arthritic hip. The fact that I was seventy-eight didn't help either.

Wait. I turned and stared at the bell again.

More specifically, I stared at the rope that hung from the bell. It had to be long enough to reach to the bottom of the tower. Lordy. I had all the brains that God gave a stump. Wetting my lips, I walked back over to the bell and put my hand on it to stop the thing's silent swing.

I wasn't fit enough to do an unaided descent, but with a rope . . . Maybe. I might as well haul it out of the hole. I could always think better of it before I did it.

Hand over hand, I pulled the stiff brown rope up, coiling it on the floor, before I realized what I was doing. It was funny how movements that I hadn't done in decades came back so natural.

Shaking my head, I hauled on it until the end came snaking up out of the hole. The rope was probably a good twenty-four meters long. Not long enough to get me down to the ground, but it ought to be more than enough to get me to the roof.

The end was spliced onto the bell pull, but I checked it for weakness anyway. Checked the yoke the bell was attached to as well, and everything seemed sturdy. I kept staring out the windows as I worked, praying to the good lord above that someone would walk down the street. You'd think being in a church would do me some good, but I might as well have been in a desert.

Bristles broke off the rough rope and found their way into the creases of my hands. It was stiff and not as malleable as climbing rope. This was going to wreak havoc on my hands.

I sat down on the stairs. Shucking off my shoes, I pulled my socks off. Or, rather, my compression socks, because I had the circulation of a seventy-eight-year-old. They were sturdy and thin and long enough to tie around my palms. It wasn't perfect, but it would do.

Once I got my shoes back on, I grabbed the railing and hauled myself back to my feet. Grimacing, I threw the rope out of the window. It landed with a slap against the roof of the church and slithered down to the side. My heart felt like an entire mob of greyhounds was running laps around my ribs. I stared off down the street, hoping that someone would miraculously appear. Nothing. I took a second to look out the other windows, but I was as alone as when I started.

All right then.

I straddled the rope, lifted it, and passed the end around my hip. Then I lifted it again to drape it over my left shoulder, around the back of my neck, and then over to my right hand. In theory, the friction of the rope against my body would break my descent. In practice, the rope was so stiff and coarse that I was a little worried I wouldn't descend at all.

I hopped up on the sill, and the wood dug into my ass. I was dumb even to be trying this. But they still had Tristan. And now Jax had gone to try to find Tadevi at Adusandika Hall with no notion that the assassin was heading there—no. Probably already there by now.

Carefully, I stood, half-crouched, on the window ledge. My weight shifted as the bell rolled to the side with an enormous clang. I could hardly catch my breath.

The rope was tight, and before I could think better of it, I stepped back and down. The rope held me as I placed my foot on the rough stone. I took it slow and steady. Just like in the textbooks of forty years ago, I fed the rope out with each step and kept my gaze fixed on the stones I was rappelling down.

My arms burned holding my weight. My fingers burned from the rough scrape of the rope. My thighs burned from bracing against the building. My whole body seemed lit on fire.

But Tristan. And Jax. And honest to God, I didn't want to fall.

My foot touched the roof. I almost let go of the rope in relief, but I had to get down to the fire escape. Comparatively, it was easy.

And after that—after that, I had to hail a car without an active subdermal.

Dusty and disheveled, I got off the streetcar at Adusandika Hall. There had been no hailing of an autocab, but, thank God, Vatri was a modern city with a robust and free light rail system.

Adusandika Hall was a beautiful old theater, with the graceful arching colonnades typical of Sati Herl architecture from two centuries ago. The long banks of sandbags that had surrounded it when I'd last been here had been banished to memories, and the grit that had coated the theater's murals had been washed away. They had been painted by some famous fellow and named after another, but I couldn't remember much more than that.

A cascade of steps surrounded the building, so it stood raised and apart like a monument. There was probably a ramp somewhere, but I went for the shortest path and hauled myself up the stairs. At the top, great double doors with etched glass opened onto a nearly empty lobby.

When I'd been here before, there was no glass. The archways had opened onto the ground floor with no doors so that any citizen could enjoy the performances. But the elite had the ticketed upper levels.

Which was where Seyeli and the lawmaker and Tadevi would be.

A Herl police officer came out of the shadows and stopped me before I got to the door. He said something in High Herl, and it took me a minute to parse. "Do you have a ticket?"

"Free seat." I pointed to one of the arches. "Down. Please?"

Frowning, he waved a metal wand over me, and when it didn't make a sound, he stepped back and waved to the door. As I went through, I heard the word "dirty."

He wasn't wrong.

Strains of music swirled out of the auditorium, but I had no idea where in the program they were. And really, all I knew was that there was a dignitary—a Herl lawmaker—and that Seyeli was going to shoot them at some point when no one would hear the shot. It wasn't a helluva lot to go on.

But I knew that Seyeli had a ticket, which meant upper level. And a box seat. Grimacing, I headed for the stairs to the second floor and had the only miracle that I was likely to get. An elevator sat open and waiting. I limped in. Pushed the up button and slumped against the wall. God, I was tired. Couldn't remember the last time I'd eaten, even.

The door slid open silently onto a wash of music. I stepped out into a long, curving corridor that followed the arc of the theater, then around out of sight. At intervals, arches led into the theater itself. Maybe I could grab a program and see where they were at least.

I stepped into the first arch and—Jax. My knees went weak with relief at the sight of his spiky hair. The line of his shoulders was tense and silhouetted against the light of the theater. Choral voices wrapped their way around him, filling the auditorium. I limped forward and tapped him on the shoulder.

He spun, eyes wide and mouth open as if he were about to shout. His shoulders sagged visibly at the sight of me, and he stepped forward, pulling me into an embrace. "Are you okay? I've been trying to reach you and—"

"Long story. Listen. There's an assassin and—"

"I know." Jax grabbed my arm as he stepped back and pulled me with him. He whispered and pointed. "He's up there."

"How the devil do you know that?" I followed the line of his arm as he pointed to a box seat in the dress circle above us.

"When I got here . . . Remember in the hotel, that Herl who came to our door while Desta was there?" Jax slipped behind me and shifted so I could sight down his arm. "There. See him?"

"Sure enough." It was Seyeli. "Seen Tadevi anywhere?"

Jax took my shoulder and turned me to look across the theater. Directly across from Seyeli, Tadevi sat with a tall, elderly Herl woman. Even in the dim light, the silk ribbons wrapping her torso shone reflected light at the stage. I would bet almost anything that she was the lawmaker Desta had told me about.

I nodded and stepped back from the arch, toward the main corridor. "Got it. Have you talked to him yet?"

"I tried. I had to use a translation app, and I couldn't get them to let me past."

I grimaced. Tadevi might not know that the attempt was going to be tonight. "You know this piece? Is there a part that's real loud?"

"I don't—but there's a cymbal player in the percussion." He stared at the orchestra for a minute. "Why?"

"That's when he's taking his shot."

Jax grabbed my arm. "What about Tristan?"

"He's alive. I heard him. But I . . . I couldn't get him." I pressed my hand over his and then headed for the elevator to the dress circle. "Keep an eye on Seyeli. Let me know when he moves."

I was already in the elevator before I remembered that my subdermal was off. I turned, and the doors shut between us. Damn it all to hell. I shifted my weight from foot to foot, waiting until the door finally opened on the upper lobby. The walls were etched with bas-relief, painted in subtle gradations of blues and greens, so it felt like I had stepped into an undersea grotto.

Outside one of the boxes, a cluster of uniformed Herl police officers stood at parade rest. I swallowed and headed for them. One of them looked toward me, no doubt seeing the complete mess I was, and stepped away from the wall. He held up his hand and spoke to me in High Herl.

Gritting my teeth, I pulled up a memory of sitting in the exercise yard, surrounded by Herl laughing because my Herl was flat and uninflected. But I used to be able to speak it. In old, very broken High Herl, I said, "I speak with Inspector Shivsati. Important."

He replied, and all I caught was "no" and "return to your seat."

"Shivsati. Please. Important. Sorry. Very important." I pointed past him to the door. "Please. Need him. I need him."

Another officer stepped away from the wall.

"Please. Ask him. Tell him Bonnyjean Stephens are here." What was the pleading movement here? Memory seeped up like blood, of kneeling and begging. I lifted my hands, palms sweating, and spread my fingers wide. Two semicircles out. "Please."

He snorted through his air sacs, and for a minute I thought I'd gotten it wrong, but he made a very clear *wait* gesture and walked over to a Herl officer whose uniform was heavy with rank buttons at the collar. I couldn't hear a thing they said, but even with different body language, it was pretty darn clear that they weren't going to let me in to see him.

The music that was swelling out of the auditorium had sped up. Strings swirled in bright flashes of sound. Drums thundered under them. Was this the climax? Sure seemed like those drums could drown out a gunshot.

The younger officer left his superior and walked back to me. He made eye contact with me and carefully shook his head. Speaking High Herl slowly, he said, "No. Go now. I do not want to hurt you."

I grimaced but backed away. If they arrested me for making a disturbance, I wouldn't get to see Tadevi and couldn't do anything for Tristan.

But I did know where the assassin was.

Everything ached as I turned my back on the officers and walked down the corridor, following the curve to the other side of the theater. The officers disappeared behind me, and it was hard to tell how far around the bend I'd gone.

I slowed when I thought I was pretty close to opposite where I'd been. A padded door closed off each of the private boxes. Easing one open, I peeked inside. A young human couple watched the stage.

Beyond them, the Herl orchestra leader was flicking the end of a long plume, like an extension of his crest. It fluttered over the orchestra, urging them to new heights. The choir's voices thrummed through their air sacs, filling the space.

I shut the door and went to the next, sliding it open. Nothing. This box was just empty. Onstage, the cymbal player leaned forward and picked up the pair of flat brass discs.

Oh hell. I left it swinging open and ran to the next.

As much as I wanted to yank it open, I still had to be cautious. A family of Sati Herl watched the orchestra, except for one teenaged Herl who drew by the dim light of the box.

Through the open door, I heard Jax. His full-throated scream ripped through the auditorium. "ASSASSIN!"

Cymbals crashed.

A gunshot.

The next box. I ran and yanked the door open. On the other side, Seyeli skidded to a halt.

Holy hell. His crest flared to surround his head with angry plumage, and he had one hand inside his tunic, where a shoulder holster would sit. I tightened my fist and swung it at his face. He dodged back, so I just brushed his chin.

He yanked his hand out of his tunic, pulling a gun from its holster. Before he could get it aimed, I lunged forward, swinging without any art at all. Just to keep him from aiming. Just to keep him from getting away. By luck, I caught his nose, crushing one of his air sacs.

With a gasping wheeze, he flinched away and stumbled over a low stool. I picked up the stool and swung it at his head. I missed, but he brought his arm up to block the stool. The leg of the stool slammed into his hand.

The gun clattered to the floor.

He dove for it, and I went right after him. We rolled across the floor. He slammed an open palm against my ear and chopped at my windpipe. I just got my chin tucked in time, but that flinch gave him time to scramble to his feet.

Seyeli climbed onto the edge of the balcony. Damn it. He was going to jump to the next box. The one with the family.

No. No one else's family was going to get hurt. I pushed to my knees and grabbed for the fellow's ankle—

He slipped.

Double-thumbed hands grasping at empty air, he screamed and fell. I staggered to my feet and grabbed the edge of the railing. Below me, Seyeli lay crumpled on the floor. Audience members were shrieking and backing away.

My hands shook on the rail, and I had to clench it to keep from tumbling over after him. I scanned the audience, looking for Jax. There—he stood just inside the door where I'd left him, staring up at me, his face pale with strain, but unhurt. Thank God.

Lifting my head, I stared through the dark to the other side of the theater. In the lawmaker's box, police officers were buzzing about.

But I couldn't tell who had been shot.

The dress circle corridor was a chaos of folks all trying to get out. Glittering theatergoers scurried from their boxes in swishing layers of fabric, weighted at hems and cuffs with jewel-toned enamel buttons. Their flared crests made a wild forest of fear, and everywhere were the deep thrums of nose sacs expanding with alarm. Police officers were trying to control their movement.

I was pretty sure that panicked rush was the only reason I hadn't been grabbed as an accessory. It wouldn't take long for the police to come find me, though, and I had no confidence that they'd listen to a thing I had to say.

But I needed to know if Tadevi was all right.

"Bonnyjean!" Jax sprinted up the stairs, dodging through the folks who were trying to get out.

I pushed over toward him as Jax threaded his way through the theatergoers. There were other humans in the crowd, but not a lot of them, and people started turning to stare at us. Even if I weren't human, I stood out, with the bruises, and dirt, and rope-torn clothing. My heart hadn't settled down, and adrenaline still made my body tight with lingering panic.

Jax grabbed me by both arms. "God, are you all right? He didn't—"

"I'm fine." That was probably the biggest lie I'd ever told. "What about you? I heard you."

"He had a gun out and . . ." He grimaced. "I'm good at being loud. It was the only thing I could think of."

Around the bend in the hall, a knot of police moved toward us, crowding back the theatergoers.

Even without understanding the language, I could hear the agitation in the crowd—crests flaring like anemones under the sea-green arch of the hall. Moving with them was Tadevi.

I was glad that Jax had me by the arms, because I think I might have dropped to my knees with relief.

Tadevi's face was tight with concentration. His gaze darted everywhere, looking for new threats. But he was unharmed.

He was walking with the same tall, elderly Herl woman. Blood soaked the cloth of one sleeve, but she kept waving her aides away. Tadevi saw me and stopped, crest flaring in alarm. He said something to the lawmaker and then broke from her and hurried toward me.

Even in the map of wrinkles, I recognized that look of fear. I held up my hands, and the High Herl I hadn't been able to find before just fell out of my mouth. "I am well."

He reached for me with inner thumb and finger, the way a Herl touches something delicate, but stopped before touching me. "You look injured."

I touched the bruise over my right eye and switched back to English. "Well . . . I reckon I am, but it's not bad."

His mouth tightened as if he were biting back words. Then he turned to look at Jax. "Well done."

"I . . . I just shouted."

"The right shout, at the right time." Tadevi gestured back to the lawmaker. "Please. She wants to meet you."

No, no! We didn't have time for this. Bureaucrats took forever with everything. My heart tied itself in knots. "Tristan—" I grabbed Tadevi's arm, touching him for the first time in forty years. For a moment, it silenced me. "The Varnhams were at St. Mary's Chapel. I heard Tristan's voice."

Tadevi's air sacs flared. He looked at the lawmaker and then back at me. "She is a good person to have owe you a favor. Please. Greet her and then I will go with you. You and your grandson will be my only priority."

Jax nodded. "Let's get it over with."

"Thank you." Tadevi led us to the small cluster. Compressing his lips, he turned to one of the lawmaker's aides and said something in High Herl. About the only word I caught was my name. The lawmaker cocked her head and looked at Jax and me. Her crest smoothed.

The lawmaker nodded to me and stretched out her hands to Jax, then winced and lowered her wounded arm. In English she said, "You have my gratitude and that of my province."

She kept her focus on Jax, and that was fine by me. It looked like no one had clocked my part yet. That was also fine with me. It wouldn't be the first time I'd had a secret like this. With a graceful flourish of her neck, the lawmaker pressed Jax's hand. "I should like to thank you for your quick wits."

Jax swallowed, looking to me for help. "I didn't . . . All I did was "

The lines around the lawmaker's eyes crinkled, and she patted his hand again. "You do not have to sing your own praises. Allow me to honor you at the embassy. We had a small reception planned for after the performance, but now . . . please do come."

"Maybe another day." Jax gave a bow, with a Herl-like twist of the head that showed he'd been paying attention to local body language.

Another aide cut in, and the police made all sorts of comments in High Herl, and the next thing I knew, the lawmaker had been bustled out of the hall with other dignitaries surrounding her. I needed a chair. My brain had just about shut off and felt as dead as my subdermal. What the hell were we going to do?

"Come, please." Tadevi gestured at an arched door to one of the private boxes, where Woodard stood as if he'd just cleared the small room. "Conversation will be, perhaps, easier in a somewhat more private space."

Inspector Idusvati, from the spaceport, joined Woodard and took up a position outside the door. I followed Jax and Tadevi inside the box. Beyond its rail, the floor of the auditorium had been cleared of its audience, and only some police officers occupied the space, guarding the remains of Seyeli.

Tadevi settled onto one of the low kneeling stools and looked up at us. Next to him, Jax sank onto a stool, knees up at awkward angles. As much as I wanted to sit down, I would never be able to get up again if I tried one of those stools. I leaned against the wall and crossed my arms. Waiting.

With his air sacs filling, Tadevi looked at me and then did a sort of double take. "A moment." He turned to the door. And there were times when subdermals seemed like a goddamned superpower, because the door opened and a police officer came in carrying a human chair. He set it down next to the inspector and vanished as quickly as he'd come.

Putting a hand on the chair, Tadevi leaned toward me. "Sit. Please. You are exhausted, but I need to know everything. Hold nothing back." He turned to Jax. "Hope is still in the room."

I limped to the chair. I half fell into it and started to talk.

Everything ached, but the fact that Tadevi had someone bring in water and doughy spiced balls filled with truddra helped. I'd written myself a prescription for an analgesic that was human-safe, and after Woodard picked it up, things just ached. Of course, I wasn't doing anything more than sitting and talking right now.

Tadevi leaned forward on his kneeling stool, fingers pressed together as he listened to Jax and me tell our stories.

"Seyeli recognized me from the hotel and the church. We tussled, and then I reckon he was trying to get to the next box. He jumped. Missed." In memory, my hand brushed his ankle. He screamed. I blinked to clear my vision and reached for a spiced doughball. "Everything after that point, you know."

His air sacs filled and he snorted. "Tali Province." His hands tightened. "If they are going to try to kill their lawmaker, I wish they'd do it in their own province."

"Wait " Jax raised his hand, almost like a kid. "That's who you think is behind this?"

"It wouldn't be the first time." Tadevi shifted in his chair to look at me for a moment, but all he said was, "How well do you remember the politics?"

I peeled a strip from the dough ball, but my mouth was too dry to think about eating. "Well enough. A fellow in Sati wanted to change the line of succession. Bombed the shit out of his own country to mask killing the lawmaker and pinned the blame on Tali. Invaded Tali. Dragged the whole bloody planet into the fight."

The fellow's name had been Mashadyavati. And before people knew that he was behind the bombing, a joint evac team was supposed to try to get him and his wounded honor guard safely back to Sati. My evac team.

Tadevi had been part of his honor guard.

The public didn't find out what Mashadyavati had done until years after the war. Tadevi and I found out on that trip.

Tristan always said I saved the world, because he was six, and that was what he thought soldiers did.

But he didn't know what I'd done. I hadn't shot Mashadyavati. I'd just let him bleed out.

Crumbs clung to my shaking hands. I bent down to pick up the fragments of dough that I'd dropped on the floor.

Against the wall, Woodard suddenly straightened, his eyes darting to the side the way folks sometimes do when a call comes in on the subdermal. "Inspector—you should take this call."

"Pardon me." With a very human nod, Tadevi accepted the call, ducking his head so that his conversation was not as obvious, but his air sacs pulsed in time with subvocalized speech.

I sat back in the chair, tempted to close my eyes for just a moment, but Tadevi's crest flared. I glanced at Jax, who had been slumped on his stool. He sat up as the inspector stood.

"Goddamn it all to hell." The human phrase rang in the air as Tadevi turned to Woodard. "The Varnhams are at the Tali embassy."

Jax was out of his seat like a shot. "Seriously?"

I pushed against the arms of the chair and almost shouted as my body stopped me from standing. "They'll have Tristan with them."

"Let me get this straight." Jax was vibrating with more anger than I'd seen from him in over a year. "The lawmaker is Tali. So the person whose life I saved is involved in kidnapping my son?"

"No. No . . ." Tadevi held up his hands, rotating them outward in a Herl gesture of supplication. "The lawmaker is the target. The Varnhams will have other accomplices in the embassy. Given the political factions in Tali, likely the ambassador, though not in any provable way."

"As for Tristan . . ." Tadevi turned back to me, his crest fluttering as it settled back against his head, but his air sacs were still puffed with tension. "It is possible that he is there, but not certain. But our thumbs are bound. We can do nothing."

You could have knocked me down with a feather. "Why the hell not?"

"We must respect the embassy's extraterritorial sovereignty rights."

"Wanna say that plain and real simple, like I'm stupid?"

He tapped his two-thumbed hands together. "We are required to treat the embassy as if it were a piece of Tali. To go in without invitation would be seen as an invasion."

Rage powered me past all the pain, and I pushed to my feet. "So they can fucking kidnap little kids and ain't no one going to do a damn thing? Oh, hell no." I spun on Woodard. "What can Earth do?"

"Potentially, we could appeal to the Interstellar Service Corps to start a procedure, but . . ." Breaking off, Woodard glowered at the floor. "The Unification complicates things. With the vote coming up, we have been instructed to remain hands-off on local politics. The ISC does not want to agitate the political landscape."

"I'll agitate their ass."

"Let me think." Tadevi walked in a small circle, crest rustling. Was he counting his steps in English?

He stopped, staring across the theater to where the police officers had now removed the body of the assassin. His fingers flexed at his sides. "Your grandson is the key. Woodard, as a citizen of Earth, if he is present, then that would—"

"If?" Jax looked like he was about to punch someone. "You know he's got to be there."

"I *hope* he is." Tadevi held up his hand, fingers wide. "But I have conjecture when what I need is proof."

Proof.

My mind was working slowly, but it was still working. They needed proof that Tristan was inside the Tali embassy. They couldn't go in without causing diplomatic problems. But Jax had just been invited, hadn't he?

"Will you let me call the embassy?" I grimaced and tapped my temple. "But I'll need to borrow a handheld. This is still off."

Tadevi and Woodard stared at me. After a moment, Woodard said, "I can arrange a handheld."

Jax cocked his head. "What are you planning?"

They were staring at me, and I didn't blame them. I smiled at Jax. "Figure on calling the lawmaker herself."

Tadevi shook his head. "No. The line will be tapped, and the Varnhams will know that you are asking about Tristan."

"I ain't a blamed fool." Not much. "We were invited over, weren't we? So I figure if we're inside, we can get you your proof."

Tadevi stared at me, air sacs pulsing with each breath. His crest rustled and he swore in High Herl, and I recognized every word. Then he switched back to English. "Get her a handheld. And someone bring a goddamned contact remote."

Woodard probably sent the commands even as he was walking to the door. Tadevi crossed the space between us and looked down his long, leathered nose. "Let me be clear. I am patching into your subdermal because there is no way in the thrice hallows that I'm letting you go in there without being able to track you."

"Understood." I'd just volunteered Jax and me to go behind enemy lines. And I'd essentially volunteered Tadevi to be my evac team.

Woodard stepped back into the room with the handheld. "Contact remote is on the way." He gave the handheld to me.

Tadevi settled back onto the kneeling stool. "Speakerphone. Everyone else, absolute silence."

Woodard nodded. "Patching the call now."

In my hand, the handheld chimed, and a Herl woman picked up on the other end. She spoke in High Herl, but I just had to trust that at an embassy, whoever answered was multilingual or had a good set of translation modules on her subdermal.

I almost put on my old-money Southern voice, but I suddenly realized that the Varnhams might have someone listening for me. I dialed it all the way down to broadcast neutral. "May I please speak to the lawmaker?"

The Herl made a little huff like she'd just cleared her air sacs. In lightly accented English, she answered, "I am afraid that is not possible."

I was having none of that, but I kept my voice polite. "Well, I understand that she must be terribly busy, but I sure would appreciate it if you'd just let her know that"—I caught myself before saying Jax's name—"that . . . the fellow who saved her life wants a word."

And by gum, it worked. "I see . . . Would you hold a moment?"

The handheld switched to the sort of insipid hold music that every culture seems to inflict on folks. With luck, she'd gone off to fetch the lawmaker or at least an aide. I handed the phone to Jax.

He took it, swallowing. "I thought you were going to talk to her."

"She'll pay more attention to you. You'll do fine." I nodded to the phone. "Just thank her for inviting us over and say that we'd like to accept her invitation for tonight after all."

A moment later, the phone clicked as the transfer finished happening. The lawmaker's rich voice rolled out of the handheld. "What a delight. I thought I would have to press my invitation again."

Jax let out his breath, and when he inhaled, he drew on the mask of Jax Low, star of Math Turtles. His voice dropped and growled with smoky silk. "I don't need any thanks, but I did want to come by to make sure you were all right."

"Of course. Thanks to you."

"With everything that happened, I forgot that we're taking the orbital elevator out tomorrow morning. And I do want to reassure myself."

"So kind! Of course, of course. And you can meet the ambassador, who will be too, too pleased. After all, you may have stopped a war."

"That sounds wonderful. We'll see you soon." Jax sounded like a rock star when he answered. I couldn't have been more proud of him if he were my own child.

He disconnected the phone and sagged, all the bravado draining out of his stance. Lifting his head, he looked at me. "Let's go get Tristan."

The autocab that drove us to the embassy dropped us off at a large, modern building. A postwar construction of glass and steel, it still had the curving lines that Herl architecture favored, but the murals were painted with light across the surface of the building. They evolved slowly as the lights shifted from greens to blues to waves of purple undulating like an aurora.

I opened the door of the cab on my own, but it took everything I had to swing my leg out. I hissed as my hip protested.

Reaching down, Jax took my hand and helped me out. I clutched his shoulder while I got my feet under me. "I'll have the surgery when we get home."

"Well, that's one good thing to come of this."

I snorted like a Herl. "Just—" Biting my lower lip, I stopped talking. This wasn't the time.

"What?" Jax offered his arm like something out of an old-fashioned movie.

He knew I was afraid of anesthesia-induced confusion. No reason to let him know that I was afraid of forgetting Sam. No reason to let Tadevi hear our private business, not with him patched in and listening to everything. At least, not now. "Just keep me steady till I loosen up. That's all."

We started up the steps of the embassy. Under my hand, Jax's arm was tense enough to be made of stone, which was a good thing, because I had to lean on him heavily to make it up the four shallow stairs. Why does everyone throw ornamental stairs in?

The door slid open as we approached, to reveal a liveried Herl woman with silken ribbons crisscrossing her tunic and binding the cloth close around her chest. She bowed to us, then led the way through an atrium, farther into the embassy. Past the main atrium, the walls were arched and tiled with blues and greens, backlit by a slowly shifting wash of color. It really did feel like being under the sea or deep in a bamboo forest—not that they had bamboo here, but there were big ferny things.

As we walked, strains of music came out to greet us. Clusters of Herl and the occasional human or fuzzy orb of a Fealif. It made me grateful that we'd taken time to clean up a little before coming here. I'm not sure how Tadevi managed to requisition a flowing mid-hip tunic overlay for me, but it covered the worst of the damage to my clothing.

The servant showed us into a parlor, where a small quartet played a series of Tali instruments. I didn't know the song, but the overall effect was like listening to water pattering on the shore.

It was hard not to gawk around the place, looking for Tristan. On the other hand, maybe the gawking was fine, since I'd never been to the embassy before and it truly was architecturally amazing.

An aide turned toward us as we came in. His air sacs filled, lines crinkling around the corners of his eyes as he hurried across the room. "Good evening. Come this way, if you please. The law-maker awaits with pleasure."

As the aide led us across the room to another arch, the music ended, and the audience made a buzzing-humming sound like a bajillion bees had flooded the room. The hair on the back of my neck rose like it was a Herl crest before I recognized the sound: the Herl equivalent of applause, a roomful of air sacs fluttering as they hummed.

Jax's eyes were wide, but he didn't send a peep over the subdermal. In a place like this, every transmission would bounce through the house system on its way out to the larger network. Sure, everything should be encoded and private, but neither of us was stupid. Well, I was, but I tried hard not to be.

The aide led us through a crowded doorway into what, on Earth, would have been a small ballroom. Here the glass tiles were accented at intervals with screens that showed scenes of natural beauty around Namhatanu. The tile around each installation took on the colors and carried them away to bend with the rest of the light display.

As we walked through the room, folks began to take notice. The buzzing hum rose again and trailed after us. I saw more than one person watching Jax and making that sound. Maybe some of them were Math Turtles fans, but in this context, I was betting that folks recognized him as having saved the lawmaker.

Speaking of whom, the lawmaker was seated on a low sofa, in a splendid new tunic with immaculate satin ribbons binding the cloth close to her narrow chest. To look at her, there was no sign that she had been wounded earlier.

She looked up, crest smoothing with pleasure, and stood. As she crossed the floor with her hands outstretched, it looked as if the wounded arm didn't stretch out quite as far. "Welcome! Welcome."

The ambassador—who I only recognized because Tadevi had given us the rundown on who to expect—followed close behind the lawmaker. He was a squat Tali Herl whose oiled skin did not hide the leathering of age.

The lawmaker turned to him, beckoning the ambassador closer. Her words were careful and pointed. "I want you to meet the young man who saved my life at the concert."

The ambassador strode forward with a very human smile and bowed, which looked more alien on him than anything. "Honored sir, you have rendered a great service to our country."

According to Tadevi, this fellow was likely the one behind the attack, ultimately. But he had no proof, only patterns that led to hunches, and he could do jackshit with those.

The lawmaker kept her gaze fixed on the ambassador for a moment longer. "I trust you will honor this *human* with all the respect he deserves."

For a moment, his crest looked as if it would flare, but he simply bowed his head. "Of course, Lawmaker."

"Excellent." She twisted her head to Jax as if the ambassador had ceased to exist. "My daughter has informed me that you are the famous Jax Low, of Math Turtles?"

Beneath my hand, Jax's arm twitched, but he kept the public mask up, and if anything seemed to settle into it. He gave a slow, almost sheepish smile. "That's me."

The lawmaker leaned in, voice gentle. "Would I be rude if I asked you to sing? You must be honest about etiquette in this instance. Please."

I opened my mouth to cut in and demur for him, and then some nonverbal part of my brain sent up a signal flare that would have painted an MRI in every color of the rainbow. I'd planned to ask for a tour, but this . . . this beautiful opportunity was better. "Jax would love that. Wouldn't you?"

Jax turned his head, brows coming together. "I'm a little rusty. And I didn't bring my guitar . . ."

"Nonsense." I squeezed his arm and hoped he would follow me because I didn't quite feel safe sending him a ping. "You can sing a cappella, just like a papa to his son."

The lawmaker held up her hands. "Only if it is not too much trouble. I already owe you so much, but my daughter is a fan and would not forgive me if I didn't ask."

"No. No, it's fine." It took him a minute to drag his attention away from me, but I was pretty sure he understood. "I'm always happy to sing for friends."

As they were talking, the ambassador turned to the gathered guests and switched to High Herl. Shocking me, I understood pretty much the whole thing. "Honored guests, tonight we have a special treat. . . . Jax Low, of the famous Math Turtles, will give us the gift of song."

There were murmurs of appreciation as the crowd moved closer. As folks rearranged themselves, I let their movement seem to draw my attention so I could look around the entire room without being too obvious. Two doors led into the room, the far one of which seemed to lead deeper into the embassy.

The ambassador addressed the lawmaker. "Please Lawmaker, sit here in front so you can get a good recording for your daughter."

Crest ruffling for a moment, the lawmaker looked at Jax. "Is that all right? I promise I will not let anyone see it but her."

"Absolutely okay." Jax gave a lazy wink, as if he was sharing a secret with a dear old friend. "And I'm fine if you broadcast. You know. For mom points."

The lawmaker cocked her head, then gave a small chuckle. "Mom points. Yes. Thank you."

From somewhere, the butler had managed to produce a guitar. A real, human guitar. Jax took it, and all the tension in his frame just added to the intensity of his smolder. It wasn't hard to understand why Sam had fallen for him. It looked like half the Herl in the room were under his spell. They'd all be lost when he started singing.

I worked my way, casually, through the crowd, trying to edge toward the far entrance while pretending that I just wanted to make sure folks could see. It helped that everyone was fascinated by Jax—not just the fact that he'd saved the lawmaker, but also because of the Math Turtles. I'd bet anything that all these folks had looked him up the moment the lawmaker had introduced him. All of them were probably pretending that they'd always known who the Math Turtles and Jax Low were.

Some of them were probably looking at pictures of Sam.

Jax adjusted the guitar over his shoulder, jaw tight. He glanced up and found me for a moment. I didn't need a subdermal to know what he wanted. Same thing as me: Tristan.

He played a few notes, trying out the guitar, and my heart split down the middle, one half staying here with Jax. I hadn't heard him play the guitar since before Sam died.

The other half of my heart, I carried with me to look for Sam's son.

He strummed a chord. The room hushed. I stood with my shoulder against the door, ready to push through except for the silence.

Looking up at the ceiling, Jax played the opening notes of "Don't Borrow Trouble." He drew a breath and sang at full voice.

Louder than the room needed, reminding me that he'd met Sam when they were both studying opera. God, my child had had a voice to make angels weep, and Jax had been one of those weeping.

I pushed through the door.

Behind me, the song followed into the corridor.

> *"When I was lost in the darkness,*
> *my fate a set course,*
> *my grandma found me . . ."*

He'd changed the lyrics. Please, dear God, let his voice carry far enough for Tristan to hear.

> *"Lifted the shadow*
> *and pulled me back,*
> *by offering this key."*

Tristan wouldn't be on the first floor. I wouldn't have much time before security cameras started flagging me, so I tried to move through like I was looking for the bathroom. First set of stairs I came to, I took. Didn't matter that it hurt, I just dragged my right leg after me.

The stairs curved around a central column. Jax's voice faded behind me but was still clear and rich.

> *"Don't borrow trouble.*
> *That's a spiral down, down.*
> *Turn around now, turn around.*
> *Don't borrow trouble.*
> *Don't spiral down, down."*

The second floor didn't have the illuminated tiles that the first floor did, just the curving halls. I hugged the wall as best I could without trying to look stealthy. Overhead camera by the light, another in the far corner. Probably one behind me, too. I tried to be as doddering as I could, opening doors like a lost old woman.

> *"Still, I told my son to whistle*
> *so his grandma could*
> *find him, find him."*

He'd changed the lyrics again, that brilliant man.

"Well, goll darn it. Gotta be a bathroom somewhere in all this highfalutin—" I opened a bathroom door.

Well, shit. What an excellent ruse you chose, Bonnyjean. I stared at the bathroom for a second, not even able to pretend that I didn't recognize it because it was built for human anatomy. Of all the times for an embassy to be gracious hosts, this was not one that I needed.

Wasn't much else I could do, so I went into the gleaming white enamel room. All the edges were square and awful and hard.

> *"And my brave boy did.*
> *But I warned him,*
> *please don't risk life and limb."*

I'd just have to go into the potty and then pretend to get turned around when I went out. I pushed the door closed—

A whistle.

Faint and wavering, but clear. I jerked the bathroom door open. Stumbling into the hall, I tried to locate the whistle. Come on, baby boy, keep it up. It seemed to trickle down from above.

I sent a ping to Tadevi. *That's Tristan.*

My HUD returned *local access only.*

They'd blocked me, which in hindsight, was an obvious choice. Damn it. I bit the inside of my lip. Judging by the whistle, Tristan was at the top of the stairs.

That was fine. I could do more stairs for my grandson. There were rails on each side of the curving spiral staircase, and thankfully close enough that I could put my hands on both. 'Cause lord knew I needed the help to haul my aching body up. With each step, Jax got quieter, and Tristan's whistle got clearer.

My breath was hot in my throat as I limped upward.

On the stairs below me, footsteps.

I ground my teeth together but kept moving. The cameras were too well-placed here to create a blind spot. And the way my hip was working, I wouldn't make it up before they got to me.

Tadevi had better notice that I was cut off and get his ass into the embassy. But until he did, I was on my own. Seventy-eight years old and exhausted—but I had the high ground.

Five more steps. They were right behind me. I pretended to miss a step and stumbled. I let the movement sit me down on the stairs. Eyes wide, as if I were hurt, I faced back down the stairs. The fellows coming up were two Tali Herl.

I clenched the handrails. "Oh, thank heavens. I'm all turned around."

"You need to come with us." The one in the front had a bulge under his tunic, like a shoulder holster.

"Of course." I pushed to my feet and held on tight to the handrails. Swinging both legs out, I caught the fellow in the chest. He stumbled back a step and slipped, colliding with his colleague. They went down in a tangle of limbs.

The doctor part of my mind wanted to go help, but I scrambled up the last five steps like a dog chasing a rabbit. Tristan's whistle came from the hall to my right. I limped down that.

And the thing is . . . I knew it was a trap. They were letting him whistle. I stopped and assessed the hall, looking for exits and anything I could use as an improvised weapon.

It was long, with doors off each side. It was less lavish than the downstairs, but there were tall, thin metal vases on a side table. I dumped the flowers and water on the floor and proceeded with one in each hand. My hip was ancient, but I could still wallop someone if I needed to.

There. A plain arched door set in a plain arched wall, and my grandson was behind it. I grabbed the knob and half fell through the door. I'd been braced for it being locked. Why wasn't it locked?

Inside, Tristan sat in a chair, face scrunched up and whistling.

For a second, the shock locked me to the floor. Only a second. I sprang forward at the same time Tristan jumped out of his chair. Letting the vases hit the floor, I dropped to my knees in front of him and pulled my grandson into my arms. Lord knows what I said, all I knew was that he was alive and he wasn't hurt.

Behind me, a gun cocked.

I clutched my grandson, keeping my body between him and whoever was behind us with a gun. Tristan's head was exposed, over my shoulder. My heart was trying to beat an opening in my rib cage to tuck him inside and keep him safe. If that gun went off, I wouldn't be able to move fast enough.

There was nothing useful in the room, at least not close. It was a small bedroom, and besides the bed itself, the room only had low kneeling stools and a small table. None of it was close enough to use for a shield.

Wetting my lips, I drew a careful breath. "Better think twice about using that gun—plenty of folks downstairs, and police are just outside."

Cloth rustled, followed by a footstep as someone stepped farther into the room. A voice spoke with low urgency. "He's just a little boy. Let him go. Please."

Human. Speaking English and posh. Emma Varnham.

Noah Varnham drawled an answer. "Of course, Emma . . . Of course. We'll take him out of the embassy now. No need to fret."

I risked a glance over my shoulder. He stood silhouetted in the doorway, gun leveled at us. To the side of the door, just inside, Emma Varnham stood with her arms wrapped tightly around herself. Her eyes were red and puffy, as if she had been crying.

Noah walked into the room, and in my arms, Tristan flinched. I was going to kill Noah for scaring my grandson. Jaw set, I wanted to keep my arms around Tristan, but I was going to need my hands free. Squeezing him, I kissed his cheek. And then I slowly released him.

That might have been the hardest thing I'd ever done. I turned slowly, still kneeling, and kept an eye on Noah.

The bastard smiled at me. "Now then. Let's all be reasonable, shall we? You won't make a fuss as we leave, will you?"

"You've got a lot of nerve, asking me to be 'reasonable,' you miserable—" I tried to rise, and my right leg completely failed. Pain shot down my leg and up my spine all the way into the back of my skull. Unable to stop a cry, I toppled over. I slapped a hand against the floor and just caught myself.

"Grandma!" Tristan crouched next to me, wrapping his little arms around me.

I patted his hand. Not that I could do much to reassure him.

Leaning down, Noah spoke past me to Tristan. "You're a good boy, aren't you? I'm sure you don't want your grandmother to be hurt."

My grandson was trembling, and tears streaked his chubby cheeks, but he stared up at Noah like a soldier. I was going to kill the man. Rage lit the inside of my head, washing the entire room in red. It was hard to breathe past the hate and fury. In the distance, Jax's voice wound through the embassy.

> *"Don't borrow trouble*
> *That's a spiral down, down.*
> *Turn around now, turn around.*
> *Don't borrow trouble.*
> *Don't spiral down, down."*

Spiral down. I tried to slow my heart rate. I had to keep Tristan safe. Nothing else mattered. Glaring at Noah, I managed to nod.

He smiled a little, and visions of stabbing him with a scalpel filled my brain.

Straightening, Noah tucked the gun in his pocket but kept it obviously pointed toward us through his suit. "Now then, we'll all walk down the stairs together, just a happy group of friends. I've had the car brought around back—and we'll go together to the spaceport. No heroics, I trust."

"Quiet as a mouse, Tristan." I turned to look at my grandson and wiped the tears off his cheek. "I need you to be real quiet, okay?"

He nodded, eyes wide and terrified. I was going to kill Noah Varnham.

Closing my eyes, I tried to get myself under control. *Don't borrow trouble. That's a spiral down, down.*

Noah stepped back, with that goddamn pleasant smile on his face. "Shall we?"

Rolling onto my knees, I got my left leg under me and tried to stand. My body was just done, and my muscles trembled but wouldn't lift me off the floor. Grimacing, I looked up at Noah.

"I might need some help here."

He laughed. The bastard actually laughed. "You must be joking. Do you think I'm going to fall for the helpless old lady bit again? You already broke the leg of my colleague."

Dead. Noah was a dead man walking. I tried again, and it wasn't even pain stopping me. My hip just wouldn't move.

Emma took a step toward me. "Daddy, I don't think she's faking."

"Why risk it?" Noah held out a hand to stop Emma. "If she can't stand, then she'll slow us down."

"So . . . so we'll have to leave her behind."

Noah did not turn to face his daughter, so she didn't see his face or the smirk. "Yes . . . yes, we'll just leave her."

Honestly, getting killed by him was the least of my worries. But no way in hell was I going to let him take Tristan without me, and if I didn't get off the floor, that was what he'd do. I needed a hand or something to brace myself on. The chair was the closest piece of furniture in here. So I crawled to it.

Tristan stayed right by me, fist gripping my shirt. I put both hands on the chair and pushed up. Ice picks drove into my hip and the base of my neck where the old scar was.

As I struggled to stand, Tristan put his arms around my waist as if he could push me upright. Such a good kid. Sam would have been so proud of him.

My breath shuddered as I tried to get my balance. I rested a hand on Tristan's shoulder to steady myself, and he tucked in closer, burying his face in my side.

"See. I told you she could stand on her own." Noah gestured for the door.

I limped toward it, grimacing with each step. Noah took up a position on the other side of Tristan.

Emma was watching Tristan and reached out to take Noah's arm. "Can't we just lock them in and go?"

"Why? So your crush will be grateful to you?" He shrugged her off. "Don't be stupid. We need the insurance they provide."

Emma half crumpled, because there's no cruelty like that of a parent to a child. We all walked through the door, Emma trailing behind.

Downstairs, Jax finished the song, and the thrum of Herl appreciation filled the embassy. Someone started clapping, human-style, and it sounded like the whole crowd joined in. I actually heard someone yell, "Encore!"

Which meant that if I hollered, they'd be able to hear me. But Tristan was between Noah and me, so I kept my mouth clamped shut. The stairs down from the third floor were too narrow for all of us, so Noah let Tristan and me go first. It was a little easier to go down, but I had to rest all my weight on the handrail when I moved my right leg.

The applause died down, and Jax strummed another opening. His voice wound up the staircase to us.

> *"Pennies from heaven, tears in rain*
> *keep coming round, but you remain."*

At the base of the stairs, blood stained the floor. I'd plum forgotten about the fellows I knocked down. That must be from the broken leg Noah had mentioned. Good. I glanced over my shoulder. He gestured for me to wait and then took up a position next to Tristan again. The stairs to the main floor were wider as they spiraled down.

> *"When it thunders, when there are clouds,*
> *and I'm buried, wrapped up in shrouds"*

Walking had helped loosen up my hip a little, not a lot, but enough that I could take my hand off the rail. I kept one hand on Tristan as we walked down, Emma trailing behind the three of us.

> *"Your laughter glitters through the dark*
> *as strange and charming as a quark."*

Jax's voice called to us, smoky and full of sorrow. We had about a dozen steps left to go. Spiral down. Time to borrow trouble.

All of us were in a line on the stairs. I pushed Tristan back up a step, stepping past my grandson toward Noah. His hand came up, tangled in his coat pocket.

Gunshot.

No cymbal to mask it. Nothing to mask the bright bolt shooting through my midriff. Momentum carried me forward, and I grabbed Noah's jacket, pulling him toward me. My useless legs tangled into his, and we both fell.

In a crash of limbs and pain, we spiraled down.

Someone screamed. I don't think it was me. The marble floor slammed into us with a crack. The pain in my hip whited out the room. Couldn't breathe. Tristan. Keep Tristan safe.

Noah struggled to extricate himself, but I was on top of him. People were running out of the parlor, and the man still had a gun.

I rammed the heel of my hand into his nose.

He shrieked, blood spattering everywhere, and brought his hands up to protect his face. One hand held the gun.

I grabbed for it. We wrestled, tumbling over.

Amid the people shrieking, I heard one clear voice.

"Daddy!"

Noah rolled over me, setting off the fire in my hip so I could hardly see. We fetched up against something hard. A table? A stool? He had me pinned.

"Tristan!" Jax grabbed his son, and that was all I could see.

Pushing as hard as I could, I couldn't get Noah off me. He

brought the gun around between us, and I was too blamed weak to stop him.

So, I stopped trying.

I put my hand over his, right on the trigger. With my other hand, I grabbed the back of his neck, lifting myself off the floor, closing the distance and pinning the gun between us.

Gunshot.

I didn't know where the bullet went. All I knew was that Noah's limp body weighed me down. Or maybe that was my own body. The room was dark and spiraling.

Down.

down

Someone was singing.

I lay on a bed that spun around me. The air had a comforting scent of disinfectant, and a man was singing. "Pennies from heaven . . ."

A child's voice wandered through the dark. "I drawed this for Grandma."

"Good job, buddy." Cloth rustled, or maybe that was paper. "That's a great spaceship."

"Look. There's a mecha."

We must still be on the shuttle. How long would it take to reach Piper Nine Station? If I slept, maybe we would get there faster.

The ceiling was blue. I blinked a couple of times and sandpaper scraped over my eyelids. That was definitely the ceiling and not the sky. The inside of my mouth felt like it had been scrubbed with a dead possum and hung out to dry.

My whole body was a litany of aches, but I didn't much care. I blinked again. Probably an opiate derivative.

I turned my head a little. Jax sat in a chair next to the bed, with Tristan curled up on his lap, reading.

"Hey." Even that single syllable made my throat hurt. Must've had a breathing tube in.

Jax and Tristan lifted their heads in perfect synchronization, like they'd practiced it. For some unaccountable reason, Jax started crying. But Tristan tumbled out of the chair, grinning like a cat with a new mouse.

"Grandma!" He grabbed the rail on the side of my bed. "You're awake."

"Mm-hmm." Not by much, though. I turned my head, looking

around the room. It had murals on all the walls and reminded me of something. Couldn't quite place it, though. "Where's Sam?"

Jax made a weird choking sound. "What?"

I turned my head back to him, and the room spiraled after. Why the hell did he look so wrung out? I cleared my throat and tried again. "I said, 'Where is Sam?'"

"Sam is—" For a second, Jax closed his eyes.

Tristan piped up. "Bibi is dead."

Everything in the room froze with those words. Had I known that? I must have. How could you forget that your own child was dead? I clenched the sheets. A thin keening sound filled the air. My throat burned.

Jax stepped forward and caught my hand. "A doctor is on the way." He brushed my forehead with the other. "It's okay. You're just confused from surgery. It's okay."

Sam was dead? My chest cracked open, and it felt like a lifetime of grief poured out. Sobs racked my body. I couldn't make them stop.

Tristan started to cry, too. He flung himself at me, but the bed rails kept him away. "Don't cry, Grandma! Please don't cry. I'm sorry!"

It wasn't his fault. Goddamn it. I tried to hold on to my breathing, but I couldn't stop making that awful goddamn noise.

My baby was dead, and I'd forgotten.

A Herl leaned over me. I pressed back into the bed. No, no, no . . . I'd tried to stay out of trouble in this goddamn camp, but they kept coming back for me. Most of the POWs were Herl. I was one of only a handful of humans. The number fluctuated depending on who had died recently.

Easier to teach vulnerable spots on me than on a mannequin.

"It's a common reaction to anesthesia at her age. And with the other injuries . . ." The Herl straightened and turned to Jax. I didn't know him. Where was Tadevi? "It just takes longer to recover."

Where was Tadevi? I pushed up onto an elbow and looked around the room. Did they have Tadevi, too? My heart slammed against my ribs.

Where was Tadevi? I had to find him. I grabbed the rail of the bed and hauled myself up to sitting. Everything hurt, but Tadevi was missing. I had to make sure he was safe.

The covers tangled around my legs, and I scrabbled to free them.

"Whoa, whoa!" Jax leaped forward. "Bonnyjean, what are you doing?"

"I have to find Tadevi." There was an IV line in my arm. I picked at the tape holding it down.

"He's fine." Jax caught my hand, pulling it away. "He's at the embassy with Tristan."

"With who?" I had to go. I had to get out. I twisted my hand away from his grasp.

He looked like I'd slapped him. "Friends. He's with friends—doc?"

A Herl came around the bed. No, no, no. I couldn't go back into the pen again. I balled my hand into a fist and swung it at him. "Don't touch me!"

His crest flared, but by a minor miracle, he stopped, holding his hands up and out to the side. "No one is going to hurt you, but you need to stay in bed."

"Fix me up so you can beat me again?" I yanked at the covers. "I have to go."

"Where are you going, Bonnyjean? Doc, why don't you step out?" Jax grabbed me by the shoulders and pulled me back. "Hey . . . hey. Where are you going?"

"I don't know!" I twisted, trying to get away from him. I was missing—who was I missing? I had to find— "I have to go. I have to find Sam."

His fingers tightened on my shoulders. "Sam's just down the hall. In the cafeteria." Jax's voice had that rough edge he used on some of their songs. But I had to go. I had to get out of here. "You don't want to go without Sam, right? So just lie back and wait. Okay? C'mon, Bonnyjean. You can do that for me, can't you? Just wait for Sam to come back."

"How long?" I lifted my hands and pressed them against my face. "How long do I have to wait?"

"I don't know." He pulled me back, and I let him guide me down to the bed. "I'll sing to you while we wait. Okay? Just close your eyes. . . ."

In the darkness, Tadevi stroked my forehead, with his soft fingers and thumbs spreading out in symmetrical circles. "You are safe. Shh . . . shh . . . You are safe. I am here. You are safe."

My lids were too heavy to open. "Again, in High Herl. I gotta practice." Partly because if they took him, I would be on my own in this damned camp. But mostly because I loved the way his voice sounded in his native language. The humming undertones beneath a rattling, burbling waterfall.

I could hear his smile in the extra resonance of his voice. "*Lu-bonnyjean. Bhu evacha. Bhu evacha. Dhe ala. Bhu evacha . . .*"

"*Dhe evacha. Bhu ala.*"

He drew circles across my skin. "Yes. I am here. *Kuma. Dhe ala syavrati.*"

I was almost asleep again. "What does *syavrati* mean?"

"Always. I am here. Always."

I followed his spirals down.

Down.

Sam sat on the edge of my bed, pixie-cut hair softening an angular face with curls. "Hey, Mama. How're you doing?"

I grinned at my child and struggled to sit up. Something held on to my wrists. "Well, hey, sweetie. What are you doing here?"

"Just thought I'd stop by. Guess who's been invited to perform on Mars?" Sam's grin lit up the room. "Can you believe it? I'm giddy. In fact . . . I'm over the moon."

I groaned. "Lordy, and I thought Jax would have the lockdown on Dad jokes."

Sam waved a hand through the air as if brushing that away. "Speaking of . . . While we're away, will you look after Tristan for me?"

"Course I will, sweetie." I tried to pat my child's hand, but my wrist was bound. Why was that? "Of course I will."

". . . sleeping now." In the dim room, Jax's voice was little more than a murmur. "Mm-hmm. Yeah. Thanks for coming by before, it calmed her down a lot. She's . . . the confusion has been hard. Thanks. Thanks. I appreciate that. Yeah. I'll tell her."

My eyes were dry as dust. I blinked once or twice and tried to lift my hand. A pressure on my wrist stopped me. I lifted my head. Restraints. Soft beige wrist restraints bound me to the hospital bed.

"Well, hell."

"Gotta go—she's awake." Jax stood up from the chair he'd been sitting in by the side of my bed. "Sorry to bother you."

Poor guy. He looked utterly wrecked, with dark circles under his eyes and his hair matted against his head.

"How many times did I try to get out of the bed?" My voice still felt rough, but my throat wasn't as sore. And it felt like I could string two thoughts together, which was an improvement.

"Twice." His eyes narrowed as he studied me. "How are you feeling?"

"Lucid. I think." I stretched in the bed and stopped that shit almost immediately. "Feel like I fell down a flight of stairs and got shot."

He snorted, like a Herl. "Funny thing, that."

"Tell me you had them replace my hip while they were at it." I waved a hand within its restraint. "Because I do not want to have to go through this shit ever again."

"Yes. You broke it in the fall." And the gentle way he said it made me think that he'd had to tell me multiple times what had happened.

And probably would again. My mind felt fairly clear right now, but the way this worked, as soon as I got tired again, I'd get "confused." I gave a half laugh, which was all I could manage. "Patients always figure 'confusion' will be like getting high. Sorry you're getting the dementia variant."

"It's okay. The doctor said it should only bother you for another couple of days."

"Well, it's no fun for you."

"I dunno. The conversation about the tree scarf was pretty cool." He ran a hand through his hair. "You need anything?"

"Wait—tree scarf?" I closed my eyes, grimacing, and tried to sort through the scattered haze of memories. "What the tarnation is a tree scarf?"

"I have no idea, but apparently I'm knitting one." The bed creaked as he sat on the edge of it.

I opened my eyes. "Do you knit?"

"Not even a little." He hesitated, wetting his lips for a second. "Sam did."

I inhaled grief that felt fresh. "I know . . . I remember."

Five days later, they let me out of the hospital. All told, I was in there for seven days, although the first few were spotty at best. Probably just as well, in fact, given the few things I could recall. The rest of the time, I watched quiz shows that I knew none of the answers to, napped, and thought. I thought a lot.

Jax picked me up and took me, not to a hotel, but to the Earth embassy. Because it turned out that our role in thwarting the assassination was well enough known that there were concerns for our safety. Lovely.

We'd been given a guesthouse cottage designed by someone who missed the Earth. I was torn between being charmed by the wainscoting and wishing that I were staying someplace that felt like I was on Namhatanu.

And also, the front room was filled with an entire hothouse's worth of flowers.

"You open a florist shop?" I stumped into the room, shoving my walker in front of me. A week ago, I'd just been seventy-eight. Now I was old.

"Whoa." Jax turned from shutting the door. "These . . . these weren't all here when I left for the hospital."

Tristan came running out of the bedroom, waving a comic book in one hand. "Grandma!"

Like a sportsball player, Jax jumped in front of his son and caught him up, swinging him around in a circle. "Easy there, buddy. Let Grandma get settled in, okay?"

Behind him, Agent Woodard hurried into the room. "My apologies! And welcome back."

Seemed like an age since I had met the agent, and I bristled for a second—but that was fear talking and masquerading as anger. I pulled on my Southern charm like armor. "Well, now. It was real good of you to sit with Tristan."

"My pleasure." His smile looked genuine as he glanced at Tristan in Jax's arms. "Inspector Shivsati thought it might make you feel more secure than a regular babysitter."

"But to be here the whole time? I mean, your regular duties?"

Jax shook his head, and I could see that he'd told me this before. "The Woodards have a little boy Tristan's age. He's been having a sleepover."

"We're just here because you were coming home." The bell to the guesthouse rang. Woodard's eyes nearly crossed with frustration, and he ran past us to the door. "Sorry! It's been like this all morning. Word got out that you were being released, I guess. Grateful nation and—oh, Inspector Shivsati."

Tadevi stood in the door of the guesthouse with a guitar case and a gift basket. He looked past Woodard to me, and his crest ruffled. With that Southern drawl of his, he held out the gift basket. "My apologies. I had intended to drop these off, but I'm afraid my credentials . . . They thought this was official."

"And it's not?" My heart was racing faster than it ought to. "I reckoned you still needed to debrief me."

He hesitated at the door, gaze flicking down to my walker. "I . . ."

"He already did, Bonnyjean." Jax stood with Tristan cradled on his hip. "Before you went into surgery, you told him what happened."

"Oh." I tightened my hand on the walker. "Well, this whole confusion thing sucks eggs. Come on in and set a spell."

Tadevi shifted his weight with a shushing as his crest settled. "I sincerely do not want to intrude."

"You aren't. But also, I can't keep standing, so come on in." I turned and stumped over to the nearest chair. I dropped into it. Gently. Because the bullet wound in my side ached every time I bent. I had bruises, and stitches were everywhere. But my hip didn't hurt, and that felt like a miracle.

Jax followed me across the room, a text lighting up my HUD. *I can make him go away if you're tired.*

Don't you dare.

"Thank you." Tadevi crossed the threshold, and Jax took the gift basket from him. "I thought a taste of home might be welcome. It's some Earl Grey tea and shortbread cookies."

I laughed, and the pain in my side only made me wince a little. "I'm not from that part of Earth."

"True, but I recall someone telling me that your part of Earth has started wars over barbecue and I thought that unwise." Tadevi held the guitar case out to Jax. "And this comes as a gift from the lawmaker, with her profound thanks."

Jax still held Tristan and looked at the guitar case with about five different emotions battling for attention. Slowly, he set Tristan down. "Please tell her I said thanks."

Tristan ran across the room, straight to me, still with that comic book in his hands. Looked like it was about mech pilots. Mey vs. Atah or some such, but I'd never seen it and it was a step up from Space Mouse, which made me feel like the hospital had robbed me of a beat of my grandson growing up. But then the six-year-old was back.

He stopped, suddenly shy, and stood on one foot. I ignored everyone else in the room and held my arms out for my grandson. "C'mere and give Grandma a hug."

The shyness vanished, and he leaped forward, grinning. I pulled Tristan into my arms and, yeah, he squeezed too tight, but nothing had ever felt as splendid as having an armful of six-year-old smelling like macaroni and cheese and joy. Grown-ups were talking, and I didn't give a hoot what all they were saying. I closed my eyes and rested my cheek against Tristan's curls. I could stay like this forever.

Except, my grandson was already squirming to be away.

It was never going to be easy to let him go, but I did and sat back in the chair as he scampered off again, leaving an ache that had nothing to do with my injuries. My eyes were wet, but it wouldn't be the first time that Tadevi had seen me weeping like a baby.

He and Jax were the only adults in the room. Woodard must have gone while I was holding Tristan, and thank God for that. Unfair, but my territorial instincts were probably never going to go away.

In my silence, Tadevi turned toward the door. "I should go."

"Don't you dare leave." I wiped my eyes on my arm.

After a look at Jax, who shrugged as if to say that he was too smart to get in my way, Tadevi sat awkwardly on a Herl-style stool opposite me. "Given that you don't remember talking to me, I imagine that you have questions."

I did. Like, had he really come to the hospital, or had I dreamt that? But what came out of my mouth was, "Why didn't you come in? To the embassy."

He pulled his head back, crest ruffling. "We did. The moment your subdermal went offline, we moved in."

Jax set the guitar case down by the sofa and knelt next to my chair. He glanced at Tadevi. "Sorry. I did tell her." He put his hand on my arm and spoke to me like I was a child. "They'd just secured the first floor and the room I was in when you . . . when you came down the stairs."

My face burned with embarrassment. I cleared my throat. "I'm sorry." No amount of forehead rubbing could pull that memory out of the morass. And I realized that while it wasn't what I wanted to talk to Tadevi about, I also wanted to know. "Let's just pretend that I don't know a blessed thing that happened between then and now."

"Of course." Tadevi pressed his fingers together, beating his thumbs against each other. "A summary then, and you may inquire more on those things for which you want more detail."

"That'd be fine." I settled in deeper into the chair, stretching my right leg out in front of me. Needed to keep the tendons from healing too short.

"So." Tadevi spread his hands. "We had cleared the first floor, including two of Noah's associates who, I gather, you had pushed down the stairs. One of them later confirmed that the ambassador had instigated the plot to murder the lawmaker in an effort to affect the vote on Unification, so it is good that you did not kill them as well."

"Noah is dead?" I thought he was, but just wanted to confirm it.

"Yes." His wrinkles were deeper and his crest flat. "We could not get a clear shot. I am sorry that you suffered injuries because of that."

"Pretty sure I suffered most of them because of the stairs."

"Be that as it may. I have regrets."

"They can't be bigger than my regrets." And I wasn't talking about any of the events of the past week.

Ducking his head, Tadevi shifted in the chair. "Other things that you may wish to know. Emma was in our custody and has since been removed to a secure location, for her own safety. She was not involved in the plot and, from Tristan's testimony, took very good care of him."

"Why the hell were either of them involved?"

"Ah . . ." Tadevi sighed, expanding his air sacs with an old familiar expression of contempt. "Their name is not Varnham, but Reyes, although the details you were told about the estate were accurate. The Reyes estate is in the highlands of Sati, with valuable geothermal rights. It is also on the border with Tali, and the Unification treaty would have required its surrender to the state. Had they been Herl, they would have been compensated. As humans, who had acquired the estate under dubious circumstances . . . Well."

For a brief, wild moment, I felt sorry for them. As a neurosurgeon, let me tell you that brains are weird. The only one who deserved pity was Emma. Losing her father, her home, and her freedom all in a matter of days.

"Got it." I tilted my head to the side, feeling like a Herl. "What else should I know?"

"The ambassador has been arrested and removed back to Tali, where he will stand trial. His plan has entirely backfired, and while I have no official opinion on the matter . . ."

I raised my brows, trying to prompt him to keep going. "But this is just a social call."

"Indeed." Tadevi's air sacs pulsed with his quiet laugh. "As an unofficial, entirely personal opinion, I am pleased that the

Unification vote went ahead and that the Tali ambassador's plans came to naught. Messy though the process will be, Namhatanu is a single polity now. I cannot be sad about this."

We sat there in silence, and the weight of forty years of apologies got wadded up in a tangled ball in my throat. I cleared it. I swallowed. I wet my lips, trying to find one end to untangle.

Jax stood up, looking from me to Tadevi. "I'm going to go check on Tristan. He's been quiet too long. . . ."

"Always dangerous." Tadevi laughed. "I remember that age with my own. They are very similar."

I watched Jax walk out of the room, because it gave me a little longer to try to sort out my thoughts. The edge of the ball of apologies snagged on something he'd said. The familiarity with six-year-olds. "I'm sorry . . . I've realized that I don't know anything about your last forty years. You have kids?"

He tilted his head in an affirmative. "I do. Three, in fact. They are grown and out of the house."

"What're their names?"

"Eroevi is the oldest. About Jax's age, I think. He's gone into medicine. Redrivu is our only daughter. She's a mechanic in the military. And Ideneki . . ." He spread his hands and chuffed a laugh. "He flocks to his own ideals. Currently taking time off from university and, well . . . his heart is good."

"He sounds like me before I went into the ISC's marines." I played with the piping on the edge of my chair's upholstery.

"As I recall, you were quite organized." He tilted his head, regarding me gently. "And you just had Sam?"

I stared at him for a moment, before realizing that he'd probably read a file on me and Jax and already knew all the things. "Yep. I was in a marriage that didn't last and then just . . ." I shrugged. "Between work and being a mom, I didn't find anyone else I wanted to get close enough with to make another baby. How about you and your spouse?"

He steepled his fingers and looked down, and his crest was flat against his head. "Symiranu died about a decade ago. An autoimmune disease."

"I'm sorry to hear that."

"The sadness does get better." He looked up, holding my gaze the way he used to do in our bunk. "It never goes away, missing her, but the frequencies of acute pain have become farther apart."

I nodded, looking at the flowers on the sideboard because the care in his eyes was too intense. "Listen . . . before we go on, I got to apologize. I should have looked for you after the war. I should have returned your call when you came to Earth. I should have kept you in my life." Swallowing, I looked back at him, and his crest was raised just a little. Agitation or happiness, I wasn't sure, because the rest of him was completely still. "I'm sorry I didn't."

Tadevi leaned forward on his stool. "Bonnyjean . . . I also did not look for you after the war." He ran a hand over his crest, smoothing it. "I understand."

"But when you reached out on Earth . . ." I grimaced. "I just . . . Truth to tell, I panicked. All these memories of the camp came flooding back, and every time I went to call, I found myself outside. Sometimes a klick away from the house."

"Believe me, I understand. And if it helps, at the time I was honestly relieved that you didn't return my call." He shifted in his chair. "I made the call because Symiranu had heard me talk about you so often that she stood over me until I did it."

There was a different guilt, that Tadevi had shared that part of his life with his spouse and I . . . I had erased him. "That's a good spouse."

"The best."

I asked about her and learned that she'd been a highly regarded muralist. That led to conversations about art and then some of the good shared memories. Talking with him was as easy as if we'd never been apart. Every now and then, Tristan would come running into the room with a drawing, and once with his Space Mouse plushie.

Watching Tadevi admire it with such serious regard made my regret at having erased him from my life rise in a new wave. He was gentle and quietly funny. His hands were as graceful as they had always been.

As Tristan ran back out of the room, paper fluttering in his hand, I yawned.

I didn't mean to, but a wave of fatigue just came out of nowhere and grabbed me.

Catching the yawn, Tadevi stood. "I should go."

"Sorry." I tried to straighten in my chair and realized that I'd slumped until I was almost lying down.

"I have this memory of someone telling me to . . . what were the words? 'Sit your ass down and rest.'"

I barked a laugh. "Not fair. Using my words like that."

"Be well." He twisted his head, as one did to show respect on Namhatanu. But he added the double-tap on the heart that meant affection. "Let me know if you need anything at all."

"Come back?"

"Always."

As Jax saw Tadevi to the door, I sagged back in the chair. I was exhausted but felt lighter than I had since Sam died. There had been days when I'd had fun, but fun was not the same as happy.

Happy felt so strange, it felt like an alien.

After Tadevi was gone, Jax stood there for a minute, one hand on the doorknob. Straightening his shoulders like he was picking up a weight, he turned back to me with a gentle smile on his face. He'd gelled his hair back into its usual spikes, but the skin under his eyes was still gray with fatigue.

"You look more worn out than me." I needed to go to bed before I dropped asleep in my chair. "Anything I can do for you?"

"The last week is just catching up." Jax sat down on the sofa where Tadevi had been and put the guitar case on the coffee table in front of him. It looked so natural, watching him handle the case.

"Sam loved watching you play." I grabbed my walker. "She said that you had hands like an angel."

He looked up, long fingers resting on the case. "Thank you."

"For . . . ?"

Tristan ran into the room, arms spread out like an airplane. Jax reached out and snagged him, pulling him onto the couch. "Remember what we said about running?"

"No running because Grandma is old."

My laugh made my sutures hurt like fire. "Well, ain't that the truest thing."

"Can I show her now?" Tristan pulled a wadded-up piece of paper out of his pocket. "It's not running."

"Maybe later." Jax kissed his son on the cheek and shot me a look that made me feel downright ancient.

I needed a walker, sure. Today. For the next three weeks, fine, but I wasn't dead and had no plans to be. There was a point in my life where I'd thought that every day might be my last. I'd made it through that. Tadevi and I both had. "C'mere. Let me see what you've got. A picture?"

He ran over to me, grinning as if the past week hadn't happened at all. Tristan thrust the paper out. "Me and Daddy are writing a song."

My heart stopped in my chest. "Is that so?" I wet my lips and smoothed the crumpled paper, glancing up at Jax. He was suddenly very fixated on the guitar case. Felt like I was trying not to spook a feral cat. "Will you sing it for me?"

"Daddy? Daddy!" Tristan ran back to his father. "Can we sing it?"

Jax cleared his throat and stood up. "It's almost bedtime, Tristan."

"Pleeeeeeease? I'll sleep better." And really, that face and those huge brown eyes—and the memory of the past week. Jax didn't stand a chance.

"All right. And then we need to let Grandma get some rest." He sat and snapped the latches of the guitar case open.

I just about stopped breathing, watching him pull out the guitar. He slung the strap over his neck and slid to the edge of the couch, one leg tucked under a little to make a rest for the belly of the instrument. The fingers that Sam had loved strummed across, checking the tuning.

"What's your key?"

Tristan hummed a note. "Is that okay?"

"Works for me." Jax adjusted his hand on the neck and kept his gaze on Tristan.

"Showtime!" Tristan did a little flamenco on the carpet as a way of introduction, and Jax matched it with a rhythmic strum. Then he stopped and struck a pose that made my heart beat sideways.

Just the way Sam used to stand at concerts, with Jax nearby cradling a guitar. Sitting in a chair on a planet around another sun, I could see my child's joy like reincarnation in the way Jax watched his son. In the way Tristan rooted his feet and held an imaginary microphone in front of his mouth.

"Play it again, Sam.
No one ever said that,
but I'm begging you.
Play it again, Sam."

ACKNOWLEDGMENTS

My first thanks go to Alfred Hitchcock. I was working on another novel and trying to get a handle on suspense, so I turned to the master. I watched movies, I studied shooting scripts, and somewhere in there, I came up with the idea for *Apprehension*. You'll see a couple of obvious plot nods to *The Man Who Knew Too Much*, even though these wound up being very different stories, and you can probably spot a few other influences.

A lot of what he did, with controlling where the viewer's gaze goes, works on the page, and other things . . . wow, they really don't.

I also owe Jim Henson a creative debt. In my brain, the head of the Herl look very much like the Mystics in *The Dark Crystal*, albeit with rather different bodies. But those images are baked into my creative core.

Many thanks to Alyshondra Meacham for some really terrible puns and insight into six-year-olds. My assistants, Marie Parks, Jes Honard, and Sarah Sward, keep things running while I'm head down in a manuscript. My editor, Joe Monti, asked fantastic questions and really pushed me to expand Bonnyjean's wartime experiences.

Thanks to my late mother, whose hip surgery inspired Bonnyjean's hip and her recovery from anesthesia. Bonnyjean's humor and fortitude came directly from my mom's time in the hospital as did the tree scarf. Thanks to my dad for a lifelong love of music that made Jax an easy character to find.

Thanks to my agent Seth Fishman and, of course, to my wonderful bookmate Sam J. Miller. It was Sam's idea to put easter eggs of each other's work into these books.

As always, thanks to my husband, Robert, who keeps me steady.

RED STAR
HUSTLE

SAM J. MILLER

LONDON   NEW YORK   TORONTO
AMSTERDAM/ANTWERP   NEW DELHI   SYDNEY/MELBOURNE

1230 AVENUE OF THE AMERICAS, NEW YORK, NEW YORK 10020

This book is a work of fiction. Any references to historical events, real people, or real places are used fictitiously. Other names, characters, places, and events are products of the author's imagination, and any resemblance to actual events or places or persons, living or dead, is entirely coincidental.

First Saga Press trade paperback edition October 2025

SAGA PRESS and colophon are registered trademarks of Simon & Schuster, LLC

Simon & Schuster strongly believes in freedom of expression and stands against censorship in all its forms. For more information, visit BooksBelong.com.

For information about special discounts for bulk purchases, please contact Simon & Schuster Special Sales at 1-866-506-1949 or business@simonandschuster.com.

The Simon & Schuster Speakers Bureau can bring authors to your live event. For more information or to book an event, contact the Simon & Schuster Speakers Bureau at 1-866-248-3049 or visit our website at www.simonspeakers.com.

Interior design by Lewelin Polanco

Manufactured in the United States of America

1 3 5 7 9 10 8 6 4 2

Library of Congress Control Number: 2025939771

ISBN 978-1-6680-9915-5
ISBN 978-1-6680-9916-2 (ebook)

For Maya
nuestra erizo
наш ёжик

· · · · · · · ONE · · · · · · ·

PSYCHO STALKER EX

ARAN

Nothing creeps me out more than actual gravity, the way it grabs hold of your bones like a psycho stalker ex whispering that you belong to him, and you always will, and no matter how far you go, you'll always end up in his clutches again.

The port stank of rain and smoke and the citric tang of negative-matter manufacturing, and I couldn't believe I was on a planet again.

I was there for work, of course. Mostly I could pick my gigs, stick to space, but being top tier didn't just mean more money—it came with certain responsibilities as well, and this was one of them: getting sent to weirdo backwater planets because you're the favorite client of a big-deal filmmaker who was going to be the belle of the ball at an intergalactic cinematics festival.

Startling, how much it hurt. The brute force of physics; the tug of something so massive. I watched the rain from beneath the theater marquee and let the wind whip through me and looked out to where the ocean darkened in the storm.

The sea. Another ex. A better one. A kind and beautiful boy,

who always took good care of you and cheered you up when you were down, but who you knew you could never be with because he'd never get his shit together enough to leave the crummy dead-end-nowhere place where he was born. Staying with him would mean staying there, and that would kill you.

And just like running into an ex can send a whole day swirling down the toilet, the sight of the sea unleashed an unwanted, complicated kind of melancholy in me. Every five seconds I turned to look down the block, to a gate hub in a small park: dozens of standing circles, person-sized wormholes propped open and held fast, each twinned with another somewhere on the planet or across the universe.

Easy hops to faraway places. People came and went. I was fiending for it, that freedom. It would be so easy to ditch this grimy globe, return to the systemist space stations where hate and actual gravity had no power over me. The gates called out to me with the same siren song that drugs sang to junkies, and booze to drunks.

I should know. My addictions are myriad. And I was as desperate for a drink as I was for escape, but that one at least had an easy solution: the flask in my back pocket, strong smoky whiskey.

One deep sip unspooled warmth along my arms, kindled fire in my belly.

One sip and I was okay; I was safe; I was grown. I wasn't planetstuck anymore. I'd left a shitty backward xenophobic planet and forged a good life for myself in space. I could go anywhere; do anything. Eighteen more hours on Cinematropolis and I'd be hopping away significantly richer.

My jaw bug buzzed with a ping from Molybdita. My intelligence handler.

From the cold, wet twilight I entered the theater, warm and dry and smelling of spilled cherry soda and popcorn and cheap fake butter and carpet cleaner. All elements of the cinematic experience that dated back to our origins, still obsessively clung to twenty thousand years after we left our home.

Planetstuck people obsess over Planet Zero, invoke it everywhere they can. Copy its practices even when they're inefficient, outdated, destructive, idiotic. In space, on a ship or station, Planet Zero is anathema. Bad luck just to mention the place, and forget about bringing something aboard that actually came from there.

In the movie theater's dark red velvet depths was a phone booth, decked out with new bubble tech to keep conversations secure. Once I was in and shut the door, the whoosh of noise-canceling kicked in, a soundless full-body sound as sweet and familiar as the omnipresent hum of the tech on a space station.

I took a full minute to breathe in, breathe out. Bask in the vacuum. I had forgotten just how destabilizing it is for me, to actually be on a planet.

Call Molybdita, I subvocalized, and Cinnamon—my AI mate—scrambled to comply.

"Why aren't you in the hotel lobby?" she asked, on-brand by being annoyed right off the bat. "Eavesdropping in the bar, chatting up the rich and powerful and lonely?"

"Wanted to go for a walk," I said.

"Honestly, Aran, you make me weep. How can someone be so good at half his job and so bad at the other half?"

"My clients don't complain," I said.

"Your *clients* won't give two shits about you when you're no longer the sexy young thing you currently are," she said. "You don't work for them. You work for yourself. And you need to be

planning for the future. Sex workers have a short shelf life. I can't believe I have to keep reminding you of this."

Here's the dirty little secret of outer-space sex work. Rent boys barely make a third of their income off the actual selling of their body. Especially—if you'll forgive the brag—the higher-end ones like me, who meet the most *fascinating* people, *important* people with more money than sense, more access than acumen.

I had a flesh handler who booked my gigs and vetted my clients and monitored my safety. Llopa: In less enlightened systems she'd be called my pimp. Molybdita was my intelligence handler. She paid me a small flat fee for every scrap I brought her, and the real money came in after she'd fenced it. Not so long ago I'd gotten a quarter vibe just for telling her the name of the man who'd paid me to punish him in an Amhara Monastery cell . . . and then received six hundred vibes seven solar days later, when his corporate competitors deduced from his presence in that sector that it was the next space for a product rollout, and they rushed their rival commodity to market a week before his, neutralized millions he'd spent on target-space research, made a billion.

"Was that all you wanted, love?" I asked cheerily.

"You know it's not, you little asshole."

I laughed. I couldn't help it. A third of the time I hated her; the rest of the time I adored her.

"How's your client? Opple."

"He's fine," I said. "Stressed. Apparently this new movie is insanely controversial. And really nasty. There've been death threats. His backers are very nervous. Talking about pulling it, or taking it away from him and making cuts. But! It's also the most buzzed-about film at the festival this year. So Opple is riding high and scared shitless all at the same time. So you see I *have* been paying *some* attention here, Mother."

"I'm not your mother, thank the stars. You left him in the hotel room, then?"

"Yeah, he wanted to sleep and didn't want to be disturbed. Told me to take a walk."

This part wasn't true, but she didn't need to know that.

"You should go back. A lot is riding on this film, Aran. It was apparently partially funded by a consortium of—"

"I don't want to know all that," I said.

"Because you are bad at your job!"

"Message received, Moly. Go back and fuck dude into a state of blissful chatty oblivion. Be nosy. Got it. Going."

"Opple will be surrounded by powerful people who are on his side," Molybdita said, "and others who hate his guts. Just listen, okay? Go to the cocktail parties and smile and be clever, cute arm candy and take fucking notes? Please? For me?"

"Bye, Mom."

I hung up on her heavy sigh.

Here's my problem. Why I won't be the zealous spy Molybdita wants me to be.

Obviously, selling intel screws people over. And of course I always scrub whatever I've got, before I sell it. Getting people killed is bad for business, and just generally a shit move. I have lines I won't cross. Lots of pleasure workers don't—and stars know they make a lot more money that way—and, I don't know, maybe it's dumb, but I actually tend to kind of care about the people who buy my body, provided they treat it with respect, which honestly almost all of them do.

Molybdita said that was the planetstuck part of me. Sentimental, still rooted in outdated notions of familial piety, accountability to abstract notions of "clan" and "tribe" and "country" that had evolved as a survival strategy millennia ago, and had been

left behind the day we first learned to spawn wormholes and keep them open and use them to spread beyond the shitty little doomed rock we started from.

She wasn't wrong. I'd left my planet behind a decade before, but I carried it with me wherever I went.

I carried it with me now, walking downhill to the port when the hotel was uphill, letting actual gravity decide my path. *Where the hell are you going, Aran?* asked the Molybdita in my head, but she could go fuck herself.

Full night, now. Actual night, not a scheduled dimming of banked lights. The city glimmering beautifully beneath a sky so full of smog I could hardly see any stars. A song was playing somewhere through a shitty speaker. The wind smelled of petrol, salt water, garbage, woodsmoke. Lemons.

A heavy, mournful nostalgia hit me so hard I had to stop.

And take another swig from the flask. And wait for the whiskey to loosen the grip that real gravity and melancholy nostalgia had on my heart.

I'd hated my home planet. Its shabby small-mindedness; its limited options and hostility to any place with more. Humanity had come so far, in most space-based settlements—with hunger and exploitation banished from so many—but on the planets, it was like we'd never left the scarcity and forced proximity and messy bloody history of Planet Zero.

And mine was one of the worst, and I'd hated it, but I'd also low-key kinda loved it. Its sweet-smelling nights; its vast unknowability. The wild free spaces in the shadow of the long-defunct terraforming towers. All the familiar sights and sounds and scents I'd never see or hear or smell again.

Because I could never ever go back.

I'd never see my brother again. If he was alive at all.

Thinking about home was what did it. What steered me away from Molybdita's very clear instructions to head back to the hotel. Instead I headed for the park, with its gate array, and walked through a wormhole bound for the nearest mega-hub. My Mapp tab told me there was a tavern in a space station seven hops away that checked four of my boxes: a tattered tawdry aesthetic; a speakerboxxx loaded with lots of corny old dance songs; cheap drinks; a predominantly working-class clientele but also an unusually high degree of cross-class commerce.

An addict doesn't need a reason to get obliterated, but they'll usually find one. That night, mine was an attack of crippling nostalgia.

It's the only reason I'm not dead right now.

TWO

OFFICIOUS LITTLE PRICK

IMADI

It wasn't that I wanted to use. Three years clean and the fiending hardly ever came anymore. I'd done the meetings and the steps and survived the night sweats and cut myself off from the people-places-things associated with my addiction. And I was good.

But sometimes. Sometimes something or someone rubbed me the wrong way. Or caught me off guard. Stressed me the fuck out. And I felt the twinge again. Not the urge to use, but the tremor that came before it. The little voice, which probably won't ever vanish altogether, that whispers, *Fuck this shit, there's an easy way out of this problem, there's a drug for this.* Couple times a week, something came along to get her started.

Like this asshole.

The man who met me at the crime scene was slick, professional, expensive. Instant hatred flared. Frustration at being an actual adult with a job who had to interact with other actual adults, who were so often fucking awful. The twinge was triggered.

"I represent the Lesser Magellanics Trade Federation," he said, and pinged me his card, which I resolved not to inspect.

"We were the primary funder of the victim's last few films, and we are responsible for his personal security contract."

Gar Opple. Apparently a significant filmmaker of the zhà xiè school (I'd never heard of him or that cinematics ideology, but that didn't mean much; it was a big universe, and I had never been big on narrative entertainment modalities). Killed by a rough-trade rent boy who was currently on the run. Apparently.

The body was gone. A musky animal smell still filled the air, beneath the reek of blood.

"Our bots estimate eighty-eight minutes between intercourse and time of death."

"We'll want to run our own," I said.

"Of course."

I uncapped the sleeve, let them out. They zipped busily through the air. Nano-miasma was thick in this station, as it always is in spaces for rich people. An invisible cloud of networked nanites, holding info and transferring data and powering devices . . . Parameters populated the chart on my tab, next to the data the station bots had logged. Most of the values matched up: This was a luxury outpost, after all, which meant it would be on the front edge of tech.

I walked the room, looking for the things my bots might miss. A smell of petrol and burning in the air. The victim's things had been shredded, stabbed, set on fire, strewn about. The random violence of a kid on a toxic trip.

But . . . not random. Not quite. Something crossed a threshold, set off the quietest of warning bells.

"What was he doing, do you think?" I asked. "After the murder."

A nod, a tell. A prepared sentence being presented as off the cuff. "Kid was on drugs, went nuts, and trashed the joint after he

got finished stabbing the dude to death. Shine will do that. Kids cut it with spiderwebbing these days."

"How do you know? That he was on drugs? Neither my bots nor the station environmentals detected anything to indicate that."

He shrugged. Officious little prick. "Must have been. To do something crazy like this?"

"There's an order here," I said. "Or, not order, just . . . this was methodical. It's supposed to look like it was done in a frenzy, but it wasn't."

Eye roll. "I can't speak to the exact kind of crazy this kid was, but Opple liked to court danger. It's well documented. His sexual tastes ran to hoodlums and thugs and other violent young men. What I believe they call 'rough trade.' This is, alas, not an uncommon result. As a matter of due diligence we maintain scrupulous records on all the pleasure workers our most important functionaries patronize, of course. I've pinged your concern a copy of the file on the boy who did this—an Uqbari refugee named Aran. Drug addict; petty criminal. Several of our trade representatives frequented him. He should be relatively easy to track down. And then you can ask him about the . . . methodical? way he trashed this room after murdering his client."

His patter was practiced, a magician's distraction. *Look what I'm doing with this hand, not what I'm doing with the other.*

"Lots of people didn't want this movie to be seen," I said. "Stream chatter says Opple received death threats. Why wasn't that in the dossier you provided to Blue Circumspect Tomorrow?"

He smiled. "I appreciate your thoroughness, I really do. We expect nothing less, given your organization's reputation. It's why we contracted you, and happily pay such high rates. But this was a crime of passion, not politics."

"How do you know?"

He shrugged, like none of it actually mattered in the least. The suit, expensive artificial sharkskin, shimmered. He wasn't wearing a red armband, but that didn't mean anything. He could still be Intelligence. Maybe he had something to hide, and maybe he simply hated the security concerns instinctively. That's pretty normal. Intelligence hates security, and we hate them. And we coexist, the blue bands and the red. The way two apex predators in the wild will pay careful attention to each other, but rarely engage directly.

"You're the expert, of course," he said obsequiously. "I will send you a full dossier."

"I appreciate that. Walk with me," I said, not waiting for him to get over his annoyance at being bossed around.

Starburst cracks in the smartwalls: a dozen of them. "These bullet holes were from an expensive weapon. Hard to come by. Not what drugged-out rent boys carry."

"Young punks love weapons. We don't know what he was packing."

"Not that, I assure you. And neither was the filmmaker. When artists and sex workers carry weapons, it's usually for self-defense. This was a show-off weapon."

"Perhaps." Here his tone edged back into imperious, remembering who was technically the hired help in this exchange. "You'll contact me, won't you? If you have any further questions, or when you have something to report?"

I bowed, smiling as smugly as I could muster.

Once he was gone, I saw it clearly. I'd been so eager to one-up this asshole, I hadn't noticed one very obvious, very bad thing.

This kid didn't do it.

Fuck.

Fuck, fuck, fuck, fuck.

I was super insanely fucked.

It had seemed like such a simple task, when it came across the streams. Straightforward.

This wasn't. This was six hundred kinds of wrong. Professionals had killed the filmmaker, intending to frame the sex worker. And his people didn't want me to dig any deeper, which raised all the red flags in my mind.

But. And it was a big but.

If I couldn't close this case, I was a little bit very fucked.

For three years I'd been doing my own thing. Being the baddest bitch. Daughter of the ancestral matriarch of one of the largest security concerns in Stratum Chín; ex-champion-mech-fighter warrior with an expense account as big and deep as her ego. I never had to answer to anyone or file a time sheet or report home for a staff meeting.

And the first time I dropped the ball, Mom could send for me. Maybe she wouldn't. But she could. And if she did, she'd find out the thing I was hiding from her. And this was a woman who'd killed her own uncle to get command of the company, and promoted plenty of lieutenants on the basis of betrayal or bloodshed. It was standard operating procedure for the security concerns that serve as the only law in space, and I knew it too well to think it'd have any mercy on me because we were family.

I scanned through the file on Aran. Nice kid, seemed like. Kind eyes. His so-called criminal history was stuff like an arrest for assault after he'd come to the aid of a drunk who some rich kids were stomping the shit out of.

But someone had gone to a lot of trouble to fit a frame for

him. And taking the time to find out the truth risked exposing everything I'd worked so hard to keep secret.

It wasn't fair. It fucking sucked. But if I hadn't stuck my neck out for my own sister, I damn sure wasn't going to do so for a stranger.

THREE

AN ERECTION IS A LIABILITY IN
COMBAT SITUATIONS

ARAN

Seven hops, from the drizzly park on Cinematropolis to the tawdry space-based bar that Cinnamon had selected for me by calibrating all my known tastes and predilections against my current mental-wellness metrics and microbiome activity.

Full night when I left Cinematropolis, but bright morning on the station I hopped to. The clock is the only constant in space. Still pegged to Planet Zero's solar cycle. World-based civilizations set their clocks to the local star, but almost every space station and system outpost sticks to the ancient twenty-four-hour cycle our simian ancestors evolved under.

I shivered, to be free of that planet's pull. My shoulders still damp from seaside rain; my bones still taut from gravity's tendrils. One more swig of whiskey to whisk it all away.

Echidna Junction, Cinnamon whispered in my implant as we hopped the last gate. *Created to breed the eponymous mammal when they were all the rage as companion animals in Stratum*

Hai Mười Một. In my viz she lit up the way to a bar called Snake Nymph.

I still had half the flask in my pocket, but I wasn't *only* fiending for intoxication. I needed people, the safe, warm buzz of space-based crowds, a long, cool sip from the well of togetherness.

Snake Nymph was trash; all the whiskey was made in space. Something about generated gravity throws the distilling process off. At least Snake Nymph had decent aromatics: sawdust top note; amber or balm for the heart note. So the place had been fancy once, and fallen on hard times. And the smell of booze—even shitty booze—was always enough to give me a bit of an erection. Just one more red flag in the never-ending parade of How I Know I Have a Problem.

I sat down at the bar and typed my order into the robot bartender. Told myself I was only there for one drink. A quick shot, then back to my life. Back to Cinematropolis, my rock star filmmaker client, intelligence gathering, doing Molybdita's bidding, tapping into my inner illness so I could start building toward the possibility of an independent future.

But by the time I'd downed that shot, I knew I needed another. So I tapped my empty glass against an ancient faded sticker that said MATH TURTLES.

Another point in Snake Nymph's favor: It had a hottie. Big guy at the opposite end of the bar from me, probably six foot five, bearded and muscular with thick black curly hair. That was how I tallied him up in my head, at first, but that's backward problematic planetstuck thinking: categorizing people by physical characteristics. Body shape; skin tone; the size of your eyes or nose: For planet-side people, they were all just ways of sorting out whether or not someone was "one of us"—like ice planets controlled by corporations who bred their gene pools for red hair

and extra heft, where anyone who looked different got treated with contempt—or, way back on Planet Zero, when people hated whole populations based on physical characteristics derived from where on the globe their ancestors came from.

Systemists describe people in terms of how they make you *feel*. And this guy made you feel like if he was standing by your side, no harm could ever come to you. This guy made you feel like his furry forearms could stop bullets, sweep away cancer. His garment was something a priest or soldier would wear, precisely tailored to show off his impressive musculature but also somehow austere, a single full-body piece with a hood and elaborate stitching that probably conveyed complex information about his position in an ancient and noble organization.

I couldn't keep from trying to catch his eye—because my biggest, oldest, most dangerous addiction is to being desired—but he seemed pretty focused on his beer. So I focused on my whiskey.

And of course I wasn't alone in my lust. Two older guys in a booth were eyeing my hottie with predatory intent. Which, honestly, my own intent had felt pretty predatory, so I couldn't blame them. But I had desisted after a couple abortive attempts at eye contact, and these two were whispering in a way I did not like at all.

You get a feel for things like this. People who are up to no good. You've got to, or you won't last long in space—which is mostly great and cool and full of awesome free people, but also has pockets of atrocity and oppression that would put any planet-based slave empire or sex-cult-turned-asteroid-republic to shame.

The other thing you develop? A sense of obligation to the other folks out here who are vulnerable to exploitation. When you see someone in trouble, you help out, however you can, and you pray that someone will help you out when you're inevitably in the same position.

Aran, Cinnamon said in my ear, her voice edged with urgency. Had I programmed that emotion? If so, what kind of crazy trigger had I set for it, considering it had never been triggered before?

The security checks you set me to routinely scan for, she said. *Concerning urgent developments around your client, their business interests, and the locations of your assignations? Several of them have been set off.*

Take *that,* Molybdita. Maybe I *do* have some sense.

Go ahead, I subvocalized.

She paused.

Overwhelmed by the volume of information she had to process? Challenged by where and how to start? Or for dramatic effect? It sounded like the kind of thing I would do—most people program their AI mates when they're pretty young, a rite of passage for figuring out the basics of programming, which are as essential as reading a station map in space. It's great, but it means there's often lots of bugs in the works, ancient mistakes you forgot making.

Your client has been brutally murdered, Cinnamon said.

And,

You are the primary suspect, Cinnamon said. And,

Station security identified you from registration and has authorized a search.

Space stood still. Time stopped.

A claims collector from the contractually bound security concern has been dispatched to hunt you down.

Down the bar, the two older men had arrived at a decision. One hung back, but the other sat down on the stool beside my future husband and put a hand on his shoulder. He looked up

and blinked, and I saw that he was blind. Sclerae clouded over with some kind of roiling metallic nano light shield. I couldn't hear what they were saying and it wasn't my business anyway and holy hell I had more important things to worry about.

But that's the thing about a crisis. Sometimes it's too scary to face. Sometimes you'll take any opportunity to postpone responding to it.

Cinnamon was showing me footage. Horrific. Unspeakable. Opple's suite, splattered and smeared with crimson. A knife and a truncheon on the bed. Beside a body I did my best to avoid seeing.

My pack, on the desk, being picked through by humans and machines. Holding everything I value in the whole wide portalverse—like most pleasure boys, my home is minimalist and I'm hardly ever there. And anyway I could never go back there again.

I thought, *At least there's nothing there I can't afford to lose—* and then remembered.

An Uqbari tlön. A coin from my homeworld: the last thing I had left from there.

The place I would never see again. The place that was gone forever now.

I stood up. I took a very long sip of whiskey. Slowly, calmly. Like nothing at all was wrong. Like I was neither guilty nor afraid.

Because lots of people would be looking for me. They'd scan gate logs and payment records and eventually they'd find this bar, watch this scene.

From sheer force of dumb muscle-memory habit, I took out my Mapp tab and stared at it. Was it even safe to use? Would the security concerns be able to trace it, track me down? Molybdita gave all her pleasure-worker intelligence assets some very

sophisticated encryption software, but the security concerns would almost certainly have the best of the best icebreakers.

At the end of the bar, Mr. Hottie was trying his hardest to politely signal disinterest, a marvel of tact and grace that his interrogator aggressively refused to register.

And then: fuck.

The other guy put something in his drink.

Fuck, fuck, fuck.

It wasn't my problem. I had to get hopping, far and fast. Last thing I needed was pissing off a couple of possible human traffickers.

But then the guy took a sip. A big, long gulp.

And, really, it's the code of the trade. We're all just scared, lonely kids lost in the starsprawl, preyed upon by the powerful and the sick and the hate-filled, and we help each other out when we can.

I could do this. Give him a quick heads-up—help him exit if he needed it—and hop to safety.

So I walked down to his end of the bar and played my best move. Which was not a very good move.

"Hey!" I said, clasping the hottie's left shoulder. "Wow, brother, it's been so long! So great to see you!!"

The vulture clinging to his right shoulder receded slightly, smiling hateful daggers at me.

"Hi?" Hottie said.

"You would not believe who I just saw last week! And what she said about you!" And here I leaned in, like the gossip was just too good, and whispered, "You're in danger. Dude just put something in your drink. There's two of them."

Hottie laughed like the gossip really had been that good. So maybe he was hot *and* not stupid.

Abruptly, he stood. "Can you help me to the bathroom? I can give you a message to send back to her. That absolute *bitch*." To the vulture, he turned and said, "Keep an eye on my drink, will you? I'll be right back, and we can continue this conversation."

Vulture looked suspicious, but also gratified.

Hottie offered his elbow, and I looped my arm through it. Feeling a throb, at the heat and sturdiness of him. Another symptom of my addictive personality: The right tangle of male pheromones makes me forget all my fears and stresses. To say nothing of common sense. I should have been figuring out how the fuck to save my ass, not give it away.

He stumbled, stepping into the hallway. His legs wobbled. "They're following us, right?"

I looked behind us. "Yup."

"Are you down to fuck them up a little?"

I laughed, from giddy fear but also because his deep voice started me tingling. "Yeah, but . . . you should know I am *really, really bad* at fucking people up. A lover, not a fighter, and all that."

"No worries, I'm super good at it. I ran an internal scan, which I wouldn't have known to do without your heads-up, so, thanks for that. I'm about twenty percent incapacitated. I've got four, maybe five minutes, before I'm fully unconscious." I marveled at whatever tech told him all that; my first hint that he was really Somebody. "Take this"—and he handed me a zip stick—"and as soon as we're out of sight, sprint ahead and turn at the intersection so *you're* out of sight. Keep an eye on me, run up and zip them if it looks like I need help. But probably I won't. Still down?"

"So down."

For literally anything, hot stuff.

"You're sweet," he said. "Name's Resh."

"Aran."

"Get the fuck outta here, Aran."

And, yes. He slapped me on the ass as I went. Like some skin-cinematic jock dream come true. Once I was out of sight, I uncapped the zip stick and watched it throb to life to distract myself from what he'd done to me. Because I don't know much about fighting, but I have to assume an erection is a liability in combat situations.

When I peeked, Resh lay on the ground at an awkward angle, like he'd collided with a wall and went down sideways. The guys turned the corner a second later. They squatted like two practiced predators who'd done this before, and wedged themselves under each of his arms to lift him to his feet.

"Who," Resh said, slurring absurdly.

"It's just us," one of them said.

"I don't know you."

"You're drunk, big guy," the other one said loudly, for the benefit of any mechanical or human listeners.

He let them struggle with him for a bit, and then: Resh came alive.

All I can say is, it was incredible. Like the best beam fight you ever saw, out on one of those far-flung stations where fighters spend their whole lives training, eating sleeping breathing the deadly ballet of battle. It couldn't have lasted more than ten seconds, but it took my breath away.

Resh let them take on part of his weight, sandwiched between them with his arms across their shoulders. Then he lifted his legs, weighing them both down so suddenly that they stopped, staggered—and he had his hands knotted in their hair, was smashing their heads together—

They fell to the side, both bleeding from scalp wounds, and

in truth he could certainly have gotten away at this point. Which was not what he did.

He extended his arm, the way you would to hurl a projectile, except his hand was empty.

Except it wasn't.

His garment. The hooded soldier-priest uniform. It *moved*. It *flowed*. His sleeves surged, a living stream of programmable matter that obeyed him like something in a cinematic—becoming water, becoming a single fluid blade, piercing the first guy's leg—a dead-on perfect-aim femoral artery puncture, and all without being able to actually see his target.

The guy dropped, and Resh stood up—tall and confident and nowhere near as drugged as he'd seemed an instant ago. He raised his hand, and the programmable matter flow arced in midair, straight for the neck of guy number two, penetrating the carotid.

I'd never seen anyone manipulate polymer like that—faster and more complex than crude subvocalizations could ever manifest. This was no random musclehead, no nobody fuckboy.

Resh turned to where he knew I was watching, and grinned triumphantly. Then he took five steps and dropped to his knees, as the full surge of the drug washed over him.

I hurried over, keeping the zip stick aimed at the screaming/gurgling bad guys bleeding to death on the ground, even though I was pretty sure they posed no threat.

"My hero," Resh said as I helped him to his knees. "Help me to my hab?"

"Sure," I muttered, trying not to look at all the carnage.

Then Resh tilted his head slightly, as if seeing me for the first time—*but he can't see, Aran, that's fucked up, wow*—and said, "Whoa, brother. What are you?"

And I didn't know how to answer it, other than, *whatever you want me to be*, so I didn't say anything, and then he shrugged, chuckled drunkenly, and stood up just enough to hobble down the hall with me.

Halfway to his hab, he kissed me on the cheek. His beard brushed my skin like starfire, which made me delirious-dizzy—and then—

A wind of crushing sadness swept me. Remembering Opple. My client. His own beard; his own cheek kiss. Silver hair and kind eyes, smelling of pine and lavender and leather. He was in his sixties, kept himself together, still a total charmer. Poised to conquer the whole damn cinematics universe. Brutally murdered. I'd almost certainly be dead myself now too, had I gone back to the room instead of hopping here to get a drink (wow, for once my drinking problem did me some good). For some reason that part was a purely intellectual fascination, the fact that I'd almost died. It didn't make me feel anything. Mostly all I felt was sadness, for this kind, sweet dude I'd barely known and now had allegedly murdered.

· · · · · · · **FOUR** · · · · · · ·

IN SPACE THERE'S ALWAYS SOMEWHERE

IMADI

Waking up was the worst.

Every morning my eyes sprang open and my hands made fists, ready to fight.

I never dreamed of her, but my mother was always waiting in the in-between. The space that was neither sleep nor wakefulness. She wore a different demon shape each time, but it was always her. Two or three times a week, for our entire childhood, she'd jolt my sister and me awake for some unspeakable unpleasantness. Combat training. Front-row seats at a bloody interrogation. Screenings of graphic footage gleaned from contractee cams. Toughening us up for when we'd fight her—and then each other—for control of our shitty empire.

Now I carried her with me wherever in space I went.

Vespertine read my cortisol levels, spent a solid thirty minutes doing her best to calm me down. And then she reminded me of my next appointment.

Ninety hops and an hour later I was sitting in the rec room of an old orbital station named Blue Buzz Place. Set up ages ago

to support an ecoformed planet, which had reached full self-sustainability a millennium ago. Now the station housed mostly pilgrims and photographers looking to get shots of the wild and weird Planet Zero species that had been de-extincted down there. Posters listed them. Some pretty wild stuff.

"Hey!" Trist said, when they saw me.

We hugged.

"You don't have to come to these every week, you know," Trist said.

"I know," I said. "And I won't be able to come super consistently for a while. Just caught a really complicated case at work."

We sat. Addicts in varying stages of dishevelment and sobriety shuffled in. The meeting would start soon.

A month ago, I'd attended a collective-help meeting for addicts, as I did from time to time when the twinge hit me especially hard. I'd met Trist there, and been harrowed by their story. Orphaned refugee of a massacred people, fending for themself since the age of nine, Trist at thirteen had plumbed depths of addiction few adults would ever reach. They didn't share specifics at that first meeting, but I could tell from the tremor in their voice that the trauma was real.

After the meeting I chatted them up. Bought them dinner. Asked where they were staying. Found out they were rootless.

In systemist space, no one is truly homeless. Not like on some planets, where poor folks sleep in the streets of big cities and are at the mercy of the weather and the cops and the monsters who would try to hurt a defenseless sleeping person.

In space, there's always somewhere. Mapp can find you a designated safe space, and the accommodations won't be great but there'll be a bed and some food, and it's easy to spot the ones where something creepy is going on.

But lots of people in space are rootless. Hopping from place to place, unable to set up shop somewhere and trust your stuff will still be there when you return. Unable to scrounge together the currency required to rent something; unwilling to make the compromises required to live in one of the consent communities where all are welcome as long as they follow the rules. Which usually means joining the cult.

Getting sober is hard as hell in the best of circumstances, but without a fixed safe place it's practically impossible. So I did for Trist what I've done for several addicts over the years: I put them up. Pinged them the coordinates of a cheap motel in Stratum Mười, and messaged the management to give them a monthlong credit. It wasn't fancy but it was safe, and they owed me some favors, so when I sent freshly sober addicts their way, they took care of them. And lots of times I never saw those folks again—they relapsed just as soon as they got the chance. But Trist was doing great, and we got together for lunch a couple times a week and I went to their meetings whenever I could.

Trist's people were Jal Fal—one of those nations where children chose their gender when they turned eighteen. Until that point, it was taboo to refer to them as anything other than "they." Among friends, kids would try on pronouns for size, for fun, seeing what felt right and what rubbed them the wrong way, and many knew from a young age exactly what they would choose, but for an adult to gender one was considered supremely creepy, bordering on sexualization.

"I was reading about you," Trist said, over cardamom coffee after the meeting.

"Oh stars," I said. "Don't trust a word of it. Any halfway competent mech pilot gets a whole lot of rubbish written about them."

"I watched some of your fights. You were good."

I rolled my eyes. Didn't challenge the use of the past tense.

"Is it weird if I ask, what's the deal with your sister?"

I laughed, and hoped it didn't sound as fake and panicky as it was.

"What did you read?" I asked, finally.

"Mey Imadi. Your twin sister—nineteen minutes younger than you. The two crown princesses of the legendary Blue Circumspect Tomorrow; minor industry celebrities; mech pilot savants, beating the best in the biz at an early age. Your sister was brilliant, by all accounts, but—bad. From birth, some people say. Ran away at seventeen. Abandoned the empire she was set to inherit, *and* the mech championships she would certainly have won. For years she was gone, popping up periodically to make the whole company miserable. But for years now, no one has seen or heard from her."

I said—

"I don't like talking about my sister."

—but I said it significantly harsher than I'd meant to. And Trist's face fell.

I didn't know their story. Not the whole thing. Just that it was ugly. I'd avoided reading too much about the Jal Fal; I wanted to treat Trist as a person, as an addict trying to get sober, and not as a narrow survivor of a brutal genocide.

But whatever Trist had seen or experienced, it had scarred them deeply. And sometimes they simply . . . went away.

Like now.

And Trist was a good kid. With more than a bit of a hero-worship thing for me going on. And I knew I had shut something down inside them. I remembered moments like that, from my own youth. The thousand times somebody made me feel like shit

for asking an honest question. How it all adds up to fear conquering your curiosity, your wide-open heart shutting down.

"But it sounds like you got the basics pretty well," I said, trying to placate them. To be less of an asshole. "I love my sister Mey, but I can't help her. She's"—and I stared out the fore screen at the endlessness of space—"rejected all my attempts."

A long time later, Trist asked, "Are you in touch with her?"

"Why are you asking?"

They shrugged. "I'm curious. And maybe a little bit jealous. I had a sibling. I don't now." She didn't volunteer the story, and I wasn't about to probe for it. "So you two never talk? That's so sad."

"We last talked three years ago," I said. "It's not good for my sobriety to spend time with people who can't get clean."

"But . . . not even a call? You never try to reach out?"

I put my hand on Trist's to signal as gently and as kindly as possible that there was not a single other word I'd be saying on this subject.

AN EVIL TRICKY MOTHERFUCKER

ARAN

Atheism is a point of pride among the spacebound. The Systemist Creed says it best: *Belief in divine beings is a barbaric vestige of primitive Planet Zero thought, a manifestation of humanity's faith in its own supremacy and right to exploit, but projected outward onto imaginary figures.* Etc.

And even though I aspire with my whole heart and mind and soul to be a systemist through and through—and I've spent years killing off every backward and planetstuck part of myself I can put my hands on—I know there are some things about ourselves that simply can't be changed. And for me, one of those is believing in gods—or God—or the Supreme Self—or animist spirits pervading every piece of material reality—or *something*.

To the core of my soul I believed in that *something*, and knew with the same soul-deep certainty that this *something* was an evil tricky motherfucker constantly trying to fuck me up.

How else to explain me getting this glorious hunk back to his hab ship—his AI mate savvily assessed the situation and took us sixty randomized hops to safety—and helping put said glorious

hunk to bed, while hunk keeps on grabbing me by the wrist and torso and trying to pull me down into his arms, hearing him plead, "Come on, please"—and his sheets were exquisitely soft and his bed was as big as anything I'd ever been in and I wanted him so bad and there was no way I could let this happen.

Also, he was insanely rich, if his ship was anything to judge by, and it usually is.

"You've been drugged," I said, for the thousandth time, folding his grabby hands gently onto his chest. "You don't really want this."

"You have no idea what I really want. Is this a self-esteem thing? Because I can tell by your voice that you're adorable, Aran. And don't let this hot body fool you, it's barely even mine."

"It's an 'I don't fuck dudes who've been drugged' thing, Resh."

He pouted, but relented enough for me to finally wiggle free and step out of his reach.

Only then, briefly freed from the agonizing torture of resisting his desire, did I remember:

Someone you care about was brutally murdered
You're wanted for the crime
You're a fugitive
You can never go home
You've lost everything
Again

Jeez, Aran. You're almost as bad with dick as you are with alcohol. Once it's on your brain, it blots out everything else. From the moment I helped Resh up off the ground, the smell of his body and the heat of him against me had triggered a junkie's fiending.

"Is this ship bricked?" I asked, trying to sound casual. "Can I

be certain none of my devices"—*or implants or tracking chips or nanites I don't even know about*—"is transmitting my location?"

"Of course it is," Resh said.

"And the station where you were docked . . . any chance they would have clocked my exit with you?" Some systems have special bricked docks, where people can pay a little extra to evade a public record of their passing through.

"I think it's a little early in our relationship for such a personal question, Aran," he said, and laughed. "But if you must know, I might or might not be engaged in extensive activities for which discretion and secrecy are essential—and I might or might not have extraordinarily powerful enemies. So yeah. I try to cover my tracks as much as possible. Now that we're practically engaged . . ." and he reached out boldly for my crotch.

"Stop that!" I said, swatting at him.

"Sorry, Aran."

"You got any dopamine blockers in this . . . insanely lavish hab?" I asked. "Purgatives, pathway clearers? Black coffee? Anything to sober you up?"

"I don't like messing with that stuff," and, wow, that was a total addict red flag right there. "Is it okay if we just talk?"

"Fine," I said, wishing I was strong enough to get up and go. He really was superhumanly hot. Like statues you see in cinematics set centuries ago.

"Those two guys in the tavern," he said. "They were probably working for my father."

"Really? Your dad's trying to sexually traffic you?"

"I don't think it's anything so tawdry. He's just trying to kill me, is all."

". . . oh . . ."

"He's not really my father," Resh said. "He's my original."

"You're a clone," I said, as nonjudgmentally as possible, because I'd met a lot of clones in my day and many of them were supersensitive on the subject.

"Zap," he said, pointing laser finger guns at me. "Pew, pew. Right."

Then he laughed, an odd high sound. "When I get drunk, I can make jokes about it. But he's a fucking monster and he's hurt me more ways than I care to count. In fact, it's probably *why* I get drunk so much."

In the totally non-awkward silence that followed, I finally had a chance to check out the surroundings. The velvet, the chrome, the intricate stone carvings framed on the wall. I breathed deep, a lungful of air that smelled as warm and rich and sacred as the inside of the oldest stone church on my home planet.

"Pardon the invasive question, but what's your aromatic setup here? It smells incredible. I wanna say the heart-note is sandalwood, but it's so earthy. . . ."

"No setup. It's an actual ventilation shaft that routes through a gate connecting directly to the Third House of the Sanctum. What you're smelling is the actual inside of my people's holiest place."

"Resh. Who the fuck are you?"

He laughed and shucked off his shirt, revealing a hairy, sturdy chest that made me want to weep. "I am the genetically identical heir of the twenty-fourth Exilarch of Mar Zutra—hereditary autocephalous Leader of the Captivity since the conquest of Iskawi and our dispersion throughout the Terfezian Empire. But don't let the fancy facts fool you—I'm not special, Dad makes dozens of me."

"Do they all get sweet hab ships like this one?"

"Right up until he kills them."

"He sounds like a real piece of shit."

Resh grunt-laughed. "Gotta keep trying till he gets it right. Although nobody knows what he's trying for. Spoils some of us, sells others into slavery, indentures us into military service . . . watches us from afar, until we disappoint him, at which point he pulls the plug. Surely one day one of us will give him what he's after. But I'm by far the oldest."

"Why's that?"

"He sent me to the empire's officer school. And I was dumb enough to take the risks that make people think you're brave—and in spite of widespread, intense prejudice against my people, I got command of a Terfezian flagship for my first assignment—fought my way onto an enemy heartship in the heat of battle, seized control and turned it on the rest of the enemy fleet and kinda single-handedly stopped an invasion—it's a whole thing. There's cinematics about it. So the Mar Zutra rank and file really rallied behind me—and the Exilarch himself is hopelessly corrupt and lives in fear of his own people, dares not show his face outside the Terfezian elite circles that richly reward their lapdogs—so he couldn't just kill me the way he killed all my variants. He's gotta be sneaky about it."

"I'm sorry. And I'm sorry to say I never even heard of the Mar Zutra."

His laugh now was much more bitter. "My people's plight is small change. Ninety trillion human settlements, and every day a handful of nations or cultures or planets get displaced or exterminated or taken into captivity. But—what about this? What if you stay over there, but you keep talking, and I just jerk off? You have a really nice voice. Is that okay, or would we run afoul of your 'I don't fuck dudes who've been drugged' thing?"

"I think you know it would."

He made a noise of frustration, a groan and a moan at once, which told me he was extremely vocal in bed, which made resisting him even harder. "Tell me *your* life story, then, Aran."

"Do you have anything to drink?" I heard myself ask, and prayed he wouldn't, and knew he would.

A stone carving on the wall slid aside, responding no doubt to more of Resh's weird expensive Exilarch nano-enhancing.

Whiskey. Good, good whiskey. So smoky I could feel drunkenness creep in as soon as I took a sniff: all the thousands of sips I'd swallowed in my life, ghosts in my bloodstream, converging like a flock of crows summoned by a smell on the breeze.

"Pleasure boy by trade," I said, tilting the glass into my mouth. Letting the smooth liquid lie there, numbing my tongue, filling my soul.

"I knew it," he said. "Knew someone with a voice that hot had to be a professional. But surely there's more to you than that."

"Planetstuck," I said, and it had to be the scotch talking, already working its way into the architecture of my psyche, loosening the load-bearing pillars that held up my resolve never to speak of this. The scotch, or the heat of him. Only addiction could get me to say, out loud, to another human: "Born and bred in a place called Uqbar. Home to an especially virulent anti-offworlder movement. Real scary fascist shit, smashing gates and breaking into homes to terrorize and"—*breathe*—"kill people they said were collaborating with the evil systemist bloodsuckers who steal the resources of hardworking planets. Escaped at sixteen; started working the skin trade right away. Fourteen years in the game now."

He turned toward me, head tilted again, the way he had when he said, *What are you?*

"Uqbar," he said. "I've heard of it. Supposedly home to some gnarly crazy tech."

"Yeah," I said, surprised. "Copper, cobalt, manganese. Planet packed with all three of the most important minerals for technology."

"You, uh . . . know anything about that?"

I shook my head, but his stayed tilted. Like he was . . . listening to me. Finally he smiled and shook it off. "Been home since?"

"No," I said. And I was silent. And he let me.

I wondered if he knew. If he'd heard of Uqbar, he might have heard of its fate. It was pretty well-publicized, for an insignificant backwater. Maybe he knew, or maybe he was just a decent person and could tell when someone was skirting something profoundly traumatic.

"I'm sorry," Resh said. "I'm getting sleepy. Not because you're boring, but because I'm starting to suspect someone drugged me." He ducked the polymer glass I chucked at his head. More tech? "And I'd sleep a lot better with a warm body in the bed with me. I promise no handsies!"

I should have shut it down right there, but . . . if I left . . . where was I going? What would I be walking into? I was a wanted man; I didn't have the luxury of turning down a free night's lodging. My life on the run could wait one more night to begin. So I muttered, "No anythingsies" as firmly as I could, which did not feel super firm.

This motherfucker actually clapped his hands. "No anythingsies."

I was so tired. I was so alone. I stripped down to my underwear (he groaned, "It's not fair!" but then left it at that) and got into bed.

The room went dark, obeying his wordless command. The

stone temple smell sent a shiver through me. I felt sleep come flooding in; my fragile stretched-too-thin body and mind gratefully checking out.

"Can we spoon?" he whispered, in a small sleepy voice.

Wordlessly, I slid into little-spoon place. I could feel the heat of his erection against my backside. "Sorry," he whispered, but I didn't wiggle away.

And if he'd done absolutely anything, moved his hips a millimeter or whispered *please* or pressed his lips to the back of my neck, I'd have done whatever he wanted. But he didn't do anything. He was a perfect drugged gentleman and I wanted him so bad.

And god was real, and she was punishing me for my sins. For the murdered filmmaker I should have died with—for the family I abandoned—for the father whose life I couldn't save. We sank into sleep together, down to the dark where the monsters waited—the savage father who stalked him, and the brutal bounty hunters who were almost certainly already scouring the portalverse in search of me. . . .

· · · · · · · **SIX** · · · · · · ·

A VERY FAMILIAR KIND OF HOT MESS

IMADI

This. This was the good shit.

They'll never tell you this in recovery. It probably goes against every rule of sobriety psychology. But I think staying clean is about finding safe addictions. The ones that add to your life instead of subtracting from it.

I'd found several. Arborism; I was low-key obsessed with trees—kept an actual oak in the center of my heartship. Watching old mech fights. Actual mech fighting would have been, if it didn't stir up so many fucked-up memories of my sister. Helping other struggling addicts was right up near the top of the list.

But this. This was the tippy-top.

The hunt. The search. The sweet, safe sweep and roll of data, assembling a dossier.

Blue Circumspect Tomorrow's proprietary mycotic-derived data-scrubbing AIs went to work. Scouring footage from millions of our own cameras, planet-side and systemist alike. Bartering and invoking mutual-aid contracts with thousands of

other security companies to scour *their* footage and hand over any Aran imagery they turned up.

I watched the clip bin populate: thousands of haunting ghostly glimpses.

Much as I hated the red bands, I had to turn to Intelligence Class. A flesh-trade buddy back in my mercenary days told me most sex workers make barely a third of their income from actually selling their ass—the rest comes from selling the intel they get off their clients. So odds were, this rent boy had an intelligence handler. And odds were, this rent boy's intelligence handler had competitors.

I had Vespertine rev up one of my catfish identities, a retired beam fighter named Mega Maude, struggling to make it as an independent inter-station food freighter. I've got dozens of these fronts, each one procedurally generated by my AI mate herself, and at random intervals she sock-puppets them all to life to leave a trail on the feeds and in gate logs and store receipts and messages to friends. Who might or might not *also* be catfish fronts.

As Mega Maude, I put feelers out in the Intelligence feeds for word on prices of rhubarb, one of the major exports of the Lesser Magellanics—the industrial region of space the filmmaker was from. Specifically wondering about sources of instability that might lead to price shifts.

It's the stock-in-trade of most Intelligence Class operatives: selling small information to small operators. And the filmmaker's own people had admitted that he'd frequented Aran for a long time. Which meant that whoever the kid's handler was, they'd have a real edge on commerce intel from the region.

A ping from my gate array: Trist. I'd given them a gate directly to Vespertine, so they could come visit whenever they needed some sponsor support. "Admit," I said, and the gate

folded inward from where it hung free outside the ship—so that any unauthorized entrants would blunder through into the vacuum of space instead of Vespertine's vulnerable insides.

"You won't believe this!" they said, and flicked a clip to the fore screen. "This is the brother of the guy the rent boy killed."

"*My brother was not murdered*," said a balding silvery gent, emotion thick in his voice. "*Gar Opple was assassinated, in an attempt to scare distributors into stopping release of his latest film,* The Nine Hundred Days of Hygrophorus Station, *which recounts the horrific behavior that followed the merger of Stratum Båy's top ten security rackets. Powerful interests lobbied hard to prevent it from receiving financing, and then fought to stop it from being filmed, and now they've resorted to violence to keep it from being released. . . .*"

I killed the clip. "Big whoop," I said. Shook, and trying hard not to show it.

I had to close this case. Whatever horrific conspiracy was at the root of it, I didn't need or want to know about.

"What are you talking about? This is huge, it could mean—"

"It could mean that this dude is trying to drum up attention for his bro's film, did you think of that?"

Trist nodded, crestfallen. I scanned their face, panicking that I'd triggered their trauma response again.

"It's good work, kid," I said, at great personal cost. "Keep scouring the feeds. And find me that film, I'm curious to see it."

"It's *sick*," Trist said, perking up. "I watched half of it already. I looked it up, and the history pretty much checks out. . . . Basically, once these security companies merged, they were so powerful no one could stop them from doing whatever they wanted, and a bunch of these sicko executives formed a secret committee and kidnapped a whole bunch of nubile hotties of all

genders and took over a whole station, turned it into this sick sex-and-torture palace? They literally show this one dude sticking a—"

"Okay, so, cancel that request, I am no longer curious to see it."

"They're calling it 'obscene, anti-security-concern propaganda,'" Triet said. "And 'part of a disturbing trend that points to a concerted hostile smear campaign that spans multiple strata.' So you should probably be offended, Imadi. As heir to one of the biggest security concerns going."

"Probably," I said, on autopilot.

Watching clips of Aran moving through space stations and planet-side forests. Churches and transit hubs and bars and pubs. Mostly bars and pubs.

Watching him belt back shots and guzzle from pitchers. Watching him chase drunkenness like it was the only thing loud enough to drown out the ache inside.

We'd never met. We couldn't have been more different. But Aran was a very familiar kind of hot mess. I felt a flash of fondness for him. Pity, and empathy. I'd staggered and smiled and blundered my way through life exactly like that. And it was pure blind dumb stupid luck that I'd never had the misfortune to be hunted by someone like me.

SEVEN

ENTER THE HEDGEHOG

ARAN

Resh's arm was around me when I woke up, hugging me tightly to him. Thick with muscle; densely furred; hot from the blood pumping through him. Neither one of us smelled great—we'd both tumbled into bed without bathing—and I exulted in our shared stink. And this moment, the safety of it, the bliss of two bodies at rest.

I subvocalized to Cinnamon, *How long did I sleep?*

Assuming you fell asleep as soon as you took off the clothes I'm presently still inside of? Eighteen hours.

Shit.

Indeed, she intoned.

Can you confirm that this ship is fully free from listening logs, tracking algos, data drones, etc.?

Locked up tight, and the little asshole actually laughed at me. *To a terrifying degree. Are you inside a stash vault right now? Belonging to the Nadav Federation?*

I didn't get the reference, but I did remember doing Cinnamon's settings and enabling references I wouldn't get. A way to prompt me to learn more about systemist culture, become more

classy. A magnificent waste of time: I was still the same old stupid planetstuck hick I'd always been. One so dumb he lets himself get framed for murder.

Craving some kind of connection to something safe and familiar, I logged in to Back Page, the hyper-secure sex-worker stream and social space. The only connection to my old self I felt safe making. My inbox had blown up, of course, with concerned and curious acquaintances wondering what was up, if I'd been caught or killed, and whether I'd actually done it.

And, listen. I had a lot of buddies. Fuck buddies and getting-fucked-up buddies and exes-on-good-terms and crushes-that-never-went-anywhere. Etc. But I had precious few friends. People I could contact and feel confident they wouldn't snitch me out.

In fact, there was only one. Newt, a lady pleasure worker, less than a year older than me but system-born, had been my guide and life coach when I first came unstuck and needed someone to show me the way of surviving in space.

Please tell me you're okay, was all her message said.

I'm okay, I said, and it wasn't true, and my heart ached to be unable to hop over to her and share my sorrows and get good and drunk. *I'll be okay. I'll keep in touch as much as possible. I miss you.*

Love you bitch, she said—immediately. *Stay safe and let me know if there's anything I can do.*

That made me feel better, but I still fucking needed a plan. And for that, I needed my AI mate. But I'd used Cinnamon too long, taken her too many places; there was no telling how many trackers she'd picked up along the way.

I desperately wanted to go see Molybdita. My intelligence handler would be able to help me out, clap her hands and hand me a new identity, maybe even tell me who'd actually set me up and why. But I couldn't run the risk of getting there.

I did have one option. An old friend I hadn't seen since a year after I first left my planet behind. A very, very stupid friend. But better than nothing.

I shut my eyes, reveled in Resh. In his smell, his heat. In this moment, which would end any second now.

I wanted to stay. Drift back to sleep, wake up again to him nuzzling my neck, kiss (mouths closed for morning breath reasons), make slow tender aching love.

But that probably wouldn't be how it would play out. He'd wake up with the drugs swept from his system and be utterly uninterested in me. And I couldn't handle that. Better to extricate myself now, leave with the *possibility* rather than take the gamble of finding out for sure.

So I squirmed my way out of his glorious grip—and he protested most pitifully, but he was still asleep, I could have been anyone—and grabbed my clothes and went to the bathroom to do all the tiny quiet morning-toilet tasks of the man who's sneaking out before the other man wakes up. With an extra level of furtiveness from being a fugitive.

I took my fist-sized lump of programmable matter from my pocket, placed it on the counter in front of me.

"Sorry, bud," I said to Cinnamon, and wiped her.

And her backups.

Basically murdered her.

It took me way too many tries to remember the password I'd used back then—but eventually I got it, and the polymer shifted into a familiar spiky shape, and a cheerful voice came through my gonial jaw implant.

Hi, Aran!

Hello, Professor Hedgehog, I subvocalized.

It's been, she said, and paused. *Wow, it's been a while!*

So, you figured it out. *The Otter-Man Empire* had been my favorite cinematics serial when I was a kid. And I'd been especially obsessed with the evil mastermind villain: Professor Hedgehog, who created the race of human-otter hybrids to be her captive workforce on the river world she called home, but they rebelled and escaped and she spent six hundred episodes chasing them across the starsprawl—so of course when I got off-world and crafted myself an AI mate, I modeled it on her. Because I am profoundly and irrevocably basic.

What can I do for you, Aran?

I wanted to say:

Find out who framed me for murder.

Give me my life back.

Get me a gun and some target practice.

But those all felt equally impossible.

"You weren't a dream," Resh said from the doorway, dressed only in underwear. His body somehow more magnificent under the diurnal light setting.

"How's your head?" I asked, and I'd fully been intending to put up an all-business front but just couldn't keep from lobbing the ancient gay joke his way.

"Haven't had any complaints," he said, and curtsied, job well done, part well played. "But it hurts like a motherfucker. Nanobots ran the bloodwork, turns out that was some basement-grade striatum hackery."

"Should we get you to a medic?"

"No, it's mostly flushed from my system, and I've got teeny-tiny bots repairing my ravaged liver for me even as we speak." He stopped. "You sound like you're getting ready to go."

"Sorry," I said, realizing he was right, my motions were abrupt and hurried. "Things to do. You know."

"Sure," he said, and did he sound sad about it? He came closer. Still almost entirely naked. "Hey. It wasn't the drugs. I still wanna fuck you. But I feel six kinds of sick right now, so let's put a pin in that, eh? And sometimes it's good to take your time, you know?"

"Yeah," I said, not letting my giddiness show on my face. The habits of deceit run deep, even when they're not needed, because Resh was blind and couldn't have seen my expression anyway.

And, yes. I know. I know! Insta-love is not a good look. But falling hard and fast for guys I just met is totally a pattern with me—part of what makes me so good at my job; the connection comes easy, the emotions are often unfeigned.

Because you are addicted. To men, to dick, to attention, to life's whole rich pageant of desire and dominance and degradation and affection, the masks we strip off when we shed our clothes, and the new ones we put on—

We got dressed together, fast and wordlessly. At the end, he popped a pill from the bottle that sat alone on his dresser.

"What's that?" I asked.

"Angusticeps. First drug I ever did, and I've been hooked on it since I was fourteen."

He shut his eyes, swallowed, shivered. Opened them again, his face somehow less gentle.

I guess that was it. That beat, that glimpse. Addict recognizing addict. It should have been a red flag, but instead it—I don't know—broke a wall, made Resh more human. Less unattainable. He ceased to be the military hero prince, and became just another sloppy fuckup. So I could almost believe it, the look on his face when he said, *Sometimes it's good to take your time, you know?* I could almost accept the possibility that he might somehow be interested in me.

But still, I needed to get to hopping—there was no reason to trust him, to mix him up in this, to tell him about the danger I was in—

"I'm in danger," I said.

"Relatable," he said.

"I've been framed for murder, and I'm on the run from a whole bunch of really scary motherfuckers."

"Okay," he said, and grinned sheepishly. "Promise you won't be mad?"

"I'm already mad," I said, because, how dare he be so adorable.

"I didn't look you up. I swear! Grizzelda did—my AI mate. She's *extremely aggressive* when it comes to assessing potential threats—she's got to be, with more than just my dad out to kill me—and she gave me the data dump when I woke up."

Without a word or gesture, one wall decohered into a flat-screen packed with stories from the feeds about the murder, mug shots from my past arrests. Details on Opple, scenes from his scandalous cinematic, comments from representatives of the Lesser Magellanics Trade Federation about how dangerous I was.

"And this," Resh said, "is the security contractor assigned to your case. Apparently kind of a big deal."

My jaw dropped when she came on-screen, a fact sheet thoughtfully assembled by Grizzelda. Though most of its facts were not needed. Once upon a time I'd known them all by heart.

"No," I whispered.

"No . . . ?"

"Are you fucking kidding me? You've never heard of Atah Imadi?"

"Not before five minutes ago, no."

I tried not to judge him too harshly. I sometimes forget that

most people actually don't give a shit about the awesomest activity in the portalverse.

"She was my second-favorite mech fighter pilot, back when I was a planetstuck fanboy. Fucking iconic."

"Who was your first?"

"Her twin sister, Mey. The bad twin. She had a little more badass panache. Could do moves her sister never pulled off. Vanished without a trace several years ago, and after that Atah retired from fighting."

The roiling of his eyes intensified, and then he laughed. "I think you might have an outsize idea of her importance," he said. "Feed chatter ranks her below ten thousandth, among the most culturally relevant and best-compensated mech pilots of the past twenty years."

"Fuck cultural relevance," I said. "The Imadi sisters had style. Grace. Guts. Of course the masses didn't get it."

"Well, Atah Imadi is your worst enemy now. So get over that fanboy shit, 'kay?"

"Yeah," I said, and my voice sounded impossibly small to me, but Resh had no trouble hearing it and kissed the back of my head. "It's okay," he said, and put one heavy marvelous hand on my shoulder. "You're safe, okay? I'll keep you safe, Aran."

"Why?" I finally mustered up the strength to whisper. "Why stick your neck out for someone who might be a murderer?"

"I'm a sucker for a pretty face. Even one I can't see." He laughed, and I did not, and he stopped. "I know you didn't kill anybody, Aran."

"How could you possibly know that?"

"Because you're a good person. You took a risk, saving my ass in that bar. Especially now that I know you're on the run."

"Maybe I just wanted to get in your pants myself," I muttered, unable to accept it, this kindness, this faith. Reminding

myself he was a people pleaser, just like me, it was automatic, it didn't necessarily mean anything.

"But you *didn't* get in my pants! Even when I begged. You entire asshole."

"That's true," I whispered, feeling quivery.

His hand turned in the air, and the ship started moving. Took us through six gates, then docked. "This is a mega-hub," he said. "Scrapyard. Mar Zutra mech fight pilots love this place. You should be able to get wherever you want to go from here."

"Thanks," I said. "Do you have secure communication channels on this ship?"

"Of course."

"I need to make a call."

And five minutes later I was accessing the untraceable secure convo-space Molybdita had made us all memorize, to be used only in emergencies and with the fake handles she'd assigned us and following a strict intricate code to shield both sides. Resh had constructed a soundproof programmable-matter cube around me, a kind of phone booth so I could have some privacy—complete with comfy chair—truly he was such a find—

Unless he's working for your enemies—

Which was absurd. I'd found him after dozens of random hops; the chances of ending up in the same bar as someone waiting to play me were infinitesimal . . . but being suspicious of absolutely everyone probably wasn't an *un*safe strategy for someone in my situation.

"*Well,*" Molybdita said emphatically, her face thick with the signature makeup that made it impossible to tell if she was fifty or eighty. "If it isn't the man of the hour. Good to see you, Aran— we had a bit of a pool going on whether you'd been shot dead and fed to a composter somewhere."

"Good to see you too, boss. You got any idea what the fuck is going on?"

"I've been working my assets mercilessly trying to find out. Not to save you, necessarily—don't get an inflated opinion of your importance to me—but from simple curiosity. And to make sure I'm not myself somehow the target of something."

I laughed out loud—her customary abrasive all-business fuck-your-feelings demeanor was actually exactly what I needed to summon a momentary sense of normalcy. "And?"

"Well, I can only admit this to you because you're friendless and alone and on the run, but—I'm stumped. Don't spread that around; can't have people thinking there's literally anything I don't know."

I did not for a second believe she was stumped, but evasiveness is her default. It didn't necessarily mean she had anything to hide.

That was the thing about Intelligence Class: Out in systemist space, where there's no big-picture government authority and every station takes care of its own, with the security rackets serving as law enforcement and military alike, the red bands had formed a de facto priesthood whose power was widespread—and unchecked—and invisible. Independent operatives, allegedly, but powerful ones, who aligned in secret to devise and carry out ambitious malevolent plans . . . according to the conspiracy cinematics, anyway.

And I could see I wasn't going to get anywhere appealing to Molybdita for information. "What do I *do*?" I pleaded.

"Do you have money? Shelter? Are you alone?"

"I need money," I said, avoiding the other questions.

"I'm tabbing you plenty," she said. "One of my unmarked accounts. Should be accessible from any transfer kiosk. You remember your user login?"

"Of course," I said. "Thank you."

"Find someplace to go to ground. Cheap, but not too cheap, or it'll be under heavy surveillance and full of snitches."

"I *know*, Mol, jeez."

"Well, forgive me for thinking that you might be off your game. I don't know what could have given me that idea, perhaps it was the fact that you allowed yourself to be—"

"I'm clicking out now."

"Keep your head down and wait it out. That's the only saving grace to being caught up in somebody else's grand schemes—the situation is by its nature volatile, and ever-changing, and at any moment your enemies are likely to go down in flames spectacularly."

"But if I don't know who they *are*, I won't know when they've gotten got."

"True, but *I'll* know who they are. Soon. You can be damn sure of that. Lie low, Aran, and check in with me when you're able, when you're sure it's safe. You've got someone you can trust, who can help make secure calls? That programmable matter booth you're in isn't something broke fugitives can typically afford to access."

Nothing escaped her eyes. Or her scanners or her AIs. "I'm fine," I muttered, since she wasn't the only one who could be evasive.

"Jolly good," she said, and hung up on me.

When I stood, the booth decohered.

"I should go," I said, making my voice hard, hating the sound of it.

"Yeah," Resh said, rubbing the back of his head. I watched the metallic clouds swirl in his eyes and ached to hug him. "Because it's a major Mar Zutra meet-up spot, this place is packed

with de-extincted cave bears—our emblem, and the sigil of our royal house. So, I hope you're not scared of massive wild animals with jaws strong enough to crack bone. Also . . . I put an everfind ping on your Mapp. I hope that's not too presumptuous."

My jaw dropped. It was an astonishing intimacy. I could always find him, though it did not work in reverse. "That's . . . amazing. Yeah. Thank you."

"I want to see you again."

I pinged him my Back Page address, the best I could do under the circumstances. "Likewise."

I didn't know if it was true. Whether this was just the sick, tender, wounded animal in him, the needy throb of his drugged hungover head. But then he pulled me close and kissed me, and that felt real, and even though it's my job to make people feel things are real—so I know how easy it is to fake it—I held close to it when I turned and walked fast toward the docking gate and onto the mega-hub, into the safe, swallowing buzz of a massive crowd.

EIGHT

ANIMAL MURDER'S MORE PAPERWORK
THAN KILLING A PERSON

IMADI

Stars, it felt good. The thrum and throb of attack mode, the heft of the fully decked-out unit, the buzz of the imminent capture.

He'd be mine in under an hour.

I'd hopped back to one of our home-stations and hooked my heartship up to six war modules, real badass ones brimming with stealth shielding and weaponry, and they couldn't coalesce into anything particularly badass-looking, but this was an arrest raid, not a mech battle, and if my ship showed up on scans looking like a clunky, janky war raider instead of a space gorilla or fire-breathing robot lizard, it wasn't the end of the world.

Then—best part, honestly—I'd staffed it with a dozen tacticals. Rough folks, battle-hardened and bloodthirsty and a ton of fun to be around. These days Mom's full battle complement is over six thousand soldiers, and it's always a bit of a crapshoot, but the ones I ended up with were terrifying in all the right ways, and none of them seemed to resent me for being the boss's daughter. We'd been in the mess pod slurping down noodles and then

everyone was downing shots of liquor like the universe might run out of it, but also everyone respected me when I said I was sober and no one tried to get me to drink after that and there were moments, short, sweet little stints when I came unmoored from the who and the what I was just then and I was back to those sweet, sweet gutter-punk rock-bottom days when I'd been miserable but I'd also been me, not this ticking time bomb of a secret in the shape of a human woman.

I was riding high on impending violence when a shiver went through me:

This is her.

This is how she programmed you.

Your mother's talons are sunk so deep in your flesh you'll never pry them off.

She wasn't done hurting me. She never would be. For three years I'd been on the run from her, but wherever I went—there she was.

Me and the muscle slurped down the last of our noodles and finished getting geared up. Six stayed behind to staff the modules. We weren't expecting much opposition, but expectations tend to get you screwed.

Also. Something was off about the intel I'd gotten. The lead on where Aran was. It hadn't come to me through Mega Maude. Meaning it wasn't in response to any of the feelers I'd put out.

Not so odd, that someone might reach out to me directly. This was a high-profile case, with feeds and streams across five strata talking about it. Everyone knew I was assigned to the case.

But still. It could be a trick. A trap. If a hostile anti-security-concern coalition was mobilizing against us, and Opple's assassination was an opening move, embarrassing or even killing the

heir apparent to Blue Circumspect Tomorrow would be a pretty brilliant next step.

We boarded a docking module, which took us the fifty klicks to the station bay—our whole raiding rig being too clumsy to safely dock itself and get away in a hurry, which we'd probably need to, because this mega-hub had a rep for wild characters, and lots of them wouldn't like tacticals busting in and taking captives.

And my sympathies were with them, much more than with myself. The people who lived here were scrappers, and so was I, underneath whatever bogus legit life I was trying to lead.

We were passing through a scrapyard now: glorious chunks hanging in space. Shards of wrecked mechs. Statues used for target practice. Towering animals, monsters, heroes and villains of history and cinematics.

Then the module turned and I had to shield my eyes, we were so close to the star. The scrapyard mega-hub was smack-dab in the center of a stellar array: hundreds of thousands of energy panels floating in space around a red dwarf star, beaming its energy through massive wires that vanished into gates and were then distributed throughout the portalverse. An old system, this one: dating back to a time when the dimmer light and more sluggish activity of red dwarves made them a safer bet for orbital construction. Advances in programmable matter have made bubble-shielding easier and also allow arrays to shift effortlessly out of the way when a flare threatens, and the higher energy output of yellow dwarves makes them a much more natural fit. But the old stuff still sticks around. A couple thousand stations were probably still living off the light from this star.

My mind went there, the way it always did when I gave it half a chance: to the darkest, loneliest spaces in the portalverse, the

places the poor and desperate go to scrounge out a living until they can't anymore.

Once you've been stuck in a place like that, a part of you never really leaves.

Off the module; our big crew splitting spontaneously into smaller groupings to scour the station separately. Leather; grease: a scrapper stink that fired me up even further. So much so that I took my time prowling through the wide bays and sooty corridors, wanting to remain in this moment for as long as I could. The hunter hunting.

Hunger was my baseline state; I'd mostly subsumed and sublimated my thirst and need, and it felt so fucking good to indulge it.

Almost disappointing, when a ping came in from one of my flanking pairs: they'd spotted Aran in a crowded cafeteria inexplicably packed with cave bears and hyenas and thylacines.

Here was a dilemma. I had needed the tacticals to guarantee success, but having a bunch of observers who were on the company payroll meant I couldn't just walk up and shoot the kid in the head. I'd been hoping to force a firefight in which I could "accidentally" take him out, but the beasts gave me pause. Animal murder's more paperwork than killing a person in most parts of the portalverse.

I'd have to bag him, store him in my heartship's brig, pay the warriors, and send them on their way. Once we were alone again it'd be easy enough to give him an escape opportunity and shoot him in the back when he took it, so with great sadness I had everyone switch to nonlethals.

But even non-lethals weren't necessary. Nor were the tacticals. Because I came from behind and the sound of the crowd drowned us out, and all I needed to do was put my hand on Aran's shoulder and say, "Don't let's make this any messier than it already is."

• • • • • • • NINE • • • • • • •

THE KIND OF PERSON WHO OBJECTS
TO KILLING INNOCENT PEOPLE

ARAN

Her brig was basically just a converted toilet stall, complete with bars made of rusted metal stitched together by programmable matter. A drain somewhere had stopped up, and the air smelled faintly of sewage and I was gonna die and I wanted a drink and I wanted drugs.

I knew I'd been taking a risk when I walked away from Resh and stepped defenseless into the starsprawl, but I seriously thought I'd last longer than an hour and a half.

But I was also proud of myself. You never know how you're going to act when the hammer comes down. Will you beg and cry and embarrass yourself? I'd debated fleeing but knew it might turn the whole crowded mess hall into a bloodbath—who knew what lengths these tacticals might go to, to bring me in, if they were part of the mAsSivE iNtErGaLaCTic cOnSpirACY? Stars knew the list of my flaws and sins was long, but a willingness to put innocent people in danger to save my own ass wasn't on it.

That was something. A nice insight into yourself, right before you die.

"I wonder if you can hear me," I said, standing up to look for obvious listening or watching devices. Even though obviously they wouldn't be obvious.

I debated telling her what a huge fan I was but figured that it'd sound like bullshit coming from the brig. Prisoners will say anything.

"I know this is useless and stupid, but I gotta state for the record that I didn't kill Opple. Just on the off chance you're the kind of person who objects to killing innocent people."

Silence.

Three hours of silence.

So . . . she probably wasn't.

She'd been a beautiful, terrifying chunky creature, back there in the mess. The kind whose face said, *I will not hesitate to utterly annihilate you.*

And of course it did. That was the mask. The person the gig required. In my line of work I always got to see the mask, and then I always got to see beneath the mask.

But if there was a way to intuit what was beneath the mask before someone let it slip, I hadn't learned it yet. 10,957 tricks—Cinnamon kept track for me, in spite of the fact that I never asked her to do any such thing—and I'd found no tells, no secrets, no foolproof ways to spot a monster—or a decent human being—if they didn't want me to know it.

So I had no idea whether there was a good person inside Former Mech Pilot Superstar Turned Badass Bounty Hunter Atah Imadi.

"Can I get a drink?" I called.

Another hour of silence.

And then—the ship shook. The matter shield burst. A shrieking boomed through me.

I felt it in my stomach: the drag and lurch as the ship started moving. As alarming as actual gravity. Thrusters firing on full. Alarms in the distance. People shouting. People screaming.

The *ship* screaming.

A loud clang, from the metal bulkhead. I couldn't be sure, but if I had to guess, I'd say it was the sound of a fully suited tac hurled against it hard. While I watched, the bulkhead began to— shiver? Ripple? Something metal shouldn't do.

Flakes began to peel off. Slow at first, then faster, as the flakes themselves formed a kind of cyclone shredding them away, and in twenty seconds or so a hole had opened up.

And Resh walked through it.

"Fuck," I said. Shocked. Swooning. Scared. "How . . . ?"

Resh didn't answer. The door to the brig dissolved as effortlessly as the bars had, and I followed him out into the corridor. Terrified and turned on and full of questions.

Two tacticals rounded the corner behind us, shouted, fired guns. I turned around in time to see the bullet hit an invisible wall and burst into harmless flakes two feet from me. A light sprinkle of metal dust fell across my face. They kept firing, but Resh was not concerned enough to speed up or turn around. They ran at us, firing all the way, until they hit his polymershield and it disassembled them both as swiftly as it had shredded those bullets. Their dust was just a lot more gruesome.

Ten paces on he veered to his right, even though there was nothing there but bulkhead, and he walked through it. His gnarly nanos shredded even the thick outer hull of the module where we'd been housed, as well as five more bulkheads as he continued on the straightest walk to the bridge.

Atah Imadi sat there, uncannily still in the pilot's chair. Held there by force, I saw, coming closer, so I could clock the micromotions of her body struggling.

"What . . . the fuck . . . ?" she hissed, through jaws that couldn't open all the way.

The gray roil of Resh's sclerae seemed somehow pronounced, more agitated, giving him an unsettling air of otherness. Of diminished humanity. He couldn't see her, of course, but he was regarding the space she occupied and perceiving *something* with the aid of scanning tech, and he wasn't liking it at all.

He lifted a hand, and I hated what I saw on his face.

"Resh?" I squawked. "Don't kill her, Resh."

"Why not?" Resh whispered emotionlessly. "Surely you can see that she was super going to kill you."

His voice had changed. A tiny tweak no one who wasn't as lovestruck as me would ever have noticed: Resh's normal speaking voice had the most minuscule sliver of a lisp to his *S*'s. But now they were clipped and precise and perfect. And utterly, horrifically wrong.

"Okay, buddy," I said calmly, uncalm. "But . . . we're not her?"

"If we leave her alive, she'll keep coming for you. And *she* won't blink before finishing the job."

"Okay, but . . . if we kill her . . . they'll come for both of us."

"I am not afraid of them."

"I know, buddy. But, uh . . . do it for me? Maybe?"

I regretted saying it as soon as it was said, this raw naked pleading humiliating expression of need and—yes—love . . . but to my surprise it pulled him back. He turned away and actually didn't kill her.

And then, because I'm a dumb simian who's super easily

distracted from even moments of life and death by something shiny, I said, "Holy fuck, is that an actual oak tree?"

Because she had one, growing in a corner of her heartship's bridge. Twenty feet tall, full of thick dark green leaves. I don't know why it struck me as so strange—pretty much everyone has plant life on their ships, and few are as big or tall or old as this one was, but it still wasn't so unusual. Something about it was off, and I couldn't put my finger on what.

Imadi looked at me like I'd insulted her, and did not answer.

"Let's just go, buddy," I said. "Okay, Resh?"

He kept moving, like it really didn't matter to him one way or another whether or not he killed the woman who was hunting me.

I followed him out of the heartship, but halfway through the door, I turned to face her.

"I know this is probably useless, and you don't give a shit about the truth or the big picture, but . . . you really do have the wrong guy. There's a big conspiracy here, and I'm just some dumb putz caught in its crosshairs."

The bulkheads reconstructed behind us, leaving weird drippy too-pale circles whose ability to hold against the vacuum of space I was skeptical of.

But they did hold, when Resh effortlessly ejected Imadi's heartship from the ship config. I watched it drift lopsided away from us, her thrusters and weapons all dissolving into dust. Tiny and dark against the backdrop of a red dwarf star. A second module followed, in which he'd stowed the remaining tacticals. And then I watched his own familiar hab ship swing into view, summoned and controlled by Resh, its outside emblazoned with the gilded script of the Mar Zutra alphabet.

"What the stars *are* you?" I whispered, but he gave me the

same answer I'd given him when he asked me that question, which was silence.

I'd been right, imagining he had unspeakably powerful tech inside him. Every moment of what I'd witnessed required field control stronger than anything myth or rumor had ever hinted at.

"What's your favorite mech config?" he asked me, and his eyes still scared the shit out of me but his voice had regained a sliver of its old Resh-ness, the lisp was back, and I was so happy to hear it I hugged him so fucking hard.

"I was always partial to dragons," I said. "Something serpentine."

"Watch this then."

Outside the porthole, things began to move. Pieces broke out of the drift and orbit they'd been following for centuries.

"You know this is unnecessary," I said. "I was totally *already* going to fuck you."

A thousand chunks of space shrapnel and unclaimed wreckage swirled together, while nanopolymer glimmered in the air in front of me to reveal in miniature the full picture I couldn't see because I was deep inside it: a dead ringer for the legendary dragon mech Red Gas Giant, star of a thousand fics and cinematics.

"Obviously it's your heart I'm trying to win here, Aran."

HOW TRAUMA KEEPS ON
TRAUMATIZING YOU

IMADI

I was fucked.

This was big, and this was bad, and this was public. That Studly Fucker had bested me in full view of a massive mega-hub. Robbed me of victory in one of the biggest claims that our concern had collected on in at least six quarters.

A conspiracy at play—Intelligence Class scheming to take out the security concerns—and I'd just made a crucial fumble.

Which meant it was over. I couldn't hide from my mom any longer.

My shoulder ached where she used to grab me. Where her talons dug in, to drag me from sleep. Me and my sister. I'd come so far and grown so big and badass, but I was still a tiny helpless thing in her clutches.

I should have been scheming a counterattack, or planning my flight into hiding. Instead, all I could think about was the thing I couldn't say.

I had to say it.

I was drowning in a secret, and if I didn't speak it I'd die. Simple as that. I'd spent years swallowing the words, little toxic doses that were slowly poisoning me. I'd killed people to keep from saying them. Cut myself off from everyone who could have helped me.

And there, in the darkened belly of my half-dead heartship, listening to my oak tree's leaves rustle in the randomized wind from the life support's ventilation system, I knew I had to say them.

Which was why when Trist pinged me six hours later, I greenlit the query.

"Hello?" they called, stepping into the shadows. "Vespertine, lights!"

The darkness did not diminish.

"That contradicts a standing order from me," I said, and I knew I sounded like shit from the horrified look on Trist's face in the light from the far side of the gate they'd just walked through. The safe warm glow of the world I'd locked myself out of.

"Atah!" they said, and hurried to my side. Sat on the floor beside me. "I was so worried. It's all over the streams—the report the tacticals filed—"

I was happy some of them had lived to get to safety and make a report. And I was sad that this was just the second time I'd thought about them since Studly Fucker hijacked me. He could easily have sent their module spinning into the red dwarf sun. Or mine, for that matter.

And why hadn't he? Because Rent Boy told him not to. Because not everyone is as bad a person as you are. Not everyone jumps to murder as the best way to solve a problem.

Trist put an awkward arm around me.

"Are you okay? Did he hurt you?"

They were a good kid. Sweet, kind, scary-smart. Plenty damaged already. They didn't need me burdening them down with my own toxic bullshit.

But I was weak. I'd always been weak.

"My sister is dead," I said. "She's been dead for three years."

"Mey? Your twin?"

I shut my eyes. This was wrong. A play straight out of my mother's book: burdening a child with adult ugliness; handing them something sharp and jagged they had no idea how to use, which would only end up hurting them.

Or was it? What if this was trust, connection, human bonding, the kind of thing a recovering addict and a genocide survivor needed most?

That's how trauma keeps on traumatizing you. Makes you doubt yourself at every turn: What's real and good and *you* and what's the legacy of the harm you've survived?

I tried to stop, and failed. "My sister's been dead, and I've been keeping it a secret."

"Holy shit, Atah."

"I can't tell my mom. She would fucking kill me. And that means I can't tell anyone. You don't know what they're like, these snakes who work for her. Grown-ups are the fucking worst. Promise me you'll never get any older, yeah?"

"Promise," Trist said. "Tell me what happened."

"Fuck," I whispered. "No. It was selfish and stupid of me to tell you anything at all. Now *both* of us have gotta live with it."

"Man, listen," Trist said with a laugh. "This is a thing we do. Me and my friends. We tell each other our secrets. Super therapeutic, honestly. Because keeping somebody else's secret isn't like keeping your own. It can't destroy you. If anything, it makes you feel way better about your own marginally less-fucked life."

I laughed. And kept going.

"You know she was an addict," I said, and, stars, I could feel it happening, the weight lifting off my chest, the hollow feeling filling. "Worse than me. The bad twin. Right? My mom had cut her off, because every cent she had, she spent on drugs. She kept signing up for super-scary tactical gigs, like doing shady shit that was pretty certain to get you killed."

Trist's hand moved up and down my back, firm consistent pressure.

"And then, silence. For a long time. Until one day I got a message. Sounding scared, desperate, hurt. She'd gotten herself into some trouble she couldn't see a way out of. Gave me her location. And I went. I made the trip as soon as I could, but I was a pretty big mess myself in those days. Took me a while. When I got there, she'd been dead for less than an hour."

"Did she—was it—?"

"I don't know," I said honestly. "But honestly, even if someone else pulled the trigger, they did it because of the decisions *she* made, the positions *she* put herself in."

"I can't imagine," Trist said. "The pain of losing your twin. *And* having to keep it secret? Atah, it's a wonder you can function at all. And. Also. I don't want to sound insensitive here. . . ."

I laughed, eager for some insensitivity, a sharp slap in the face, a get-the-fuck-up-off-the-ground.

"As shitty as it sounds to say it out loud, I think everyone wrote your sister off a long time ago. You've basically said so yourself. No one, from your mother on down, thinks any good could come of Mey Imadi ever coming back."

"You don't know my mom" was the only thing I could say. "All this time, her anger's just been on hold. Waiting for an excuse to explode. And for the thousandth time in my life, my

sister's not there to take the hit. So it'll all land on me. And I can't tell her. I can never look her in the eyes again."

"I get that. But *you* get that your sister fucked you over, right? She did you wrong, Atah. Mey stuck you with a shitty fucking bag, and you've been holding it for all this time. But you don't need to hold it any longer."

I nodded. Trist was right. I knew they were. And that was what started me crying again.

﹒﹒﹒﹒﹒﹒ ELEVEN ﹒﹒﹒﹒﹒﹒

THE HEAT AND ANGLES OF HIM

ARAN

Don't be mad," he said, once we got back to his hab ship bubble.

"Mad?" I said, laughing. "You just saved my life, you magnificent son of a starfucker, why would I be mad?"

"Clone of a starfucker," he said. And grabbed me, one big hand on my upper arm, and pulled me close. Kissed me, his mouth impossibly warm and needy, lips opening and closing around mine like I was a food he couldn't get enough of.

"We . . . kind of could have avoided this whole vulgar display of power?" His eyes were on me, and they had calmed down from the swirling frenzy I'd seen before. And there was no trace of those horrific un-lisped *S*'s—although I still couldn't say why they had felt so fucking wrong to me. But something was still missing, an infinitesimal overall diminishment, like he'd been sapped of something deep and vital. Which, of course he had.

"How so?"

"When you called your handler, Grizzelda determined that the callspace you accessed was logging spatial positioning. Which it shouldn't have been, if it was the secure channel she had promised.

Quite sophisticated tech, actually, which I guess makes sense if she's involved in a horrifying massive Intelligence Class–led conspiracy. Sophisticated enough to home in on your AI assistant and log its call signs, then flag her whenever it pinged through anyone's entry hub."

It shouldn't have been a surprise. It shouldn't have felt like a sucker punch. I shouldn't have had trouble breathing.

"Molybdita . . . ?" was all I could say, and that barely.

"Of course I can't say for sure whether she was originally part of the conspiracy, or she just recognized your value once you were enmeshed in it. Either way, she betrayed you."

Breathe. In. Breathe. Out.

"I probably should have told you. Warned you. But I wasn't sure what Molybdita was up to. So I figured I should stay put, keep an eye on you. Help out if I had to. I'm sorry I put you in a position of unnecessary risk."

His voice quivered. I'd just seen him do the impossible, but the impossible comes with a cost. Resh felt flimsy and exhausted and vulnerable in my arms.

I let him swamp me in one of his superhuman hugs, felt the heat and angles of him. The stress and fear of capture and certain death were beginning to come crashing in on me; they'd been forestalled by adrenaline while I was actually in danger, but now . . . I wanted more than anything to be embraced and cradled and protected by Resh, but this was not the moment to make him be the big spoon. Pleasure worker 101: Read your lover's body energy, and go from there. They'll try to tell you what they want with words, but their body knows better than they do what they need. And after what he'd just done—how much it must have taken out of him—he needed to be treated with tenderness.

It's a primate thing. Mammalian. We think because someone is bigger and stronger than us that they're superhuman, have all the answers, live without fear. And desire blinds us to who people really are. When we want them, we only see what's good. But Resh was just a person, as fucked up as me—as much of an addict, I was just beginning to piece that together by then—and I had to pull myself back from the brink of helpless adoration. That, too, was an addict's baseline: falling so hard so fast they ignore every red flag.

"You're not mad?" he asked.

"No," I whispered. "Are we safe out here? We only went one hop. And this big-ass dragon isn't exactly inconspicuous."

He laughed. "I'm sorry, did you miss what I just did? Anyway, I've set a trigger field five thousand klicks wide. Nobody's sneaking up on us. And anyone who tries will swiftly wish they hadn't."

We sat. On his bed.

I took off his boots, and he groaned some more. Tried to pull his foot away when I started peeling off one sock—"My feet stink like . . ." he mumbled, and I told him, "Shut the fuck up, stupid, I know exactly what they stink like"—and from there on out he let me do my thing with no more commentary than near-constant groans.

"Are you okay?" I said, climbing into bed once we were both down to our underwear.

"Yeah," he said. "I'll probably sleep for like a million years, but I've bounced back from bigger efforts than this."

"That must have been impressive," I said. "I wish I could have seen it."

"Me too," he said, and we both laughed. I grabbed his hand in mine, felt our fingers intertwine. *This is really fucking finally fucking happening.*

"I love topping as much as bottoming," I said. "You got a preference?"

"Most guys want me to top, on account of my size," he said.

"Is that what you prefer?"

"I like to go with the flow."

"Ugh," I said, delivering a very light mock slap to his bearded beautiful cheek. "Tell me what you want, Resh."

"I want you to fuck me, Aran."

"Yeah you do," I said.

My mind raced with scenes I was desperate to play out with him, extravagant extended sessions: Resh on his belly on the floor or riding me reverse, but I was in no rush, and we settled into something slow and sweet and tender, nose to nose and mouth to mouth, and I told myself there'd be time for all the wild weird stuff.

TWELVE

MAYBE THIS WAS A NEW HOLLOW DEADNESS

IMADI

The company sent a fleet of buzz drones through the scrapyard gate to fix my ship while I slept. I woke up to the thousand comforting sounds of mechanicals at work. Whirring and piston-hammering and sclerping and sawing.

I lay there listening. Remembering. Other ships; other gigs; other lives. The times when I'd been . . . down in it. Wallowing in the glorious muck. Instead of up here. The crown princess of the whole concern. A safe good life for as long as I didn't weaken.

A message from Mom came through. Only briefly stopping my heart.

Impressive how you keep finding new ways to be a disappointment.

But she still hadn't formally sent for me. So that was something.

A message from Mar-Tek, my mom's right hand, head of operations at Blue Circumspect Tomorrow. He idolized my family, so I always took his hyperbole with a grain of salt. But he was the closest thing we'd ever had to a father, and I loved him. Mostly because he never bought into the bullshit about Atah Imadi being the Good Sister and Mey being the Bad One.

He wasn't writing to scold me. Just to see how I was. And forward a massive file they'd assembled on recent industry developments . . . and on the Studly Fucker who'd fucked me up and taken my bounty.

Every week, Mar-Tek sent me an intelligence briefing. Which I was absolutely not entitled to receive. My mom would have fucking hated it if she'd known, and it said something about how much he cared for me that he kept the secret from her. Somehow, he believed I'd run this show one day, and he wanted me to be ready. And I didn't have the heart to tell him how that was never going to happen.

I barely read it. Like always. But then a phrase caught my eye, and I went back to pay better attention.

An alarming increase in targeted attacks on our contractees.

The six largest security concerns in our bracket have all seen the same approximate uptick.

Someone is trying to destroy us. All of us.

Aran had said, *There's a big conspiracy here, and I'm just some dumb putz caught in its crosshairs.* For a split second I wondered if so were we. But I didn't have time to chase that thought down its rabbit hole.

I thought I'd feel different, now that I'd told Trist. I thought having someone to share my secret with would change me. Maybe it had. Maybe this was a new hollow deadness. Or maybe it was the same hollow deadness as always.

So I dulled it with work. Reading through what Mar-Tek sent me on Studly Fucker. Learning everything I could about the seventy-eighth known clone of the twenty-fourth Exilarch of Mar Zutra—hereditary autocephalous Leader of the Captivity since the conquest of Iskawi and the dispersion of her people throughout the Terfezian Empire.

THIRTEEN

SUPPOSEDLY DESTRUCTIVE BEHAVIORS

ARAN

I woke to Resh getting out of the bed, wobbling slightly.

"You okay?" I asked, alarmed for him even as his presence filled me with joy. "How's your head?"

"You tell me," he said with a laugh.

"It's fucking fantastic. But something tells me you already know that."

"What can I say," he said. "I love what I do."

"Same," I said, rolling over onto my stomach, reveling in the many ways my body ached. The aftereffects of sex were one of my favorite things; these little twinges we carry through the boring hours of vertical life, reminders of how alive we have been. And will be again.

At breakfast, a fist of polymer tentacled across the room and took the shape of a cave bear on the table between us.

"Meet Grizzelda," he said, and the bear took a bow. "She's ten kinds of too much, first of all. The programming tutor my father assigned me was a secret radical anti-Terfezian, certain it was just a matter of time before our imperial benefactors decided

they no longer needed to prop up the Mar Zutra aristocracy as a sop to the laboring class, so paranoia is built into her DNA. She's constantly scouring headlines and economic reports and gathering intel on ministry staffing patterns, waiting for the day when they try to wipe us out and return our people to a state of open slavery."

"What fun for you."

He laughed. "I mean, I set up most of those six hundred daily communiqués to auto-archive, so it's not too much trouble. I showed you mine, you show me yours."

"Ugh," I said, ashamed in advance, and zipped up my own polymerload into its baseline form.

"Is that—is she the guy from *The Otter-Man Empire*?"

"Professor Hedgehog!"

"She terrified me when I was a kid."

"I fucking loved her," I said.

"See? I knew you weren't as virtuous as you seem! I figured there had to be a little villain in there somewhere."

Professor Hedgehog and Grizzelda danced together, acting out elaborate subroutines and responses we'd programmed ages ago. The bear thrusted and Professor Hedgehog evaded; Hedgehog took in air to swell to three times her size and Grizzelda tentacled forward to puncture her, but a hole opened up around the tentacle.

"What do they do, your people?" I asked. "You mentioned how valuable they were to the Terfezians. If *that's* an acceptable third-date question."

"I'll allow it," he said, looking less jokey now. "We make dust. Programmable nanomatter. Only a handful of techniques have been developed to accomplish that, and ours is by far the most

functional. Our artisans use machinery developed centuries ago on Iskawi, which not even the most sophisticated imperial scientists have been able to replicate. The Terfezians have a total cone of silence on it—I'm committing treason by telling you it exists—because it's been a decisive factor in multiple military engagements throughout the history of the empire. That's why they treat us so well, by the standards of other captive workforces."

"Do you hate them?" I asked.

He nodded. "Intensely. But honestly, the majority of our people are not unhappy. Culturally, we value the work—it's at the core of our religious practices, all kinds of mystical underpinnings about the machines working only through the grace of the Name and our continued obedience to it—and the Terfezians understand that, and give it the respect it's due. Like most empires that have lasted longer than five centuries, they understand how to keep their subjects happy."

Grizzelda shivered, and then spat out a pill. Resh popped it into his mouth.

"Angusticeps again?" I asked.

He nodded, swallowing it without water.

"You said you'd been on it since you were a kid. What does it do for you?"

He grinned. "Tough to say. Like, it's so much a part of me. But sometimes I stop taking it, on purpose or by accident—because life gets too crazy—and it's like, the world hurts? Everything is full of jagged edges, every surface is sharp, every puff of wind makes my skin itch."

I swallowed the last of my mycosteak. Chose my words carefully. "Are you on anything else?"

Resh laughed. "Oh my, yes. Right this minute?" And he rattled

off a bunch I'd never heard, capping it with, "Spiderwebbing, *of course*. And it ebbs and flows, you know? Sometimes I'll be on something for a couple months before I drop it, shift to something else or take a break altogether."

He sensed the *something* at the root of my questions, and sat down beside me. "Why do you ask?" and sucked on a couple of my fingers while I fumbled for the words.

"I'm an addict," I said finally.

"All the best people are. What's your substance of choice?"

"Alcohol. Sex. Drugs. Relationships. You name it."

"I have to assume there's a reason you're telling me this," he said, his voice sounding way too small for his big body. "And that it's *not* because you think I give a shit, because you know I don't."

"I'm telling you because it's something I'm struggling with. I really want to get clean, and stay that way."

"You spent—what—sixteen years on a planet?"

"Yeah," I said, fighting the hackles rising. "What does that have to do with anything?"

"Because it's a total vestige of planet thinking. The whole concept of *addiction* as this pathologized set of supposedly destructive behaviors. Rooted in shame-based attempts to govern our behavior and limit our potential, keep us backward and beholden to our communities. Honestly, it's the kind of shit humanity should have left behind on Planet Zero."

I wanted to see it like that. I really did. But I didn't.

And I wanted to ask him, *So you don't think* you *have a problem?* But I couldn't.

"I don't want to belittle your feelings about this," he said. "If you want to change your behavior, cut out things you think are harming you, I absolutely support that. And I'll do whatever I can to be helpful in that process."

To prove his point he took two of my fingers, rubbed them in the last of the sauce, and stuck them back in his mouth.

One of his gates pinged.

"I reached out to some of my friends who have connections to intelligence. To try to see what we can find out about the people who framed you. I hope that's okay."

"Of course."

A young man in the soldier-priest garment came tumbling through, and dropped to his knees and touched his forehead to the floor and rattled off a string of multilingual honorifics my gonial translator could not keep up with. *Aechmalotarches*?

"Enough with that bullshit," Resh said, and the young man stood and Resh swallowed him up in one of those patented hugs I'd gotten 100 percent addicted to. So much so that it twinged, slightly, to see him give one to someone else.

Stupid, stupid shit, Aran. You literally just met the guy. He has a life outside of you. Cool it with the insta-love.

There were actual tears in his eyes when Resh released him.

"Hail to the Name's anointed, Leader of the Captivity, last link in the Line of the Monarchs, who alone has the right to enter the Holy of Holies of the Third House of the Sanctum."

"That's blasphemy *and* treason," Resh said, kissing his forehead and then slapping his face. "My father is the reigning Exilarch, to whom all those names apply—and on whose head may all glory accrue, etc."

"Your father is a traitor and a usurper who broke his house's pact with the Name by killing his own children, and as such has forfeited all right to life and power. The fact that he's helped our oppressors punish people for daring to question the mighty Terfezian Empire is just the olive in the cocktail."

"I didn't want to talk politics," Resh said. "Okay, well,

actually, I totally did. Just not *those* politics. Also, I want you to meet my new boo, Aran. Aran, meet Imm Eskehek."

"Well, isn't *this* a delightful surprise," Imm said, shaking my hand and then pulling me into a pretty decent hug. "It's been ages since Resh thought me worthy of meeting a boo, and a famous one at that! Depraved brutal rent boy, assassin of cinematics-makers, refugee from security-racket justice—is there anything this triple threat can't do?"

"Tea?" Resh said.

Three chairs cohered from programmable matter; a table crawled across the room. Resh felt for the handle of the teapot, then tipped it out into space, a cup cohering as he poured to catch the deep green liquid. ("Show-off," Imm said, and Resh blew him a kiss.) I took mine and breathed in the cool sweet smell of mint; the bitter freshness of the green tea leaves. Good sugar, from one of the plantation planets where machines worked the island fields of endless archipelagoes where cane had been seeded centuries ago.

"Okay, so, Aran—I trust Imm one thousand percent to keep this all secret," Resh said, sitting down, hostly duties completed. "And to help us figure out who's at the bottom of it."

"Trust is dangerous," I muttered. "I *trusted* Molybdita. But I get that that was stupid. And . . . not everyone is stupid."

A flicker in Imm's eyes when I said her name told me it was not unfamiliar. But then again, it was always in a red band's interest to deceive you about what they did and didn't know, so the tell could have been a lie.

"His intelligence handler," Resh said. "By all accounts a villain worthy of any cinematics serial. She gave his location up to the security concern that has the contract on the filmmaker, which would have resulted in his immediate arrest if he didn't

happen to be in the company of a bad bitch who can make a dragon mech out of literally space junk."

"Ah. Well. Cheers to that bad bitch, eh?" Imm raised a glass mockingly.

"Basically, Resh thought you might be able to help us see the bigger picture," I said. "And why the fuck I'm in the middle of it . . ."

"There's definitely something spooky going on," Imm said. "The largest security concerns are shitting themselves—their clients are being targeted specifically with terror attacks, largely from planet-based anti-systemists. And they're deploying some crazy sophisticated and expensive weapons to pull off their attacks. Far and above anything we've ever seen them wield. Which means someone is arming them. The logical culprit would be a coalition of the smaller security concerns, trying to take out the big fish."

Resh said, "But . . ."

"But the way they're doing it is incredibly unstrategic. Like, scorch and burn, calculated to call into question the entire *idea* of security rackets. If it's the smaller companies, they're doing it all in an extraordinarily dumb way."

"And surely you have a theory . . ." Resh said.

"I belong to several Intelligence Class consortiums and caucuses. They spin out fucking reports on everything. Mid-level functionaries in Stratum Một start wearing feathers and they're putting out a dossier on the cultural antecedents and deeper political ramifications. But on this? Silence of the stars, baby."

"So you think it's the red bands," I said.

"That's my current working theory. A big, powerful, far-reaching Intelligence Class alliance is behind this. They've always been pulling strings and moving the pieces around the board, but if I'm right, this would be the kind of mega-coalition

not seen since the fall of the Great Amalgamations eleven hundred years ago."

"Why would they do that?" Resh asked. "They seem pretty happy with the status quo. Why push for something that could be so destabilizing?"

"That's what I'm trying to find out," Imm said. "They could be responding to a threat we're not aware of—I wouldn't put it past some of these security rackets to decide the red bands are dangerous and should be destroyed. It's also possible that some intelligence players have started to develop a conscience. Many security rackets *are* super abusive, so taking them out—or transforming them against their will—would be the right thing to do. I've just never known too many of my fellow Intelligence Class operatives to get too hung up on doing the right thing." He stood up and swallowed the last of his tea. "I've already scheduled a meeting later, with a friend who I know has a grudge against some of the more tyrannical security outfits. If I'm right, and something's going on, she'll likely be involved."

"Be careful," I said, and Resh laughed out loud. "What's so funny?"

"Imm Eskehek takes caution to ridiculous extremes," Resh said. "Trust me, we don't need to worry about him."

"I know what I'm doing," Imm said, clinking his empty teacup to Resh's. "Next year on a free Iskawi."

"Next year on a free Iskawi."

"He's so embarrassing," Resh said, after he was gone. "A true believer, which is common enough among the Mar Zutra soldier-priest caste. But I, alas, am not one. Imm was also the best friend I had for many years, when I really needed a friend."

"I think it's adorable. Your people love you."

"Some of them," he said, dropping to his knees between my legs. "Not a statistically significant percentage."

"Hey," I said, putting a hand on his forehead to pause his greedy grabbing. "Are you sure you're up for this? Helping me? It's not your fight—there are crazy risks—you could just walk away. . . ."

"Shut the fuck up," he said, tugging down the beautiful pants his ship had printed for me. "I'm bored, got nothing better to do. Also, in case you missed it, I am kinda super into you."

He grinned and then demonstrated that quite convincingly.

"What *were* you doing, anyway? Like, with your life. Besides getting drugged in bars."

Resh lifted his mouth, looked hurt that his oral skills hadn't silenced me.

I knew the answer already. I'd done my research—which was allowed because his AI mate had researched me for him. I just wanted to hear how he'd put it.

"You know. Live a cushy life. Do a ton of drugs. Organize terrorist attacks on our evil oppressors, in support of the goal of reclaiming Iskawi and resettling our scattered people."

I nodded, glad he hadn't tried to hide it. He was Public Enemy Number One across the fifty-seven worlds of the Terfezian Empire, the subject of innumerable leaked official communiqués. A better rent boy than me might have been bothered by the whole terrorist thing, but I tend to feel like violent colonizers deserve a little payback.

He tilted his head in my direction. I wondered how much of my inner world he could see, thanks to his tech. Biometrics, chemical releases, whole entire emotions? Did he know how I felt? Did I?

"Hey, Aran," he said, and I knew that look, the look of, *I gotta say this, and it's not gonna go great*, so I didn't say anything, and eventually he smiled and the look went away and he said, "Are you going to let me suck you off or aren't you?"

"I know better than to come between an addict and one of his addictions," I said, and I said it like a joke, but it wasn't.

CRACKED, CRAZY, WAY PAST HUMAN, BUT ALSO SOMEHOW FAMILIAR

IMADI

Ugh. Incense. Always the fucking incense with these people.

The Exilarch's hall was massive, a high roof held up with columns of amber-colored stone, a floor of tiny octagonal polished tiles. Bright real light from high glassless windows filled the space; occasionally, the flapping of a bird's wings echoed like little gunshots. And everything stank to high hell of frangipani incense.

I was in a foul mood, and I blamed the gravity. I fucking hate actual gravity. It's invasive, all-consuming, climbing up your bones and tugging on your blood vessels. Smothering.

At least the process to see the Exilarch was surprisingly straightforward. I showed up; I spoke with the scribe, who wrote my name down on *an actual scroll,* and then I sat and waited. And waited. While supplicant after supplicant went in to see him, to have their cases adjudicated before a fellow member of the Mar Zutra.

And, stars, what stupid shit it was. A man alleging that a woman had cut down a date palm belonging to him. A woman

who claimed that her wife was traveling via gate during the Day of Rest, and didn't the Old Ways explicitly prohibit that? An old woman who said the Exilarch's own servants had stolen her wood and had built a smoking-hut out of it. No one was calling numbers, but my fellow supplicants seemed to have an acute sense of who was ahead of who. Every time the tall door opened, the right party rose even before the verger cried out their name.

I'd read up on who this guy was, how it all worked. The brain-numbingly dull ancient history. The Mar Zutra had been subjects of the Lycoperdon League when the Terfezians defeated the Lycoperdans at the Battle of Kar-Che-Mish and laid claim to all their vassal systems and planets. The reigning monarch of the Mar Zutra, believing false reports that the battle had significantly weakened the Terfezians—most historians agree that the Terfezians themselves had spread those reports—decided she would not pay the Terfezians the annual tribute that had been forced upon them by the Lycoperdans. At which point the Terfezians sacked the Iskawi capital, torched their fields and salted the earth, and carried tens of thousands of them away into captivity. Along with their famous machines. A generation later, in reward for obedience, they permitted the Mar Zutra to return to Iskawi to gather the pieces of the destroyed Second House of the Sanctum and rebuild it on a new homeworld where the captivity would be centered. They also proclaimed the monarch's granddaughter the Exilarch and granted her imperial administrative power, a titled place in their court, even reestablished the captive aristocracy.

"Excuse me," said a timid-looking scribe—not the one I'd registered with. This one was young, with a shaved head and ornamental chains around her wrists. To indicate novitiate status, I assumed. "I'm sorry, but it appears we have no record of your

family or house name in our logs. Is there any chance you misspoke, or I misheard? Atah—Imadi?"

"I won't be in your logs," I said. "I'm not Mar Zutra."

She blinked several times. This was not a response she'd been trained to handle. "Then . . . why have you requested the gift of our Exilarch's time?"

"I'm the one with gifts, sister. Tell him I've got information he wants. About his . . . I guess 'son' is the right word. His son Resh."

She blinked some more.

"Say it," I said.

"His son Resh."

"Good!"

She hurried away. And very shortly, the careful, orderly system of the Exilarch's arbitration court came to a screeching halt.

The tall door opened. A wealthy-looking businessman on my left stood up. And the verger called—my name.

Instant gasps! Shaking fists! Old fuckers up and on their feet and shouting faster and louder than you'd have thought they could! Oh, the cruelty! Was nothing sacred! Etc.

I stood and walked between them, and didn't even try to hide my smug smile. Through a door and into a room every bit as opulent, except full of—animals. Dogs, wolves, cave bears. Lots of bears. Hyenas. Crazy de-extincted shit. Monarchies love charismatic megafauna.

"Atah Imadi," said the man on the throne.

It was Studly Fucker. But way older. And a little bit smaller. And less hot.

"Are they drugged?" I asked, pointing to the animals. "How are they all getting along so well?"

"Pheromone synching. They all recognize each other—and

me—as members of the same species. Of course, members of the same species quite often kill one another, so we make sure to keep them well fed. And my retainers and I can intervene if needed."

Nine soldiers stood along each wall. None of them were armed. No weapons anywhere in sight.

"Let me guess," I said. "You can paralyze them with a thought." *Just like your clone did to me.*

"Precisely," the Exilarch said, standing up. "So am I to presume you ended up on the wrong side of my errant son?"

"Precisely," I said, mocking him, but it went right over his head. He was very old and a little rheumy-eyed, and something set my teeth on edge, made me sick to my stomach in a way this harmless old creep could never have done on his own.

"Resh has caused me no end of trouble," he said, and turned to his retainers and said, "Leave us" very softly.

The briefest of pauses—the request was unusual and probably ill-advised, but they were well-trained—and then they filed out.

"You want him dead," I said, when we were alone.

"Yes."

"He's protecting someone I need. If I help you get your man, will you help me get mine?"

The Exilarch laughed, an old and sick sound. My unease deepened. "I have offered professionals astronomical sums of money to deliver what you are offering, and they all failed. Your price seems very reasonable, provided you can deliver."

"I can deliver. I've got a tracker on a known associate of his." I pinged my card to a screen on a rostrum before his throne.

"Why do you want him so bad? With all due respect, you're old as shit. I can't imagine you've got a ton of time left. Shouldn't you be, I don't know, preparing for . . . succession?"

The Exilarch laughed, and now it was not a weak man's sound. The look on his face was cracked, crazy, way past human, but also somehow familiar.

And, there. The thing that was freaking me out.

Something in his eyes—in his tone of voice—was way too much like my mother. Who wasn't quite this deranged but was well on her way.

The Exilarch was an addict. Hooked on power, which didn't fuck up your face like crystal but did twist your mind sideways just as hard, turned you into something toxic. Was my mom the same? Was she where I'd gotten it? For the first time I was *grateful* for my rock-bottom moments. What would I be without the loss of my sister? And all the other shit I went through, that almost broke me, that *did* break me, that made me into something less great than what I was but still way better than this fucking psychopath?

"My people are profoundly disloyal," he said, smiling at the shiver that went through me. "Many openly call on the Terfezians to strip me of my title and bestow it on him. I would never give them the satisfaction. I will cling to life and power for as long as I can, and the only succession I am planning for after my death is bloody chaos."

• • • • • • • FIFTEEN • • • • • • •

MORE PAIN AND ANGUISH THAN YOU'D HAVE THOUGHT COULD FIT INTO A HUMAN UTTERANCE

ARAN

I wish I could say we had a plan, but plans have never been my strong suit, and while Resh, to his credit, kept trying to get me to actually figure out some next moves, it was hard to focus on clearing my name and exposing a nightmare conspiracy when we could spend endless hours sprawled in Resh's endless bed instead, sharing our favorite cinematics, then discussing them, then fucking, then repeating the cycle ad infinitum.

I also made Resh listen to the commentary on every Imadi fight. And then compare them to the current superstars, pointing out how they were all wack and graceless. And problematic. Like Chthona, who had been the biggest in the biz but retired in disgrace after her pilots were discovered to be colluding with fascist planetstuck anti-systemist terrorists.

Stars, those were good days. Sex and mech fights with my man.

But Grizzelda and Professor Hedgehog did keep on working, crunching a couple nebulas' worth of data a day, giving us updates—

Assassinations and attacks were still unfolding, targeting the clients of the major security concerns. And now shareholders at those companies were calling for votes of no confidence in the management. Issuing press releases—eerily similarly written, as if the Intelligence Class masterminds pulling their strings didn't care enough to hide their fingerprints—decrying the failures of corporate leaders to keep their contractees safe, citing declining stock prices as the need for drastic action. Loss of profits always motivates the powerful more than loss of lives.

I tried to pay attention. But Resh's very well-developed chest made a hell of a pillow, and he was stroking my hair and I was rubbing his belly when a call came in.

Resh ignored it. But they tried back twice and finally he groaned, "Put it through, Grizzelda."

A man, sobbing. Trying to speak and not making a lick of sense. Resh sat up suddenly, his whole body rigid.

"Bar, breathe. Okay? Calm down. Breathe."

Bar breathed. Bar stopped sobbing. Bar started up again. We sat and listened, in slightly embarrassed silence. Holograms hung in the air before us: the Amharic melodrama we'd been watching, on pause, something about their war with the Xuya. Whoever Bar was, I could tell by Resh's expression he wasn't the type to cry. This was big. This was bad.

Eventually, Bar managed to gasp, "It's Imm."

Fuck. Fuck, fuck, fuck.

Resh stood up, hurried to his wardrobe. His face reddening rapidly. "Bar. Speak. What the fuck happened with Imm?"

"Imm's dead, buddy. They fucking—"

Resh's roar was the kind of sound you spend your whole life hoping not to hear from someone you (*love*) care about. More pain and anguish than you'd have thought could fit into a human

utterance. And that was me, wasn't it? My fault, my damage, my fucking problem Resh had been trying to fix, a problem so big and scary that even an Intelligence Class mastermind like Imm Eskehek was in over his head, and I sat there on the bed hugging my knees to my chest while Resh and Bar sobbed together and why oh fucking why hadn't I just been lucky enough to die with Opple in the first place, and spare so many people so much useless pain?

SIXTEEN

YOU LOOK LIKE SOMEONE WHO'S THINKING ABOUT USING

IMADI

Fuck, I'd missed this.

Nothing in the ninety trillion worlds compared to the thrill of prepping for a mech fight.

Setting up my subroutines; assembling my modules; feeding Vespertine data on the other belligerents likely to be participating.

This was actual combat. Not a show fight. Not a staged battle in a set space, with rules and wagers. The Exilarch's forces were going to war, and I was along for the ride.

The delicious frenzy of prep was why the news was six hours old by the time it got to me. I'd been hopping across eleven systems, gathering everything I needed for the battle, with Vespertine set to pass on only mission-critical updates.

Mar-Tek had traveled to the site of a terror attack on one of our contractees. A minor bomb planted in a major hub, twenty injured, six dead. The red-band conspiracy at work again.

But the first bomb was a trap. A trick to lure in claims assessors and collectors from the eight different security contractors

who represented individuals caught up in the blast. And when they were all on-site, the second—actual—bomb went off.

I couldn't stop to grieve or cry or call the hospital at headquarters for updates. Instead, I took the single split-second clip of Mar-Tek—swallowed up in a sudden soundless blossoming of flame—and set it to loop in a corner of my AR viz as I worked, to remind myself of the stakes of this struggle.

Trist sat and watched me prep. I tried to engage them as much as possible. But something was up. Something was wrong. Even through my prep-overwhelm and my fear and worry over the possibly mortal injuries of the closest thing I had to a decent parent, I could read the vibes Trist was giving off.

"You okay?" I said, after the fifth time Trist answered me with a monosyllable. "I gotta be real and tell you that right now you look like someone who's thinking about using."

"No," Trist said, but they shivered when they said it, and they avoided eye contact.

Maybe a better sponsor would have stopped everything. Taken Trist directly to a meeting, or a treatment center. But I was distracted. And I wanted to believe Trist was strong, capable, they could figure this out on their own.

Which makes what ultimately happened entirely my fault.

SEVENTEEN

SETTING OFF A SIGNAL FLARE
SAYING, "COME KILL ME"

ARAN

We can't," she said, her hand on Resh's shoulder.

"We have to."

Nine of them had come through the gate, Resh's most loyal soldier-friends, all of whom did the forehead-to-floor hail when they first laid eyes on him. Led by this one, the only one whose name I remembered: Imm-Lo Izkeriki, sister of the deceased, currently trying her best to talk Resh down from some kind of ledge.

Of course I was drunk. Of course I'd needed to dull the pain of seeing Resh in so much pain.

"It's suicide."

"That doesn't matter."

Imm Eskehek lay on the bier before us. Mouth open in a silenced scream, fingers digging deep into the flesh of his face like he'd been trying to claw out something beneath the skin. His body weirdly bloated and veined with green.

"It's exactly what your father wants," Izkeriki said calmly. "If

you hold a formal keening ceremony, you're setting off a signal flare saying, 'Come kill me.'"

"I will not send my friend and comrade into the void unkeened because of my own cowardice," Resh said. "It's as simple as that. I'm afraid—of course I'm afraid, of course I know you're right—but we're going to do this anyway. So we better do it in the safest way possible. Okay? We know the combined power of him and his nine retainers is the only way he could potentially overpower my field control—so he'd have to do it himself, he can't send flunkies. And he wouldn't attack during the ceremony itself—to profane an act so sacred would mean throwing everything away, the soldier-priest caste would then be empowered to strip him of all authority, imprison him, potentially execute him. So we need to be ready for a devastating assault as soon as we leave the sanctum. Am I understood?"

The Mar Zutra keening ceremony could not be performed with fewer than fifty-seven members of the soldier-priest class. And when Resh put out the call, three hundred gathered. They filled the space station chapel, howling and drinking and telling stories and crying—and the formal ceremony hadn't even started.

We stood in an antechamber, flanked by adjutants. Resh was on eleven drugs to keep him from crashing, on top of the nine drugs he'd taken to numb himself. Once or twice in all the frenzied prep he'd squeeze my shoulder or kiss the top of my head, but he never slowed down to do it. Which *of course* I was fine with, what kind of needy monster would resent his awesome boyfriend for prioritizing his grief and his responsibilities to his comrades? Certainly not me, wow.

"Intelligence update," said one of his comrades. "Looks like your plan is bearing fruit. We're hearing whispers in the Terfezian polyumvirate that they're taking seriously the possibility

that you are connected somehow to the Intelligence Class conspiracy against the security concerns, and that it'll mean significant resources for the resistance. They're panicking, sir. Military deployments have already been reconfigured, to form smaller battalions across more points of vulnerability."

I was barely listening, wouldn't have thought twice about it, if Resh hadn't sucked in the tiniest gasp of air—if he hadn't stiffened the slightest bit—if I wasn't an expert pleasure boy well-versed in reading all the body's tells.

"Resh," I said, seeing it, getting it, but needing him to say it. "What plan are they talking about?"

"Aran," he said plaintively, but he didn't say anything else.

He didn't need to. I got it. I was an idiot not to have gotten it sooner.

"Is it the plan where you set me up to get captured, then swoop in to save me before the eyes of a crowded mega-hub?"

"Aran," he said, and he'd been hurting so bad already, and I was hurting him more, and I hated it, didn't want to cause him any more pain—I wanted to stop, but I was drunk, I was drunk and angry and on the run and my life had been ripped away from me and I couldn't trust anyone and I couldn't stop.

"The plan where you met a vulnerable boy and thought to yourself, 'Hey, here's an opportunity to scare my imperial overlords by making them think my raggedy little resistance movement is a power player in the massive strata-spanning power struggle this boy is at the center of'?"

"Aran," he whispered, coming so close our noses almost touched, and his pain made me relent just long enough to hear him say, "I cared about you before I knew anything about that. And I thought I'd be helping you just as much as me. And I was confident you wouldn't be hurt. I'm—"

"I know, I know, you're amazing, you're the Name's anointed, you can shatter warships with a thought, you can do anything, even make rent boys believe you care about them."

Rage fizzed and bubbled inside me, stronger and purer than I'd ever felt before, pulling from deep inside, things I'd buried, moments I'd blocked—me, bleeding, on the floor of my fathers' home, forced to watch, helpless—

But I wasn't helpless anymore. I let the rage come, let it throb through me.

Unthinkingly, I moved both my hands from Resh's face to his chest and pushed. A weak, ineffectual gesture from my scrawny arms against his muscular body, but he—howled. And for just a split second, the roiling metallic clouds covering his sclerae— cleared. Revealing blue-tinted whites, a ravaged shattered black-brown iris like a star mid-supernova (*spiky like a hedgehog,* I thought, irrationally, idiotically). Then the clouds returned. I'd have missed it if I hadn't been staring into them.

His retainers leapt to their feet, weapons drawn and aimed in an instant.

"It's okay," Resh said, gasping, clearly not okay.

I'd hurt him. Badly. Somehow. Weak puny me had hurt massive mighty him. The pain and confusion in his face broke through the shielding of my rage, demolished my moral high ground. I'd been weak. I'd resented the way his work—his dedication to liberating his people—took him away from me. I'd lashed out—tried to do damage—succeeded.

I remembered his head tilt, the drunken question *What are you?*

What *was* I? And where had it come from, the sudden lust to hurt?

Outside, a murmuring. Impatience in the crowd. "We need to start," Imm-Lo said softly.

Resh put his hand on my shoulder. "They can wait," he said. "I'm so fucking sorry, Aran. I want to talk about this. I want you to know it's not like that."

"We'll talk later," I said, well aware there might not be a later. I was about to squeeze his hand reassuringly or say something else when I remembered the brig on Imadi's heartship. The place he put me. The sewage stink and the certainty I was going to die. And I just stepped out of his way, watched him walk into the amphitheater.

Inebriated, I could marvel at the lovely strangeness of it all. The Mar Zutra military and religious establishment were one: The ability to make war in the defense of their god was the highest expression of spiritual faith, and while the terms of Terfezian control prohibited the Mar Zutra from forming their own military, the priestly warriors had all signed up as soldiers with other ethnomes and nations and colonies and systems.

In spite of Resh's resistance to being treated with the reverence that was due to his father, he was legitimately the highest-ranking figure in their sectarian hierarchy, and as such it fell to him to lead the services. Which he did with eloquence and a lot of weeping.

The "keening" of the ceremony was literal. A high piercing wail, which everyone assembled would let loose at apparently random moments. Whenever the spirit of grief struck them with particular force. And when Resh keened, as leader of the service, the congregation clapped once.

A strange sensation, sitting there, drunk, experiencing it. The keening got to you. It really did. I felt like shit about Imm

Eskehek's death, but I hadn't really known him, wasn't experiencing true loss. But the more I sat there listening to these mournful utterances, the more they crawled under my skin, kindled something that felt for all the world like actual grief. Once, as a kid, my dads took my brother and me to a wolf planet. There's lots of them—other animals live there too, of course, but the wolves are what's really special to a kid—and one of the tenders showed us how to howl. And when we howled, the wolves howled. They didn't know we weren't part of the pack. And, because I was a dumb kid, I thought maybe that was all it took to join the pack. Just to howl, and hear your howl echoed.

Stupid, but that was what I thought about. I'd never be one of Resh's people, but I could feel the beginnings of true spiritual connection.

An hour in, everything went to hell, like we'd all known it probably would.

Soldiers stepped into the chapel from the main gate, dressed in ornate complex armor raiment, and blew three ram's horns as one. Everyone dropped to their knees—even Resh.

That's how the Exilarch makes an entrance.

And then they were up, dozens of his soldier-friends forming a circle around Resh.

He won't do it, Resh had said, throughout the planning. *He won't profane a sacred ceremony—not because he has any respect for the holy, but because to do so in front of a big audience would be a huge error in judgment, threatening whatever legitimacy he has left. Every member of the Mar Zutra would turn on him. He'd be throwing his throne away to take me out.*

Which, maybe. But it appeared Resh had also made an error in assuming his father *wouldn't* throw his throne away, because the Exilarch came through the door—a horrifying vision of Resh

made monstrous, all gnarled limbs and jutting bone and seamed skin. "Arrest him!" he shouted.

Gasps, all through the room. Cries of horror, anger.

Fuck him up, Resh, I thought, in the pregnant pause of all these armed warriors wondering who would make the first move, and I watched for him to do to his dad what he'd done to Atah Imadi on her heartship.

And he did step forward. And I saw his muscles tense, preparing to unleash hell.

And nothing happened.

Resh was their ace in the hole, the only hope they had of surviving the assault they'd all imagined would come after the keening ceremony. But Resh had nothing.

He turned his head, to the door to the vestibule where he knew I'd be standing. I saw the question on his face—*What the fuck did you do to me?*—when one of the Exilarch's retainers stepped forward to shoot him with some kind of tiny electrified bolt.

I yelped, but Resh barely blinked.

Now his friends drew guns from inside their garments. A ghastly sin, to have brought them into the chapel during the ceremony, but allowing their leader to be taken into captivity would have been a far worse sin.

Imm-Lo, who was standing very close to the Exilarch, screamed, "You have broken your house's covenant with the Name by harming your own blood! You are a traitor and a fraud!"

"Fraud!" the crowd echoed.

"He has conspired against the Terfezians," the Exilarch said, "by whose grace and generosity we live and worship and complete our noble work each day. I'll not harm him. I'll hand him over to face their justice, for his terrorism against them."

Blood stopped flowing inside me.

His voice: It was Resh's, but it wasn't.

He spoke without a lisp.

Whatever dark thing Resh became when he tapped into his power: His monster father was at the root of it.

"The Terfezians are our oppressors!" shouted Imm Lo. "You side with our enemies against your own people—your own blood—and you turn a deaf ear to our cries—and that is why the Name has withdrawn its favor from your brow, and why you will die like a dog in the streets of a dusty nameless world!"

The Exilarch opened his mouth, but the spell was broken. His power was gone. Shouts of "fraud" and "traitor" drowned him out.

Through the great mycoplastic windows of the hall, we watched hundreds of ships and drones flank into battle positions. Resh's people had come prepared, but so had his enemies.

My heart soared and sank, at the sight of the massive mech that accompanied the Exilarch's forces. A vision from my childhood dreams, and my present-day nightmares.

Vespertine. Atah Imadi's fearsome monstrosity.

Stars, she was beautiful. The mech she'd assembled for this fight was eight core modules, and a battling body of eerie artistry. Head like a stylized skull; bone-like lines along the brutalist limbs. Lit up blue in the light from the stars. Magnificent.

She had come for me.

We were super screwed.

EIGHTEEN

TRADE ROCK BOTTOMS

IMADI

Like dancing.

Like fucking.

It felt that good. That free.

So much time had passed, since the last time I'd fought. And this felt better than it had ever been, an ecstatic swirl of physical and mental dominance.

I told myself it was because this was real fighting, life and death, instead of the staged safe bouts that had been most of my battle track record.

But I knew it wasn't that.

For the first time in my life, I was fighting and my sister couldn't see. Wasn't watching now; wouldn't look later. Couldn't judge, or criticize, or be impressed. I was fighting for myself now. I'd always thought it would feel empty. It felt fucking great.

I was proud of the fighting body I'd assembled. Limbs spindly where they connected to the torso, thickening to barrel ends. Weaponry at the end of my arms; thrusters in my feet and along my spine and at my joints. This was a fight where structural

Integrity wasn't the primary concern—speed and heft were. I thanked the stars for the miracle of mycoconcrete, which let us assemble incredible shapes in astonishing time.

My presence confused Resh's fighters, as I'd intended. What the fuck was this big wasp-looking monstrosity doing in the mix?

So I could lurch in fast and hard, plasma sword swinging. Through flocks of drones glinting and surging, complex meshes of rival robots painting the starsprawl with railgun pulses and laser arrays, occasionally bursting into bright flowers of flame and metal and mycotics.

Pivoting my hips abruptly, I swung into a butterfly kick that flung one fighter into another. One of my favorite moves.

I screamed. I howled.

I launched a telescoping probe, glommed it onto the myco-plastic window at floor level. Three tacticals charged through the umbilicus with me, cut a hole I walked through into the great hall where the keening ceremony had become a battle-ground.

War raged outside the windows, but inside it was still a standoff. Both sides, ostensibly, respected the sacred space. Both sides stared at Resh. Waiting for him to flex his mental muscles and crush the bad guys.

His face contorted with effort. But Resh was suddenly re-markably unable to wreck shop.

Finally he said, in a high loud voice, "I will have no blood shed in this sacred space, as we send our brother into the void. Stand down, everyone. I will go willingly. Complete the cere-mony. Honor our fallen brother."

The Exilarch's soldiers closed in.

This time, Aran fought. He'd come quietly when I arrested him the first time. But now he screamed and raged and swung his

fists and kicked his feet. It took all three of my tacticals to hold him down and cuff and ankle-cuff him, and even then he still squirmed and writhed so much they had to throw him over their shoulders and carry him back to my heartship.

I wondered what had changed. I figured it was Resh. Aran had something to live for now. Someone to fight for.

I'd had that once. I'd had my sister. And now I didn't.

I paid the tacticals. They hopped home.

Which left me alone with a handcuffed kid and the Suddenly Very Big Question of What the Fuck to Do with Said Kid.

Because I was pretty sure I couldn't kill him. For a lot of reasons. Like that he really clearly actually *was* innocent, and because I was pretty sure the keening ceremony had been recorded by a dozen different drones, and Aran wasn't friendless anymore, and my plans to shoot him in the back became a little less tenable when there was footage of him being taken into custody.

And because he'd talked Resh out of fucking murdering me.

But the biggest problem was that ever since my confession to Trist, I'd been rethinking a lot of things. Like the lengths I'd gone to, to keep the secret. And what that might have done to me. I'd been so alone, and so in pain, with grief I couldn't speak of and a secret I couldn't share, in the shadow of a sister I'd loved but also hated, that I'd done a lot of awful things—and now I had the chance to do something different. Make better choices.

I could use someone to talk to. I pinged Trist, but Trist did not respond. Which was also unsettling.

I marched him to the brig. By now he was calm, knew there was no getting away. And without Resh he had no way of eating through the new metal bars.

Although Resh himself probably couldn't do it either, now.

And I thought about what the Exilarch had told me, the

fabled biotech that lived inside Resh's body like a second nervous system, linking up with any network to convey information of astonishing complexity back and forth between his mind and the environment.

But don't worry about that, the Exilarch had assured me. *For years I've kept his connectivity artificially limited. And now I can sever it completely.*

I'd helped destroy something fucking amazing.

I swung open the door to the tiny cell.

"Tell me the truth," Aran said. "This used to be your toilet."

He wasn't wrong.

I gave him a gentle push, and he got in. Tear lines framed his face.

"Do you have any alcohol?" he asked. "Being drunk would really help me make peace with your deeply uncomfortable hospitality. No offense. And also, if you're going to murder me instead of putting me in for processing, I'd love to not be super sober when that happens."

"Sorry," I said. "No booze on board. I'm in recovery."

He blinked, like I'd just become a person. Instead of an ogre. Which, fair play. I'd been pretty monstrous up to this moment. To everyone. Including—especially—myself.

"For real? How long?"

"Three years."

"Fuck me, man," he said, and I saw the Adam's apple wobble, the lips tremble.

I saw him, and I knew him. Just as I'd known him in those cam clips.

He was an addict, and he was in that place where I'd spent so long: knowing you need to quit, and not knowing how. "What's your secret?" he whispered.

"Rock bottom," I said.

"I've hit rock bottom so many times," he said. "Then it turns out there's a bottom below that. And below that. There's always further you can fall, until . . ."

He trailed off, and I had to finish the sentence. "Until you're dead."

"Yeah."

I imagined it would be fun to trade rock bottoms with Aran. We'd probably both have some good ones.

I put my hands on his bars.

What the fuck are you doing, Imadi?

Honestly, it was idiotic. I didn't know this kid. Didn't owe him anything. He was my mark, my target. My claim. But he was also an addict and he was suffering and every addict who's been lucky enough to get sober actually *does* owe something to other addicts who want to do the same.

It was the point and the power of meetings. Of mutual aid and accountability. Of the sponsor-sponsee relationship.

Stories have power. Stories can heal.

I heard my own voice:

"For me, the real rock bottom came when I lost something that I had never appreciated, but that I loved and needed with my whole heart. I didn't lose it—lose her—because of my addiction, but if I hadn't been an addict, I might have been able to behave differently. I might have been able to save her."

He flinched. Took a step back.

"What?"

"Oh, stars," he said, his face anguished, his voice close to cracking. "It *is* you."

"Yes . . . ?"

"Watching you fight," he said, his eyes welling up. "I thought

maybe. But it seemed impossible. But now—just now, what you said—I see that it's true."

No, something screamed, in the back of my mind. *No, no, no . . .*

I wanted him to stop talking, but I couldn't make him.

"I'm a fan," he stammered, a mile a minute. "Have been since I was a little stupid planetstuck kid. Didn't wanna tell you before, when you got me, because . . . I'd say anything, wouldn't I, if I was in captivity? To try to get on your good side? And I wasn't going to tell you now for the same reason. But. Stars, I'm sorry, I don't fucking know how to say this. I'm sorry for your loss?"

No

no no no

"She died, right? Your sister? She must have. When I saw you do that butterfly kick, I thought—Atah Imadi could never pull that move off. She tried a bunch of times, and she never nailed it."

I shook my head. As if to say, *No she never could,* as if to say, *No, stop, don't say any more,* as if to say, *It's not possible, I've kept this secret so long, it couldn't be that easy to figure out.*

Aran said, "Atah Imadi died, and you took her place. That must be an agonizing way to live." He stuck out his hand. "It's an honor to meet you, Mey Imadi."

And I was prepared for this. I'd been expecting it to happen for years now. Snappy retorts and devastating comebacks had been composed ages ago.

But now I was defenseless. Disarmed. I hadn't wagered on what it would feel like. No one had called me by my real name in so fucking long.

NINETEEN

THE SACRED SPACE OF
A BRIEF TRANSACTION

ARAN

As soon as I started talking, I knew I should stop, but stopping was never my strong suit.

The whole story had just kind of assembled inside my head—pieced together who knows how, and apparently not as full of shit as it seemed, because now she was crying, and so was I.

"It's only because I *just* rewatched all your fights, when I found out you were the bounty hunter—I'm sorry, I mean 'claims collector'—assigned to my case. One-in-a-trillion chance. Someone who was a huge fan of yours at a formative age, who internalized all those moves, *and* recently refreshed hours of fight footage?"

"Just my fucking luck," she said.

"When you 'collected' me the first time, I almost told you, 'Wow, Atah Imadi, what an honor, you're my second-favorite mech pilot of all time, I've watched your first Orbitapalooza fight a couple hundred times, the only fighter better than you is your sister, Mey.' But I figured that would just seem like me being super shady, so I didn't say anything."

She laughed, and wiped her eyes. And sat down, beside the clear programmable-matter walls of the new cell (the old one having been demolished by Resh when he rescued me).

I sat down as well. And we cried, together, without it being weird, without either of us being embarrassed—because this was a kind of intimacy I had with my tricks, sometimes, and I imagine she did with her claims as well—the knowledge that both people are caught up in the sacred space of a brief transaction, after which neither party has to see the other again—and you can say things that you can only say to a perfect stranger.

I cried with her, over the trauma of what had happened to her, of losing her sister and living a lie—but I also cried over having crippled Resh, and seeing the ceremony interrupted; watching him get dragged out of there by his father, who was definitely going to murder him.

He'd played me, lied to me. So why did it hurt so fucking bad to know I'd lost him?

· · · · · · · TWENTY · · · · · · ·

ON TOP OF CORRUPT,
SHE IS ALSO INCOMPETENT

IMADI

For forty-five minutes I sat there and let myself feel. Allowed myself to be raw, to be helpless, to be broken and open. To be with him, this stranger, this person who had somehow seen through to the truth of me—and responded to what he saw with kindness and empathy.

And then. Right when I thought my world had already fallen as far as it could fall. It fell further.

My jaw bug pinged. A message from Trist. I leapt up, excited—I'd been worried about them, leaving them messages; their sobriety had seemed so imperiled—and before I was on my feet the message played.

Fuck the stars, Imadi, I'm so sorry, they said, their voice sounding grim and hollow. And dazed. And disconnected.

High.

This gets blasted out across every ansible spectrum in five minutes. I made it part of my deal with them—that I could give you a tiny bit of heads-up. But I know it still totally fucks you. I'm sorry, Imadi.

"Be right back," I told Aran, and sprinted for my bridge.

A 'cast clip came with Trist's voice memo. I played it through my AR lenses.

A familiar balding silvery gent in a studio somewhere. The murdered filmmaker's brother. The slick 'cast's scroll at the bottom of the display said his name, and *Grieving activist exposes security racket corruption.*

"Before my brother's assassination, I never paid much attention to the security contractors that are the only law in systemist space. I thought they were like oxygen gating—expensive and prone to failure but absolutely necessary to sustain human life in space."

Slick cut as he turned to face another camera.

"But since the brutal murder of my brother at the hands of security contractors bent on silencing his devastating cinematic critique of their behavior, I've been learning a lot.

"The rich can afford expensive contracts with so-called security concerns, glorified gangsters who cause as many problems as they solve. For the poor, there is nothing. If you can't afford a contract with a security racket, anyone can harm you with no consequences. Sure, there are inexpensive security concerns. But their work is a joke. And yeah, many stations have contracts that protect everyone on board, but what happens if you go somewhere else? Freedom from fear of violence should not be a privilege of the wealthy."

Standard stuff. Accusations we'd heard a hundred times. Things I agreed with, actually.

And then: My mother's face filled the screen behind him. And I was glad Aran wasn't there to hear me whimper.

"I've connected with dozens of different networks of activists—millions of concerned citizens, toiling tirelessly to expose the

misdeeds of some of the worst players in the security space. A lot has been written and 'casted about Blue Circumspect Tomorrow—the largest security company in this stratum. Check the show notes for links to some of their greatest hits, like the time their illustrious leader, Amm Imadi, was caught accepting a bribe to arrest and execute *the wrong woman* for murdering one of their clients."

Slow, thoughtful pivot back to camera one. I needed him to get to the fucking point.

"But now it turns out that on top of corrupt, she is also incompetent."

And, *there* was the point. *I* was the point. My face replaced my mother's behind his. Mine, and my sister's.

Fuck.

Fuck.

What the fuck, Trist.

But even then I couldn't be mad at Trist. This was on me. I was Trist's sponsor, and I'd failed them. Handed them something immensely valuable—something a savvy addict could parlay for a massive amount of currency. I was not brand-new. I should have known better than to give that to someone in such an early stage of recovery.

"We've just learned—and are officially leaking it right here and now—that Amm Imadi's daughter Mey has been dead for three years. *And. Amm. Did. Not. Know.* That's right—you're finding out at the same moment she is. Every security concern is fundamentally wicked, and profoundly inept."

When Mom saw this, she'd come for me. Guns blazing. We were under attack and every security concern had their shareholders baying for blood and I'd given our enemies a brutal weapon to use against us.

She wouldn't kill me—probably—not right now. But I'd have to look her in the eye. I'd have to explain to her. How *this* outrage, this unacceptable transgression, this betrayal broadcast for octillions to see, was only half the story. Not even the worst half.

She'd see me and she'd know that things were even worse.

Her favorite daughter was the dead one, and the worthless fuckup had taken her place.

"Vespertine," I said, out loud, which was how stressed I was. Deep breath. Be smart.

"Jettison every gate in our array." It hurt to give the order. But half of them were registered to the company, and the other half could well have been bugged or flanged at any point. Which meant tacticals could come pouring through them at any moment. "Then take me sixty completely randomized hops away from here, terminating in a high-density transit nexus."

I watched my gates go, spinning out into the stars. Felt the thrusters rev.

I'd done it before: walked away from who I was, become someone different. I'd have to do it again.

"Completely scrub the registry, call sign, uplink identity, transponder frequency. Every identifying mark. Choose from one of the randomized backup identities you developed for me."

"Including our external appearance?" Vespertine asked, also out loud.

"Yes."

We went through the first gate, and I knew the programmable matter scrubbers on the hull were already hard at work transforming us.

I had no idea what to do next. I couldn't think five minutes into the future. For now my priority was making myself as safe as I could, by scrapping every trace of my old identity. I had

currency stashed, squirreled away in a dozen different dead drops and fake accounts. I could do literally anything.

But what the fuck would I do with Aran?

"Twenty hops," said Vespertine.

I watched wild spacescapes flicker through the porthole. Swirling nebula; ring planet orbit; stellar corona.

"Thirty."

Accretion disk of a naked singularity. Rust-red damocloid.

"Forty."

Fuck.

I went back to my brig and decohered the programmable matter box I'd locked Aran into.

And took a deep breath.

"You can go," I said.

He turned to me, looking as confused as I felt. "Wait . . . what?"

"I jettisoned my gates, so you'll have to do it the old-fashioned way and go through the door. I'll dock briefly at a cluster port and you can walk out, hop to wherever you want to go."

"You . . . jettisoned your gates? Imadi, tell me what the fuck just happened!"

"I kinda lost my job? So I've got no incentive to keep you. Or reason to kill you, for that matter. And you saved my life, I guess, so? We're even?"

"Imadi." He patted the floor beside him. "Sit down and take five deep breaths."

I did. It helped.

"What now?" I whispered.

"Five more deep breaths. In through the nose. Out through the mouth."

I felt like an idiot. A child.

But I was into it. I hadn't been a child in forever.

"You do this a lot for tricks who freak out?"

"Tricks, friends, boyfriends, myself."

"People freak out around you a lot."

"What can I say," he said. "I'm just that magnificent. You wanna tell me what happened?"

I gave Aran almost all of it. My mom's monstrosity; the secret I'd told Trist—which was only half the horror, which he alone knew in its entirety—Trist's traumatic past and why they'd snitched on me; the broadcast telling the whole portalverse my fake secret. He rubbed my back very sympathetically throughout.

"Just your dumb luck I was assigned to you," he said, "and the next thing you know you're in the crosshairs of the same conspiracy."

"Sixty," said Vespertine, and we both leaned forward as the thrusters slowed us down. Out the porthole we could see a massive asterisk station: eight evenly spaced arms of equal length, jutting out from a central hub. Thousands of ships docked along each arm, hundreds more buzzing by us. We could go anywhere. We could do anything.

"Do you need money?" I asked. "I don't have a ton stashed away, but I could loan you enough to—"

"Imadi," he said, and he took my hand in his, interlaced our fingers. "Mey. I get it, if your instinct is to run and hide somewhere. Hope this all blows over. Keep on hopping for the rest of your life, trusting they'll never catch you. But we can fuck these fuckers up! We already have, me on my own, and then me and Resh. . . . Together, you and me stand a chance of stopping them, exposing the conspiracy, having a shot at a normal life again."

Oh Aran. Poor beautiful young happy naïve simple Aran.

You'd think a pleasure boy would have a deeper and more accurate sense of just how awful the human race is.

"You and me are nobody," I said, pulling my hand away from his. "This is too big, and too connected to too much institutional fucked-upped-ness for us to be able to do anything about it."

"*On our own* we can't," he said. "That's why we need Resh."

"Resh is . . ."

"Resh can do crazy things—you know this, you've seen it! You've, uh, been the victim of it."

I tried again. "Resh is . . ."

He was standing now, excited. Thick dark curls bounced atop his head, whose sides and back were faded high and tight. "I don't know where they're holding him, but I think I know how to—"

"Resh is broken, Aran. They shattered him, okay? That thing they shot him with—it's special tech the Exilarch developed, and it completely fried the secondary nervous system that let him do all that amazing stuff. He's as powerless as you or me. Okay? Resh is dying in a Terfezian prison cell and there's—"

"Shut up," he said, and even though he said it very, very softly, I stopped talking. "You don't know that."

"Aran, the Exilarch *told* me—"

"His piece-of-shit dad would have said anything to get you to help him kill his fucking son. Which, you did."

He sat back down. He'd forgotten, for a minute. What I was. What I'd done to his man. He was a sweet kid and an adoring fanboy and he'd forgotten for just a moment that what I'd done was unforgivable.

We sat in silence. Right outside the porthole, a million different paths awaited.

"Help me try," he said. He was that desperate. No one to help him but someone who'd hurt him bad. "Please?"

He had hope. He believed the wrongs could be righted, that balance could be brought.

I didn't, but I'd taken enough away from him already. So what the fuck was I supposed to say? Except yes.

KNOW HE'S NOT DYING ALONE

ARAN

Imm's sister Imm-Lo rolled up with a micro-squadron of three thorn fighters, real badass little pods basically just big enough to house the human fighter pilot inside, but bristling with weaponry.

"They're not enough to take on the pleasure dome that houses the whole Terfezian royal throne complex," she said, "but it's all I could whip up for now."

"And we're sure that's where they're holding Resh?" I asked.

"One hundred percent confirmed," Imm-Lo said, and then paused like she was weighing how honest she could be. "He's been their biggest boogeyman for years now. All their most embarrassing military defeats were at his hands. So . . ."

"So they're making a spectacle of his capture," Mey said.

"Capture, and . . . punishment. They've been broadcasting it throughout imperial space. Cinematics of his interrogation and suffering. Currently he's chained to a pillar in the center of their primary entertainment complex, starving, dehydrated, beaten . . ."

Fucking idiotic of me, to be so sick with pain and fear for him. Why did I want so badly to believe him when he'd said that he actually cared for me—that I hadn't just been a tool for him to use in his struggle for national liberation? Was I hopelessly naïve? Or totally desperate?

Neither one was a good look, but I couldn't help it. I cared about him, and I would do whatever I could to help him, even if I was 97 percent sure I couldn't.

"In less than twelve hours there will be a public execution—the first in living Terfezian memory. Ten thousand people already in the amphitheater; it'll be at capacity by chop time."

I practiced on programmable matter, as I'd been doing with my downtime for days. Tried to repeat whatever the hell I'd done to Resh. And of course I couldn't. I figured strong emotions were the key, and once I made myself super sad before I tried, but (a) it didn't work, and (b) I felt so miserable I started fiending for a drink, so, no more of that.

I sent a message to Newt: *Miss you, whore, hope you're having oodles of fun and making tons of money. Don't worry about me, babe. I got this. The bitches who set me up are ON THE RUN, or they will be soon if they know what's good for them.*

Sometimes it feels good to lie so someone who loves you will relax.

"Seventy thousand representatives of the Terfezian elite will gather for the execution," Imm-Lo said, "including their whole royal house."

"Sounds like a great time for a death strike," I said.

Imm-Lo laughed. "Yeah, no. Not with the biggest, baddest mech ever made, or a whole arsenal of nukes, let alone the rinky-dink little arsenal we've got at our disposal. Or haven't you noticed that the mighty Imadi here has become a refugee, completely

stripped of weapons and power and resources? Terfezian space is permeated with an incredibly dense miasma of nanopolymer—created by and stolen from my people—controlled by hundreds of Terfezian warriors with cerebrospinal connectivity. Resh could have overpowered a couple dozen of them before, but even *he* would have been no match for the combined field control of the entire guard. And anyway his connection to the nano-field has been broken. So . . . anything we threw at them would get turned around on us."

"So . . . what's the point?" Mey asked. "Why are we here?"

Imm-Lo looked at me. We were basically strangers, we'd met twice, but love for Resh united us. How honest could she be with me?

"*I'm* going because I want to bear witness," Imm-Lo said. "I want them to see us out their windows. Know we're watching, seeing. And maybe Resh will hear them talking about it, know he's not dying alone. It's idiotic, I know. But it's the best I can do. The Iskawi resistance is real, and it's big, and it will survive without him. It has to."

Imadi asked, "How do you know they won't just blast us to bits as soon as we show up? If they're as well-armed as you say."

"Engagement protocols. Away from the battlefield, they never fire first. Terfezians pride themselves on the genteel magnanimity of their empire. As long as we don't engage, we'll be okay. I just want them to know we're there, that we didn't forget him."

"Fuck that," I said. "You have no idea what he's capable of. Right? So he's shattered—we don't *actually* know what that means, or how the Line of the Monarch's hereditary tech *actually* works. There's a chance, is all I'm saying. And you know it. If you just wanted to bear witness, you wouldn't have brought weaponry. Am I right or am I wrong?"

Imm-Lo nodded. She admired my hope. She didn't share it.

We were about to lose someone who meant the world to us. My puppy love was bad enough, but Resh symbolized her entire resistance movement, her hope for overcoming exploitation, and he was about to be brutally butchered in public.

"We're going to observe," she said. "If anything happens, we'll respond to it. But nothing is going to happen."

I nodded. Unconvinced. Idiotically in love.

"Then let's get hopping," Imadi said.

ALL I EVER ASKED FOR FROM LIFE

RESH

I was thirteen years old when my father blinded me—the age of accountability for Iskawi children, when the transition ceremony relieves their parents of ethical and legal responsibility for their actions—the moment when we're branded with the mark of the Facet of the Divine we have chosen for ourselves—mine was the Bear Herder, I didn't get to choose, the cave bear is the emblem of the Line of the Monarchs—I had placed my hands in the manacles and my feet in the hobble like we're supposed to, focused my breath the way we're trained, didn't scream when they seared the mark into the arch of the sole of my left foot—and in the instant afterward, that sweet blessed instant when the fear of the pain is gone and the pain itself is fading, my father himself stepped forward and grabbed my face and kissed my forehead and tilted my head back to drip a single drop of something into each eye, and the pain didn't come right away but when it did it soared, reached dizzying heights far in excess of anything I'd ever experienced, and I didn't scream, but it didn't stop, and then I was screaming, and screaming, and it didn't stop, and my father staring into my

face with a weird wonky smile was the last thing I saw, for the entire time it took my vision to sputter and falter and die—

—I spent years trying not to hate him, and even now I don't, because the Terfezians put him in an impossible situation—and he was too weak to resist and too fond of his luxuries to ever jeopardize them, but I knew from the age of six when Ashrei, my hand-to-hand-combat instructor, first started to tell me the real story, share the cinematics, the forbidden texts, the sobbing testimonials of workers broken on the wheel, her own twin sister slaughtered as a ringleader when she stood up against the overseer who cut their daily water rations—I knew that I wasn't going to be like him, I was going to choose differently, and I probably wouldn't succeed but I would die knowing I hadn't helped hurt people who didn't deserve it—and I knew that the Terfezians *did* deserve it, the hurt, and I'd make them hurt, and I didn't care that I'd get hurt myself in the process—

so I always suspected I'd end up here—not here, exactly, but somewhere in the clutches of my enemies, weaponless and broken—and I trained for enduring agony, it's part of every soldier's training but I took it to extremes, stayed in the pods longer than was safe—and when their blades and hooks pierce my skin I can absent myself, when their blows strike my body I can vanish with my out-breath—though I scream when they expect me to scream because I have no shame or pride, no performance to enact—

so from the pain I'm safe, from their laughter I'm immune, the scorn and the stares, the children laughing in the resounding amphitheater—

what I can't defend against is the withdrawal, the agony of not having the angusticeps, this idiotic drug I've been on for so long I don't even know what it does anymore, except tick, tick,

tick in my head like a bomb for my entire life, waiting to explode: a deadly swarm of hornets filling my head, a feeling like the world is made of porcupines (*hedgehogs*), sharp spikes throbbing everywhere, wet and glistening—the present so unspeakably palpable that the past is absent, the safe wide beautiful universe a dream I've awakened from—

—except when the orbiting of this station tilts me toward Terfez, the star of my enemies' home system, and its light shines on my face and I feel them twinge inside me, the ghosts of memories: pleasure, love, a boy with hair like a hedgehog—or a boy with a hedgehog on his head?—

But love was a dream—pleasure was an illusion—I'll never press my lips to the hedgehog boy's again—this—this is all that's real—

time passes and the withdrawal gets worse

nausea making me shake and shiver

nothing to vomit up, no food or water in days,

while the space around me continues to crystallize

sharpen

resolve into pinpricks and scythes and swords and daggers

a sharp endless forest of harm cutting into the dead nodes and wells of my secondary nervous system

this gift the Divine gave me

strung through hundreds of thousands of threads as thin as hairs, all through my body, and as fragile as hair as well, as easily cut,

to keep me humble before this gift

that I scorned, failed to safeguard

strength is nothing without wisdom, Ashrei always told me, and wisdom is what I lacked, which is how I got here

here

cold chains binding my hands above my head, back scraped by the rough stone of the pillar

the steps leading down from the altar they've set up on the stage

the expensive seats

the cheap seats—the pinpricks and rough raw blades slowly resolving into shapes, into *things*, and I can—almost—see them, see! not with my eyes, but with the air around me, with the miasma of nanopolymer, which I can feel, breathe in, breathe out, like I could before my shattering, but also *not at all like that, like something totally new, like that gift that made me such an unstoppable foe, the scourge of the Terfezians, only beatable by betrayal—was itself a tiny fraction of my actual gift, my true power—*

power I'd been blinded to, dulled with the drug my father got me hooked on at an early age, so I'd never see, never know what I was capable of, the angusticeps a muzzle I'd willingly put over my mouth every day of my life to stop my song from being sung

my foes fill the space now, and I can feel them—their faces, the data on their devices—I know who they are, the Terfezian nobility and military leadership and ruling polyumvirate, gathered here to delight in the death of their greatest enemy, blind to the fact that

I can split this station wide open

suck them all out into the vacuum of space.

I'll die myself, but I don't care. This is all I ever asked for from life. The power to deal the fatal blow to my foes. To give my siblings-in-arms the moment they need to break the back of the empire. Free our people. Reclaim Iskawi.

I scream. They hoot, imagining that my final despair has come upon me. And all the while I'm reaching out, forming shapes in the chaos, tentacles of nanomatter that even their most sophisticated minds can't perceive, making ready to pull down the pillar, see (*not see*) their faces as my scream turns to laughter in the last second of their lives.

TWENTY-THREE

I DIDN'T WANT TO NOT WANT

ARAN

I once spent six hours masturbating.

Wild, what pops into your head while running dark, floating silently in space, waiting to maybe die trying to rescue your maybe boyfriend. But it'd been hours of doing absolutely nothing, so I had a lot of time for reflection, which invariably turned sexual, which invariably turned to self-loathing.

Then Imm-Lo gave the signal: We were entering the final hour before Resh's execution. Time to power up the engines, come out of the darkness, sync our orbit up to the great clear mycotic dome of the amphitheater, looking up/down on the spot where he'd be killed.

But even that just turned out to be more of the same. Sitting. Thinking. Saying nothing.

Six hours masturbating. It was a long time ago, and even then I'd had the good sense to be ashamed of it. I'd been browsing blue cinematics, scouring the endless accretion of centuries of skin, marveling at the way fashion and grooming and narrative modes had changed over time, but—let's be clear—my primary interest

was not aesthetic. I wanted bodies, beautiful bodies doing terrible wonderful things, and once I reached orgasm I wouldn't want them anymore, so I didn't want to ever reach orgasm.

I didn't want to not want. That was the definition of my addiction. The shape of my unique damage.

"Soooo," Imadi said at last, sitting down on the floor beside me.

"Are we allowed to talk?" I whispered.

"Yeah, idiot. There's no stealth here, they can fucking see us. We're up to our necks in the miasma cloud."

"Right. Hey, what?"

"It's not fair. You know my most traumatic shit. And I don't know anything about you. So, spill it. Tell me something fucked up about the hooker with a heart of gold."

"You're just trying to get my mind off . . . things."

"Yes. Exactly. Spill."

I told her about the time I killed someone, a bizarre spontaneous decision that came out of who-knows-what-part-of-me, the right call but one I never would have imagined myself capable of making. She told me about one of her rock bottoms. We swapped rock bottoms for a while. Eventually I got there.

"I had three dads," I said, shutting my eyes, letting it happen. Not fully knowing why? "That's pretty normal in systemist space, but it's crazy taboo on most planets—outright illegal in lots. Don't know if you know this, but planet-based civilizations tend to have a very strong reproductive mandate. 'It's our responsibility to make lots of kids, help our society succeed, spread to tame this wild world,' etc. Real sick stuff, straight from Planet Zero, rooted in a mindset of open antagonism with plant and animal life. That's why a lot of planets ban or frown upon any forms of romantic or sexual relationships that don't lead to childbearing.

"So, my dads did their duty. They all accepted the childbearing

mate that was matched to them by the regulatory AI; they submitted to the spousal ceremony; they got their womb-bearing partners pregnant; they raised the kids. But they loved each other, and they weren't without resources, so they bought a big house where they all lived, along with their partners and the kids—if they wanted to, one of their mates wasn't into it—and it was a super brave and ballsy move. They got so much hate from the neighbors, and alarmed, confused messages from the algorithms. But me and my brother were dead happy there."

I looked up, straining to see if I could recognize Resh beneath the mycodome. But it was a chaos of glinting lights and moving figures and reflected starshine.

"One of my dads was a refugee. Uqbar's southern continent hadn't consolidated politically the way the northern one had, and it was full of squabbling nation-states always invading or bombing each other. He grew up feeling helpless and vulnerable, and his family were fisherpeople who'd gotten exploited terribly by the space-based systemist trade federation that bought their goods. So he had some . . . anti-off-worlder sympathies. Went to some meetings. Got marginally involved. Nothing terrorist-y, just peaceful demonstrations, leafletting, that kind of thing."

I could still see him: Poppa to us, Drill to his friends. Smoked shitty cigarettes. A skinny guy who smelled like salt and rooftop tar; fidgety, earnest, kind.

"But he was naïve, and he thought that just because he wanted the same things as those people he was in meetings with, they'd all be buddies. But some of them were really nasty motherfuckers, and when they heard about his living situation, they didn't like it at all. Thought he was bringing shame on the movement, or that maybe he was a systemist plant sent to discredit them."

"Fuck," said Imadi, knowing where this was going.

"They showed up one night, long after midnight. Kicked down the door. Carrying weapons. I ran to hide in the closet with my kid brother, Drommeda. Clamped my hand over his mouth to keep him from screaming, crying. And then he wiggled out of my grip, ran out—and I followed—and they had rounded up my dads in the kitchen, and were going to make Drill choose which one of the other two would get to live—said that's what it meant to be part of the movement, being willing to give up everything for the goal. He refused, and then my brother charged in—tried to tackle a guy with a weapon—some kind of weird percussive projectile device—and he saw Drommeda coming a mile away, would have shot him right in the head if I hadn't tackled him, so the explosive hit the wall above us, pumped me full of weird shrapnel, which kept me in the hospital for a month. Then they shot my biological father in the head.

"My brother never looked at me the same after that. I'd been his idol up until that moment. He said if I hadn't tackled him, he could have stopped the bad guys. I knew it wasn't true, but that didn't make the hate in his eyes diminish. Two years later, I ran away from home. Hopped a gate to systemist space and haven't looked back since. But he caught me, the night I was leaving. Drommeda. He called me a fucking coward, told me to go hide from our problems like I always did."

"That's rough, buddy," Imadi said, wincing at the inadequacy of the words. But, weirdly, they did the trick.

"Are you two gonna fuck or what?" Imm-Lo said over the wireless.

"Only if you're not interested," Imadi said, without batting an eyelash or letting a nanosecond of silence slip in.

"Sorry, honey," Imm-Lo said. "Sex is not my thing."

"It *is* pretty overrated, isn't it?"

"Sorry to interrupt your tender moment, but wanted to share that we made the broadcast."

She pinged us over a clip from Terfezian news: *Anti-colonial extremists show solidarity for condemned terrorist.* And there we were, tiny blips seen through the dome. Below us, the message we'd been beaming in their own military binary code: *Mar Zutra will be free.*

"I'm shocked that such a subversive message would be included in the royal reporting," Imm-Lo said. "Maybe some kind of internal power struggle is going on?"

"And could we—"

That was when the world caught fire.

PROGRAMMING THAT
OVERRIDES WHO HE IS

IMADI

The mycodome cracked like an egg. A caustic surge of fire shivered through the amphitheater, splitting the clear ovoid down the middle—and then shattering it into a billion pieces.

"What the fuck," Imm-Lo bellowed, rolling us out of shrapnel range, engaging her programmable matter shielding. I did likewise.

Corpses spun through space. Lavishly dressed nobility, already frozen solid, long cloaks twisted from the first flourish of the concussive blast, utterly still now.

"It's Resh," Aran said.

"That's impossible," Imm-Lo whispered.

And we couldn't see through to the stage where he'd been chained, because green-veined red fire still surged around it. How could there be flames, with the dome gone, in the oxygenless vacuum of space?

"I'm engaging," Imm-Lo said.

"Fuck yeah!" I cried, swinging in behind her and the other two thorn pods.

Bodies were clustered so thick that our shield bubble stretched and swelled and deformed around them, pushing them clear.

Terfezian harriers swung into view; Imm-Lo and her friends broke away to take them on directly. Ten total: big clunky perimeter defense vessels. You wouldn't have thought the tiny Mar Zutra thorn pods would have the firepower to hold their own, but they unleashed three arcing lines of railgun fire that crippled the gun arrays of half the enemy ships.

"Go get him," Imm-Lo told us, and for the first time I could hear hope in her voice. "If there's anything left to get."

Vespertine screeched a warning, braked so suddenly the grav stabilizers couldn't compensate and I fell to the floor.

"There's a bubble of nanomatter occupying the space in front of us," she said. "If we attempted to breach it, we'd certainly be shredded."

"Resh," Aran said.

"Maybe," I said.

"Who else would be capable of bubbling that whole space?"

"Resh *isn't* capable of that," I said. "Not anymore."

Abruptly, the fire went out where the dome had been.

"The fuck he isn't," Aran said.

For there he was. Impossibly. Floating in space, stripped naked, chains floating freely now that the pillar he'd been tied to was gone. And then they dissolved, same as the bars of my brig cell.

Bodies shifted, moved through space. But not bodies: living people, held in bubbles. High-ranking officials in the Terfezian empire, to judge by their attire. Resh had them, all lined up. He shifted each one slowly toward his own floating body. He looked them in the eye, one after another. He couldn't see them, but

they could see him. His smile. And then he popped their invisible bubbles, without moving a muscle. One at a time, they moved forward—struggling mightily—and then went eerily still as the vacuum killed them.

"Weird that the perimeter defense harriers are still the only response," Imm-Lo said. "They keep at least six flotillas on standby. The silence means no one's giving orders."

"Or they're giving orders and they can't be followed," Aran said. "Because Resh has the whole fucking fleet in the palm of his hand. We've got eyes on him, and I can assure you he's very alive and very badass."

"We've taken out all the harriers," she said. "Rendezvousing by you."

"There are gates inside the nave of their station," I said, reading through Vespertine's scans. "We can get him to safety that way. Try to hail him, see if you can get him to move in that direction."

"Resh?" Imm-Lo said. "We're here for you, buddy. Can you get to the nave?"

The nave exploded in a glorious green-red fireball. Gates gone.

"Sorry, fellow soldiers," Resh said, his voice on every channel. "I'm not coming back."

Aran's eyes gleamed, to hear his man's voice again, even the hollow emotionless husk of it. And then we watched as three massive imperial warbirds broke apart into a dozen perfect vertical cross-sections.

"What the fuck did they do to him?" I asked.

"This has always been a thing," Imm-Lo said, sounding weary and defeated in a way I couldn't have imagined her sounding fifteen minutes ago. "Whenever he taps into—whatever it is

that lets him do all this. It's like he's running programming that overrides who he is."

"His father," Aran said sadly, authoritatively. "That's his father's voice he's speaking with. No lisping on the *S*'s. His father must have . . . embedded? something? inside of him."

I remembered Resh in my heartship. How easily he could have killed me. How little it would have mattered to him.

"I'm taking them all out with me," Resh said, his voice mechanical and cold.

"It shouldn't be possible," Imm-Lo said to us. "At his most powerful, he was capable of . . . two? Three percent of the damage he's done here? And we saw his secondary nervous system get fried."

"He's tapping into something else now," Aran said. "I fucking told you you were wrong to write him off!"

"Forgive me for thinking I knew the limits of the tech I've spent a lifetime studying, Aran."

"There's got to be a way," Aran said, off comms, to me. "To grab him, take him on board, get him to safety."

"None of these ships have air locks," I said, "let alone enough programmable matter to make us spacesuits—or tentacles—to go out and pull him in. And I jettisoned all my away-gates. To say nothing of the fact that *he doesn't want to be taken in*, and I don't really feel like pissing off a guy with godlike powers and bottomless rage right now."

"What about your docking gate?" he asked.

"What about it?"

We turned to look at the internal half. Its mate was affixed to the exterior of the ship, and could be propelled to a space station's docking bay to let someone hop aboard without an actual docking craft.

I got it. What he wanted to do. And it was fucking crazy.

"That's literally our only way off the ship," I said. "And you want to launch it out into a shrapnel-field war zone, at Resh, in the hopes of aligning it perfectly to hop him onto our ship? If it gets damaged, we have no way of exiting, except hoping we can get to a safe haven and have somebody cut us free—which could compromise my heartship forever."

But I couldn't stop looking at it.

It *was* possible. It was a super long shot, but it was possible.

"If we open it in the vacuum, it'll suck out all the oxygen from the ship—and us with it."

"But Resh has preserved oxygen and thermals in his bubble," Aran said. "We have a razor-thin window of timing, to launch it at him and then iris it open and shut while it's inside of that."

"But his bubble fucking destroys everything that collides with it. He'll shred the gate on instinct."

"Unless I can get Resh to let it in," Aran said.

"Maybe you could get *Resh* to let it in," I said. "But that guy—right now he's not Resh."

"But Resh might be in there!"

Every piece of the shattered imperial warbirds burst into flames, one after the other. A series of gracefully executed explosions.

"Come *on*," Aran said. "This seems like *so* your thing. A very dumb, very dangerous maneuver! Am I wrong?"

He wasn't wrong and he fucking knew it.

"Imm-Lo," I said into the wireless. "Do you have enough polymer to run interference on our docking gate, if we launch it at Aran to try to bring him on board? Protect it from shrapnel and projectiles?"

"Fuuuuuck," she said. "That is a very impressively dumb

idea. I think we do, yeah. We can declare victory out here—it's a fucking graveyard, not a single Terfezian left to fire on us."

"Not now," I said. "But reinforcements will probably be here any minute." He'd devastated the military units—no gates left for bad guys to come through—but a sprawling Terfezian outpost drifted in the distance, and there were probably portals there. Unless Resh had already broken them too. In which case we were dead, there'd be no getting home.

"Then let's fucking hurry."

"Yeah!" Aran said.

We turned to the fore screen, which showed a zoomed view of Resh in his bubble in the middle of the wreckage and drifting corpses. Hands clasped together behind his back and head tilted up, in a posture I'd seen in friezes in the sanctuary where we'd interrupted the keening ceremony. Some soldier-priest meditation modality.

"Oxygen's depleting," Aran said, panic at the edges of his words.

"Vespertine," I said, out loud, so Aran would know what was going on and hopefully feel less freaked out. "Pivot so our external docking gate is pointing directly at Resh."

Thruster sweep, the slightest stomach lurch with our swift speedup and slowdown into position.

"Do your thing," I said to Aran, flipping on the wireless. "See if you can get him to allow the gate to enter the membrane."

"Resh," he said.

Silence.

"Resh, I know you can hear me."

Silence. And then: "I'm sorry, Aran." But he didn't sound sorry. He didn't sound human. "I've done what I was created to do. All I've ever wanted. My work here is done."

"Resh, you can sense us, right? You can feel Imadi's heart-ship?"

"I suppose you still don't want me to kill her."

So there was some Resh left in there. Aran laughed. "No, we're cool now. She risked a lot to come and rescue you."

"Then I'm sorry to disappoint both of you."

"We're going to send something to you. I need you to admit it into your polymer membrane."

"Don't bother, Aran. I'm so . . ." And *something* happened, who knows what, because he sounded almost himself again when he said, "I'm so tired. I hurt you, Aran." A long, aching pause. Did I detect the slightest hint of a lisp? "I used you. Because that's what I am. I'm a weapon who wanted to believe he was a man, who wanted to have beautiful things, who wanted to have lo—" He choked on the word, had to repeat himself. "Who wanted to have love. I was happy while I believed I was human. But I don't believe that anymore."

"You're not thinking straight," Aran said, now about to cry. "You've been hurt, tortured, made into a public spectacle—and I couldn't save you from that. But I can help you now, if you let me."

"You have to let me go," Resh said, sounding a little more like a person. A sad, broken person. That's what they were: two broken things crying out to one another in the endless darkness. That's what love was.

Aran shut his eyes. Took a deep breath.

"I'm not fucking playing with you, Resh."

He'd made his voice hard, sharp. His whole posture and body language had changed. Aran took up more space, felt wider, taller. He felt powerful. He was someone to be obeyed unquestioningly.

"We're launching a gate at you in thirty seconds. You're going to let it into the polymer bubble. Aren't you, Resh?"

And I got it. This was Aran's skill set: the ability to become whoever the scene called for. The bossy dom; the needy sub; the gentle lover; the savage sadist. What was needed now was someone brutal. Someone imperious.

For all his muscle mass, and the unquestioned military leadership that made his comrades in arms worship him, there was a part of Resh that was soft and gentle and wasn't ashamed to be weak. A part that took pleasure in being vulnerable, being commanded. Aran had plumbed the depths of Resh, and found that part, and given it what it needed, and he knew how to reach it now. Love let you do things like that.

"Don't make me fucking say it again, boy," Aran said.

Silence.

"Do it," Aran said to me. "Launch the gate."

"He hasn't said yes yet," I said. "Even if you've shaken him out of his funk, the automated membrane defense protocol might still be in place, and it'll destroy the shield and leave us fucking trapped in here."

"He'll allow it in," he said.

I wasn't convinced. But I didn't need to be.

I wanted to hope. I wanted to believe. I wanted to think that people weren't fundamentally fucked-up doomed selfish primates from a blighted planet who had accidentally spread throughout the universe.

"Launch the gate, Vespertine. Straight propulsion, on an intercept course with Resh."

The gate's external thrusters fired up, launched it away from the vessel.

We watched it on the fore screen. A bubble of protective polymer formed around it, under the command of Imm-Lo and her squadron mates. But it wasn't much. A couple solid strikes

would shatter it, leave our gate helpless. I rerouted all our own onboard polymer to merge with it, leaving us with nothing.

I said, "Open the internal gate, Aran."

He disengaged the clamps, swung the protective rectangle away. Through it, we could see the irised-shut metal of its mate, currently speeding through space. That steel was all that stood between us and the vacuum.

"Vespertine," I said. "On my command, open and close with a three-quarter-second iris."

"Fuck," Aran said. "You can't give him a full second?"

"Bubble's too small," I said, watching the screen map the gate's trajectory toward Resh. "If it's open for even a quarter second past exiting the membrane, it could suck so much of our oxygen away that life support for three people would be compromised."

"But if it closes on him, he could lose a leg! Or like his whole fucking body below the neck!"

"Then we'd better make sure to time this right, yeah?"

On the screen, the gate approached the edge of his protective membrane.

"It's coming, Resh," Aran said, voice shifting effortlessly from pleading to imperious. "And you're going to fucking take it."

It worked. It fucking worked.

The gate passed through the bubble like a stone through the surface of water. The protective membrane Imm-Lo had thrown up around the gate was absorbed into Resh's.

"Now!" I shouted.

The gate irised open. A smell of meat and burning filled the heartship: the smoky air from the bloodbath carnage inside the Terfezian amphitheater, caught inside Resh's bubble and now passed through the gate to us. Looking down, I could see the

starsprawl through the internal gate, and Resh's body looming in front of us as large as life—

—and the alignment was off, a minuscule differential that would have bounced it off his hip—

—and Vespertine fucking corrected for it, the tiniest thruster jolt from one side, to angle its propulsion slightly enough that it swallowed him whole, and I don't know what crazy quirk of programming gave her that intuition, something I'd coded when I was a kid, probably, or an emergent behavior she evolved on her own by collating and cross-referencing innumerable other commands.

All in under .75 seconds.

Resh spilled through the inner docking gate. Hung in the air for a nanosecond, before succumbing to the ship's grav and falling to the floor.

The gate slammed shut.

Resh lay there, eyes closed, utterly immobile.

"We got him!" I shouted, and the cheering of the Mar Zutra through the wireless was deafening. Aran cried, "Baby!" and rushed to his side.

"Vespertine, recall the docking gate," I said.

Because I'm smart. I'm just not fast.

Two seconds had gone by, maybe three. The exterior gate had exited the protective membrane. And in the instant I issued the order, a piece of space shrapnel broke it into a billion bits.

We were safe. We were also stranded. Trapped in Terfezian space with no way out.

"You guys okay?" Imm-Lo said.

"Barely? We're kinda fucked here, without a docking gate."

"How's Resh?"

"He's . . ." I looked at Aran, who had his boo's head in his lap. He gave me a tiny head shake. "Unconscious."

"He needs serious medical attention," Aran said. "Like a dozen different kinds."

"Nothing here could help us," Imm-Lo said. "The nearest station or settlement is a week away, at full thruster capacity."

"He won't last that long," I said.

"Look," Resh said, his voice so low it wasn't even a whisper. But we all heard him just fine, since it was amplified over all our comms channels.

An explosion, in the hub at the center of the Terfezian outpost. And then, something. Moving toward us. My fore screen magnified it, showed us what was coming.

"I did that," Resh breathed.

A bubbled gate. Big enough for my heartship, and Imm-Lo's needle squadron.

"You're amazing, big guy," Aran said, and kissed his forehead.

"I hurt," Resh said, and then slipped back into unconsciousness.

TWENTY-FIVE

WORRYING WAY TOO MUCH ABOUT THE WELL-BEING OF RAGAMUFFIN FUCKBOYS

ARAN

Imm-Lo had a lead on a field-ready regen bath from a Mar Zutra combat medic whose unit was between engagements, and somehow managed to get medic and tank on board Imadi's heartship in less than two hours from the moment we hopped away from the carnage that had once been Terfezian headquarters.

They slid him into the bath with a wet slurping sound, and he groaned as the electrolytic nutrient slime engaged his internal systems.

"I told you he wasn't shattered," I said to Imm-Lo and Imadi for the thousandth time.

"He *was* shattered," Imm-Lo said. "I just don't know what the fuck *else* he is."

No plan. No destination. Just hopping. Nothing driving us but the need to keep moving, to keep away from the innumerable forces that wanted us dead. I was impressed, actually, at the rate at which we were acquiring enemies.

We watched stations stream by, saw the very colors of space

shift as our hops took us past galaxy filaments and quasar super-groups and protoplanetary nebulae. We had a really good view of all this through the rectangular hole Resh's people had had to cut in the side of Imadi's heartship to get us out after the rescue left us trapped inside, sealed now with clear programmable matter.

Really unsafe, I thought. *But Resh will patch it up good as now, when he wakes up, just like he did the last time he punched a hole in Imadi's wall.*

But what if Resh doesn't wake up? Or if he isn't Resh when he does? Or if he is, but he can't do what he once did?

What if he's his father—

Five days out, Resh opened his eyes.

"Well, well," he said.

I was in the middle of giving him a sponge bath, and, yes, *maybe* I'd gotten a little inappropriate with it—nothing strenuous or excessively stimulating, just paying a lot of extra attention to the parts of him that pleased me the most—the soles of his feet, his armpits, his inner elbows, the soft skin of his sides, his inner thighs, okay, pretty much most of him, it was a really long sponge bath, but very chaste, I wasn't excited and it wasn't sexual, just . . . fascinated.

Addict behavior. But for once I wasn't ashamed of it. Susceptibility to all-consuming obsession was part of who I was, and it wasn't always ugly. I could choose when to fight it and when to give in. I gave in then, because it was beautiful.

"Hey, boo," I said, booping his nose.

He smiled, put his hand on the back of my head. Pulled me closer. I kissed him—but I lost my balance and my shoulder hit his chest and he cried out in pain around my lips.

"Sorry," I said.

"It's okay. I just . . ." And then he must have remembered

something, because his mouth went slack beneath mine, and his hand loosened its hold.

He had good moments. But not many.

He'd wake up screaming himself so hoarse at night that he couldn't eat for the next day and a half; he'd sweat through every sheet and towel and article of clothing in sight. He'd dissociate and think he was somewhere else, back there, in the clutches of his enemies, and I wasn't his boo then, I was something he scrambled away from in blind shrieking panic.

And I didn't mind, knew it was normal, never resented or doubted or hated him for any of it—

Who I doubted was myself. Whether I was strong enough to do this. Be who he needed me to be. I wasn't tempted to use, or drink, not yet, but there were so many hours and days ahead, who could say how he would change, and what kind of toll it might take on me.

One day, while he slept, I found Imm-Lo at the noodle canteen of the military outpost where she'd squirreled us away for a week. When I sat down at her table she just kept eating, until it was clear that I'd come to talk to her.

"Hello," she said.

"Hi."

Up to this point, our interactions had been extraordinarily minimal. Like I don't think we'd said five words to one another that weren't part of a bigger conversation with Resh or Imadi.

"Is this okay?" I asked. "I don't want to bother you."

She softened slightly. Set her bowl of noodles down. "It's fine, I'm sorry." She was older than Imm, probably fifteen years older than me, with a big sister's brusque exterior protecting a predisposition to worrying way too much about the well-being of ragamuffin fuckboys.

"This is probably out of line, but I realize I know very little about Resh. I"—*love*—"like him a hell of a lot, and it feels mutual, but I've fallen for boys before who love-bomb you for the first six weeks or months and then ghost or go feral or *whatever*. Anything you can tell me about his past, that I might need to know?"

She sighed and took a swig of some frothing green liquid. I caught a whiff of sweet tarragon. "He was the love of my brother Imm's life, I think. And Resh reciprocated. But . . ."

"But?"

"Resh's heart is as big as his people. He wants to do everything for them. Back then—this may not be true now—but back then he couldn't have been anybody's boyfriend. Not really. His commitment to the cause took precedence. Imm tried to stick it out, be the supportive boyfriend, but when it became clear that he'd never get more than ten percent of Resh's attention on any given day, he told him they'd work better as friends than lovers. They were still kids then, mind you. Not even twenty. And Resh loved my brother just as hard as his best friend as he had as his boyfriend, which is to say—with his whole heart, and an animal intensity, in very small doses."

"I'm not looking for a way out," I said. "I just want to know what I've gotten myself into."

"That's smart. Resh is a different person now. But still. There will always be demands on his time and attention, and he'll always honor them. That's who he is. That's what makes him a great leader, and a difficult boyfriend."

"How are you doing?" I asked. "This must have been a pretty wild week for a patriotic progeny of Iskawi. Who might or might not be a leader in a certain resistance movement of which we won't speak."

She laughed. "Yeah. I had a front-row seat for the most decisive victory over our oppressors in our history, and now I get to be in fucking meetings all day every day, trying to figure out how to take advantage of it, find the other political strongholds of the surviving leadership. Speaking of which . . ."

Imm-Lo hailed Imadi on the comms, asked her to come to the canteen.

"We've got some new intel that will inform our next moves," she told me, and, wow, that felt good, to know that there were next moves and I might be part of them.

"The Exilarch is missing," Imm-Lo said, when Imadi showed up. "He's hopped away, probably looking for new imperial protectors now that it seems likely that the Terfezian Empire will fall and the people who hate him—our people—will be in a position to take him out. And the Terfezians are freaking out about it, since it could mean a disruption to their primary military weapons supply, but they're way too stretched-thin and worried about baseline survival to keep unruly colonies or puppet monarchs in check."

"That's the good news," Imadi said, and gestured for the bad news.

"Our intel is better than the Terfezians' is. We actually have an embedded loyalist among the Exilarch's core retinue, one of his nine retainers, who reported back that he's being harbored in a manufacturing facility built for the purpose of developing our nanoweapons on a massive scale. By what appears to be a very well-connected and powerful alliance of red bands."

"Fuck," Imadi said.

"Who might or might not have been behind me getting framed."

"Precisely," Imm Lo said.

"And now they might be able to get their hands on your crazy fucking nano-magic-whatever-the-fuck?" Imadi asked.

Imm-Lo nodded.

"Then security class is fucked."

"Almost ironic," I said. "That Resh used me to insinuate your resistance into the conspiracy, and now the conspiracy has embraced your archnemesis, his evil father."

Imadi asked, "Has your embedded retainer been able to tell you the location of this manufacturing facility?"

"No. We assume the royal retinue has gone someplace bricked and shielded. And that it's just a matter of time before they succeed in leaking the location to us. So we need to be ready."

"So I need a better mech," Imadi said.

Imm-Lo raised an eyebrow, impressed that Imadi was still interested in supporting their struggle. Was it just me, or was there something electric in their eye contact?

We started a long series of hops that brought us to the kind of station mech fans fantasize about, with giant robot krakens and dinosaurs and samurai and dragons and spiders floating in space around a ramshackle agglomeration hub, where the mech heartship docking gates had affixed themselves.

Even more mind-blowing on the inside: food carts with billowing smoke that smelled like fish balls and five-spice powder; coal dust and dirty leather; algal biodiesel and armpits and cheap good vat-brewed beer. Wanted men that we were, me and Resh had been suited up in mechanics' coveralls and mouth masks and protective visors, and we didn't feel half as conspicuous as I'd imagined we would.

My basking in the raw wild taste of the place was interrupted

by barks from black-geared tacticals pouring through a gate, weapons raised, aimed at us—

I stood still and put my arms up. Resh did not do likewise.

"It's okay," I whispered. "Don't do anything dumb on my account, okay? You're damaged, you're still recovering, you don't know what might happen if you try to go full avatar state on these assholes."

But the tacticals marched right past us.

"What the hell!" Imadi shouted, as they grabbed hold of her.

"You motherfuckers aren't welcome here," someone said. And all through the massive low-ceilinged space, everything had stopped. Everyone was silent, taking hold of plasma saws and wrenches and whatever else. "Let her go, and get the fuck out."

But even I could see it was over, and I'm fucking idiotic when it comes to battle strategy. There were twelve of them, all armed with guns—and not the nonlethal kind—and their path back to the gate they'd come from was pretty wide open. If everybody in the room ran at them at once, we *might* have had a chance at winning, but a lot of people would have gotten killed. And no one in the room looked like they were in too big a hurry to die for someone they didn't know.

"It's my mother," Imadi said, and it was the first time I saw her look scared. I wondered what kind of monster her mother was, to scare someone so awe-inspiringly badass. And I thought of Resh's asshole father, and I thanked my lucky stars to have had kind, supportive, loving, useless dads who didn't run a massive evil corporation or descend from a genetically modified supernaturally powerful monarchy.

Even if one of them got another one killed.

Resh raised one arm—and my heart swelled, thinking he

could do this, cripple all twelve tacticals at once—but all he did was make a small whimper and then drop to one knee.

"I fucking *told you* not to try to *do anything*," I said, kneeling to feel his pulse—racing—and his forehead—suddenly cold and greasy with sweat.

"How can we help you?" I called out to Imadi, as they marched her toward the gate.

"You can't," she said. "I'm sorry, Aran. And Resh. And Imm-Lo."

And then she was gone.

TWENTY-SIX

THERE'S MORE THAN ONE VILLAIN HERE

IMADI

How's Mar-Tek?" I asked, but the tacticals were probably on orders not to speak to me.

"How'd you find me?"

Pretty easy to figure out, though. I'd very visibly piloted a mech recently—not too much of a stretch to think my mom would scour fighter scrapyards for me. I'd known it was a possibility when we came. I'd weighed the risks, taken a gamble, and underestimated how badly she wanted to punish me.

Well, that's not exactly true. I knew she might come collar me, which was why I had the plasma knife nestled in its pocket up the inside of my sleeve. A real gnarly little fucker with a three-foot blade. Just in case I happened to find myself presented with a very specific head that needed lopping off.

Ah, the good old densely forested pathways of Cerulean Causeway Prime. Walking way too fast toward where my mother waited.

It had been three years since she'd seen either of her daughters. I'd changed a lot, inside and out. Would Mom recognize

me? Know at once that the story Trist leaked was a lie, a cover for something even worse? Any other mother would know immediately which daughter was staring her in the face, no matter what name she had been living under. With mine I couldn't be sure.

We'd made a game of it, as kids—trying to trick her. Trading clothes, mannerisms, favorite words. But the game lost its fun, because she never seemed to care which one of us we were. We were both held to the same impossible standard. She bought into the Good Twin/Bad Twin bullshit as much as anyone, but she at least didn't give Atah a break because of it. I got screamed at for not knowing any better, and Atah got torn up because she knew better but didn't *act* better. That kind of thing.

I knew it would mess me up: being home. The smell of the pine trees and flowering dogwood. The specific caress of the station ventilation's wind randomization. Chestnuts toasting somewhere, always. When I stopped beneath the blue lilacs outside my mother's suite, one of the tacticals elbowed me in the side and spoke—"Keep it moving," the first words any of them had said to me—but it was too late, I had a head full of flowers and I was ready to meet my mother.

Her office hadn't changed. Too many screens on the walls, too many tabs stacked on every surface, the smell of burned coffee so strong it choked the unprepared. Lilac underneath, my mother's signature.

She sat at her central desk, staring down at a series of screens. Aggressively ignoring me. For all I knew she was actually doing work, but her taps and types all seemed excessive to me. Performative. My handcuffs decohered, fell to the floor as an inert lump of polymer, and slithered to an amassing node in the wall somewhere.

I said nothing. I'd be damned if I broke the silence first.

We let it stretch, drag, thicken. Two stubborn assholes.

"You're such a fucking coward," Mom said eventually, and even though it was idiotic I felt the smug pride of victory, for not being the one who spoke first. "If you weren't, none of these dramatics would have been necessary."

"I wasn't scared," I said, making my face rigid so she couldn't see what a lie that was. "I just didn't have anything to say to you. I still don't."

I faced her. I stared at her. Willed her to see me.

Look up, Mother. Know the truth.

Your favorite daughter is dead. Has been for a while. You're stuck with the weak one, the Bad One, the one who wanted no part of your empire.

But no. She wouldn't look up. And every screen on the walls went black. And then the largest one flickered to life.

And my heart broke all over again.

My sister. Staring into a camera.

"This is an asshole move, Mey. I'm sorry about that. At least it's my last asshole move. You won't have to deal with me and my bullshit anymore."

This was it. This was the end. The suicide note I'd never seen.

"I can't do this by myself anymore. I can't live this life, work for her, be what she wants me to be. I've always envied you, how you don't give a shit what anyone thinks about you, your ability to just walk away from what causes you pain. I don't have that ability."

Atah was wrong: I wasn't strong enough to walk away.

This was on me. I'd abandoned the business, left her a burden too big to bear alone. She'd said as much to me in a hundred messages in those last few years. And it broke her.

And *then* I'd finally shouldered my share of the work. Become the Good Twin. The heir to the throne.

If I'd been able to do all that before, Atah Imadi would *still fucking be alive*.

Grief wasn't what brought the tears to my eyes. It was rage. Cold blue fire sparking to life all through my body, singeing my central nervous system, scorching away my self-control. My fingers curled around the edge of the plasma blade up my sleeve, centimeters from the sensor that would bring it to blazing life.

I'd always wondered. Whether or not she'd killed herself.

"You knew," I hissed, tears already rolling like lava down my face. "All this time. You knew. She left me a message, and you stole it, and you let me—"

My plasma blade surprised us both, springing out of my sleeve and into my hand and blazing to life aimed straight at her.

Finally, my mother looked up from her screen. Her eyes met mine. Found fire.

"Am I the villain?" she said, but I could hear it in her voice: the struggle to keep calm. "Am I the one who chose not to come home, be with my family, mourn and grieve and celebrate her together?"

I stepped closer. The blade was close enough that she could feel its heat. A single step forward and I could sink it into her heart or neck.

"Mom, we both know there's more than one villain here."

For sixty seconds we stood there.

"Don't tell me the mighty Amm Imadi doesn't have a weapon at hand," I said. "Blade or blaster or zip stick? Draw it and let's find out. How successful you were in making me a monster."

She tried to smirk and did not succeed.

"I don't know why I'm surprised," I said. "That she left a suicide note via cinematics, and that you hid it from me. Let me

guess—you had her chipped? Got a little ping when her heart stopped beating, sent some tacs to collect her. But—no. You didn't collect her. You left her where she lay. Where I found her. So, no tacs. Too sensitive an operation. Couldn't have anyone else knowing. So you went yourself. Wow, what an ordeal *that* had to have been, leaving your safe little bridge. You took the tab where she recorded this message, and you left. *Draw your fucking weapon, Mother.*"

She stood up. Which meant I'd pushed her past her smug comfort zone, which meant this was not going at all as she'd planned. Which didn't give me even a flicker of satisfaction.

"I told myself you'd come to me when you were ready to lead," she said. "To take the reins of this company the way you knew you'd have to, one day. I'm a patient person, Mey. I was in no rush. You were useless to me unless and until that happened."

"It's the rehearsed script for me, Mom. How many times have you played this conversation out in your head? How cool did you think you would sound when you said it? But you just sound sad to me."

There were a lot more ugly words I could have used, but there was no point. She was what she was and she knew it. And now so did I.

My hate for her had always been informed by fear. The child's terror of her bully. And so I'd always dreamed of doing what you do to bullies, which is give them back the violence they've given you.

My mom had shrunk, when I saw my sister's message. She ceased to be the supermassive ogre at the center of the galaxy of me, the thing I dreaded more than anything. She was weak and scared and fraudulent like me. For years I'd beaten myself up over taking on my sister's identity, but now I could see that I'd

done that for Atah's sake, to keep her alive and well (*and undamaged, unbroken*) in the eyes of everyone who knew her. I'd kept that crushing pain to myself. And I hadn't spent years making myself feel bigger by making others—my own daughters—feel smaller.

I held the knife tighter. I stood up, looked my mother in the eye. Saw her weariness. The lines of her face, way out of proportion to her years.

Was this what she wanted? To taunt me into taking her out?

I killed the plasma blade, and stabbed my metaphorical one as deep as I could.

"Why hasn't the alarm gone off, Mom?"

She blinked. Took a breath.

"You thought I wasn't paying attention, but I remember your lessons. There are always drones scanning. A weapon gets drawn in your presence, hell comes raining down. But it's been four whole minutes and nothing. Is it true you killed your uncle for control of the company?"

It seemed like a non sequitur, but me and my mother both knew it wasn't. Her eyes flicked away. Looked at the floor. Had it been that easy to break her? Had she been this flimsy all along? She asked, "That's the story they tell?"

"You know it is. Is it wrong?"

"He forced me to," she said. "I always thought it was perfectly obvious that he basically committed suicide with me as his weapon, because he was a deranged old man who couldn't keep going and couldn't stop. I thought everyone saw right through me from the start."

"You played the part so well that everyone bought it," I said. "Including me and Atah. But I finally figured it out, just now.

Why your tacticals didn't pat me down and take this weapon away from me on the way here. Why the heat didn't kick down the door the second I pulled out my plasma blade."

She didn't look up again. She wouldn't smile, wouldn't beg, wouldn't speak to me human to human. She wasn't strong enough.

"*You're* trying to commit suicide, with *me* as your weapon," I said. "Because you're a deranged old woman who can't keep going and can't stop."

"Mey," she said.

"This company is toxic," I said. "In ways I never had the vocabulary or perspective to communicate before. We deal in violence and brutality and we *are* violent, we *are* brutal, and corrupt and greedy. That's what my time out there taught me. We're part of the problem, and I won't continue to be part of it, and you don't have to either. You can just stop."

"Mey," she said again, but could say no more.

"I'm assuming I'm free to go."

My mother nodded. Almost obediently.

"So. I'm leaving."

I stopped to breathe, beneath the lilacs, outside her office. Burnt algal coffee still scorched my nostrils, but the floral scent had been there all along.

There was a person under all of that. Beneath the harsh exterior of the head of the largest security concern in Stratum Chín, there was a mother who loved her daughters, in her own broken, damaged way, who'd never allowed herself to mourn an unspeakable loss. Just like me. Maybe someday we'd be able to see each other as people, capable of great love as well as great harm, and, I don't know, hug it out, punch each other in the face and cry and move on.

But today was not that day. And somewhere in the vastness of space I had a conspiracy to help crush.

Vespertine hummed in my head, mapping my way home to the heartship. I stepped through the first portal feeling as light as the dust of a ring system.

A DEEPLY SHITTY PROBABLY DOOMED PLAN

ARAN

I'm so, so sorry," Resh said, for the thousandth time.

"I know," I said, each time. "It's forgiven, Resh."

"I don't deserve that. And I don't forgive myself. I care so deeply about you, Aran. I can't believe I let myself put you in danger, use you for political advantage. I used to take this drug called spark, it's like shine but more so, a lot of military officers use it when they need to be razor-sharp and unsentimental for strategizing. And I can see now how it made me make bad decisions. I won't ever take it again."

And there it was. Addiction. But the gulf was too wide, the talk too terrifying to have now. "What did I . . . do to you?" I asked. "At the keening ceremony?"

He shivered. "Honestly, I don't know."

"The day we met, you asked me what I am. Why?"

"Okay, so, this is going to sound super creepy, but . . . I couldn't feel inside you. My whole life, my internal systems have automatically delivered detailed readouts on every person who steps into close proximity. All the ways they could be destroyed,

if I needed to. But you're a total blank. You're the first person I didn't feel afraid I might split wide open if I sneezed wrong, or had a panic attack or stroke or whatever. You have no idea how fucking liberating that was."

And he kissed my forehead very tenderly.

"I can see you staring at me."

Which, busted. I was propped up on my elbow, surveying the magnificent mess we'd made. My semen shining on the knots and hills and curves of his muscled torso. Saying it, it sounds gross, but it looked beautiful. It felt sacred.

"How . . . can you see me?"

"I don't know." And he shuddered. "Ever since I was cut off from my angusticeps, it's like there's this whole other spectrum of things to perceive."

"Is that . . . good?" I asked.

Resh shivered, shook his head. "It scares me, Aran. It goes so fucking deep. Every time I try to probe its boundaries, I push further. See more. Feel more. I always dreamed of what it would be like to see again, and now I can, and I fucking hate it."

"That sounds really, really scary," I said, helpless to help him find a way out of what was hurting him. "Is it something you want to talk about?"

"I do. But I don't know what to say. I just . . . I need to make it stop. I need something to make it stop."

"Okay," I said, knowing what he was asking. "We'll figure something out."

I hadn't shared with him the new corner I'd turned. Back when I thought I'd lost him forever. I wanted to be sober. I was ready. And Resh wasn't. And now wasn't the moment, when he was hurting from a wound I couldn't fathom or help him heal from, and drugs probably *were* the answer, but there was a safe

therapeutic solution—which would take forever to find—and an unsafe, self-destructive, self-medicating way to do it, which would be as fast as the nearest bottle or gram of amph or drop of spiderwebbing.

I dipped my finger in the splattered fluid on his body, sketched lines and letters across him. Wards and runes from millennia ago, to keep him safe from himself and every other threat out there.

A busy hum, from elsewhere in the mech Imadi was assembling around her heartship. She'd strolled back less than two hours after she'd been kidnapped by jackbooted tacticals, with the most half-assed explanation ever ("family bullshit"), but she'd seemed fine and I didn't want to pry.

And now we were ground zero for frenzied preparation, as Imm-Lo and Imadi put together a deeply shitty probably doomed plan to wage war on wherever the Exilarch and his Intelligence Class keepers were headquartered.

And then—way before I was ready—we were ready. We got a data dump from Imm-Lo's operative embedded in the Exilarch's retinue.

"Fuck," Imadi said, zooming in on the coordinates they'd gotten, for the site of what would hopefully be the final fight. A red ball veined with blue. "Why did it have to be a fucking planet?"

TWENTY-EIGHT

YOU DON'T WANT TO HEAR THIS

IMADI

We had a lot of work to do. People to visit. Asks to ask. Weapons to assemble. Last wills and testaments to be compiled. Eleven hours, basically, to turn a whole bunch of abstract conversations very concrete.

I was alone on the heartship when Vespertine spoke up.

You're happy, she said in my ear.

I'm excited to be about to battle again, I subvocalized.

I definitely detect the brain chemical levels that accompany excitement, she said. *But that is* in addition to *the brain chemical levels that indicate true happiness. I mean, what do I know, I've only spent tens of thousands of hours charting your emotional state in relation to your activities.*

She hardly ever entered therapist mode. I'd disabled most of that functionality—half of it was Atah's, snuck into Vespertine as a gag at age eighteen.

That meant: This was her, talking to me. My sister, speaking through code; a practical joke or sisterly gesture of love from

when we were teenagers. Pegged to a level of happiness I hadn't reached since then. The realization took my breath away.

When did that start? I asked. *The, uh, true happiness.*

After you left your mother's. Serotonin off the charts.

Why are you telling me this?

You've always been very bad at processing your feelings and understanding what you're experiencing.

"So . . . I'm happy," I whispered.

You're happy.

Thanks, Atah.

Vespertine didn't answer. She didn't know I was talking to her. And whatever Atah love bomb I'd stumbled upon didn't go so far as to understand when I was addressing her by proxy. But still. It was a gift. I'd snuck plenty of my own code gags into her AI mate Matutina back then, but clearly none of it had been half as helpful.

The happiness was my own. I'd fought hard for it. Won it by telling my truth and reclaiming my name and rising above Mom's weird manipulation-and-abuse game.

But this, this moment, this prompt to see and celebrate myself? That was Atah's. One of the ways she'd excelled, where I never could.

Her strengths had always felt like slaps in the face before. Attempts to prove to the world how she was the Good Twin. Now I could take them as lessons. Ways to maybe be better.

A half hour later, I found Aran in the mech's mess hall, looking like his own serotonin levels weren't so hot.

"Where's Resh?" I asked.

"He and Imm-Lo are working on some of the details for phase three of the assault. I know I should pay closer attention, but it's all very butch and intimidating."

"You're fine. We've all got our parts to play, and none of us need to know all the little details."

"Except I *don't* have a part to play," he said. But when he said it, he looked away a tiny bit too abruptly. "Snuggling is not required on this mission."

"You never know, most real fights take some surprising turns."

"I mean, I'm a fucking champ—literally—but if the battle takes the kind of turn where my skill set is needed to save the day, it's probably a pretty good sign we're screwed."

"Well, *somebody* is."

He giggled. So did I.

He was up to something. And he didn't want to talk about it. And I wasn't about to needle him for further information. The chances of it somehow scrambling our plans or introducing a significant variable were vanishingly slim.

I hoped.

"You seen this?" he asked, showing me the latest oppo report, a gnarly toothy scary familiar face on the surface of our target planet.

"Fuck. Is that—?"

"Yep," he said. "Chthona. Once the biggest, baddest mech in the business—all brawn, no brain, a very boring, very successful battle strategy—unemployed for the past five years, cooling her guns in a scrapyard somewhere, taking on mercenary battle assignments when they come along . . . and the latest assignment is for our enemies."

"Fuck," I said again. "Fuck. But then there's this," and I pinged the schematics to his Mapp tab: the mech Resh was assembling himself.

Head of a cave bear. Spines of a hedgehog all down its back. The sigil across its chest was a weird combination of the cave-bear

seal of the Mar Zutra Line of the Monarchs, and Professor Hedgehog's flag from *The Otter-Man Empire*. It was ridiculous, and I adored it.

"Maybe it was supposed to be a surprise. But. Look what your man made for you."

The goof grinned so hard he fucking blushed.

"How's Resh doing?" I asked.

"He's getting there. Figuring it out." Several seconds of silence. "And it's been really hard."

He'd told me the basics, in bits and pieces, since we'd rescued his man. Some of it I'd been able to figure out for myself. That Resh was an addict, same as him, same as me. But nowhere near ready to kick. Going cold turkey, because we couldn't take a chance on his powers being inhibited even the slightest bit for what was about to unfold, which had to make him a nightmare to deal with. Not that Aran would ever complain.

"You don't want to hear this," I said. "But your own sobriety has got to be your first priority. I know you care about him, and I know he feels the same, but you're at two different places on an incredibly difficult journey. You might be able to make it work—love can give you crazy superpowers—but this is Recovery 101: Romantic relationships can be another form of dependency, and the work of building something together is diametrically opposed to forging a whole new life for yourself, which is what an addict has to do in the early stages of recovery. I mean, fuck, it's been years for me and I'm only *just now* getting to a place where I can start to imagine myself being with someone." Like *just now* just now, like in the last week.

"You're right," he said. "I *don't* want to hear that. But that's because I already know it's true."

"Let me know if you ever want me to go with you to a meeting. Assuming we don't all die today."

Aran rolled his eyes. "People still *do* meetings?"

"Collective-accountability recovery meetings are almost as old as addicts rolling their eyes at collective-accountability recovery meetings."

"Touché," he said. "And. Hey." He pointed to the corner of the bridge, where my oak tree sat in her massive pot. And my gut dropped. It was ridiculous—he couldn't have known—and his wide handsome curious face was as innocent as ever—but he'd just aimed his intellect at the last real secret I had left. "What's the deal with your tree? When I first spotted it—back when Resh almost murdered you and I talked him out of it—something bothered me about it. I just couldn't put my finger on what. But now I remember—it's an oak tree. We had them on Uqbar. My papa planted one, when my brother was born. I tried to get a bonsai version, when I first left home, to carry something with me that had his spirit. But here's the thing: oak trees need winter. That's why you almost never see them on stations. They need the dormancy, they need the cycle. So how do you have it on your ship? Is it some kind of crazy gen-mod cultivar with no need for cycling? Because if so, it must have cost you an insane amount of money."

"We winter," I said, confessing something insane, preparing myself to confess something way worse. "The bridge is set to a seasonal cycle that matches the planet where this oak was grown. Right now we're in the summer, tapering into fall, temperatures holding steady at sixty-five, but in a couple of months we'll start to drop down into the thirties. Sometimes below. Vespertine is programmed to introduce slight variations in the day-to-day, so it's not a purely linear progression."

His jaw dropped. Because that shit is insane.

"You mean to tell me you spend months out of every year just shivering in your ship all day?"

"I have blankets. Lots of blankets. And sometimes I bubble the tree so it stays cold but the rest of the ship warms up, or bubble my hab. I'm not . . . completely crazy?"

"Just ninety-five percent."

"Ninety-one."

"Fair."

He didn't ask me why. He's good like that.

"My sister's buried there," I said.

He hugged me. And then he said, "Yeah, but there's like literally tens of thousands of species of trees. You could have used one that didn't need to winter."

"My sister," and I could see it now, could say it. "She wasn't well. She was so amazing hardly anyone ever saw it, but I saw it. She would get obsessed with things, to an unhealthy extent. And in the last couple years, she got super obsessed with Planet Zero. Sending me articles she'd read and rants she wrote about how life on stations and other planets wasn't right, wasn't how we were meant to be. And how we could only know true perfect peace on that planet. So. I try to give her that. Even tried to get my hands on soil from there—took me six hundred and twenty hops just to get to its lunar colony, but everything down there is contaminated and irradiated and infected and—"

"You would have brought Planet Zero soil on board? You, who wouldn't even let me play a scan of a cinematic from there?"

"The things you do for love," I said. "And also from crushing, soul-killing guilt."

He hugged me again.

"We have to go," I said.

"Just hug me back, stupid."

I did. It felt great, and I would never tell him that.

Over his shoulder, I looked at the oak tree. She was big and healthy and her arms were spread wide and her leaves were glorious.

My sister was still with me, still being a pain in the ass, still giving me so much.

Which is when I realized: My mom had known where I was the whole time. Whatever trackers she'd had inside Atah were still there in the soil. Stupid of me not to have suspected. For three years I'd thought I was lying low, running silent, and she'd been monitoring my movements the entire time.

"We're rendezvousing," I said, extricating myself from Aran's aggressive embrace.

Outside, three dozen ships had gathered. Of totally different sizes and shapes and makes and degrees of obsolescence. But it was three dozen times better than nothing.

Our target was on a small, densely populated planet named Cyanoxantha. Heavily industrialized; most of its surface covered in sprawling cities. Rich in iron ore, and therefore powerful, and renowned for the quality of its steel and the sophistication of its munitions plants.

Which was why there was only a single gate connecting the planet to space, and it was insanely heavily guarded. They had giant industrial ones to connect points on the surface—to transport ore from the mines to the refineries and from the refineries to the factories, and then to the off-world gate for distribution, but there was no question of using that to gain access to the planet itself. They'd tear us apart in seconds.

But Cyanoxantha was part of a crowded stellar system, and the plan was to hop to a station orbiting the next planet over and

use thrusters to get there. Which they'd see us coming from wayyyy away—but we weren't going there to hide from a fight.

Thanks to his father's identical field control signature, Resh had been able to pinpoint the place on the planet where the facility was located. So we knew where we were going, but had no idea what the defenses would look like. Our most recent scans were a week old, and they showed a pretty limited missile and cannon array, but who knew what else they had now?

"You're point on phase one, Imadi," Imm-Lo said. "We go on your signal."

The goo tank was already full and my whole body throbbed with the need to be immersed in it, to be fully assembled and out there wrecking shop. Even if—oh grossest of indecencies—I would have to be subject to planetary gravity pretty soon.

"Let's go," I said, lowering myself into the tank.

TWENTY-NINE

I WANTED TO SEE SOME SHIT

ARAN

We came through the gate, a two-hour trip on max thrusters from the target planet: thirty-eight Iskawi battle ships and the eight hundred pieces of Imadi's mech. Which assembled itself swiftly and gorgeously, a mechanical ballet of twirling pieces and micro-thrusters blasting in a billion directions, the heartship shivering as its field control expanded to encompass each new addition.

She bubbled us all up in programmable matter, and we rocketed toward Cyanoxantha like a comet whose tail was made of fighter vessels.

I regretted not paying better attention in the briefings, but mostly I was grateful to be in the dark; better to trust-slash-hope that they knew what they were doing than to know the details and see clearly how screwed we were.

Imadi was submerged in the goo tank with the hatch shut, so I couldn't talk to her. And I didn't know where Resh was. I'd gone out of my way not to know what his specific part of the mission was. So I wouldn't freak the fuck out about it.

Which, wow. *That* didn't work. Because here I was. Freaking the fuck out about it. Imagining him captured again. Picturing him dead.

I worked one of Vespertine's screens to give me an exterior view, showing the mech in all her primed and charged-up glory.

The only mechs I'd ever been inside were museum pieces. I once stayed in a toxic relationship six months past its expiration date, because the guy was a fusion engine repairman who took me aboard some of the biggest fighters of the moment, but only when they were in the shop or being prepped for postmortem prettification.

This was different. This was a battle begun, a brawl about to unfold. And not a show battle either, something pretty for the cameras. Something messy and dangerous, where success or failure actually mattered. Imadi's weapons were charged up and her shield was ready to flare into action and we could all die and I would taste every swing and hit and thrust and recoil.

But there was something I had to do. Something exceedingly stupid. My one, extraordinarily unlikely chance to free myself from the frame that had been hanging over me since Opple's assassination.

Against one wall was the escape hatch Imm-Lo had acquired for us. A gate to a crowded commercial station, in case the mech got compromised or defeat was otherwise imminent.

I was gonna hop that gate. I just wanted to see some shit first.

Imadi had no idea what I had up my sleeve, and she'd stop me if she knew. For my sake—not because I might fuck up the plan. But that would mean climbing out of that tank and bricking her mech, so.

When we reached orbit over Cyanoxantha, she didn't slow down. Just jetted right into the atmosphere—compacting the

programmable matter bubble, as it would just have been shredded by the force of entry. Everything began to rattle, as gravity reached out her long, strong fingers and took hold of us. The smaller ships had metal shielding, but we'd been built for this— she'd sourced mycotic cement strong enough to withstand atmospheric entry, an explosion of aerodynamic heat.

Her heartship had top-of-the-line grav compensation, but it was totally unprepared for the rigors of controlled entry. I felt it all through me, tugging me down. The ex I'd escaped from ages ago, who finally had me back in his clutches.

I was screaming. So was Imadi—though hers was more war whoop than mortal terror. The noise of the planet swallowing us up was so vast there could be nothing else.

With a clunk, the thermal soaks disengaged. I watched them fall on the screen, bright burning arcs plummeting straight down as our engines kept us to a steep angled entry.

The fore screen showed the ravaged surface of the planet far below us: a snarl of red rock and the scars of massive human settlement. And while we watched, a shadow fell across it. Cyanoxantha was revolving on its axis, turning this side away from its star.

Night had arrived, and so had we. Lights flickered on in the distance as the darkness deepened. We were coming in over a blue rift, now blackening: the inland sea of the planet's largest continent, on whose western shore our target had been built. To them, we'd be a burning golden god descending from the sky, reflecting the angled light of the "setting" star that they'd already turned away from.

We'd also be a prime and easy target.

They launched missiles, four at once, and the Mar Zutra made themselves useful, forging ahead into a complex configuration AI-optimized for maximum evasiveness. Spraying bullets at

the oncoming projectiles—taking them all out—but more were on the way.

Around the edges of the screen was a dizzying profusion of readouts and bars and meters and schematics, cycling through so fast I couldn't imagine Imadi actually reading them. But they were a team, her and Vespertine, and between the two of them they could consume all the intel in the world and turn it into action.

I'd dreamed of this. Seeing a mech in action. The real stuff, the inside view, the human-sized details—and the tiny lines of code that won and lost fights, not the goofy flashy six-hundred-foot-tall robots swinging swords. Although, yeah, those are cool too.

The fore screen showed the path ahead—filling up with black as we plummeted closer and closer to the surface of the water.

"Imadi, we're kinda sorta about to crash into the sea," I said, knowing she couldn't hear me, knowing she knew, had a plan, and this was part of it.

The screen was all black.

With a knee-punishing jolt, she engaged the thrusters on the mech's feet. Cones of blue fire bloomed, slowing us, fast, so close to the surface of the sea that they sent up jets of steam behind us as we skidded forward across the water like we were ice-skating.

I missed ice-skating. There were places to do it in systemist space, but it always seemed like such a kid thing to me that I'd never tried it once since I came unstuck. Now I wanted to, desperately.

Damn, I hadn't even set foot on this planet—with any luck I wouldn't—and it was already making me sentimental, spellbound by nostalgia.

A single missile made it past the Mar Zutra bullet blizzard. And one of their fighter pilots—with reflexes and a heroic instinct

so superhuman that I had to believe it was a programming decision, code they'd developed for just this kind of situation, knowing exactly what it would mean—pivoted and redirected and collided with the missile. Taking it and themselves out together.

A single unison keening cry across the comms, for their fallen comrade, and then silence. The mission was still on; there'd be time for grieving later.

This was so insanely not my scene. Way too stressful even to sit around for.

And then—on the horizon, amid the sprawl of artificial lights that was our target research facility, a new blip. Something big and bright: thrusters flaring to life.

The fore screen zoomed.

Chthona. Dolled up now in kaiju-form drag: sheathed in mycotic "skin" in the form of mottled green-gold scales, three long necks arching and snapping and wobbling.

She was here, and she was defending the target, and she was pissed.

I said, "Vespertine, relay a message to Imadi?"

No answer. But she was pretty busy scrambling missiles from her mech shoulders.

"I'm sorry, Imadi, I gotta run a quick errand," I said.

I tried my best to be stoic and forward-facing, but I couldn't keep from looking behind me as I stepped through the gate. Her eyes widened in a split-second WTF, and then rolled dramatically, and then returned to the battle at hand.

FASTER AND SMARTER THAN
I COULD EVER BE

IMADI

Aran *probably* wasn't sneaking away to get drunk or get fucked, but if he had been, I couldn't have blamed him. Chthona loomed larger and larger in my ext view, and I would gladly have been absolutely anywhere else.

Twice my size. Packing probably five times the polymer payload.

I fired up my plasma blade. Blue-green lightning lit up the darkened surface of the water, a coursing spiny sword of it.

Far off to our right, a hundred threads of smoke arced up into the air: the exhaust of smaller missiles from a secondary battery. Each like the stalk of a flower, terminating in a bright orange bloom where the Mar Zutra flanking squadron's bullets took the projectiles out, to zip in and try to deal as much damage as possible to the research facility while its primary defender was distracted.

And then Chthona was upon me. Vespertine veered us away, sharp and fast enough to avoid the long necks and biting heads reaching out, but Chthona pivoted just as fast and pursued.

Away from the target. Herding us into the city sprawled beyond. Tall skyscrapers, crowded streets. Exactly why I hated fighting planet-side. Too many people who would get caught in the crossfire.

Chthona flickered her own plasma blade to life, hoisting up her front left paw—in kaiju-form mode she was quadrupedal. The weapon was shorter than mine, spear model instead of sword, the surging fire of it pure terrifying white, thrusting straight at me.

Which didn't even matter, because it was a feint. I tightened the left hand around my blade and prepared to counter her thrust, and then her chest irised open and aimed a focused magenta laser blast in my direction.

Vespertine, faster and smarter than I could ever be, assembled the shield in an instant, programmable matter flowing into circular shape and forming molecular structures as smooth and reflective as crystal, raising my right arm so Chthona's death-ray blast was blocked, deflected—

—into the city. Strafing a skyscraper, a diagonal line cutting it fully in half. Orange explosive fire turning to black smoke—lights to the upper floors flickering out—the top portion unmoored, sliding down, and I wouldn't look, and I wouldn't do the math, on how many lives were in the middle of being lost.

Chthona surged forward, so low that her foot thrusters ravaged the roofs of buildings. Killing dozens. Hundreds. Again the chest laser—again Vespertine raised the shield to deflect the beam—but this time she was expecting it, and could angle the shield just so and bounce the deadly laser harmlessly into the sky.

Two long twisting tentacles of programmable matter shot out of Chthona's shoulders. I swung my plasma blade and sliced them off, but six more followed. A second swing stopped one,

but the rest grabbed hold of me—one on the chest, one on each limb—and lifted me up, swung me around, hurled me into the air.

Into a massive complex of what had to be worker housing. Twenty buildings—ish—with thirty stories each. Ish.

I rolled over onto my side, braced myself with both arms to push up and off the ground. But Chthona's polymer grappling hooks were on me again, holding me in place.

With a wrenching thud I could feel in my chest, in my tank, she landed in the street. Walked toward me, closing the distance with massive four-footed strides that tore through a crowded thoroughfare.

I'd hoped to hold her off for longer, but Chthona was simply too big and too good and too well-armed for me. The plan was fucked. The timeline was all wrong—it was too soon to do what I was supposed to do—but if I didn't do it now, I'd be dead, and therefore not able to do it at all.

From a vent in the thorax of my mech, a tiny little thing spat out. A small circle, lost in the smoking chaos of the street.

But then. It opened. As wide as it could. A wormhole five hundred meters in diameter opened up into space, sucking atmosphere into the void with such force that Chthona staggered back, destabilized, pulled toward its hungry maw.

Lots of other things were getting sucked through. Trees and vehicles and people. I tried not to think about it.

And then Imm-Lo roared through, her mech resplendent and sleek. On her signal, I shut the gate and the two of us turned to face Chthona.

THIRTY-ONE

YOU COULD END THIS

ARAN

Candy smell of fake cherry, thick and dizzying in the air. I'd never noticed how insanely strong it was here, before. But this had been my milieu, the fish tank I swam in, so of course I'd been numbed to all the ways it was weird.

Men saw me, made eye contact, smiled, smirked. Not recognizing me as me, just me as meat. I was home. She had dozens of skin centers, but the Miracle of the Rose was her favorite, and I'd spent an awful lot of time here sprawled out on the couches or perched on a bar stool, or dancing, or making out with someone on a dance floor or in a bathroom stall. Or turning a trick in one.

She wasn't expecting me. But she wouldn't be alone or undefended, I wouldn't be genuinely catching her off-guard. It was a dumb chutzpah move, and I couldn't not make it.

"Aran," she said, seeing me before I saw her. Molybdita sat at the head of a long table, on top of which two ballet boys were doing an exquisite Hasdaian divestment dance, all bends and flourishes and sudden snatches that tugged away one of the dozens of carefully placed swatches that covered their bodies.

It was a battle, obeying ancient elaborate rules, and the winner got to dictate the terms of their subsequent immediate very public intercourse. The hostility between the two of them was palpable—which was normal, the number of professional divestment performers was shockingly small, so most of them had beef with one another going back forever—which actually always made for much hotter performances. Sitting beside Molybdita, the guy she was working was super into the performance, staring up slack-jawed and spread-legged and visibly aroused.

Hasdaian spectacles can get pretty intense, once things progress to the secondary stage—screaming is not uncommon—and they weren't the Miracle of the Rose's standard fare. I wondered if it meant anything. If Molybdita was on the ropes here, somehow, for some reason. Wooing a new client or connect, who didn't trust her enough to visit her more extreme spaces. Which gave the proceedings an unaccustomed sense of urgency.

"Can we speak privately?" I asked her, smiling like this was just another day at work, she was my boss who hadn't sold me out, fucked me over. "I have some intel you might be interested in." She smiled and inclined her head enigmatically, eyes flicking to the mark. I said, "Judging by how many swatches they've both still got on their bodies, your dancers will be keeping him busy for forty-five minutes *at the least*. I won't take more than ten."

She stood, said, "Excuse me for a moment" to her tablemates—few of whom even noticed—and fixed me with one of her patented dagger-stares.

I followed her through the maze of tables. The element of surprise didn't amount to much—for all I knew, she could be subvocalizing commands to the tacticals to kick down the door and take me away, or for the conspirators to come kill me—but

I'd been around her enough to have a vague sense of how the game was played.

I'd resisted it, all these years. Told myself that her milieu of deception and greed wasn't mine, that I could be better, that I could stay true to myself.

But that hadn't worked for me. And if I was going to take my life back, I had to be what she was. At least a little. At least for now.

What she was is above it all. She didn't care about any of it. Lost homeworlds, murdered filmmakers, blue-band corruption— none of that troubled her sleep. The security rackets could conquer the portalverse or cease to exist, and the only issue she'd have would be how to best monetize it. So I knew she'd hear me out. And *then* decide whether to get rid of me.

The fake cherry smell was somehow even stronger in her office. I knew it was only *one* of hers, that she had dozens of spaces squirreled away where she could store data, have meetings, make calls. Murder people. The face she wanted to present here was the bawdy immoral madame, mistress of gleeful erotic mayhem.

I didn't sit when she gestured to a chair. "I know you've got all the dirt, on everyone. Everyone involved in Opple's assassination, the terrorist attacks on the clients of your targeted security concerns, and a thousand other acts of random meaningless violence. It's all up your sleeve as an insurance policy, in case anybody ever tries to come for you. Is that wrong?"

She shrugged. "If that's what people think, I certainly wouldn't want them to think anything different."

"So I'm begging you," I said. "You could end this. Expose the actual architects of the assassination. Show everyone I didn't do it. Let me have my life back. I know there's no currency in it, and currency is the only language you speak. But I'm betting you've

got enough already stored away for fifteen large and lavish life-times. So here I am, asking you to help me out. Because I made a lot of money for you, and because we worked closely for over a decade, and because I thought we were friends."

"So . . . it was a lie, out there, when you said you had intel for me."

I grinned. The same old goofy, boyish, hapless Aran. Nothing to see here. Nothing to fear. "I didn't say that."

"Drink?" she said, pouring one out for each of us. Something thick and red.

"I don't drink," I said, and she raised an eyebrow and her shot, then downed it.

"I could do what you're asking," she said. "Absolutely. Easily, even. And you're right, it would cost me nothing, and I already have far more than I'll ever need. . . ."

"But," I said.

"Exactly. But. I won't. And it's not because of the currency—it's because of the connections. My reputation as a trustworthy conveyor of information who obeys the rules of the game would be gone. My sources would suffer, because I'd be unable to sell the intel they bring me."

Of course I hadn't expected her to respond differently.

Thing was, I genuinely didn't know what I was going to do. Uncertainty was my only hope, my secret weapon. If my mind was made up on what the fuck I was going to do next, she'd have seen it a million klicks away. And stopped me. But I had no plan, no definite next steps, so there was nothing for her to sniff out.

"As for currency—I am prepared to offer you quite a lot of it. Enough to buy yourself a new identity, set up shop somewhere far, far away, make yourself a new life."

"What kind of 'quite a lot'?"

She typed onto a tab, showed me a number. It took my breath away. Made it hard to hear. Even eclipsed the nauseatingly sweet stink of cherry candy.

I thought about it. Not for a little while. I imagined the life I could live, the space I could buy, the sex-worker-owned cooperative me and Newt would be able to create. It wouldn't be my old life, but it would be just as fun and glamorous. And this time, not under anyone's thumb.

But. That life wouldn't have Resh in it.

Assuming we emerged victorious today—assuming he did not die—Resh would be a public figure. Visible, famous. Leader of the newly liberated Mar Zutra, possibly the new head of the Terfezian Empire . . . and, yeah, a victory did not seem super likely for them, but I wasn't about to plan for his failure. For a future without him in it.

And if I was on the run with Molybdita's money, I couldn't be anywhere near Resh. I'd be a sitting duck. And, yeah, he could probably crush whoever came for me, but I wasn't about to put a new head of state or rebel political leader in the position of killing people to protect the boyfriend everyone believed was an assassin.

I opened my mouth, but I had no idea what to say.

**STALK AND HUNT AND FIGHT
AND FUCK AND HOWL**

IMADI

Imm-Lo was glorious to watch.

Neither the Terfezians nor the Mar Zutra establishment had used mechs for military engagements in centuries, but she and Resh were hardened warriors, and the crash course I'd given them—and the flashed clone of Vespertine's fighting subroutines I'd uploaded to their heartships—would make them magnificent.

Her cables were braided steel, not polymer, and they couldn't be cut by anything short of Chthona's plasma spear. They blasted from her chest and wrapped around Chthona's front legs. Coiling tightly. Hobbling her.

And she was already off-balance from the recently closed vortex into the vacuum, so the first step she tried to take toppled her to the ground. Crushing an entire city block, but by then I was getting good at not running the numbers.

Imm-Lo grabbed hold of Chthona's feet, hoisted them up. Swung her in a circle, the hydraulics masterpieces of engineering—until she was up off the ground, spinning, faster and faster—

—and I felt something. A weird new wild thing, climbing up my spine from someplace I'd thought I'd lost, the connection severed, the channel blocked, the chakra sealed—

—a giddy, savage thing. A lean and hungry greedy thing, the wolf, the primate, the beast in the jungle, the thing that wanted to *live*, to stalk and hunt and fight and fuck and howl through the starsprawl—

—and it had been there all along, I'd just been under the spell of something else—the human, the miserable, the quirks of brain chemistry and the burdens of guilt and grief—I'd been sleep-walking through the cosmos, sloppily shambling my way toward death, always doing the dumbest thing, aggressively making the bad decision, the thing that would make me hurt more, because hurt was what the human thought it deserved, but the human was wrong, the human was dumb and the animal was wise—

—and I was here, I was alive, my sister was dead and it fucking sucked and I'd carry her with me forever and my life was my own and and—

Imm-Lo hurled Chthona away from us, aiming for the sea.

"Good shot," I said, seeing the splash go up. "We need to get her away from populated turf."

A million small shriekings came across the sky. More white threads of smoke; more projectiles coming from where the Exilarch was waiting. More orange blooms where our allies succeeded in taking them out—with bullets, in most cases, but also some with their own ships.

"I want to go stomp the shit out of that place," she said.

"You can't," I said. "That's not on us. Stick to the plan—we've got to take Chthona fully out of commission."

"*Fine,*" she said petulantly. And we stomped toward the sea.

Chthona had cut herself free and was standing in salt water that came up to mid-calf.

"Shields," I said. "She's got a nasty chest blaster."

We kindled ours as one, two bright glowing red translucent discs in the darkness.

Chthona walked slow—and then picked up speed. Bipedal now, half of the kaiju-form flesh on its right side scraped away. Running at us, spear raised high. We kept going, leaving the asphalt city behind and stepping into the surf. A thin band of light at the horizon lit Chthona up from behind, sent its shadow ahead for a hundred kilometers.

I stopped; braced myself for impact. Imm-Lo kept going. We didn't know what our enemy was going to do, but we trusted each other's instincts.

Chthona swung the spear downward as it closed the last little bit of distance, a blindingly fast move Imm-Lo still managed to evade effortlessly, pivoting to the side so the plasma blade plunged deep into the water. But it made her balance momentarily precarious, and when Chthona raised her spear arm to elbow her opponent in the gut, Imm-Lo teetered.

I flared my plasma sword back to life, thrust straight ahead. Piercing Chthona's midsection, driving into her left flank.

Toppling, Imm-Lo grabbed hold of her. Pulled Chthona down into the sea with her, my blade sliding effortlessly out of the breach. Massive waves surged up from the force of their impact, and Chthona had to be facing some serious internal flooding.

Imm-Lo held her still for me, hands gripping her by the shoulders as she struggled to escape. Dragon heads writhed and snapped at the air. I raised my plasma blade, bracing it with both hands this time, for a decapitating stroke.

And Chthona's chest blaster struck me squarely in my sword arm.

A searing slice, a catastrophic cross-section.

In the goo bath, neuro-connectors translated mechanical trauma into the pain of flesh. Agony seared through me, a solid ring of fire in my upper arm. Temporarily deadening all muscular activity below that point.

(Yes, it's weird, I know, most mech pilots who still use goo baths dial the pain way down, but pain has always been a helpful motivation for me.)

The mech's arm fell into the sea. Steam coursed up in a thick column where the plasma blade's surging fire met the water.

Chthona rolled, attempting to turn that deadly beam on Imm-Lo. Chthona was bigger but Imm-Lo had better mechanics, could echo Chthona's moves and stay a split second ahead of disaster. Walls of water thrust up around them as they struggled.

My programmable matter was almost all gone—what was left I needed to preserve for shielding and repairs. And my only real weapon had been severed.

So. Even though it was corny as shit. Even though it's something you've seen in a thousand cinematics and laughed at as ridiculous every time. What else could I do?

I picked up my own severed arm, with the bright fiery blade still coursing at the end of it. And I swung it. And drove it through Chthona's right rear leg, pinning her in place. Imm-Lo stood up, and we both stared down at the mightiest mech of our generation, now definitively caught and helpless before us.

"Look who finally showed up," Imm-Lo said in my ear.

Onshore, the telescoping gate had worked its magic a second time. Resh's mech towered over the undefended research facility: half cave bear, half hedgehog, all badass. Barely visible in the

thickening night, our battle having killed all power to the city. Lit up only by the fires we'd started.

I saw Chthona's arms reach out, clamp down hard on one of Imm-Lo's legs and one of mine. I laughed at the pathetic attempt—we had her, she couldn't escape and she couldn't budge us—but Imm-Lo said, "Fuck," because her scans were way better than mine.

"What?" I asked, seeing only a helpless fallen mech with a blade thrust through its leg.

"Her core," she said. "It's going critical."

THIRTY-THREE

THE BIG HEAT

ARAN

Is this meeting over?" Molybdita asked, when thirty silent seconds had gone by.

I slumped into the chair I'd spurned. Defeated, and not caring whether she saw it.

"Maybe I will take that drink," I said. Avoiding her eyes.

She looked up at the clock: only seven minutes since we left her table. Her mark would not notice her absence for a while yet. Victorious, Molybdita could afford to be magnanimous with her time. She slid the shot toward me.

I sniffed it: cherries, of course.

I was running on fumes here. No plan. No idea whether I'd swallow the shot or not, let alone what to say to my boss and betrayer.

"You don't have to make a decision now," she said. "I'll be here. I'm not going to turn you in or hand you over. You've got my word on that."

"Thanks," I said, putting the liquid to my lips. Letting just a few drops slide past. Holding them on my tongue. Feeling how

my whole body responded. Warmth flaring in my joints, triggered by memory alone. How badly I wanted this.

The thing was, I couldn't trust her word. She was as much of a monster as Mey's mother or Resh's father, and I'd been too fucking dumb to see it.

Fuck it. I thought. *Let's do this*

"I did have intel for you," I said. "That wasn't a lie."

"Jolly good," she said.

"It concerns one of the most powerful red bands in the portal-sphere. I imagine intelligence *about* your fellow Intelligence Class operatives would be very valuable to you, would it not?"

She half nodded.

"This red band is very skilled, with a massive network. A brutal, cynical old woman who runs a lot of young rent boys to gather her intel for her."

Her eyes narrowed as I told her the story.

The one I'd been able to piece together, once I finally stopped acting like some dumb stuck kid and embraced my red-band-adjacent nature.

The tale of me and Molybdita.

"And one day she finds this hustler. Cute kid. Nothing special. Refugee of a doomed world. Tale as old as time. Except. He's got something inside of him."

Both eyebrows rose, infinitesimally.

"Tech, to be precise. Something he doesn't even know about. Left in his body from a brutal attack back on his homeworld, the same one that killed his father. She detects it, because she's got the best scanners money can buy, but she keeps it secret. Because it's weird and wild and maybe game-changing. Because it renders nano-manipulation weaponry inert. Which

could completely flip the power balance in innumerable major conflicts. Stop me if you've already heard this story."

"I know a version of it," she said softly. "Intelligence is all about comparing variations of stories. I'd be amused to hear yours."

"But the kid's oblivious. He's got no idea how to use it, so she figures it's safe where it is, while she tries to figure out how to monetize it. For years she lets him live his life, until—for some reason—she decides it's time to take him off the table. Frame him for murder, get him killed, so the tech will die with him."

"Fascinating story," she said, folding her arms over her chest—an astonishing display of defensiveness I'd never imagined her capable of making.

"What do you think changed, to make her decide to kill this kid?"

"Who can say?" Molybdita said. "Red bands are mysterious inexplicable creatures. But it's possible she learned she was dying. It's possible she couldn't let that tech fall into the wrong hands after she was gone."

And I must have let a sliver of smugness show on my face, because hers hardened. And her voice, when she spoke, was a weapon. "It's even possible that she knew about the tech long before she met this hustler. That she was part of an Intelligence Class faction monitoring anti-off-worlder terrorists on this kid's homeworld. And saw what they were making."

Here my lungs stopped pumping air, exactly as she'd calculated.

"It's possible that they decided to cut the planet off completely from the portalsphere, rather than let such terrifying weapons proliferate. And blame it on the anti-off-worlders, who were all too happy to take the credit."

I gasped, struggled to breathe.

Reminded myself, *You can't believe her. Molybdita is as good at telling lies as she is at weaponizing the truth.*

But I also couldn't pretend what she was saying wasn't possible.

In the end it didn't matter. It didn't change what had to happen.

Resh's father and Mey's mother had done unspeakable damage to them. But as broken as they both were inside, they were strong. Their hideous parents had prepared them for life in the portalsphere.

I'd arrived unprepared. Easy prey for the first monster who showed me kindness. I was weak and I was naïve and I was dumb.

"I never knew what safety was, when I was young," I said. "My home wasn't safe. My family wasn't safe. People who wanted more weren't fully safe, couldn't be completely open. And when I left Uqbar, when I first discovered found family, when I got a taste of what it was like to choose the people you want to live and love and die with—well, I was hooked. Addicted."

I swallowed the shot. My sobriety clock would have to start again, but I'd be better equipped this time around.

"Don't get me wrong—found family is everything. I'd die to protect the people I love." Like Resh. Like Imadi. Even if she was an asshole. "But when you're addicted to something, you can't see it clearly. And you can't have a healthy relationship with it. So I assumed that everyone who showed me love was being honest about it, was treating me with the same openheartedness as me, wasn't trying to harm or exploit or manipulate me. And was worthy of my love. That was a mistake."

Here, her face tightened. My self-pitying speech had taken a turn toward the accusatory.

"I have no idea who I am," I said. "Who Aran is. I think he's

good, and kind, and loving, but I've never truly gotten to know him. I've let the relationships in my life—and the substances—define me. And that came really close to destroying me."

"*Who you are* is stupid and sentimental," Molybdita said, clasping her hands behind her head. The indulgent monarch, tiring of playing at friendliness. "And good. But also weak. Planet-stuck, still, in the depths of your silly little soul. Still clinging to outdated community-minded morality that evolved as a survival strategy ten thousand years ago, rendered obsolete the day we first learned to spawn wormholes and use them to spread beyond the doomed rock we started from."

I'd heard this speech before.

I took the gun out from my back pocket. The one Imadi had given me when I asked for it, telling her it was just in case I ended up in the thick of the fight somehow.

My voice was even and unafraid. "If anything happens to you, everything comes out. Right?"

Her eyes blazed.

"That's how you set it up," I said, speaking slowly. "You've got all the dirt on all the rats. That's how you kept your enemies over a barrel, all these years. Everyone in the security rackets, everyone in Intelligence Class. They all play nice with you because they're part of the same sick system. But here's the thing. I'm not one of them. I've got no stake in the status quo. And with you dead, the big heat follows. Everything comes out. Everything burns down."

She kept herself from smiling, but not completely. "I've known you since you were a child, Aran. I know what you're capable of. And what you're not."

I felt it open inside me. The power to pull the trigger.

Another disappointing discovery about myself: I could do this.

"You're going to shoot me? You really *don't* know yourself, do you? Allow me to introduce you. You're a sweet kid who likes sex and boys and partying and is not a killer."

I'd killed someone, once. I hadn't enjoyed it and it had fucked me up, but it was completely the right decision to protect the people I loved—and she knew about it. Had she forgotten? Was she trying to convince me of something she knew wasn't true? It was either a mistake or a miscalculation, and neither one of them was like her.

And then she saw it. In my eyes. The shock of seeing it probably saved me, kept her—for once—from instinctively doing the smart thing immediately. Molybdita blinked before she began to subvocalize a call for help, and in that blink I shot her in the head.

SECOND STAR

IMADI

Eject!" I screamed, and Vespertine was on it, the heartship decoupled from the rest of the mech, the thrusters firing so hard that the massive, suddenly soulless machine fell backward.

Imm-Lo was ahead of me, her reflexes faster and her thrusters stronger—but she was also a better person and she wasn't strictly thinking of herself, so she threw me a lifeline—polymer arcing out behind her, a tentacle that grabbed hold of my prow and pulled me along, zipping away from Chthona's wrecked and about-to-go-nuclear body.

"Fucking fuck!" I screamed. "We did it! Didn't we? We killed Chthona. Or made it kill itself, which, wow. Sort of better, right?"

"And we could still totally die," Imm-Lo said, flinging a viz into my readout: six concentric circles mapping out possible blast radiuses, depending on a hundred variables whose values we couldn't know—payload, ancillary explosives, the precise fusion mechanism of Chthona's engine. Two blue dots were blipping away from the center, but still inside several of the circles.

Ahead of us, the facility was in flames. Kesh's mech opened its cave-bear mouth and burning jellied petrochemicals poured out.

Something was wrong with the fire. The flames were sickly yellow, and they billowed greasy black smoke in a greater volume than felt natural.

"Whatever they've got in there, we need to get the fuck away from it," Imm-Lo said.

But we were flying right toward it.

Through an insane aerial firefight that had suddenly sprung up around us.

Missiles still rocketing from the facility's remaining batteries—our own railguns swinging to violent percussive life—the depleted Mar Zutra spraying bullets and circling the site—fighting off what finally came up on our fore screens: dozens of battle-arks, an ancient and effective tool of close atmospheric aerial combat, who had come at last through the Cyanoxantha orbital gate to assist in the defense.

Behind us, the world went white. A second star rose in the sky as Chthona's core blew; new day blessing the ravaged city, its light making every bullet and streak of smoke and shred of shrapnel in the air around us stand out with excruciating clarity.

We were still inside the last three concentric circles. Which meant in a moment we might be swallowed up in annihilating nuclear fire. An hour or a day before I'd have thrilled at the thought, but now I cut my guns to eliminate even the minuscule backward momentum generated by every explosive shot.

Imm-Lo took my lead on that.

Chthona's heartship rocketed over us, wobbling slightly from the foreshock but faster than us, equipped with the best engines security currency could buy. We were still inside two of

the circles, but the mech's payload must have been smaller than the most dire projections, because the actual blast radius did not swallow us up.

A wave of thermal and ionizing radiation rushed past. Our ships shielded us, but the people in the city would not be so lucky.

A split second later, the electromagnetic pulse hit, shorting out every solid-state electronic circuit—which meant almost every ship in the air lost power and controls—but most of the newer vessels had swift reboots built in for just this possibility. The heavy arks were not so lucky, and the ones that were flying lower fell to the earth or sea.

Imm-Lo and I had our ships back in action in a second and a half, pulling out of a plummet, continuing our course toward land. Almost reaching it.

Of course Resh's mech hadn't stopped, slowed, flickered. He didn't need electronics. He was the engine, he was the circuit board, and he was unstoppable.

"What's the plan here?" I asked Imm-Lo. "Is the goal to destroy the facility, or to salvage what we can of their weaponry and intel and *then* render the whole thing useless?"

"You know it's the latter."

"Does your boy know that? Because he's set to reduce this whole thing to ash."

Imm-Lo groaned. "Yeah. He's not responding to my hails." And then: "Incoming!" as three battle-arks swung at us from the side, lightning-guns blazing. I pivoted sharp and hard but uncontrolled, barely slipping between two wide sprays of electric death.

She unleashed eight large, inflated globs of polymer, to circle our ships and confuse the battle-arks' homing systems.

And then she banked up, and if she hadn't still been towing me I'd have been fucked, because a massive wall of water bore down on us, a tsunami thrown up by the nuclear explosion. The wave broke across the facility, and the sickly yellow flames all went out with a sizzle I could hear through my heartship walls.

THIRTY-FIVE

LAY DOWN THE STRAIN OF SELFHOOD

ARAN

For a split second I was scared shitless, the sound of the gunshot echoing in my head, convinced her security team would be on me in a minute, and maybe they were, maybe there were silent alarms pegged to her heart rate going off all over, and the bad guys were converging on me with guns drawn—even as the data she'd set up to distribute in the event of her death was wending its merry way through the feeds and streams and into the hungry maws of select journalists everywhere—but then the fear passed. Because I knew how this worked now. Molybdita, Resh, Imadi—probably everyone who was anyone—they had an escape hatch ready.

All the smart people had an easy way out for when the big heat came down. Everyone who had forged a life for themselves, something worth saving their own skin for.

Maybe one day I'd get my own.

But for now I just needed to find Molybdita's, which wasn't hard: You don't hide too well what you're going to need to get to in a hurry.

The hatch was in her bathroom. First place I looked. It took me to a busy city-station in the middle of a parade or music festival: the whole place throbbing with sound and color, people in masks carrying giant mycoprinted versions of their chosen heart animals. I found the seam in the flip-side gate, flipped it open to reveal bio-electric filaments and polyps throbbing with blue and green and purple light, and with a slight pang in my heart (gates are practically sacred in space, the thing that makes life among the stars and across distant planets possible), I tore the tentacle that powered the negative-mass loop that propped open the wormhole. Her tacs couldn't come after me, but I still hopped through another one of thousands and was gone.

Mapp said it would be eleven hops to get back to the station where Imadi'd rented a slot for her escape hatch's other half. I went there slowly, savoring the scenery along the way. Adjusting to the new blood on my hands.

It didn't feel good, taking a life. But if it had, I'd have been worried about myself. So I sat with the guilt and the gruesome spectacle of her death—the body in the chair, the tilt of her ravaged head, the shape of the spray on the wall behind her—but I also let myself remember Molybdita's stern direction and support over the years, which had become part of who I was. She was a monster, but she'd been important to me, and it was so, so strange to sit with the knowledge that her unique and terrifying energy was gone from the universe forever.

Eventually, I got to the gate back to Imadi. Pinged it with Mapp; was pleased to see it was fully operational, with normal oxygen and environmentals on the other side. Which meant she hadn't been blown to smithereens just yet.

"Well, look who comes crawling back," she said, standing there scraping goo off her body.

"Sorry," I said. "Had to go pay my power bill."

"Bullshit," she said, grinning. "Tell me all about it, when this is over and we're not dead."

"So . . . we're not done yet?"

"Not done. But our mechs got fucked."

Vespertine had docked in a scraggly public park, klicks away from where the sky was still lit up by the battle. At this distance, each new explosion—which probably meant a whole ship blown to bits, with one or more souls lost—looked as harmless and pretty as little fireworks.

Death is a thing that happens. Every life ends. I'd seen the stats once, on how many people die every second, across the entire portalverse—thousands of them—but I'd told myself then what I told myself now: *You're alive, you're breathing, live as much as you can for as long as you can.*

"Are we winning?" I asked.

She stepped into a set of coveralls, even though goo still glistened and jiggled on her hair and skin in spots. "Our victory looks assured, but we all might die. Follow me."

She pulled a flimsy lightweight gate out from the array, set it into the floor, hopped through. I went after—

—into Imm-Lo's ship, also squirreled away far from the battle, this time in a darkened block of falling-down buildings on the edge of town.

"Thank the stars you're back," Imm-Lo said, and she was so glad to see me it brought a wide dumb smile to my face before I realized it had nothing to do with me—and first my feelings were hurt—and then my heart sank.

"It's Resh, isn't it?"

"I can't reach him. Can't stop him."

On her fore screen, I could see his cave-bear-hedgehog mech

still stomping the shit out of the target facility. Stopping every few seconds to shoot lasers at terrestrial assault vehicles, or swat aerial antagonists out of the sky.

"I mean . . . he seems to be doing just fine. . . ."

"He's not in there," she said, unclamping the locks from a gate.

"Where is he?"

Imm-Lo removed the gate's panel and pointed through to a swirling, terrifying firestorm. "He's there. Inside the facility."

"What the fuck did you—"

"Easy, Aran," Imadi said. "This was his plan. *He* proposed breaching the building's defenses, plunking a gate down, using it to hop through and scour the facility himself while still controlling the mech remotely with his secondary nervous system. Way better than a goo bath, btw. We tried to talk him out of it—"

"Well, you obviously didn't try hard enough. He's in there? Walking around fighting evil motherfuckers armed with tech we don't even fully understand?"

"We don't fully understand *his* tech, but it's probably a damn sight better than theirs," Imm-Lo said, but I could see she was just as scared for him as I was.

"Except that his father might have the same tech as him, and understand it a lot better because he hasn't been kept in drugged ignorance of it for his whole life, and he's definitely in there too?"

Neither one of them had anything to say to that.

"You've got to be fucking kidding me."

"I sent backup with Resh," Imm-Lo said. "A life-sized polymer drone of Grizzelda, his AI mate, with massive storage banks so he could siphon off all the data they've gathered, and with authorization to use deadly force in defense of Resh. And with this gate embedded inside, so he could get out in a hurry."

"Fucking hell," I said. "So we're going in?"

They looked as scared as I was—which was weird, because they're brave warriors and I'm a dumb squeamish kid who hides from every fight—but I was already moving, grabbing hold of the edges of the gate and lifting my feet off the floor, vaulting myself through.

Into the inferno.

It singed my face, scorched my bare arms. Eerie, greasy yellow flames everywhere. The drone was walking behind Resh, a crystal cave bear within a swirling vortex of howling wind he controlled, keeping us safe from the flames and ensuring the toxic smoke got siphoned off into the air above us, through a long rip in the roof that widened as we went.

And I could see what he was doing. The dizzying fractal magic of his matter manipulation, moving through the air, long tongues and tentacles disturbing the dust, like he stood at the center of a magnificent starburst or ball of energy, the clear space it carved out around him—while I watched, one long curved spike of negative space thrust out through the swirling ash and across to a clear tank of something, in a lab whose wall had been torn down, and when it hit the tank it shivered and then shattered and the liquid inside boiled away in an instant cylinder of steam.

I'd never seen anything more beautiful. He wore the sacred tunic of his caste, now burned in places, so much skin peeking through, so much muscle, his posture so perfect, his body so exquisite, its motions speaking of grief and rage in equal measure, almost mechanical, almost not human, and it fully took my breath away, dropped me to my knees.

Which was when I saw it.

His father. Suspended in the air, bound in chains of polymer that twisted and tugged at his limbs while he howled in pain, his

screams inaudible above the din of destruction that blossomed around Resh. I'd been afraid his dad would be the only possible match for Resh's bottomless, incomprehensible abilities, but he was a tiny mouse in the paws of a monstrous cat that would toy with him indefinitely before deciding to kill him.

Now Resh's voice cut through the air, a booming, echoing sound amplified who knows how, like he was broadcasting our comms channel through the actual molecules of air or had repurposed the still-standing walls into speakers—

"Galuta Resh," he said, addressing his father—and, fuck, did they have the same name?—*"twenty-fourth Exilarch of Mar Zutra—hereditary autocephalous Leader of the Captivity—"*

No lisp. I remembered his voice in the Terfezian massacre—floating in space, refusing to be saved, determined to destroy all his foes and die alongside them. He'd do that now—die gladly, even if he took us with him.

"You and your forefathers have conspired with our enemies to oppress your own people—"

Resh raised one arm, and I could see the shock wave thrust out, widening as it went, until it hit a wall that cracked and crumbled beneath the onslaught. While I watched, a human body, possibly already dead—and possibly not—was shredded in the ebbing of the surge, flesh dusting off bones and then the skeleton blowing away.

"That is why the Name has withdrawn its favor from your brow—"

Had his father's subroutine taken over? Or had it just awakened something that was already there, given center stage to the abuse and oppression and trauma Resh had lived his whole life with?

And didn't I have that same thing inside me? The damaged

core, the wound of my lost homeworld that didn't stop bleeding? Didn't every addict have that? A burning need to be free of the torturous burden of being alive—*a plague I call a heartbeat*, to quote an ancient song scrap a musician ex was fond of? Not every addict had suffered trauma like mine or Resh's, but they all yearned to lay down the strain of selfhood. . . .

"*That is why you will die like a dog in the streets of a dusty nameless world—*"

Maybe it wasn't universal, that self-negating shadow-self, but I knew I had it, and that it might take me years of trying to grab hold of it and tear it out and let it rot and shrivel in the starshine—but Resh hadn't even gotten to the place where he knew it was there, let alone that it could be cured, let alone that *he* could cure it.

We were on the same journey. But we were not in the same place.

Grief and rage and fear and sadness bubbled up in me, and I called his name again, didn't yell, didn't scream, didn't even say it out loud, just thought it, *Resh*, all up my spine, echoing out of the bottomless well of my knowing how much healing we both had to do before we could be together, from the fear (*from the certainty*) that it might never happen—

I saw it move through the air. An eddy in the dust; a spiraling sloppy wave of wanting, nothing at all like his elegant precise snarls and fractals—but it was real, I could see it, it had come from me. From my damage. From the shrapnel of my father's murder.

A starburst behind my eyes; a smell of sandalwood and candy-apple lollipops.

The disturbance in the dust faltered and faded before it reached him. But I could trace the river of it back to the source, feel the tributaries that fed it run through me, and I stepped

forward and I raised my hand and I summoned all my love and all my rage and said—without saying—*Resh!*

And I touched his shoulder. And I felt it surge out of me again, stronger now than before, an electric crackle—

And he stopped—

And he turned his head and his eyes met mine; the silver swirling fire vanishing, revealing those blazing brown-black starburst irises—

Aran, he said, without saying it, and the world stood still. Dust eddies paused and even the flames froze, held their shape, like all of reality was a construct of Resh's mind, and he smiled, and I smiled.

And I loved him. And he loved me.

"Let's go home," he whispered, swaying unsteadily now that the exertion of the assault was over, his nano-connectivity temporarily stilled by whatever the fuck I had inside me.

The thousand-armed octopus of negative space around us blew away. His father fell forty feet to the ground, howling all the way. I heard more than a couple of bones break, but he was still alive and screaming when Imm-Lo put a bullet in his brain.

AFTER ORGASM OR A BRUSH WITH DEATH

IMADI

We should go," I said at last, and it was all logistics from there.

With the uncanny clarity that always comes after orgasm or a brush with death, I savored the smell of the cocoa butter on Imm-Lo's skin and the beeswax in her hair.

"You were pretty good out there," she said, as Vespertine took us away. I hoped her senses weren't as sharpened as mine, because I was pretty sure I stank. "You might have a future as a fighter pilot."

"I don't know," I said. "It's a pretty expensive hobby, and I'm presently unemployed."

"You could go pro," she said.

"I'll sponsor you," Resh said, his voice faint but firm. "I'll be fucking loaded once I finish conquering the Terfezian Empire within the week."

"That's a spooky dude," I said.

I picked chunks of dried vat goo out of my hair and tried my best to look glamorous doing it.

She wasn't into sex, but sex wasn't everything. Maybe nothing would come of this, the electric tremor that she stirred up inside me, but it felt good just to feel it, sit in it.

"You're okay," Aran was saying to Resh. Over and over again.

A ping had come through while I was away: a status update, finally, on Mar-Tek. I opened it immediately, before my brain could generate an endless list of potentially devastating things it could say about the man who'd been like a father to me.

He was alive. He was out of the regen bath. He was healing and he wasn't going to die.

I didn't switch off the comms channel, even though I was crying. Because I wasn't the only one.

COMMON TROPES IN THE
STORYTELLING OF SOBRIETY

ARAN

His whole ship was lit up crimson. We'd docked at one of the pleasure motels surrounding the Red Rectangle Nebula, basically the galaxy's hottest make-out spot: dying binary stars with a ladderlike system of diamond "rungs" expanding out around them. They filled the huge portholes, dyeing our bodies the color of bright impossible cherries.

I grabbed Resh's red head with my red hands and pulled him down to kiss me.

I was on my back, my legs resting on his shoulders as he plowed me. His body was slick with sweat and his face was a mask of ecstasy and the improbable perfection of it all edged over into absurdity and I laughed out loud.

"What are you laughing at!" he said, in mock outrage.

"You're so beautiful," I said. *I can't believe you're real. I can't believe you're mine.*

"You are!" he said, and he couldn't see anymore, he'd found

the right drugs to dull most but not all of the abilities he'd acquired when he went off the angusticeps, but I knew he meant it.

Three weeks since Cyanoxantha; Resh's recovery was almost complete, and now I was the exhausted one who lay back and let *him* do all the work.

Meetings all day. Research. Professor Hedgehog churning out business plans.

Me and Newt were actually making it happen. Starting the sex-worker collective I'd always been too afraid to dream of.

Because we'd both suddenly found ourselves with quite a lot of money in the bank.

Part of Molybdita's in-the-event-of-my-death automatic response was an immediate redistribution of all her financial resources, divided up equally among her intelligence assets. And even though she had a *lot* of assets on her roster, she must have had a truly staggering amount of currency—because our shares were enough for the seed money for a new enterprise, something Newt and I could build together.

Also, it turned out she hadn't been lying about being terminally ill.

All of which made me feel way worse about fucking shooting her.

"I'm close," Resh said, and I stopped stroking, used both hands to grab his arms, his back, his butt, his thighs, every marvelous perfect all-mine part of him. "You don't want to come together?"

I shook my head, pulled his down to kiss him. "I want to focus on you right now."

And I did. And it was magnificent. And then he spent another forty-five minutes getting me to mine. Which was incredible,

epochal, unlike anything I'd experienced since my first few wild terrifying transformative fucks.

After that we slept pressed close, face-to-face, our bodies stuck together with sweat and cum and still-throbbing need, in the dim red light.

And I swear to fucking stars I was stealthy as hell, extricating myself, needing to go pee—and stopping by the big hab portholes to admire the nebula on my way back. But I guess I wasn't stealthy enough.

"I think I love you," I said, hearing him come up behind me.

"There's no *think* about it for me," Resh said. "I love you, Aran."

"You're the best thing that's happened to me since I came unstuck," I said.

"But."

"But."

He knew. Most of it, anyway. He had to. But he was going to let me say it, because his suspicions were rough and shapeless and he wanted the specifics, valued my needs even when they might take me away from him. Because he was too fucking decent.

"I'm an addict," I said. "And I'm going clean. And I have to build a whole new life for myself, and that's too much work to leave space in my life for anything else. Even something wonderful, something I don't deserve. Not right now. But something I want to deserve."

"I have your back," he said, his mouth pressed to the back of my neck, his voice unsteady. "You know that, right? If you need to go sober, I am here for that. Whatever you need."

"I know you are," I said. "You've made that so clear, and it means the stars to me."

"But."

"But," I said, eyes on the bright burning X at the center of the Red Rectangle. "You're an addict too, Resh."

He didn't say anything. Not for a while. He'd never said it before. But he knew it was true, and eventually he said it.

"I'm an addict. But, Aran—I need it. I know that sounds like some shit all addicts say, but . . . it's a medical thing, right? Same as the meds you take for your depression. If I don't numb this thing inside me, I won't be able to stay alive."

"That's real," I said. "And I know you're figuring that out, the perfect mix of meds to get you to baseline. But it's not the whole thing. Part of you can't stop, can't modulate, craves escape, thirsts for more—for self-erasure, self-destruction, *something*, same as me, and that's what makes you an addict. Right? You see that, right?"

Resh nodded. "Yeah. I see that." He took a breath. "I'm an addict. But I want you in my life. And I'm willing to go fully one thousand percent sober if that's what it's gonna take."

"What it's gonna take is going to hurt a lot more," I said. "For both of us. Getting sober is super hard. We're going to stumble, and backslide, and fuck up. That's normal. What's *also* normal is that when one person fucks up, it derails the other. I've talked to a lot of folks about this. Read all the things. Seen the cinematics. I think you have, too. These are what they call common tropes, in the storytelling of sobriety. Codependency is a real detriment when it comes to relationships in the early stages of recovery. We need to be figuring out who we are separately, before we can see who we are together."

"What are you saying, Aran?" Hurt singed his words.

"I need to focus on me. *You* need to focus on *you*. We need to figure out whether or not we're strong enough to each be who the other needs."

"Is this because of what I did to you?"

"No!" I said, kissing him. "I told you, I forgave you for that. All that is for me, now, is an example of why we can't have drugs in the mix of who we are together. This is what I need. This is what *we* need."

"How long?"—and here he was on the edge of crying.

"Six months? Maybe more? I don't know. Until we both feel ready. Not fixed, not cured, but solidly sober. I'm proud of you for being able to admit your addiction, but that's the first of many really tough steps. To see what your triggers are, to tackle the traumas that shaped it . . ."

"No," he whispered. "Please? Can't we . . ."

The lump in my throat was so big I couldn't speak. We stared out at the Red Rectangle: the vivid lines—*caused by anisotropic dispersion of circumstellar material*, according to Professor Hedgehog—the X at its center. A smell like mothballs filled the hab ship, from where we'd docked to the station: polycyclic aromatic hydrocarbons given off by the two dying stars at its center.

"I'm sorry," I said at last, and I wanted to say more but did not dare.

Resh shook his head. "I get it, Aran. I really do. And I can do this. I swear to fucking stars. I can do anything. Or did you miss how I fucking single-handedly brought an empire to its knees?"

"You can do this," I said, and turned to press myself against him, feel his arms wrap around me and hold on tight. "You can do anything."

"Fuck you, Aran," he said, silver-swirling eyes locked on to mine. "Fuck you for having my best interests at heart. For being fucking mature."

"Thank Imadi, she's my de facto sobriety sponsor, she made me like this."

"Fuck you, Imadi."

"I hate this," I said. "I fucking hate it."

He was crying. So was I. But he smiled, and kissed me again, and we went back to bed and we lay awake and wordless, our hearts full and breaking at the same time, for hours.

"So like . . . cold turkey?" he whispered. "No contact?"

"I think so," I said. "We need to be on our own. And if that means you fuck other people while you figure yourself out, I get it, I hereby grant you an all-encompassing pass for the duration of our cold-turkey-ness."

He nodded gravely. His fingers interlaced with mine. "Likewise. I mean, I know it's your job, so . . ."

"We'll see whether I'll even have time for that, now that I'm making moves toward the management side," I said, but Resh was falling asleep, smiling, safe, happy, and before I knew it, so was I.

A TRANSFORMATIVE RECONSTRUCTION

IMADI

It took three weeks for Mar-Tek to recover enough that I could tell him my plan, and two more weeks to convince him to get on board.

And to do that, I had to have the hardest conversation ever. Worse than with my mom, when I had hate and rage to shield me from the full emotional impact.

He was asleep when I walked into his hospital room, and he'd never looked so old. The elegant remaining tufts of hair on his head had all been burned away, and the scattered stubble that was growing back left his cheekbones stark and his forehead lines uncamouflaged. I sat and I held his hand until his eyes opened.

And the next day, after a great deal of friendly chatter and sharing cinematics of my recent exploits, I took a deep breath and said:

"I've been lying to you for three years, Mar. Since my sister Atah took her own life. She killed herself and she left me holding the bag and I've been pretending to be her ever since."

He grabbed my hand, and held it tighter and tighter as I told him everything. He still couldn't talk, which I thought would make it easier—not needing to worry about what he might say—but his eyes were as alive and expressive as ever, and they said more than his mouth ever could.

"I'm not mad at my sister anymore," I said, when it was done. "I'm not even mad at my mother. Her patterns of violence and abuse made Atah what she was, made me what I am, but Mom's a product of the same sick system, and I don't think she could have been anything other than what she is."

He looked away. He was too loyal to my mother to hold eye contact, and too good a person to dispute the truth. Weeping openly, for my dead sister and my broken life and our corrupt world.

"But now I see that it's bigger than that. I never really questioned how we operate—how all the security rackets function. I'm not saying the red bands are better than us, just that the only way we can truly beat them is to change ourselves."

A swift and bloodless coup, as I knew it would be once I had him on my side. Fear kept my mom's hundred thousand workers in line, but love for Mar-Tek turned out to be a way more powerful motivator.

I was far away—this had to feel like *his* insurrection, *his* vote of no confidence. I was happy to leave it to him, but I wished I could have been there. We filmed it, of course, for maximum propaganda value—his first day back on the bridge at HQ after the hospital, Mom in full magnanimous mode welcoming him back—but I would have given anything to have been there in person to see the fine lines in her face, the slight widening of her eyes when he pulled out the zip stick and knocked her out.

A handful of resignations, some hostile talk from Mom-loyalists—but no meaningful challenges to his assumption of interim authority were mounted.

"I don't understand why I can't just turn the company over to you after that," he'd said, running through final contingencies and backup plans the day before. "There's ample precedent for inter-family seizure of power, in Blue Circumspect Tomorrow as with all the big security rackets. People would respect you for having the chutzpah to take out your mom."

"It would be the wrong way to begin a transformative reconstruction of the company. Everyone would see it as more senseless violence—a daughter taking out her mother to seize power. The example we set is important. Our intel shows incipient pro-worker-cooperative agitation within all the major rackets, and the largest security concern in Stratum Chín going that way would give them all some powerful ammunition."

This was like 60 percent of the reason. The rest was, I didn't fucking want any part of being the boss.

So I took a seat on his advisory board, alongside dozens of other workers who'd given their all for the company, to play a tiny role in transitioning it into a worker-owned cooperative. We kept Mom on house arrest for the duration, but I knew it wasn't necessary. She'd never admit it, but she was happy to have to step down. I'd given her what she'd never been strong or smart enough to seize for herself: a way out.

What did I know about cooperatives, governance, interminable meetings? Not a fucking thing. I was there to give the stamp of approval, establish continuity, access the gene-locked systems Mom had put in place to keep power in the family.

And advocate for Blue Circumspect Tomorrow to do what

no security concern had done before: sponsor a mech in the upcoming circuit season. And repair my damaged heartship; and pick a crew; and sketch out what my magnificent monster would look like.

And figure out what shitty pickup line I'd use on Imm-Lo when I got over myself and asked her out.

And catch the hourly updates blaring out across every feed, watching Resh dismantle what was left of the Terfezians. And hope he and Aran could make it work . . . because tearing apart an empire was easy compared to forging a sense of self as a newly sober human person.

And do what I'd actually become kinda good at, somewhere along the line of my three-year impression of my sister Atah: tracking down someone who didn't want to be found.

Because Trist was out there. Making bad decisions and causing harm and putting themself at risk—because they were scared, and angry, and because they'd been through something horrible and thought that meant they were broken forever. I knew the feeling way too well, which was why I hadn't reached out to help them before, but I was well enough now, and I was going to break the cycle.

All I had was a flimsy lead, to start with—Vespertine had logged the address Trist called me from, when they gave me a head start after snitching. Almost definitely phished or phreaked. But still. Something.

I revved my heartship's thrusters and started hopping. And maybe I'd never find Trist. And maybe they wouldn't want my help even if I did. That's okay. You can't save someone who isn't ready for saving. I hadn't been, until I was.

ACKNOWLEDGMENTS

As always, first gratitude goes to Juancy Rodriguez, for the love and support and ridiculousness that helped me survive the harrowing roller-coaster ride of writing (and hustling) a novel.

Pier Paolo Pasolini is the patron saint of this book. I spent years trying and failing to write a fictionalized version of the conspiracy surrounding his murder . . . and this isn't that, but it couldn't have happened without that—or without the exuberant, engaged eroticism of his films.

Thanks too to Seth Fishman, for finding such a perfect home for this book, and for all the ledges you talked me down from along the way.

And to Joe Monti, for publishing *Red Star Hustle*—and for helping me polish it to a diamond shine—and for including it in the launch lineup for such a marvelous new (old) format.

And to Mary Robinette Kowal, the best bookmate a writer could ever hope for. *Apprehension* is magnificent and I'm so excited for folks to wander our worlds together.

Profoundest gratitude, finally, to Natalya Podgorny—and to Maya, whose joy and wonder and love are constantly helping me to see the world with fresh eyes.